SOULS OF STEEL AND STONE

SOULS OF STEEL AND STONE

TODD WOODMAN

Sami Mark, Cover Art
Vincent Woodman, Cover Design

Todd G Woodman

To Vince, for inspiration
To Lisa, for years of patience and support
To my mom, for teaching me to love books

I

In the small hours of the morning, Kellyn stood in a narrow alley, reaching out with her hands to gauge the gap between the two closely packed buildings. No more than four feet—perfect. She braced her hands against the coarse wooden planking at just below shoulder height. Simultaneously, she pushed herself up with her hands while jumping, and kicking out her legs. The rubber soles of her boots hit the walls and she pushed her hands once more against the wooden planks. She hung suspended about three feet above the alley in shadow as dark as ink.

Again she pushed herself up with her hands, though her legs aided her ascent less than before, as she pushed against a vertical surface. A quick look up. No more than fifty feet to spider-climb. She'd managed more difficult climbs in training. Of course, in training, she'd never dealt with wood of such poor quality that each push gave her new splinters. With more than half the climb ahead, her left hand began to bleed.

She possessed good time sense, and though the climb felt like forever, she knew when she reached the roof of the western building, no more than a couple of minutes had passed. Unfortunately, she needed to gain the roof of the eastern building, which as it turned out would require a leap of four feet horizontally and another six feet up. A last push brought one hand to the lip of the lower roof. She transferred her other hand to the edge and pulled herself up onto the tar and gravel surface, where she laid breathing deeply for several minutes.

Once she felt able to continue, she reached into a small, leather bag tied to her belt, searching for a tiny jar of dark fluid. Both hands bled from shallow cuts; she applied the astringent, inhaling sharply at the sting. Within moments, the bleeding stopped.

Moonlight illuminated the roof through patchy, scudding clouds. She detected movement on the opposite roof: a man patrolled the perimeter of the other warehouse, strolling casually and puffing on a pipe. Kellyn waited for the man to walk beyond her position, then took a running leap, landing in a roll and sprinting to the guard before he could react to the slight noise of her arrival. A quick slap with a leather-wrapped billy and the man slumped unconscious into her arms.

Kellyn lowered the guard to the surface of the roof as silently as possible. She stood, stretching to get some of the soreness out of her muscles before heading down into the warehouse below. She turned from the prone figure toward the stairwell shack, unsheathed her sword, then abruptly reversed course to see if she'd killed the man. She reached for the man's neck, forgetting that she still held the training sword, and stopped with the blade just a fraction of an inch from the guard's skin. Moonlight flickered on the suddenly trembling blade.

"No," Kellyn whispered. She had no reason to kill. This was only a test. She had but one order: retrieve the talisman from the warehouse. She supposed other candidates might have slashed their way through any obstacle, but Kellyn's test featured a unique element. She had not only to prove that she'd mastered a warrior mage's skills, but that she had mastered herself.

She pulled back her unsteady right hand and reached out with her empty left. The guard lived. Well, as much as anything in this test lived. Everything in the test, the building, her enemies, the darkness and the damp of a dockside warehouse, complete with ships' bells softly ringing in the swell of the harbor, existed only within the testing hall. Not even the weather was as it seemed: outside the sun shone brightly in a clear blue sky, typical of a midsummer's day in the capitol. Here in the testing hall, night had fallen, and a chill like late fall raised goose pimples on her skin. At the conclusion of the test, only Kellyn and her weapons would remain. And the consequences.

How can an imaginary place possess such weight?

She remembered her first test, five years ago. She'd been just ten years old, and the test had been rather straightforward: as part of an honor guard protecting a visiting noble, she had to see the man safely through an angry mob. Had she passed, she'd no longer be a novice. She'd almost certainly have moved beyond apprentice status to journeyman by now. But no matter: Kellyn had lost control of herself, wading into the crowd swinging her enchanted sword with wild abandon, and the noble had been trampled to death in a human stampede. Luckily for Kellyn her teachers had decided to run her through the program again. Five more years, with the promise of a chance to redeem himself. Magrahim, her primary instructor, had made one thing clear: there would be no third time through the program.

Light spilled from under the door of the stairwell shack. Pausing only to extinguish the oil lamp that had bathed the shack with light, she darted down the stairwell into the poorly lit warehouse below.

Along the way, she willed her eyes to detect weak spots in the wooden stairs, gaps, anything that might make noise. The essence of magic—its diwa, in the ancient language of the Brotherhood—flowed through not just living things, but also through all materials that had once been living organisms, and through some things that had never lived at all. One of Kellyn's talents allowed her to see through the dead material itself, down into the many cracks and air pockets that filled with diwa, waiting to be released with the tread of a foot. This was a very low-level form of magic, and she could do it without fear of exhaustion. All magic came with a cost, as Magrahim never tired of telling her, usually physical and psychological exhaustion. She'd hardly used any magic at all so far, and her physical training paid off; already she felt better. She grinned, skipped those stairs that looked likely to creak, and emerged into the warehouse.

Stacks of wooden crates created narrow paths and dead ends. Unfortunately, the trick that let her see the hidden weaknesses within the wood did not allow her to see through the objects. After checking that no one lurked nearby, she retreated to a dark, narrow space. From a pocket, she produced a green stone shaped like a dragonfly. She closed her eyes and whispered an incantation, and the stone transformed into a real dragonfly and flew upward.

Behind closed eyelids, Kellyn saw what the insect saw. Along the outer wall of the warehouse, six red-robed men patrolled about ten paces from each other. By the big warehouse doors at the front of the building, two more armed men in red stood idly. Within a nearby office, seven more red-clad men lounged around a table, laughing and arguing.

There were other rooms along the right-hand wall of the building, and Kellyn directed the dragonfly to investigate when she noticed something far more important: the talisman! The diwa within the magical object was so powerful that it shone like a lantern, though it gave every appearance of being nothing more than a small bone tied to a leather cord. A single guard sat in a mostly enclosed area created by stacks of crates that reached almost to the ceiling. The talisman lay on a stool behind him. Only a single, narrow path led to this space. A smile spread across Kellyn's face as she thought about how she would attack this miniature fortress.

She set the dragonfly down upon the edge of a crate with a good view of her objective and opened her eyes. The insect reverted to a stone, and Kellyn moved quietly to a wall of crates one row over from the talisman. She thought briefly about trying to lift the talisman with the dragonfly, but the bone massed nearly as much as the insect. At best she might dislodge it from its stool, possibly alerting the guard. Instead, she climbed the crates, again doing her best to avoid those that looked most likely to make noise.

Her circuitous path to the top left her several feet behind the guard, too far for an unaided jump, so she reached underneath her tunic and grasped the amulet of strength that hung by a leather cord around her neck. Power flowed into her muscles as she silently mouthed the words of an incantation. She withdrew her billy and jumped.

She landed with a grunt, rolling to save her feet from the impact, and brought the lead bar up against the guard's temple as he turned.

The large man fell into Kellyn's arms, still extraordinarily powerful with magically enhanced strength, but already fading perceptibly. She set the man down quietly, flew the dragonfly back to her hand, and snatched the talisman from its resting place.

A bird screeched, implausibly loud. The sounds of booted feet slapping the wooden floor echoed throughout the warehouse. She should have checked the talisman for alarms; too late now. Sword in hand, she ran silently on the balls of her feet toward the oncoming men. A tiny corner of her mind screamed that she should be running in the opposite direction, but she couldn't make herself turn away. She was born for combat. Why would she run?

In an empty space at the intersection of two rows, she waited for her enemies. Within seconds four men clad in red entered the space from her left. Kellyn fingered a stone tied to her belt, pushed her personal time until she moved among the others like a hare among tortoises. The ability to manipulate time made the warrior mages of the Brotherhood a force to be feared well out of proportion to their small numbers. But like all forms of magic, it came with a cost. Already, her breath came rasping and ragged, and sweat poured down her body.

Her enchanted sword, though just a training weapon, sliced through flesh and bone with minimal resistance. One day she'd have a sword of her own, and it would be more than a weapon. A sword inhabited by a spirit, to bond with its wielder, to give her a sixth sense, almost a fifth limb, but not until she'd passed beyond her current lowly status. If she could only pass this test, despite the nagging voice telling her she ought to have escaped while she could.

When all the men she faced lay bloody and motionless on the floor, she pulled her time back to normal with a crooked smile. Her body trembled all over, flushed with excitement and the sheer ecstasy of killing. She might lie to Magrahim and call it just a manifestation of the joy of combat, the manic state many brothers experienced when fighting, but the truth was far simpler. She loved fighting, always had. She could no more stop herself now than she could fly to the moon.

Kellyn made her way to the front of the warehouse. She reached for

6 - TODD WOODMAN

a small door next to the big sliding doors that opened onto the street, but a noise stopped her. From those rooms on the right-hand side of the building, the rooms she hadn't had time to check, four men emerged, each leading a person in a gold robe.

"Put your weapons down, squint!" shouted the nearest red-robed man. Kellyn blinked at the jarring realism, as even the traditional Thurnish prejudice against her people had found its way into the test. "Surrender or we will kill the prisoners!"

Exhausted as she was, Kellyn never considered surrender. She pushed time again, pulled two charmed throwing stars from a pocket and hurled them in the general direction of her foes. As the stars flew, she took control of them, much as she did with the stone dragonfly, but with her eyes open. She controlled both at the same time, seeing the exact path travelled by each star, nudging each into proper alignment at the same time.

As she did this, her opponents in slow time began pressing their knives into the throats of their captives. The first star sliced effortlessly through the jugular of the first captor, leaving one hostage safe. The second star struck, but not until after a hostage died with a knife thrust under her jaw. From there, the stars kept travelling, but by the time they struck their targets, the last two prisoners died.

The test ended. The warehouse and everything in it, except the bodies, dissolving into dust that itself faded out of existence. All the guards lay dead, and Kellyn held the talisman in her pocket. One hostage still stood. The gold-robed man dissolved, as did the dead, leaving only the massive interior space of the testing hall.

Along one wall sat two people: Kellyn's instructor, Magrahim, and an old woman she had never seen before. From her pocket, she removed the small bone on its leather cord, the only object in the test that had been real. She held it out toward the elders with a trembling hand and a tentative smile.

She didn't need to see their pursed lips and hooded eyes to know she had failed spectacularly.

###

Kellyn had been allowed to bathe and change into fresh clothes. Magrahim led her to a small room where a bland meal of rice and lamb awaited her. Her instructor watched as she ate in silence. Kellyn avoided eye contact, concentrating on replenishing the fuel she'd burned so prolifically in the testing hall. The food, however, would not be enough. Her thoughts moved sluggishly, eyelids drooping every few heartbeats. She needed sleep to recover fully, but that would have to wait. When she finished her meal, the old woman joined them in the little room. The three of them sat upon stools facing each other around a circular table.

The chamber, like most in the Brothers' House, remained sparsely furnished and devoid of decoration, so unlike the rest of the Royal Residence. For ceremonial purposes, Temple Hall sported rich tapestries and ornately carved statuary, but the Brotherhood held aesthetics in low regard.

Magrahim introduced the woman as Trenna, a member of the Chamber of Elders, the group of mages who ran the Brotherhood and its sisters in the Order of Healing, usually referred to as the Sisterhood. She fit her position well, Kellyn decided, her robes undyed and functional, her graying, brown hair tied back in a severe bun. With her olive skin and dark, round eyes, she took the woman for a native of Thurn. Certainly, the heat seemed not to bother her.

Kellyn had often wondered what life would have been like for her if she'd been sent to the Sisters. Might her problem with violence have been better served learning to heal others, not kill them? Her elders must have at least considered bringing her to the sisters. The Brotherhood was not exclusively male, just as the Sisterhood was not a "girls only" club. But there were as few male 'sisters' as there were female 'brothers.'

Kellyn tried her best to remain calm, to look at her situation through the cold light of rationality. As with the test, she failed. Her shoulders slumped and she felt a tickling sensation in the corners of her eyes, as if she might cry. An elder had taken interest in her and she had proven she could not control himself.

"Do you know why you failed?" Magrahim said. Her teacher reached nearly six feet, almost as tall as Kellyn, but the two resembled each other not at all. Magrahim's powerful, barrel-like torso filled robes that always looked too small, while Kellyn's impressive height only served to accentuate her lean build. Long black hair lay in ringlets down her instructor's back, and a thick beard covered most of his dark-skinned face, clearly a foreigner to the shores of Thurn. Kellyn's classic northern looks—ruddy skin, straight, black hair, and amber eyes narrowed by epicanthic folds—looked nearly as out of place among the olive skin and brown hair of those native to the lands surrounding the Sea Between.

Magrahim's eyes held no hint of forgiveness. Kellyn had long looked to him as a father, but not a warm, loving figure. Her instructor demanded constant effort, precise accuracy, intellectual consistency, from himself as well as Kellyn. Like Trenna, her teacher chose unadorned clothing, but with a single affectation: Magrahim always wore black, for its stark simplicity.

Kellyn looked at her instructor, then down at her hands. "I should have examined the talisman for an alarm."

Magrahim shook his head. "We took steps to assure that you could not leave the warehouse without alerting the guards."

Kellyn opened her mouth to speak, but words refused to form.

"The candidate performed well when facing a single foe," Trenna said, filling the awkward silence. "Twice, in fact. She did not kill until she faced a numerically superior enemy."

"It is not the fact that she killed that bothers me," said Magrahim. "You healers are not often forced to take lives. Warrior mages must kill. Frequently."

"I took pleasure in killing," Kellyn said softly.

"Not merely pleasure. A kind of savage joy. You did not want to kill them. You needed to kill them, the way a sot craves a drink. Only when you kill do you feel that ecstasy." He turned to face Trenna. "I have taught the girl everything I can. For five years, she and I have been inseparable, I her primary instructor and she my only pupil. And yet I have failed to purge this love of death from her. Our options are limited."

Trenna nodded. "Protocol demands that we strip your powers, Kellyn. The least invasive method would leave your memories intact, and with your training and education, you would make a fine officer candidate for the Auxiliary Force."

"Considering your parentage, however," Magrahim said, his voice suddenly quiet, "the Chamber would certainly demand the most invasive method, taking your memories as well."

Trenna turned her gaze toward Kellyn. "Do you know why we brought you here, Kellyn, daughter of Valdis Hittrech?"

Kellyn gasped involuntarily. No one ever mentioned her father by name. She felt her eyes welling up with tears, and her cheeks burning red with shame. The Brotherhood valued emotional control rather highly, and she soon mastered herself. Still, she'd shown weakness.

"I apologize," Trenna continued. "That was unfair of me. But we do need to discuss your father. I'll answer for you. We brought you here for three reasons. First, because of your extraordinary abilities. You display mastery of nearly every talent for which we test you. The breadth of your abilities was clear even as a five-year-old. If you could master yourself, you could become an extremely able member of the Brotherhood.

"Secondly, we could not allow you to remain free, developing your talents without us to guide you. That's what your father did, and he became . . . a monster.

"Thirdly, most importantly, we brought you here to ease our guilty consciences."

Kellyn's mouth dropped open. Here sat two of the most powerful people she had ever met. Both confessing weakness. She blinked, scrambling for something to say.

Trenna smiled, but her eyes looked sad and old, very old. "We killed your father, destroyed his armies, and took you from your mother. How you must hate us."

"No! No, I—" She trailed off into silence. She had few memories of her father, just an impossibly large and powerful man, angry and terrifying, images that fled when she tried to focus on them. Mostly all she had at this point was a dim remembrance of fear.

Her mother, on the other hand—she had one very specific memory of her. The Prince's forces had been closing in, led by the mages of the Brotherhood. She and her mother, and a few of their closest supporters, trapped in a cave complex somewhere in eastern Kattenwa. Their defenses at the cave mouth had been breached, and her mother had taken Kellyn aside before fleeing deeper into the caves.

"I must leave for a short time, my daughter," she had said. She remembered every detail of her face, seen that last time, inches from her own. Her eyes, of an amber so bright as to be almost golden, the unhealed cut on her cheek weeping blood across a face pale as bone. Her hair had been cut short; she knew her mother usually kept it long, though she could not picture it. She'd been filthy from weeks on the run as the rebellion fell apart.

"The mages will come. Fight them if you can escape, but whatever happens, live! Surrender if you must, because I promise I will come for you. I won't be long, my lovely girl. I will return to you."

With those words she had fled, and Kellyn had never seen her again.

The Brotherhood had become her family. Must she now lose them, too?

Magrahim took a deep breath, let it out slowly. He had something important to say, she knew, and she wouldn't much like it. He always started out that way when he had something unpleasant to say.

"We may yet be able to save you," he said, quietly. "You're no longer the hate-filled bundle of violence you were when we first brought you here. But you still take great joy from killing. So much so that rational thought leaves your head at the prospect. Your father taught you that, and nothing we've been able to do for the last ten years has changed you. If you are to ever become a mage, you must lose that bloodlust."

Better to die showing mercy to the undeserving, Kellyn quoted to herself from the Code of the Brotherhood, *than to live denying mercy to the innocent.* "What can I do?" she said in a small, wavering voice.

Magrahim shrugged. "There's certainly nothing more I can do."

"There is one who may be able to help," Trenna said. "Felida Uffgold."

While her two elders nodded slowly, Kellyn wondered who this Uffgold person was, and why she'd never encountered him at the school before. Or 'her,' she supposed, since 'Felida' sounded like a woman's name.

"I agree," said Magrahim. "And I think she should leave right away."

"Leave?" said Kellyn. "Where is this Uffgold?"

"As it happens, she's back in your homeland."

"I have to go back to Kattenwa?"

"Uffgold is the only one who can teach you what you refuse to learn. And maybe it would be good for you to confront your demons."

Kellyn nodded, but her eyes went wide with fear.

"When do I leave?"

"As soon as we can arrange transport," Trenna said. "Not more than a week from now, I should think."

Her surprise must have shown. Magrahim reached across the table and laid a hand upon her forearm, a rare show of affection. "There is good reason for haste. Our agents have picked up rumors of a gathering of your parents' old cohorts. It may be nothing; such rumors surface often. But the Prince's men have picked up a few of the rebellion's junior officers in the last few months, men who have been in hiding for a decade."

"They claim to know nothing," Trenna said, "and almost invariably die at the first hint of magical questioning or torture. Such sorcerous conditioning argues that they did indeed know something worth dying to protect."

"What does this have to do with me?" Kellyn asked, though she feared the answer.

Magrahim shifted uncomfortably on his chair, frowning and staring intently at the tabletop. He took another deep breath. "One of your father's men lived long enough to answer a single question. We found him, here, a thousand miles from Kattenwa. When asked his objective, he answered, 'The girl.' They are coming out of hiding to find you, Kellyn, and we must know why."

2

Micah tried not to watch Garron. He had a job to do, and Garron would not look kindly upon slacking. If he caught Micah watching him instead of working, he could expect a beating. It wouldn't be a savage thrashing, the way some of the other bosses hit the boys who worked for them. Garron possessed no great store of brains, but he had smarts enough to know that injuring his worker wouldn't get more stone out of the quarry. And anyway, the boss could punish him in other ways. He had merely to threaten Micah's mother, and he would do anything, anything at all, to keep her safe. He brushed the spindly shape of Serpent, his prayer stone, hanging around his neck by a hempen cord, silently beseeching the help of a god, any god, in protecting his mother.

"I knows what yer thinkin', boy," said Garron, in an uneducated, hill country accent. The big man with thinning gray hair and a patchy beard smiled unpleasantly, showing the handful of crooked, yellow teeth he had left. Garron was a half-breed, most likely, with eyes almost as round as a Thurnish prince's, but with the ruddy skin and straight, dark hair of the Kattenese. He was digging quartz from the twenty-foot wide section of quarry wall that was his claim, but the bits of practically worthless stone were not his goal. No, he was after the pink granite boulder that had just begun to show right in the center of the rock wall he worked. Granite could fetch at least ten times as much as quartz. A really big boulder might fetch fifty times an equal amount of the lesser stone. Garron slapped that portion of the pink boulder that he had so far freed. "Yer thinkin' maybe this here pinkie's gonna be small enough ya can steal it from me, ain't ya?"

Micah shook his head and wiped sweat from his brow, fighting an urge to chew his fingernails. His mother hated the sight of his ragged nails, but they fit with the rest of him—hands scarred and calloused, every exposed bit of skin deeply tanned under layers of dust and grime, hair tangled and greasy. His mother would be sitting at home in the tiny shack the two of them shared, polishing prayer stones, and somehow remaining clean and presentable. Not Micah. He looked like any other rock dog.

Out of the corner of his eye, he could see other quarry workers watching the exchange with Garron. Envy and jealousy spread like wildfire whenever a man had the good fortune to find granite in the center of his claim. A smarter man would take the boy into his confidence, use him to find out what the men in the neighboring claims were thinking. A smarter man might talk with those neighbors, negotiate a little help in removing the big stone. Spread the wealth a little, so to speak. Garron was not such a man.

"Ah, yer lyin', ya little turd! Just ya remember, I got yer bond! An' this here pinkie, she's mine! Got it?"

"Yessir," Micah mumbled as his suddenly trembling fingers brushed the tattoo on his neck: his bond mark, and Garron owned it. If Micah ever disobeyed, or tried to run away, his master had merely to speak a few words and the bond mark would force Micah to do Garron's bidding. He'd heard the mark could hurt worse than anything in the world, burning like flame. He'd never felt its lash and didn't intend to. All he wanted was to get home.

"Good. Now git this quartz outta my way!"

Micah had a few baskets full of quartz, not really enough to bring to the pit master, but at times like this, it was best to stay away from Garron. He loaded the baskets onto the wheelbarrow and pushed them up the ramp toward Tunni's scale shack, where the pit master would weigh and inspect the rocks. Even if it wasn't fully loaded, the wheelbarrow and quartz weighed a lot more than Micah, and he was big for just ten years old. He had to be, in order to do the job well, and he never wanted Garron to think he wasn't worth his keep.

So Micah made himself big. Part of it included eating as much as he could, whenever food was available. His mother wasn't a small person, and she'd told him that his father had been a very big man. But he knew that the most important reason for his unusual size was that he had abilities other people didn't. He could make his body grow faster than it should and build muscles normal ten-year-olds just didn't have. The back-breaking work at the quarry allowed him to work those muscles hard. As a result, he wasn't tall and gangly. No, he'd nearly reached an adult's height, while still stocky and strong as an ox.

He couldn't have said exactly how he did it, but he knew it had to do with magical power, what Dimford, the local practitioner, called 'diwa.' Dimford had some magical education, and claimed he'd gone to a school in Thurn. Micah scowled. Thinking of Thurn always made him think of his older sister, the one he'd never met, whose name he didn't even know, who had supposedly gone off to a school of magic in Thurn. His mother used to talk about how she'd come back one day, how she'd free her and Micah from their bonds. But she never came back. His mother rarely spoke about her now.

"Don't need her," Micah said through gritted teeth as he pushed the wheelbarrow up the ramp. The sun rode high in the sky, its fierce heat the kind that could drop a big man, or boy, if he weren't careful about drinking enough water. He rested for a few seconds and reached for the water gourd tied to his waist. What water remained had lost all flavor, but it helped to have a little moisture in his mouth.

Dust hung in the air on this windless day. Worse were the windy days, when the dirt and grit flew into eyes and mouths, and no amount of water ever seemed to get rid of the taste. Worse still, the rainy days, when every surface turned slippery and treacherous. He'd seen a man swing a pickaxe at a wet stone, and shivered at the memory as the point slipped off the muddy boulder to bury itself instead in the digger's foot.

He recalled the time a shard of rock sent flying by a sledgehammer took out Blind Tom's left eye. Or the day the ramp collapsed and killed three boys.

At the top of the ramp, he heaved a sigh of relief. It was a lot easier rolling along on even ground. But his relief died quickly, for two groups of boys waited outside the shack. Older boys in their teens, about Micah's height if not his strength, lounged about, leaning against the shack, napping sprawled in the dirt, or sitting cross legged. Some rolled pigs' knuckle bones, gambling away wooden company coins, good only at the quarry store. Micah pushed Garron's wheelbarrow into line and stood near the older boys, but they either ignored him or sent bored scowls in his direction. Occasionally, he'd catch one of the older boys staring at him. They remembered him as a smaller boy, obviously younger. Maybe his size confused them.

Most of Micah's attention he gave to the little ones, who ran around the shack in ragged bands, playing 'catch me if you can' or 'the robber and the baron' or throwing stones at imaginary targets. He hadn't joined their games in a long time now, since the little ones seemed as confused by his unusual growth as the older ones. They'd give him odd looks and turn their backs. The last time he tried to play, Fanien, one of the bolder boys, had realized that Micah enjoyed no more welcome among the teens. He'd shown his cohorts that they could gang up on Micah and drive him away with a shower of rocks and insults. Micah, in turn, had shown Fanien the limits of his power when the boy came within striking distance. He'd thrashed the little bastard, leaving him whimpering and bleeding in the dust, and while he hated his isolation, he still relished the feel of Fanien's nose splintering under his fists.

Clearly, Fanien remembered the beating as well. The boy's face still sported bruises, and his nose looked like a misshapen, purple potato. Micah looked his way, but the other boy refused to make eye contact. Another boy, Larkin, walked beside Fanien. Larkin looked directly at Micah and flinched. Micah smirked, but the flinch struck him like a blow. Larkin had been a friend not all that long ago.

Micah sighed and sat next to his meager accumulation of quartz.

He pulled Serpent from around his neck and rubbed the stone with massive, spatulate hands. He'd named the stone for its type, serpentine, before he began to shape it. The green stone, almost as worthless as quartz, had begun its life as a roughly spherical lump smaller than an apple. Micah had worked Serpent for a couple of years now, squeezing, rubbing, even talking to it, and above all imagining Serpent as he wished the stone to be. Now, when he stretched his fingers wide, Serpent reached from the tip of his thumb almost to the last knuckle of his little finger. Of late he'd begun to work curves into the stone so that it even looked a bit like a snake.

Some other rock dogs could work stone the same way, with neither tools nor brute force, just the power of their hands and minds. As magic went, it neither impressed nor counted for much. But Micah believed Serpent possessed magical qualities all out of proportion to its size. Serpent calmed him, and when he felt he could work no more, he believed he could draw strength from the little stone. His mother scoffed at the idea, so much so that Micah never mentioned Serpent to her anymore. But now, as he sat alone, torn between feeling sorry for himself and seething at the injustice of it all, he grasped Serpent tightly, willing the stone to calm him.

He waited outside the shack while Tunni dealt with the older boys. They entered with full wheelbarrows and exited with pockets full of wooden coins. The boys laughed at something one of them mumbled, but they spared Micah only the barest of glances. Except for Newill. The older boy, tall and rangy, with a beak of a nose and a peasant's brown eyes in his ruddy face, motioned Micah over to join him.

"Hey, kid," he said.

Micah nodded wordlessly as he stood near Newill.

"Saw what you did to that little shit," he said with a nod toward Fanien. "Good with your fists, eh?"

Micah shrugged. "He's pretty little."

"Yeah, but you're not. You got some size. Wanna see just how tough you are?"

Micah blinked, unsure how to respond. Newill was hinting at the fights the older boys staged every week. They gambled as the chosen boys pummeled each other. Micah had never been allowed to attend. The fights were invite only, and his mother would probably say no anyway. "I, uh, I don't know."

"Think about it. Still a couple days left 'til Templeday. Talk to me before then if you change your mind. Right?"

"Sure."

Micah released a breath he hadn't been realized he was holding and forced himself to attend to the business at hand. He had no time to worry about the fights, and whether or not he'd even try to sneak out to try his hands against the older boys. Still, the thought intrigued him.

He shook his head, counted up what he thought he had in the wheelbarrow, figured it was about one hundred and eighty pounds of relatively low quality stone, and came to a likely total of twenty-five counters. The pit boss would short him at least two counters' worth, plus the three he'd take as his fee for a load like this, leaving, at best, twenty counters. Garron would probably give Micah no more than four or five of the wooden coins, added to the three he'd given him earlier in the day. Maybe one more run today, for a day's total of ten or twelve. Not much, but it would be enough to buy food for the next couple of days, and maybe enough to set aside a few coins for the other little necessities of life like clothing, or even soap. Maybe other boys didn't think like that. Maybe they had fathers to make such calculations. For Micah, such thoughts had become commonplace.

And what would Garron say to today's take? He wouldn't be happy, and most days Micah could expect to get slapped around. Or maybe his master would threaten his mother. Threaten to beat her, to force her to work in the quarry. Micah cringed at the thought, but those threats paled in comparison to Garron's ultimate weapon: the threat to marry Micah's mother. He couldn't stand that one. The thought of that cruel old man, putting his lips on his mother's lips, forcing her to have his children; he shivered despite the heat. Or maybe Garron would leave him alone. After all, he had the granite.

And what did Micah have? He might have a new set of friends. If he could handle himself in the fights, that is. Did he want to? What if he got injured? What if he couldn't dig in the quarry? What would Garron do then? He had no answers, and the worries failed to disperse.

The weighing went pretty much as Micah expected, though Tunni shorted Micah just one counter. Probably wanted something; Tunni never gave anything for free.

"How's Garron doing, boy?" said the old man.

"What you mean, boss?" But Micah knew what the pit boss wanted: information. But how to tell Tunni about Garron's granite without his master knowing? Garron would beat him for that, surely.

"I hear tell there's a big chunk of granite poking out of his rock face. That true?"

"Yeah, I guess," he said. "Don't look so big, though."

A great deal of granite lay behind the face of Garron's claim, but no one could see that yet. No one except Micah. Granite contained a lot of diwa, way more than quartz. The quartz made good polished prayer stones, but granite could be made into just about anything. Maybe even into the kind of magical objects Dimford made. Micah saw the diwa in the stone the way ordinary people might see a candle through gauzy curtains. The bigger the stone, the more power it held, and the brighter it looked to him. That boulder in Garron's claim shone brightly as a bonfire.

Tunni picked up a handful of quartz pebbles from his scales. "This stuff, this is nothing. But that granite, Garron could be sitting on a lot of money there. But you know what? If that really is a lot of granite, he'll have to hire dozens of men to haul it out of the quarry. It's worth more as a single piece than if it's broken up, you see?"

"Well, yeah. But we don't know how big it is yet, right? Maybe it's small enough for me and him to handle."

"That could be. But like I said, the bigger it is, the more it'll cost to move when it comes out. And if that boulder's big enough to extend into someone else's claim, then he'll have to split the take."

"So?" But Micah knew what Tunni was getting at. Garron could sell his claim now, on the chance that it might hold a big return. It might just make sense to hire a magical practitioner to figure its size exactly. But Garron would never spend money on a chance like that. Micah knew, though, that this granite would justify the expense.

Tunni confirmed his guess, offering about six months' worth of credit for Garron's claim. "Think he'll go for it?"

Micah knew the answer would be no. That kind of offer would only convince Garron that he could get more on his own. But could he? A few more quick calculations told him that, after hiring all the men it would take to move the boulder, Garron would only see a little bit more profit than Tunni was offering. In other words, Tunni's offer, supposedly based on guesswork, looked almost perfectly fair. He decided to be forward, bold even.

"That's a lot of money for granite you can't even see, yet. You know something Garron don't?"

Tunni looked down, smiling. When he made eye contact with Micah, he could see that the smile was fake as fool's gold. "I been working this shack since before Garron was born. I see a lot of things, and I talk to a lot of people. My guesses are probably better that what most folks would say they know for a fact."

Micah could see his lie as plain as day. Tunni knew. Which meant he'd sent a practitioner down to Garron's claim during the night. Micah merely nodded. "Yeah, s'pose you're right. I'll tell Garron. Now I better hurry back so I can get another run in before dark."

Outside the shack, Micah's heart raced. How would he convince Garron to take the offer? He'd never been able to convince his owner of anything. But what if someone else could do it? Newill's father, Waldsdon, he might be able to convince Garron. Everyone listened to Waldsdon. Micah resolved to ask Newill to help him, and to agree to come to the fights on Templeday, but Tunni would expect an answer sooner than that.

Garron scoffed at Tunni's offer. "He's so cheap, if he's offerin' that much, it must be worth three times that!"

"What if it ain't, though?" Micah asked, hoping he could find a way to steer the conversation without looking like he knew anything for certain. "He sounded like he knew, see? Like maybe he sent someone down here to spy one night while we was sleeping."

"A 'course he sounded that way to you, boy, 'cause you don't know nothin'!"

Micah looked at his battered shoes and nodded. Rejecting Tunni's offer represented a huge mistake. Garron would probably take the cheap and stupid route and break the boulder up into several smaller chunks so he wouldn't have to hire help. Probably he didn't think the boulder massed as much as it did. If only he could show him the granite's extent without revealing his ability to see things normal people couldn't.

Above all, he had to hide his true abilities. There was already talk about Micah's unusual size. If just once Garron thought his worker had magical talent, he'd sell him in a heartbeat, Micah knew. Then his mother would be forced to marry that swine, and probably work in the quarry alongside him. His mind's eye showed him his mother with a pickaxe through her foot, or crushed under a falling boulder. But if Micah didn't find a way to show Garron just how big the granite really was, he'd break it up. Then he'd earn less than he might have, and somehow find a way to blame Micah. He flinched at the thought. Garron had never been so mad as he would be when he realized how much money he'd pissed away. There had to be a way to show him his folly before he acted on it.

And then it hit him.

"You want me to help dig that boulder?" Micah asked. Usually, he just scooped the loose quartz into baskets, but he could see the greed in Garron's eyes. Two people could work the boulder free faster than one.

"Yeah, ya better help. Stay on that side, outta my way."

Micah nodded and began working a large awl—a bit like a five-foot long toothpick capped with an iron spike—into the quartz under the boulder and to the right side, while Garron steadily worked the left side with a pickaxe. Micah pounded the flat end of the awl with a wooden mallet, driving the tool deeper and deeper into the rock. When he'd buried about half its length in the quartz, he made a big show of trying to move the awl to loosen the stone. But he'd driven it in too deep and had to really work to try to free it. He braced himself against the granite boulder, pushing with all his might.

Of course, it wouldn't budge, and Micah didn't care. He only braced himself against the granite so he could feel it, drawing strength from the diwa within the stone, as he did with Serpent. And then he did something he'd never done before, never even tried to do until now. He reached deep within the surrounding quartz, not with a tool, but with his mind. Micah envisioned an invisible third hand probing into the stone underneath the granite, pushing the weaker rock aside and widening all the cracks he could find.

"What in blazes ya doin', boy?" Garron said.

"Sorry, boss," grunted Micah, straining with the effort. He'd never worked so hard, but the power flowing through his hands exhilarated him. Diwa poured into his body like lightning coursing through his veins. Powerful, searing hot, charged. But he didn't dare show how great it felt. "I got the awl stuck, but it's almost free."

"Ya stupid, clumsy oaf! Break my tools an' I'll beat ya, hear?"

"I hear, boss. Don't worry, I—"

Micah never finished the thought. He had moved more quartz than he thought, that or the rock surrounding the granite was too unstable to begin with, because the whole boulder moved a few inches. The shift itself wasn't dramatic, but the cascade of rocks and pebbles that followed sure was. Micah found himself buried up to his knees in pieces of rock varying in size from pebbles to chunks larger than his head. Even Garron had been half buried in the little landslide.

While his boss struggled to free himself, shouting a string of curses that should have made his ears burn, Micah just stood there, stunned at what he saw. The boulder massed as huge as ever, but it glowed in his sight as it never had before. Almost as if the granite had grown. But of course it hadn't. The shift in the surrounding stone had simply allowed Micah to see that behind this boulder sat another, even bigger chunk of granite, and in that larger stone, even more magical essence burned. It wasn't yet visible to anyone who couldn't see diwa, but he could see its power.

Without thinking, Micah placed one hand on the granite in front of him and felt diwa leap from the stone into his body. He felt a sense of power he'd never experienced, like he could move the whole boulder out of the quarry by himself if he chose. And why shouldn't he? Why not just shove it up to the rim of the pit, sell it to Tunni and keep all the credits for himself? Who was Garron to stand in his way? Just an uneducated, ignorant swine, a beast who hit a child and threatened a woman.

The thought of that pig touching his mother filled him with rage, and he decided to use that power, to display his might to everyone in the quarry. Grinning like a maniac even as the frightened boy within him trembled, he grasped the granite with both hands, drawing the whole thing a few feet from the quarry face. Micah giggled, a high pitched, gurgling sound that threatened to break free of all constraints.

The screaming stopped him, and he jerked his hands back from the boulder. He'd caused a small avalanche, and Garron's lower body was entirely covered by a thick slab of quartz. From the blood leaking out from beneath the rock that nearly buried him, it was clear that his boss would not survive. His screams grew ragged, then hoarse. He sobbed, whispering, "Help me! Help me, boy!"

But Micah did nothing. Dozens of workers stared in their direction. Quarry work threatened physical harm at the best of times, and fatal accidents were not uncommon. Most could tell at a glance that Garron had but moments to live, and that nothing they could do would help. But few of them paid much attention to the dying man. The ramp above Garron's claim had partially collapsed, revealing not only more of the boulder's true size, but the presence of the second boulder.

Micah stared, then heard another rock fall. He looked up, seeing Fanien on the ramp above him, trying to pull his wheelbarrow out of the pit that had formed on the collapsed ramp. Fanien locked eyes with Micah, who saw fear on the younger boy's face. Micah knew a little fear then, too. Had Fanien seen what he'd done? Would he tell someone? Would they believe him?

Garron died then, surrounded by men whose lust for the vacated claim showed on their faces. Micah's one thought remained rather more personal. He had just killed a man. It should have scared him. And in truth, it did. A terrified scream bubbled just under the surface, waiting to burst forth from his lips. But his head buzzed with the memory of the power that had just flowed though his hands. The power to move mountains, the power to kill.

But all those people staring made him nervous. He grasped Serpent through his filthy tunic, begging the stone for help. In a moment of pure panic, he freed himself from the drift of quartz and scrambled up the partially collapsed ramp, passed Tunni's shack without slowing down, and ran all the way home.

3

"Why can't you tell anyone?"

Kellyn sighed. Alonselle Westlyn wasn't her only friend in the Brotherhood, but he was a member of a very small club. Tall, gangly, shy, a pale foreigner from Khedria, immersed in the esoteric field of Instrumentation, Alonselle had as few friends as she. He was the only student older than her, and the only person she actually wanted to tell, but Magrahim had been quite clear about the need for secrecy.

Alonselle pursed his lips. "Come on, if we can't trust each other, who do we have? Or don't you trust me?"

"I trust you," she said, a slight edge to her voice. Alonselle always pressed their friendship a little too much. Demanded too much, clung too much. He seemed the sort who felt his social isolation too keenly, and desperately wanted friends. Kellyn wanted friends, too, but she was too distrustful, too skeptical of motives. And, she could admit to herself, she didn't want anyone too close.

But still, what harm could it do to tell him where she was going? Considering the play acting she was about to engage in for the benefit of potential spies, it was harmless, wasn't it?

"I'm going back to Kattenwa," she said in hushed tones.

"You've been expelled?" Alonselle looked incredulous, furious. "That's unjust, that's . . . that's outrageous! You're a better mage than any other student. Nine hells! You're better than half our instructors!"

"Keep your voice down! Look, thanks for the kind words and all, but I still have things to learn, important things, and I have to go back to

Kattenwa to learn that stuff. I'm not in the clear, but I'm not expelled. Not yet, anyway."

Alonselle's eyes were wide, nostrils flaring, mouth set in a grim, straight line. He grunted and rubbed his belly, likely feeling some kind of gastric distress. The poor guy could never gain weight because of some unspecified problem in his gut. If he weren't such a pathetic figure, physically, such a display of anger would be endearing, even cute. She knew he was interested in her, romantically, but Kellyn had made it clear that she liked girls. It didn't stop Alonselle from trying to change her mind, occasionally. Even now, he stood too close. She put a hand on his chest and gently pushed.

"Arm's length, remember? You promised."

"I'm sorry. I just . . . .." He backed up a step, looked at his feet, shoulders slumped, and it suddenly dawned on her that what he was really upset about was that she was leaving at all.

"Thanks, Alon," she said. "You're a good friend. And we'll see each other again, I promise. Right now, I could just use some of that good luck you're always on about."

Alonselle nodded, still not making eye contact. "Good luck, Kellyn. I'll miss you."

Kellyn followed Magrahim through the corridors of the Brothers' House. The Brotherhood's home wasn't so much a house as a fortress. In fact, the massive stone building had once been a castle. These days, it was merely one structure among a couple of dozen that made up the Royal Residence, a whole district of palaces, temples, parks and court-yards that together housed the king and his court. The Brotherhood supplied both the officers of the king's army and its elite shock troops, few in number though they were. Still, there was nothing grand about their home. Like the Brothers themselves, the old fort sat among the finer chateaus and towers like a stoic country cousin come to visit its sophisticated city relatives. Neither did the Brotherhood attempt to make their home more comfortable. In winter, the old stone held tightly to the cold and damp, while now in high summer, the stuffy heat could overwhelm the unprepared.

"That scroll will get you aboard any means of transport you can find," Magrahim said. "Once you are packed, you are to leave as soon as you find a caravan captain willing to take you. That shouldn't be hard. They're always willing to hire a trained sword."

Kellyn looked at the scroll in her hand and nodded, playing her role as well as she could, despite her relatively poor performance in her Deception classes. "How long do you think the journey will take, Brother Magrahim? I would guess at least four weeks."

Magrahim smiled a little. "Good application of book learning, young Kellyn. But you will soon see that books do not contain all the knowledge there is. Most likely you'll be travelling in a merchant caravan, not a military convoy. Factor in stops at every large town along the road and the slow pace of fully laden wagons, and your journey will stretch to at least six weeks, maybe eight."

Neither of the two mages were being particularly quiet, for the benefit of any possible listeners. But she didn't want to talk about the journey. She wanted to hear more about this Felida Uffgold woman and her plans for her continued education. Magrahim, however, had made it clear that he wouldn't talk about it, and that at no time was she to speak the healer's name. And so Kellyn asked questions about everything else she could, hoping Magrahim would let something slip.

But she had run out of questions. The silence stretched as they made their way to the barracks. Soon Kellyn would enter the students' section, and Magrahim would walk on to the instructors' apartments. Would she even see Magrahim again before she left via some secret passage? His steadying presence had been there, each and every day, for five years straight. She tried and failed to imagine life without him.

"Brother Magrahim!"

Kellyn turned, along with her teacher, toward the familiar voice of August Nigh. The king's First Minister strode briskly through the wide central corridor of the Brothers' House, followed by the small army of aides and messengers that dutifully trailed him everywhere. Among his flock stood the Master of Spies, short and thin, with small eyes too close together, thinning brown hair gone mostly gray, dressed in the beige cotton trousers and tunic that comprised his uniform. People tended not to notice the spy, which made Kellyn want to watch him all the more. But she found that she couldn't. She'd try to stare at the man, but her eyes would wander to the First Minister in the scarlet silk of his office, or to the messengers wearing red ribbons around their biceps, identifying them as Nigh's men. Her gaze simply didn't want to fall upon the little gray man.

Subtle magic, but powerful. A line from a rhyme she'd learned years ago came to her. "His vow cannot be broken, 'til his secret name is spoken." The Master of Spies had taken a Name of Power. Whatever his mother had called him mattered not at all. And none but he knew the name that bound him to the throne with complete and perfect loyalty. He could speak his hidden name anytime he wished, thus breaking the spell that imprisoned him. Freedom he would have, then, and death. All the low born men who rose to positions of influence in the king's service took such vows, going all the rest of their lives without a name, just a title. All except the officers of the Brotherhood.

And the First Minister. August Nigh dressed in court finery, consisting even in this hot, muggy, summer weather of silk robes over woolen leggings, all of it in the scarlet red that his office required. Nigh's origins as a commoner were well known, and yet he'd never been required to take a Name of Power. Instead, he'd received the reward of a noble title for his service to the king. Nigh enjoyed the title of baronet, not much above a landless knight. The title was nonhereditary, but it mattered little; Nigh had no children.

But as long as the king was satisfied with his First Minister's loyalty, why should anyone else question it? And Kellyn believed the presence of the Master of Spies in his retinue argued that the king trusted Nigh implicitly.

The old man glanced in her direction and winked a pale, rheumy eye. Suddenly, Kellyn realized that in all the time since her failure, she hadn't once thought of Nigh or the kindness he and his wife had shown her over the years. The Nighs had done all they could for Kellyn, inviting her to their apartments for holiday meals, providing clothing, books, even the occasional present for birthdays or Winterfest.

Not that they didn't help a lot of the Brotherhood's students that way. Many children's families lived too far away from the capitol for visits during the school year, and most couldn't afford to travel back and forth no matter how close they lived. Alonselle was one of those shown the First Minister's favor, too. Some, like Kellyn, had no living relatives. But almost none of the other initiates had reached fifteen years of age and still hadn't attained the rank of apprentice. Very few of them, for that matter, were even teenagers. Fewer still, within the Brotherhood, were girls. Kellyn was unique, and often uniquely miserable. The friendship shown to her by Nigh and his wife, Chahn-li, provided just about the only refuge she had from the routine of school.

And yet she appreciated them little. She'd always been a touch embarrassed by their attention. And as much as she hated to admit it, she didn't entirely trust the First Minister, despite the king's apparent satisfaction in that regard. Nor could she have said exactly why. Maybe it was just that Magrahim didn't trust any member of the king's court, and said so often. It wouldn't be the first time she'd picked up one of her instructor's attitudes.

And Nigh's exotic wife, from the far western land of Sook, constantly attended by her sorcerer-healer, inspired a certain unease in Kellyn. Many had commented upon her, few favorably. Not that Chahn-li had ever shown her anything but kindness. Still, Sook attitudes toward sorcery were famously relaxed. As one whose parents so clearly fell into the category of 'evil sorcerers,' Kellyn found she could never quite trust the First Minister's wife.

"So glad we've bumped into one another," Nigh said to Magrahim. "May I speak with you, privately?" His retinue dispersed at a flick of his hand.

"Of course," said Magrahim. He and Kellyn fell in behind Nigh and followed him out of the old castle and into the Summer Palace, to his apartments. The First Minister's living quarters consisted of large, ornately decorated rooms clustered around a central, high-ceilinged hall. Nigh led them to his relatively unadorned office. A large desk dominated the stuffy, windowless room. Nigh pulled a rope tied to a golden ring set in the wall by the door, sat and invited his guests to join him around the desk. Within moments, the ceiling fan began to turn, and Kellyn wondered briefly if either magic or a servant at a set of pedals powered the fan. She shrugged, then blinked at the sudden presence of the Master of Spies.

"I have invited the Master to join us; I hope you don't mind."

Magrahim inclined his head.

"Good. To begin," Nigh continued, "knowledge is my trade. I know that young Kellyn is being sent back to Kattenwa to continue her education." He lifted his hands. "Beyond that, I know little, nor do I want any details. But I must tell you what I have discovered of the situation to our north. Master of Spies, if you would?"

The spymaster sat rigidly at the edge of his chair, his back straight as a pike. He spoke quietly and with few of the flourishes of speech so common among most court functionaries. "My agents have detected an unusual amount of activity in Kattenwa, including more traffic on the roads than is usual in high summer, gatherings of men in tavern back rooms, and a spike in the number of coded messages sent through supposedly secure message services. Most of the information exchanged in all this traffic is unintelligible. But those messages that we have decoded point to an uprising."

August leaned forward. "The timing of the uprising is what intrigues me most. Do continue."

The Master of Spies frowned minutely at the interruption. "Yes. They are waiting for someone to arrive in Kattenwa. Someone whose arrival—or perhaps return—they have anticipated since the death of Valdis Hittrech."

Kellyn blanched at the mention of her father, her breath and heartbeat becoming quicker. Nigh glanced at her, smiling sadly, and Kellyn looked away, embarrassed at the display of sympathy. She took a deep breath and ran silently through a calming exercise.

"You say 'perhaps' return?" Magrahim asked.

The Master of Spies nodded. "Most of the messages are in an ancient form of High Yungka, a language rarely spoken anywhere except among the sorcerers of one of the lesser Mohotsan schools. Between the obscurity of the language and the complexity of the code, I cannot be certain of the translation."

Magrahim nodded, stroking his beard and looking up at the spinning ceiling fan, eyes unfocused. The First Minister broke the silence. "Given that Hittrech's supporters may be waiting for Kellyn, might it not be best to keep the girl here, and bring her new teacher to the capital?"

"If Kellyn's safety were our only concern," Magrahim said, "then yes. But Hittrech's Rebellion came uncomfortably close to success. If he'd shown a little patience, we might all be living under his yoke. His successors, whoever they might be, have had a decade to plan. What we need now is to bring them out into the open so we can strike. This time, we will destroy them at the root."

"And the girl will be bait?" Nigh asked, with a hard edge to his voice.

Kellyn, long practiced at remaining silent while her elders spoke about her as if she weren't in the room, glanced at her instructor with no particular expression on her face. Behind her placid mask, however, she rejoiced—finally, she'd get some concrete answers.

"Only a handful of people know where Kellyn is going. When she will arrive there will remain secret." Magrahim inclined his head toward the Master of Spies. He had not yet mentioned the Brotherhood's own information regarding the planned uprising in the Principality of Kattenwa.

"My people," said the spy, "will of course give the sorcerers false information. And the Brotherhood maintains a contingent of mages in Kattenwa, in the service of Prince Johann. Kellyn and her contact need only reveal themselves to an officer and they will receive all the help they require."

"But why send her there at all?"

"Minister Nigh," Magrahim said, "in order to complete this phase of her education, Kellyn must confront certain aspects of her upbringing. The diwa in specific locations within her homeland should resonate within her, perhaps call to the fore deeply buried memories. The person who will take over her education is unusually skilled at identifying those memories and finding ways to excise them."

"There will be danger."

"When is life ever safe for the mages of the Brotherhood?"

Nigh sighed. "May I at least offer my assistance? I would like to make one of my caravans available to transport young Kellyn to Kattenwa. I already have a perfect cover. My wife is quite active in court fashion, as you may know. She has located a source of high quality martin fur in northern Kattenwa, and martin will be all the rage this winter. It will not seem strange that I am rushing a few wagons north on short notice, and a new crew member won't attract much attention. What say you?"

Magrahim frowned, but the Master of Spies nodded eagerly. "Brother Magrahim, the First Minister's special cargo caravans are staffed with only his most trusted employees. I think you should accept this offer."

Magrahim glanced at Kellyn and nodded his assent.

Two days later, Kellyn found herself in a little-used storeroom within the Brothers' House. Amid stacks of crates that reminded her of the simulated warehouse of her test, she whispered an incantation while grasping a tiny, pewter key. The key began to glow dimly. As she moved about, its light varied until suddenly it shone bright as a torch. Nearby, between tall crates roughly the size of coffins, another source of light appeared: a keyhole no larger than a fly, floating in the air a finger's breadth from the wall. She squeezed between two crates and inserted the key into its hole. The crates moved away from each other, and a doorway opened.

She stepped through the portal and into a dusty corridor lined with doors. Her contact hadn't told her which door to use, so she chose one at random and walked confidently into what looked like a tiny broom closet. The door slammed shut behind her. With a clang, the closet lurched, dropped a few feet, then slid sideways. Despite knowing that such a system of secret passageways existed beneath the Royal Residence, Kellyn shouted in alarm.

The lateral motion continued for some time, turning occasionally, before the closet stopped for several moments. More metallic sounds followed before her tiny cell abruptly fell. Kellyn squeezed her eyes shut, bracing her hands against the walls, anticipating a catastrophic landing.

With a screech of metal on metal, the closet slowed to a stop. "It's not the fall that kills you," she said to herself in giddy relief, "it's the sudden stop at the bottom."

The door behind her opened, and the Master of Spies greeted her in a windowless corridor. He motioned for Kellyn to follow and led the way to a spacious office. Shelves crammed with books, loose papers, and scrolls lined two of the walls. A large table dominated half the room, and atop it sat several unfamiliar brass instruments. A small desk occupied the corner furthest from the door. On it were a few neatly stacked piles of paper, some blank, some filled with densely packed script. The Master sat at the desk and waved his fingers at another chair.

"Sit, Kellyn. We must assume you are being watched. If the rebels' spies are well informed, they will know that there are many secret passages within the Royal Residence, and that all roads lead to this office."

"So they'll know I'm here."

"But they will not know where 'here' is. Only I know the exact location of my offices at any given time. The portals leading out of the Royal Residence from here are relocated randomly, but we have a finite number of possible exits to choose from. A thorough spy network could conceivably watch all the known exits. Therefore, we have given them something to see."

The Master of Spies removed a single sheet of paper from one stack, read it quickly, and dropped it into a wicker basket on the floor. The paper ignited, but the basket remained unharmed. The burning paper emitted no smoke.

"One of my young agents has been magically modified to look a little like you, as if you yourself were disguised as a boy. He has taken your place on the First Minister's special caravan."

Kellyn smiled crookedly. "In case someone associated with Minister Nigh is part of this conspiracy?"

"Yes. I trust the First Minister as much as I trust anyone who has not taken a Name, but not all of those in his employ. Another of my agents already bears a striking resemblance to you, and no magic whatsoever has been used in her disguise. She is currently aboard a sailing vessel headed north. Both agents left yesterday."

Kellyn's smile hardened. Those agents had placed themselves in danger for her. And though all of them worked toward the same objective—rooting out the conspirators—Kellyn stood to gain the most from their success. "So when do I leave?"

"Today. We won't bother altering your appearance, since those slanted, golden eyes proclaim you as Kattenese no matter what disguise I might concoct. You will leave via a rarely used exit that will take you to the air dock by the shortest route possible."

Kellyn's mouth dropped open. "An airship?"

"Yes, one of the First Minister's, in fact."

"He knows about this, then?"

"Yes, though only he and I know how you will leave the capital. Sister Uffgold, incidentally, has been told to expect your arrival in a matter of weeks. Even she does not know exactly how you will be traveling. Are you ready to leave?"

"Now?" Kellyn should have known better, but she'd nevertheless expected to be able to say goodbye to Magrahim and Alonselle before she left. It was silly, she knew, for at fifteen she was no longer a child and shouldn't need to have her hand held. She focused instead on the most important fact: not all tests in the Brotherhood took place in the Testing Hall. She could still pass. She could still become a fully fledged member of the Brotherhood. A powerful mage, an officer within the king's army, maybe one day an Elder. And now she'd get to sail aboard an airship, a privilege only the barest handful of people could ever hope to enjoy.

"Will I have a cover identity?"

"Your Deception scores were rather unimpressive. So, no, you will not have much of a cover. 'Kellyn' is a common enough name in Kattenwa, and it is obvious that you are a mage. Just do not tell any of the crewmen anything about your family or your destination. Agreed?"

Kellyn nodded.

"Good. One last piece of advice: trust your instincts. I am told you are an excellent judge of character. This is not an ability to be ignored. If someone or something seems wrong to you, do not shrug it off. Examine all the information you have, but also listen to your gut."

Kellyn walked down the street without a glance back at the shipping office from which she'd emerged. Something about the advice from the Master of Spies' worried at the back of her mind, but all thoughts left her head when she saw the airship for the first time. Well, not exactly the airship, for what she saw in the air was only part of the vessel. Above the roofs and chimneys of the capital floated what could only be described as an enormous fish. She'd seen them floating well out above the sea, of course, with harnesses of rope holding tiny ships beneath their bellies. But this one wore no harness, and without the boat underneath she had no reference to judge its scale.

It looked more like a catfish than anything else, with whiskers surrounding its fat, rubbery lips, and fins in all the places one would expect to see them on a real fish. But its skin looked dry, not wet and slimy. She could make out individual scales, greenish brown on the beast's sides, pale yellow on its belly. She knew its body produced some sort of gas that made it float in the air, but the creature wasn't round, like the hot air balloons the Brotherhood used as aerial pickets while on campaign. It was broad, and more flattened than round.

Kellyn quickened her pace, trying not to trip on loose cobbles or the stray feet of passersby as she stared upward. The floating fish had attracted a lot of attention, however, and more than a few people had stopped in their tracks to crane their necks. She bumped into someone, and with a mumbled apology she quickened her pace, looking resolutely forward. Behind her, she heard a woman mutter a curse featuring a vile epithet. Kattenese facial features were not uncommon in Thurn, but familiarity had not bred love among most Thurnish she'd met. As worried as she was at returning to Kattenwa, she wouldn't be unhappy for her looks to pass unnoticed.

Once she arrived in Kattenwa, Felida Uffgold would teach her how to control herself, how to finally come to grips with her past. For the first time since her failure, she looked forward to the future.

4

Micah sat quietly on a wooden bench next to his mother, sweating as he waited for her to say something, anything. He'd arrived in their tiny shack of a home just a few minutes earlier, breathless from running, caked in dust that clung to the sweat that poured down his face. She'd asked him what happened, and he'd thought about lying, telling her that Garron's death had been an accident, pure and simple. He'd thought about it on the way home, and had decided to tell her that he only ran because of fear and shock at seeing all that blood. But one look at her face and his lies had crumbled, and the whole truth came tumbling out. It hadn't taken long, but in all that time she had remained silent, her face completely still.

"Someone's coming," she said calmly, as if he hadn't just told her he killed a man with magic. "Remain silent. I will handle this."

Micah nodded, trembling and fingering Serpent through his shirt. He watched in amazement as his mother's normally bland face transformed into a mask of fear and worry. And he knew, without a doubt, that this was a mask. She rarely showed emotion. The deep frown, the wide panicky eyes, the little drops of sweat that sprang from her forehead, those were all to convince whoever approached their home. Micah needed no disguise to proclaim his fear.

A knock rattled their flimsy wooden door, and Tunni said, "Reanna Lumarr, are you home? I need to speak to you about your son."

"He's here," Micah's mother said in a quiet, shaky voice. "Come in."

It was weird hearing someone call his mother by her full name.

Mostly Garron had called her 'woman' or sometimes something else, some disgusting term Micah pretended he hadn't heard. But Garron wouldn't be calling her anything ever again. For all his fear, he took a glimmer of pride in that.

Tunni stepped in, their bond servant's home crowded with three big people in it. The pit master looked around at the bench and table, the straw covered floor that served as their bed, and a pile of a few hundred small stones his mother had been polishing to serve as prayer stones. He shrugged and remained standing. "There's been a death at the quarry today."

"Micah told me," Reanna said. "He—"

Tunni held his hands up and produced a small red crystal. He rubbed it and whispered a few words. He glanced furtively at Micah but made no eye contact. "Dimford says this will give us privacy," he said. "Sure hope it works. I don't got any talents myself."

"What do you mean?"

"Garron's death was an accident. Are we all clear on that? It was his own fault. He had Micah dig too much quartz out from underneath that boulder, and that's what caused the rock to spill. We can't have the workers thinking he was . . . murdered for that granite." As he spoke, he edged as far away from Micah as he could. "His own fault, you understand?"

"I . . . no, I don't understand."

Micah watched his mother lie and wondered that Tunni couldn't see it. His own confusion was completely unfeigned.

Tunni sighed. "Garron's claim will revert to the quarry's owner, who happens to be Prince Johann. He stands to make a nice chunk of coin from this. Now, a man will come along to question you. Dimford's arranging that now. He should be here later this evening, after dark. You'll tell him it was Garron's fault, right?"

"Of course. But what will happen to us? Will we be sold?"

Micah stared at his mother; she'd put voice to his biggest fear. That they would be sold, maybe separately. That he would never see her again. He fidgeted, and his stomach growled. He hadn't eaten since breakfast, and the day had been stressful. Still, he felt far hungrier than he would have expected, and tired. Bone deep tired. His big hands, more like shovels made of flesh, shook so much that he clasped them together to stop them trembling.

"Don't worry," Tunni said. "Everything will be fine. You might have to leave the quarry, but you won't be separated. Just remember the story and cooperate. Everyone involved, including the two of you, has a strong reason to agree that it was Garron's fault. So the two of you just stay here, calm yourselves, go over the story so you call tell it without, you know, stumbling. Somebody might think you're lying. And we can't have that. See?"

Micah most definitely did not see, but his mother only nodded and said in a whisper, "Yes, I understand. Thank you, Mister Tunni."

The pit master left without another word. Micah's mother turned to him with an intense, focused look on her face. "Do as he says, Micah. Go over it in your mind, over and over, until you believe it to be true."

"But . . . but I—"

"No buts." And then she said something, something in the language Dimford always used when he worked magic, or at least something that sounded similar. All the while her eyes looked deeply into his, and he felt like he was falling into two giant, black pits. "Tell me what happened. Tell me the way Tunni said it."

"Garron had me dig under the boulder to loosen it. I dug out a lot of stone, too much I guess. But he kept telling me to dig deeper. Then it collapsed on his legs and he died."

Micah blinked. Where had those words come from? That wasn't what happened.

"Tell me again."

Micah repeated the strange story, adding details. And as he did, it began to feel true. His mother had him repeat it again and again, until the sun hung low in the west, and by then he no longer questioned the story or where it had come from. It was true, that's all. That's the way it happened, as best he could recall. He could remember being afraid, and a slight taste of that fear still troubled the back of his throat, but it had subsided. Mister Tunni himself said they wouldn't be separated.

Not long afterward, they heard horses and a wagon. Micah parted the scratchy hempen cloth that served as a curtain in their home's only window and looked outside, but there he saw something he never thought to lay eyes on. A black coach, pulled by a team of four magnificent white stallions, came to a stop outside their shack. This amazing display of wealth stunned him, with its golden door handles, glass windows, and dark, glossy paint, its beauty marred only by a thin coating of dust that clung to its sides.

The driver, seated underneath a black canopy made of some shiny cloth Micah had never seen before, climbed down and opened the door, revealing an interior that was all red cushions. From this luxury emerged first Dimford, and then a tall, thin stranger with extremely pale skin, long black hair, and a mustache and beard that both ended in sharp little points. His eyes were round, like a southerner's.

The stranger was totally clean, the way only rich people could ever be clean. His shiny, loose, blue shirt looked to be made of the same material as the coach's canopy, while his trousers seemed to be made of some kind of blue fuzz. And his hat! It was also blue, with a broad brim, and a hat band made of the same material as the shirt and studded with jewels. Only his boots and belt sported a different color, both of highly polished black leather. His skin looked dry, with no hint of perspiration or the omnipresent dust. He had to be a lord of some kind; all wealthy people had 'lord' this or 'lady' that attached to their names. Or so he believed. He'd never met a lord before.

Dimford looked like a slob standing next to the stranger. Even the driver was dressed better than the local magician, who wore the same patched, undyed robes and dusty boots he always wore. Dimford had tried to pull his long, filthy hair into a ponytail, but several loose strands ruined even this weak attempt at making himself presentable. It didn't matter though, because the stranger ignored the magician.

"It's this one, your lordship," said Dimford, pointing at Micah's shack.

The man in blue walked straight into their home as if he owned the place, and for a moment, Micah wondered if he might have bought their bonds already.

Dimford tried to say something more, but the stranger closed the door in his face and removed his hat. He stared at Micah's mother for an uncomfortably long time before finally speaking. "Tell me," he said.

His mother told the story, the one Micah now believed to be true. As she spoke, the man would interrupt here or there to ask for further detail. As Micah watched the two of them, he noticed that the man kept fidgeting with his hat, running his fingers through his hair, or stroking his beard. Micah could almost sense a pattern to his movements. His mother fidgeted as well, smoothing her peasant's homespun dress, pushing stray locks of hair behind her ears, rubbing her hands together. Not that the movements themselves were strange, but a pattern seemed to hover at the edge of his awareness.

Stranger still, the man in blue possessed an aura. Light seemed to shimmer about his hands and face, as if his skin glowed with diwa, almost like stone. But faintly, much more faintly than even weak stone like quartz. He'd nearly convinced himself that the shimmer was a figment of his imagination, or a product of exhaustion, when a loud growl emerged from his stomach. Micah gasped and clutched his belly with both hands, groaning. Neither the stranger nor his mother paid him any attention as he slumped sideways to the dirt floor. The room grew dark, as if he'd pass out, but he remained awake, if groggy.

"Dimford!" the stranger called. The magician opened the door instantly. "It was an accident, just as I suspected. I will purchase the bonds of these two. It is best that they disappear, after all. Tunni can negotiate a price at a later date."

"Yes, your lordship. Will you need them bound?"

"No. They're harmless. You two: gather your things. You will not be returning to this place."

Micah expected more questioning, or orders from their new owner. He tried to stand—it wouldn't do to have their new owner think he couldn't earn his keep, but his legs refused to cooperate. He watched the hem of his mother's dress flow by, followed by the lord's shiny black boots. He would have closed his eyes then, but Dimford hauled him to his feet.

"Come now, Micah. You belong to the Baron now. Let's get you in that coach." With the magician's considerable help, he made it aboard, expecting to be told to stay off the cushions lest his filth befoul the rich upholstery. But Dimford eased him onto one of the benches and left, and no one told Micah to move. He wondered idly if he could move on his own, if he could even remain awake another instant.

He couldn't have been less prepared for what actually happened. As soon as they were all seated, the stranger pulled dark curtains over the windows and activated a small crystal with a mumbled incantation. The little blue crystal gave off a surprising amount of light. The stranger then went to his knees in front of Micah's mother, clasping his hands and bowing his head.

"Forgive me, Lady Sarah! All these years! If only I had known, I swear I would never have allowed you to live under such barbaric circumstances!"

"I was in no danger, Lon. Uncomfortable, yes; annoyed, most certainly. But if it hadn't been for this buffoon's actions today, I could have lived there for as long as it took. This arrangement was my idea, after all."

Micah blinked, slowly realizing that by 'this buffoon's actions' she referred to the death of Garron at Micah's hands. But no, that had been an accident, right? He couldn't quite decide what had really happened, but it didn't matter. He looked at his mother's face, hoping to find some hint that she didn't really mean what she said. But she wouldn't look his way, focused instead entirely upon the stranger, Lon. And he'd called her 'Sarah.' Who was Sarah?

"Now," she continued, "please tell me that I won't have to create another new identity and spend more years in hiding."

"No, my lady. She comes. I was just about to activate my signal to you when . . . all this happened."

SOULS OF STEEL AND STONE ~ 43

His mother leaned forward, eyes wide open and a predatory smile upon her face. "When?"

"I cannot be sure. The mages may have sent at least one decoy."

Micah's mother narrowed her eyes. "What do they know?"

"Little, to be sure. My agents know less than I, and even I do not know all the details, as per our agreement. Nevertheless, some of them have been captured over the years. It was inevitable."

"They were to have died immediately. You conditioned them."

Lon inclined his head. "Yes, my lady. But the mages are not stupid, worse luck. They will have learned how to identify my agents and prepare them for questioning. One must have lived long enough to tell them what he knew. Otherwise, why would they bother to send decoys?"

A disgusted look flashed across his mother's face, one Micah had seen before, but she mastered her emotions quickly. "When will she arrive?"

"Six to eight weeks if by caravan. Three to four weeks if by sail. Perhaps as little as two weeks, if by air."

"An airship? Will the First Minister will be involved then? He owns most of Thurn's airships. Can we count upon him?"

"His attitude remains . . . difficult to define. He works for himself alone, as ever. Even your husband could not shake his supposed loyalty to Thurn, you will recall. What hope have I?"

Micah's mother—Sarah, he supposed—took a deep breath. "We go forward, regardless. What else do we know?"

"We know her destination. A woman named Felida Uffgold, a healer in the town of Roccobin. They tried to keep that little bit of information to themselves. My man in the palace took great risks to obtain her name. He also spent a ghastly amount of my gold."

"We must assume they do not know all our plans," his mother said, ignoring Lon's complaint. "They can't, or they would never have sent her north."

"My thoughts exactly, my lady."

"We have preparations to make, then. And just barely enough time, if she comes by air. Now get up off the floor." Lon returned to his seat on the bench opposite the one Micah shared with his mother. "How much longer must I wear this face?"

The realization that his mother was a stranger to him was just dawning upon Micah. That her name, even her face, had been part of a disguise. He shook his head, but he couldn't arrange his thoughts. His belly snarled again.

"My lady! You cannot be seen before the appointed hour! If you were to be recognized, word might get back to the Prince. His informants are everywhere. The ten-year anniversary of your husband's death approaches: The Prince's troops will be on the alert for anything that might look like rebellion."

His mother sighed. "You are correct, of course. You always were the cautious one, so unlike me or my husband. So, what more can you tell me? Why is she returning now?"

"My lady, your daughter has finally been allowed to take the test again, and she has failed, as we knew she would. This time, apparently, she will not be sent back through the program. Beyond that, I have no idea if she has been expelled from the order, or sent here for more training, or something else entirely. Our agent in Thurn says only that she will be here soon, to see the healer. Your wait is almost over."

"My daughter! Oh, I have waited so long! Ten years, Lon, ten years as a peasant. I will not return to that life."

"There will be no need, my lady. You will sit upon a throne soon enough."

Micah's mother smiled, but there was no warmth in it, and no attention for him whatsoever. It was, he realized, the smile of someone thinking about revenge. Her world sat poised to go back to what she had enjoyed before his father's death. But not for Micah. His thoughts and emotions boiled together, leaving him confused and exhausted. His mother used to tell him that one day his sister would make everything better, but now that her return approached, Micah seemed at best a bit of trash blown along in her wake. Would she have any attention left over for him, once her daughter arrived?

But he remembered how it had felt to crush the life from Garron's body, even if he was a little confused about the details. He had power, power he no longer had to hide, and this sister was no sorcerer. She had failed. She was weak. *I can stop her*, he thought. *I can make it like it used to be. Just Mother and me. No one else.*

Micah fell asleep before they reached their destination. He was shaken awake by the driver, and found that his mother and Lon had left him there alone. And his bond mark hurt. He put one hand over the mark and cried out wordlessly, clutching Serpent with his other hand.

"What is it, young lord?" the driver asked. He was a big man, even by Kattenese standards. Easily six feet tall, broad shouldered, and broad faced. A nose many times broken dominated a face scarred by acne. His eyes were not the amber of Kattenese nobility, nor the light brown of the middle classes, but a brown so dark as to be almost black: peasant's eyes.

"My bond mark! Someone's activating it! It hurts!"

"Not to worry. It's been removed. Either your mother or the Baron got rid of it."

"I thought . . . I thought they were permanent." Not to mention the fact that he had killed the man who owned his mark. Hadn't he? Or maybe it had been an accident; he wasn't sure.

"Not for first rate sorcerers like the Baron and your mother. Anything's possible for the likes of them."

Micah nodded, but the spot where the mark had been was still sore. Maybe removal caused that. Whatever the case, the driver seemed unworried, so he tried not to think about it. Momentary panic faded quickly, replaced by awe: their destination was the biggest building he'd ever seen, a palace, or at least a mansion, not that he really knew the difference. Massive pillars supported a roof over a wide porch. A marble staircase led to the porch, flanked by statues of warriors, dragons, and creatures Micah had never imagined. Everything he could see gleamed white in the light of a full moon, every window and corner decorated with fine carvings. The whole thing must have been big enough to house a hundred people, if not more.

"Come with me, young master," said the driver. "They'll want you to bathe and get rid of those rags."

Micah blinked. "These are my only clothes," he said as he climbed down from the coach. As he stood on wobbly legs, he caressed Serpent. He would have sworn a slight surge of strength flowed into his body then, but maybe he imagined it.

"No longer. We've a seamstress who'll make you a fresh set in the morning. Meantime, you can have one of my nightshirts. It'll be a bit long on you, but you're a big one." The driver looked around for a few moments. "Come with me to the stables."

Micah, feeling weak but slightly better for the sleep, climbed up onto the driver's bench where he sat with the stranger while he drove the carriage around the back of the palace. Wings of the building that couldn't be seen from the front extended from the rear of the massive structure, doubling or even tripling its size. When they finally arrived at the stables, handlers took the carriage into a stone barn, and the driver led Micah into the palace through an entrance with none of the decorative flourishes that adorned the rest of the structure. He stumbled as he walked, the physical exertion bringing back hunger and weakness.

"Who's the Baron?" he asked, to distract himself from his discomfort. "Is he that man in blue?"

"Yes. Baron Lon Ypreille of Norringeir, to be specific. And this place is his palace, Engvar House. My name is Chase, young master. Are you hungry?"

Micah was always hungry, but he'd long since learned to live with the discomfort. Still, he'd been ravenous before he fell asleep, and right now he felt like he could eat four or five meals. He nodded vigorously.

"Come." Chase led him to a large kitchen where a whirlwind of activity was in progress. "Della!"

A girl appeared, clothed in a gray dress that reached the floor. She was pretty, Micah decided, in an ordinary way, with her smooth skin, brown eyes and straight black hair. Not that he'd seen many girls in his life; only boys and men worked the quarry. But he'd been to town a few times. She clasped her hands in front of her and cast her eyes down.

"This is Micah. He's the son of our lord's guest. Feed him. When he's finished, escort him to the minor guest wing. I'll have Randall prepare a bed."

Chase left without another word. "What do you prefer, my lord?" asked Della.

Micah stared all around, at brass pots and pans, silver utensils, and other cooking implements he had no name for. This baron clearly possessed wealth beyond imagining, and yet he had knelt before his mother like a servant. "Whatever you have."

Della pinched her bottom lip with the fingers of her right hand, studying Micah with obvious confusion. He didn't mind it, though, since he was pretty confused himself. 'My lord,' she had called him. Was he important, too? And if so, why had he been brought in through what was apparently the servants' entrance? And where were his mother and Lon?

"My lord, I think you had better come with me," she said. She led him to a long table in a room near the kitchen. A few other servants sat at the table, eating and rubbing at sleepy eyes. "Do you mind eating here?"

Micah shook his head.

"Good. Drasky, come stand next to Lord Micah, if you will."

A man about Micah's height stood from the table and moved quickly to do as he was told. He was a thick set man, much like Micah.

"Nevin, get Roma out of bed. Have her make a set of lounge clothes for Lord Micah, using Drasky as her template. She can fit them properly later. We'll have to rouse the cobbler in the morning for new shoes. Lord Micah, if you would please sit, I will wait upon you. I believe there is stew and bread from this past evening. Would you like butter and honey for the bread, or will you prefer dried bread cut up in your stew?"

"Butter and honey, please!"

Della bowed her head and walked briskly into the kitchen, leaving Micah stunned. He'd never had both butter and honey at the same time, and in fact he could only remember tasting honey once. He sat on a bench, though collapsed might have been a more accurate term, and within a short time, Della set a plate in front of him with white bread and the promised butter and honey. It was, without doubt, the best bread he had ever tasted. No sooner had he finished the bread than Della took the plate away and replaced it with a bowl of stew. Again, he had never had better. Thick and hearty, with chunks of beef, vegetables that weren't potatoes for a change, and a savory taste that sported more pepper than salt: a far cry from the gruel dished out at the quarry. He washed it down with a cup of watered wine and a grimace. He'd found wine disgusting the few times he'd tried it. But even that failed to take away from the amazing meal. He gladly accepted a second bowl when offered, and another chunk of bread. With his belly groaning, he would have thought himself well satisfied. But he still felt hungry and couldn't imagine why.

Della gave him no time to dwell upon his situation. "Come, my lord. I've had a bath drawn for you."

Micah followed, eager to see more of the palace. And yet a nagging doubt dispelled any joy he might have felt. Surely, there had been some mistake. At any moment, Lon would discover the error and eject him from this heavenly place. Worst, he feared that his mother would stay with Lon, sending Micah back to the quarry and some master a hundred times worse than Garron. He tried to calm his breathing as he followed Della to a wooden staircase, and up two floors to a landing at least as large as the shack that had previously been the only home he'd ever known. He stopped with hands on knees, fighting to regain his breath as rivulets of sweat poured down his face.

Della opened a door and they exited into a wide hallway lined with paintings and statues. Glowing crystals in golden sconces lit their way.

"It was faster that way," said Della, frowning slightly as Micah limped along. "The servants' stairs are always the easiest way to get from one part of the palace to another, Lord Micah."

"What are servants' stairs?"

"Hidden staircases throughout the palace, my lord. They allow us to move quickly and unseen so that we are always where our master needs us, without disturbing him unnecessarily."

"So Lon doesn't use those stairs?"

"My lord! Please forgive me, it is clear that you do not know . . . certain things. But you must learn. We are being a little loose with the rules tonight merely for the sake of convenience. But in the morning, you must take your place among the nobility, as is your right."

Thinking of his 'nobility' made Micah wonder just who his father had been, but that only brought him back to his predicament. His sister would be here soon. He knew enough of the world to know what that meant. The older sibling inherits everything, while the younger gets whatever the elder doesn't want. But she was a girl, and women could not rule in Kattenwa. Did that mean he would inherit? It was all so confusing.

They reached a room tiled in marble, containing an enormous bath-tub full of steaming water. Like the rest of Engvar House, the room surpassed anything he had ever experienced, with golden handles and faucets, a thick carpet beside the tub, and racks of bottles and towels. A faucet set above the rim of the tub had words printed in the tile above it, and though Micah couldn't read, the words didn't look like the loopy, rounded script of Kattenese. Chase stood near the tub.

"Leave us, girls," he said. Della and an older woman left without a word. "I don't want you to be embarrassed, my lord, but owing to the conditions in which you have lived your entire life, I felt you might need some instruction."

"I know how to take a bath," Micah said, staring at the floor with burning cheeks.

"You have not bathed as the great and powerful bathe. You will be expected to emerge from this room completely clean. You will need to scrub every inch of your body with strong soap and coarse washcloths. You will use a special soap for your hair, which you will comb when you are done. And after that, you will drain the dirty water and refill the tub to bathe again. Afterward, you will apply scented oil to your skin. This is no splash in a stream."

Embarrassed as he was, he had to admit that Chase was right.

Chase turned his back. "Now get those clothes off, my lord, and climb in. I warn you, the water will be very hot."

Chase was right; the heat threatened to cook the flesh from his bones. The bath itself left him bewildered. Before he'd half finished, the water had turned a murky brown, and still his hands stubbornly clung to their ground-in filth. He pulled the cork from the drain in the tub and experimented with the golden handles. One, he'd discovered, gave cold water, and the other hot. He filled the tub with water as hot as he could stand and scrubbed again. By the time he finished bathing, exhaustion had seeped deep within his body, until he felt even his bones would sag.

Chase inspected his handiwork, declared him acceptably clean, and handed Micah a soft towel. When he finished drying himself, he pulled on a borrowed nightshirt of soft cotton, and followed Chase to a room down the hall from the bathroom. There, he found more unexpected rituals. Indoor plumbing, for one. He'd never before done his business in anything fancier than a chamber pot, and more often in a trench in the ground near the quarry. Chase gave him a tiny brush and some powder to clean his teeth, with firm instructions to do it every day. From there, another set of servants' stairs led to another luxurious hallway, and a bedroom of unimaginable beauty. Tall windows looked out upon the palace grounds, though he could see little so late at night. Couches and chairs and glass-topped golden tables and crystal lamps and paintings and soft rugs and . . . words failed him. He stood stunned and mute, torn between wonder and suspicion. This had to be a mistake.

In the center of it all stood a bed bigger than the entire hut he'd shared with his mother. He climbed in and pulled soft sheets up to his chin, sinking into a mattress as soft as a cloud. Chase showed him a rope near the bed. Something about a bell in the servants' quarters. All he had to do was pull the rope if he needed anything.

But there was only one thing he wanted. For the first time in his life, he found himself sleeping without his mother in the same room. This night, he didn't even know where she was.

"Chase?" he mumbled around a yawn. "What's going to happen to me?"

"I don't know, my lord," Chase answered, his voice barely above a whisper. "Things will change in Kattenwa, that is sure. But as for you? I don't know."

Micah's eyes drooped shut. He slept like a corpse.

5

Kellyn stood at the front of the airship, not quite enjoying anything about her first flight. The wind in her hair, the tiny ships floating on the sea hundreds of feet below, the massive bulk of the blimp above her, all of it overwhelming, and far from the thrilling ride she'd expected. She wondered what Alonselle would make of the airship, but couldn't imagine him enjoying it any more than she did.

It's bloody terrifying, she thought. *And cold.* She'd have thought that flying so far from the ground, getting closer to the sun with each foot gained in altitude, they would get warmer, especially now in high summer out over the Thurnish Sea, where it might not rain a single drop until autumn. Just to keep from shivering, she wore quilted trousers and a jacket over a woolen sweater. Much colder, and she'd don thick gloves, hat and scarf. The wind whipped her hair around most annoyingly, so she tied it in a ponytail.

"You're not puking over the rail, are you?"

Kellyn turned to find the *Nighthawk*'s captain standing at ease on the deck, hands on hips, adjusting his stance as the ship rocked slightly in its harness. *Abbatay,* Kellyn reminded herself. A strange name, like Magrahim, possibly from somewhere on the southern continent of Mohotsa. Like her teacher, the captain had jet black hair and a full beard, both with just a hint of gray, but there the resemblance ended. Abbatay had a face tanned and wrinkled by many years of exposure to bright sun and harsh winds, a nose that had been broken at least once, judging from its crookedness and the knob in its center, and a mouth full of bad teeth which he constantly showed in a broad, easy smile. He might have been thirty years old, or sixty. With the captain's aged face attached to a body that seemed to be young, trim, strong, and agile, Kellyn couldn't tell. Before liftoff, she had watched the captain climb the ropes to inspect the harness that attached the ship to the blimp, moving with all the speed and precision of crewmen barely older than Kellyn herself.

"No, sir. First Mate Payner told me you never throw up at the front, you do it at the rear so the only ones who get splashed are any people unlucky enough to be beneath the ship."

"Aye, you listen to Payner, you won't go wrong."

Kellyn had discovered that airmen didn't go for a lot of naval terminology. The front of the ship was just the front, and the rear the rear. Starboard and port replaced right and left, and she understood the reason for it: right and left changed with the perspective of the viewer, but starboard was always to her right when she faced the front. On an airship, however, there were more surfaces than on a seagoing vessel. 'Topside' referred to the blimp's back, 'underside' to her belly, and 'dirtside' to the ground below. Thinking of the blimp reminded her: airmen would never call the enormous creature above her a blimp.

"Uh, sir? So, she's an airhee, did I get the pronunciation correct this time?"

"Almost, Kellyn. Most dirt huggers call her kind air-hee, or worse yet, blimps. You say the first part like you'd say 'eye'. And the second part is 'rhee' just like it looks written out. She won't mind an honest mistake at first, but don't take too long learning to say it right."

"No sir. I mean, yes sir."

Abbatay laughed and clapped her on the shoulder. "At ease, young mage. But don't just stand there. Walk around, get your air legs under you. Once you're comfortable, we'll put you to work. Which I expect won't be longer than another day at most, hear?"

That was a strong hint if Kellyn had ever heard one. Everyone worked while on board, even if most of the effort appeared to be busy-work, and she couldn't do anything so long as she felt like she'd fall over if she weren't gripping the rail so hard her fingers turned white. So she eased her grip and stood, trying to let her body relax, legs spread a little wider than seemed necessary, leaning slightly forward with her knees bent a little, just as Payner had showed her. Part of her nervousness, she knew, came from the relatively small size of the ship itself, maybe twelve feet wide and no more than forty feet long. Compared to the airhee above her, the ship was tiny.

"Uh, sir? Is it true what Mr. Payner said? About the airhees, I mean. He said they're intelligent, like people."

"That's certainly true. This here airhee is named Magda, though her true name is—" Abbatay made a sound that was more like a short burst of song than a name, but in a language Kellyn had never heard. "Now, I don't expect you to master their language right off. In fact, I don't even want you trying to sing to Magda on this voyage. It takes years of practice, and the fact is she speaks Thurnic far better than you'll ever speak Airheean."

"She speaks?"

Abbatay laughed. "She does. And you'll know when you hear her voice. Imagine the loudest, deepest voice you've ever heard. When you hear it, you'll know who's speaking. You'll also know we're in a world of trouble, for she only speaks our language in an emergency."

"Oh, so I, ah, I can talk to her?"

"You can, and I encourage you to do so. But not until you're confident enough to climb the ropes to her harness and speak right into her ear. Airhees have excellent hearing, but there's too much noise down on the ship, and we're too quiet for her to pick out our voices from the background chatter. You'll need to be topside."

Kellyn nodded, looking up at the spider web of ropes that attached the wooden ship to her harness. Magda massed more than any animal she'd ever seen. Even bigger than the war elephants kept in the stables outside the city, those hairy beasts two to three times the height of a regular elephant, grown to their unnatural massiveness by specially trained mages.

"No time like the present," she said, half to herself. "I'm going up."

Abbatay held up a hand. "Not just yet. I would speak with you about our mutual friend, the First Minister."

Kellyn nodded. Though she had no idea how much the captain knew about her situation, it seemed he knew more than he was supposed to. She did her best not to appear alarmed. "Yes, sir."

Abbatay strolled over to the rail and leaned his backside against it, arms folded over his chest. "Have you given much thought to what might happen to you, should you fail?"

"I . . . that is, ah—"

"Whatever awaits you in Kattenwa, there is no guarantee that you will succeed, is there? So what will you do, if the worst should come to pass?"

Kellyn stood silently, feeling dimwitted. She'd never given much thought to the possibility of failure. Mostly it meant disgrace, but beyond that her mind's eye refused to look.

"The boss controls a vast trading empire, Kellyn. With more than sixty airships, near two-hundred ocean going vessels, and river barges and caravan wagons beyond count. He has representatives—factors, he calls them—in cities all over the continent and even in Mohotsa. At a guess, I'd say more than five-thousand people are in his employ, and many more than that do his bidding from time to time."

Abbatay stopped and looked at Kellyn, but just what the captain expected she couldn't have said. "Yes, he's very wealthy. Everyone knows that."

"Alas, he is but one man. He is always looking for smart, skilled individuals to help him keep watch over his many interests. Ship's captains, we are not esteemed very highly in August Nigh's empire. A young woman of your talents could rise much higher than myself. Do you take my meaning?"

"I do. I'm sorry . . . I've never considered being anything but a warrior mage." That, however, was not entirely true. When she'd first come to the Brotherhood, just after they'd destroyed her father's rebellion, she had wanted nothing more than to become a sorcerer of such enormous power that she could destroy all the warrior mages of the Brotherhood. That had been a long time ago. Indeed, she couldn't remember the last time she'd fantasized about vengeance for her father.

"Just remember that the boss will take you in, if the Brotherhood casts you out. But for now, you have a climb to make, yes? Try not to fall, youngster," said Abbatay as he walked back to the center of the ship. "The First Minister would be rather cross with me if you should die. And take the center ropes, not the sides. Better practice."

Looking up, she could see of the airhee only her broad underbelly, maybe forty feet wide. The center ropes formed a ladder leading up to the belly, where they disappeared into a rope and leather gondola that hugged her yellow underside. Not much of a climb, only about thirty feet, and in training Kellyn had made more difficult ascents. She'd shimmied up ropes hanging from cliffs. She'd even climbed up the sides of castles with nothing to protect her from a fall. The ascent kept her mind off all that Abbatay, and perforce the First Minister, knew about her journey. Or mostly, anyway. Nagging doubts kept her from concentrating as fully on her hands and feet as she would have wished.

"Hey! There's a safety net between the ship and Magda!" No wonder the captain had seemed so unworried about her first climb. The net itself, made of some gossamer-thin material, reminded her of a spider's web more than anything else. With the net to give her confidence, Kellyn climbed quickly up the ropes, pausing to test the feel of the net where the ladder passed through a gap. Strong, certainly, smooth and slippery like fine silk; she could imagine falling into the net would be like being caught by a feather bed. A fall from the side ropes, however, wouldn't stop until she hit the surface of the sea, and from this height, the impact would not be much better than hitting solid earth.

At the top, she emerged into the gondola to find one of the riggers. She thought she'd find the crewman charged with singing the captain's orders to Magda, but the thin, wiry boy in the gondola held a looking glass to his eye, scanning the skies for danger. There'd be another boy, ship's eyes, they were called, on top of Magda, in a basket called the crow's nest.

"Ah, young man? Where do I go to speak to, um, to Magda?"

The boy never took his eye from the little scope. "Side harness to the top, then forward."

"Thanks."

The side harness consisted mostly of ropes wrapped in padded leather, but she could see no ladder to speak of, just a few ropes attached to Magda's harness at the top and to the gondola at the bottom, hanging free in between with knots every few feet. Climbing those ropes, however, would require her to climb across the beast's underside, hanging only by her hands for a good twenty feet or so before she could start climbing vertically and use her feet on the side. She had an amulet of strength hanging around her neck, but there had to be an easier way.

"Untie a climbing rope," said the boy with the looking glass, again without bothering to look up from his task. He sounded bored, and maybe a little annoyed. "Swing out to the side ropes, tie it there, and climb on up."

"Thanks again."

I can do this, thought Kellyn. *It's scary, sure it is. But fear can't conquer me. I'll just accept the fear, allow it to make me cautious, and deal with the task at hand.*

And so she untied a rope, held on tight, then pushed off with her feet. While swinging, she looked straight out, not down, and wrapped her legs around the rope. As soon as she was away from the bulk of the airhee, however, the wind caught her and pushed her back along the beast's length. She caught a stationary rope and gripped it with hysterical strength. The wind had pushed her a good thirty feet downwind from where she'd started. If she stayed on the rope she'd swung on, she'd be climbing up on an angle. Clearly, the smart thing to do would be to switch to a rope that was still tied down, leaving a vertical climb.

But first she had to tie the rope she held in place. She switched her grip to another rope, then wrapped her legs around it and began tying her rope down. Once she'd secured that, she started climbing up, staring at Magda's brownish green scales to avoid the sight of the sea hundreds of feet below.

In a surprisingly short amount of time, she reached the topside, laying on her back and panting heavily. "Can't just lie here," she said. She got to her hands and knees, and saw a walkway of sorts: A padded leather strip about three feet wide, running from just in front of Magda's dorsal fin right up to the crow's nest. She crawled a few feet to get away from the steeply sloping sides, then walked carefully along the leather walkway to the crow's nest. There she found Captain Abbatay, to her surprise.

"Have a seat. Not bad time, for a beginner," he said.

Kellyn found nothing resembling a seat in the crow's nest, which looked like nothing more than a very wide barrel, cut in half. The captain and the topside ship's eye sat upon the padded leather floor of the crow's nest. Kellyn joined them, wondering idly why Abbatay didn't bother introducing the ship's eye, a skinny boy with a girlish face, sitting half covered with burlap bags he apparently used for warmth. "Thank you, sir. So, where do you go to speak to Magda?"

"Here's the best place. Her hearing membranes are just a little in front of us, to the left and right. You don't want to go further than this; her ears are very sensitive."

"So what do I say?"

Abbatay laughed. "Airhee Magda, this is our passenger. Her name is Kellyn, and I would be forever in your debt if you and your mates would help me keep her safe."

Magda responded with a blast of low-pitched sound that she felt in her chest as much as she heard it, followed by a whistle and a rumbling that sounded for all the world like a war elephant's fart.

"Magda welcomes you and assures you that her mates would have caught you had you fallen."

"Caught me?"

Abbatay laughed again. "You don't think I would have let you climb up without a safety net, do you?"

"I thought the safety net was between Magda and the ship."

"Yes, there is that. But once you're on the side ropes, only the males can save you."

Kellyn had seen the males, two of them, clinging to Magda's sides, but she hadn't seen them fly yet. They were small compared to the female, only about twenty feet long with a body about the thickness of a large man's torso. They clung to Magda with clawed fins, keeping their leathery wings folded against their backs.

"I alerted Marshall and Spot as soon as you came aboard. They've been keeping a close eye on you ever since."

"Thank you, sir."

"Now, say something to Magda. Something nice."

"Uh, Magda? It's a real pleasure meeting you. This is . . . an amazing way to travel."

The airhee emitted another rumbling, whistling, burbling response. Abbatay laughed. "Yes, my dear. The girl certainly is nervous. But she's a friend of First Minister Nigh, and she's at least as important as our cargo."

Magda sang again. "She says you are welcome aboard, young Kellyn. And she promises that any friend of the First Minister is a friend of hers."

"Thank you." Kellyn smiled then, trying to look happy and confident.

Abbatay smiled back, looking out over the front of the airhee at endless miles of nearly cloudless sky and a deep blue sea that stretched to the horizon. "We'll fly with the air currents at first," he said. "It's not exactly a straight line north, but it allows Magda to conserve her strength. Once we're back over land, she'll have to push hard until we're over the Red Spine Mountains. From there, she'll have another easy stretch of flight."

"How does she stay aloft?" Kellyn asked.

"There's magic in it, girl, believe me. Now, she has sacs inside her that take up most of the mass of her body. She makes a gas inside her that fills the sacs, and the gas is lighter than air. That makes her float, and her tail fin propels her forward. But there's more to it than that. I'm no mage, but every pilot knows there's more than just her air sacs keeping us aloft."

Kellyn wasn't so sure about that, magical creatures being the stuff of tall tales and myths, for the most part, but she wasn't about to contradict the captain, so she let the statement stand unchallenged. "How can anything be lighter than air? Air doesn't weigh anything."

Abbatay shrugged with a lopsided grin. "I don't understand it myself. I just know it works. And this is important: I also know the gas she produces is very flammable. That's why only the ship's cook uses fire. There's quick-release knots on the sides of the harness in case the ship ever catches fire."

"What? You mean if there's a fire you'll drop the ship?"

"Absolutely. Magda's worth about ten of the *Nighthawk*, just in terms of money. More important, though, is what she means to me and the crew. If we ever lost her, well, I don't know how I could ever captain with another airhee. I'm closer to her than I am to my own wife."

Magda said something then, startling a long, loud laugh out of the captain. The ship's eye giggled then, too.

"What? What did she say?"

"Sorry, Kellyn. That was something I'd rather keep between me and Magda. Only thing I can say is this: the bond between an airhee and her captain is a lot like a marriage. We have our ups and downs, but right now, the world looks pretty damned good. And if my wife ever made me choose between the women in my life, well, I'd still be a captain is all I'll be saying."

Kellyn couldn't help smiling at that. Abbatay was in his element on the airship, completely at ease. And while she didn't exactly feel the same, she could share in the captain's happiness.

Kellyn woke to the sound of a bell ringing. She'd been aboard the *Nighthawk* for a week now, a week of hard work alternating with long periods of boredom. Other than checking the harness every day for weak spots or areas where the pads had slipped and allowed the ropes to chafe Magda's skin, and removing the occasional growth of moss or algae from the surface of a scale, most of what they did each day could best be described as busywork, including a ridiculous amount of cleaning. There were no sails to furl and unfurl and repair as there would be on a naval ship. There was no reason to look for leaks in the hull. No barnacles to scrape off. Magda did what she was told. The crew was there mostly for loading and unloading cargo, and for emergencies.

The bell that woke her was for emergencies. She ran barefoot but was otherwise mostly dressed. She knew she was not the most attractive woman in the world, but aboard a ship full of men, she took no chances that one of the crew might try to take advantage of her. Though she felt certain she could defend herself from any unwanted attention, she didn't want to hurt any of the men. Their occasional glances made her uncomfortable, but her status as a warrior mage in training must have counted for something, since they mostly kept their distance.

Up the stairs from the crew's quarters to the deck, she found everyone standing at the rails, watching something far off in the distance. There Captain Abbatay stood with a looking glass to his eye. Kellyn squinted and looked in the same direction, but she couldn't see anything. If only she had far sight, but that was one of the few magical talents she'd been tested for that she didn't have.

Out there at the edge of sight, however, she spied something among the clouds that might have been another airship. She turned to Cookie, who stood brandishing a soup ladle like a weapon, and asked through chattering teeth, "Is that a wild airhee?"

Cookie shrugged. "Could be. That'd be best. If it's an airship, might be trouble. Now git some shoes on girl, or you'll freeze yer toes off!"

Kellyn wanted to ask more questions, but the cook shrugged again and went back below, muttering something about an interrupted breakfast and a stupid girl. Other crew members went about the business of checking their weapons, or loading one of the four big deck-mounted crossbows, ballistae they were called. Two of the ballistae shot enormous arrows, five feet long and thick as a spear, while the other two shot lead balls the size of a man's fist.

That reminded Kellyn that she had a job to do, now, one to which she brought unique qualifications. She ran shivering down below the deck and donned shoes and a sweater, then grabbed her weapons: a handful of throwing stars, a sword, and a bow. She slung a quiver full of charmed arrows over her shoulder before seeking out the captain.

The captain collapsed the looking glass and strode briskly to a room in the center of the deck, called the deckhouse. A leather tube ran from the deckhouse up to the gondola, and another tube ran from the gondola to the crow's nest. Speaking loudly into one end of the tube allowed someone on the other end to hear clearly. That person, in turn, could relay the message to the crow's nest.

"Ask Magda if she thinks it's wild or tamed," Abbatay said, loudly enough that everyone on the deck could hear. He paused while the message relayed to the topside ship's eye. Magda gurgled a response. "Alright then, keep a close eye on it." The captain came out of the deck house and addressed the crew. "She's tame, and she's headed our way. All hands remain alert, weapons at the ready. Mage, to me."

Kellyn jogged to the captain's side. "Sir!"

"Airhee females are solitary folk, Kellyn. Their young stay with them for a few years, then they scatter. When adult females encounter each other, well, usually they just keep their distance. A wild female will only approach another if she's dying. Her males will abandon her and try to kill the other female's mates. But even males with healthy females will attack each other if a storm forces them too close to each other."

Abbatay paused and looked at Kellyn expectantly. Just as Magrahim would have. "We have a tame airhee coming toward us," she began. "I guess that means Magda could see the ship slung underneath. Her eyesight must be excellent."

"Yes."

"That ship's males and ours will attack each other. Their captain knows that, so he must be planning to attack us. Air pirates?"

"More or less." Abbatay pointed at the steadily growing dot. "That there ship might be pirates working for themselves, or it could be a merchant captain operating under a war license."

A war license would give a merchant captain the right to attack unfriendly ships, but the Kingdom of Great Thurn wasn't at war with anyone right now, unless a conflict had broken out in the last week. Whatever the case, merchant ships like the *Nighthawk* weren't heavily armed, while pirates would be armed quite well, indeed. They'd also have more crewmen.

"Do all airhees have just two males?" she asked.

"Usually," said Abbatay. "If the males are all siblings, she might have more than two, but more than two unrelated males would not tolerate each other. Now tell me, what weapons do you bring?"

Kellyn described her weapons in detail, careful not to exaggerate her abilities. Still, as she told Abbatay about the charmed arrows, the captain's eyes grew wide and he began to smile.

"You're not a bad climber, but not yet fast enough," Abbatay said. "I'll need you and your weapons in the crow's nest. The topside is always an airship's greatest weakness. If our friends out there can land marines on Magda's back, they can cut just enough of the harness to force me to surrender. So, I need you up there quickly; I'll need you to jump."

Kellyn took a deep breath, nodded. "I can do it."

"Good. Yuni! Come take Kellyn's weapons up to the crow's nest, top speed!" Abbatay then ran to the speaking tubes in the deckhouse and shouted, "Alert the males! We're going to have a jumper! Take her to the nest!"

Within moments, both males could be seen flying below the ship, their wide wings flapping slowly, moving in broad figure-eights as they awaited the jumper.

"Now, Kellyn!"

If she allowed herself any time to consider, she'd find a hundred reasons not to proceed. Instead, she ran to the rail and leapt out into thin air, whooping as she fell. Abbatay had told her she'd have to learn to trust the males before the voyage ended, but she hadn't quite worked up the nerve yet.

Kellyn fell for what seemed like forever, though in fact she couldn't have been in the air for more than a few heartbeats before one of the males caught her under the arms from behind with handlike fins, and immediately began pumping hard to fly back toward the ship. She knew what to expect, since she'd seen some of the other crew members practicing the move, but it was still a shock when the male let her go. Her upward momentum stopped and she hung in the air for a fraction of a second before the second male grabbed her and flew the rest of the way up to the crow's nest.

The move had something to do with the air sacs, much smaller in the males than in Magda. The first male, Marshall she later learned, had vented some of the lighter than air gas so he could dive to grab Kellyn, but the effort of flying her up to the second male had drained him. The second male, Spot, had pumped his sacs fuller than normal, using the extra lift to take her the rest of the way up with relative ease.

In less than a minute, Spot dropped her gently atop Magda's back. Shortly after she arrived breathless at the crow's nest, Kellyn was greeted by Yuni, a skinny ropeman as agile as a monkey, bearing a bag full of her weapons.

"You listen, youngster," Yuni said in a thick accent Kale couldn't place. "The males will fight first. You let 'em, hear? We take no part in that. Healthy males don't kill each other, not usually. You just sit and wait 'til you get a shot at their crew. Got it?"

"Got it."

Without another word, Yuni scrambled over to a harness rope and slid down Magda's side. Kellyn ignored him, opened the bag, and laid her weapons on the floor of the crow's nest. In very little time, she had her bow strung, quiver tied to the wall of the crow's nest, and throwing stars tucked into little leather pockets sewn into her belt. At her left hip, a sword rested in its scabbard, waiting to be blooded, so that sword and wielder could bond. She shivered with anticipation. When she looked up, the pirate airship had grown from a dot on the horizon into the distinct shapes of blimp-like fish and toy boat.

"The males won't peel off until they're almost on us," said a small voice.

Kellyn turned to find the topside ship's eye sitting half-covered in a pile of burlap sacks with a looking glass to his eye.

"I didn't see you there."

"You weren't supposed to. When there's danger, I hide in these sacks and talk to Magda, telling her what I see in case she misses something."

"Do you have a shield under there?" she asked the boy.

A 'bonk, bonk' sound issued from under the sacks as the boy knocked on the hidden shield.

"Good. You may need it. What's your name?"

"Jirra."

"Kellyn. Pleased to meet you, Jirra. Have you any weapons?"

"Just my knife. I can take care of myself."

"Perhaps, but it might be best if you went below. I don't think I'll need help, and frankly your presence might be a distraction."

Jirra scowled, his eyes flashing. "You do your job, mage. I'll do mine."

Kellyn muttered an apology and looked out across the sky. The pirate vessel had grown again, until she could now make out individual men, ant-tiny, on the approaching ship. Their airhee labored hard through the breeze, pushing straight at them, and up, apparently trying to position themselves above Magda. As she watched, ropes spilled over the rails of the ship, and men could be seen swarming onto the deck. Off to one side, four males spiraled around each other like a small flock of very large birds, not doing any obvious harm to each other.

"They mean to board us," Kellyn whispered to herself.

"Our Captain's not trying for more altitude," said Jirra. "He's not using any evasive maneuvers. That's showing a lot of confidence in you. Better not let him down."

Kellyn nodded, ignoring the sarcasm in the boy's voice, reached for an arrow, and waited. A few more moments and they'd be at the extreme range of her bow. Almost. A little further.

Now! She shot the first arrow high, grabbed another, shot it just a little lower, another and another, then lowered her bow. Four was her limit, though she'd heard of masters who could control a dozen or more. With eyes closed, she took control of the arrows, flying them straight at the pirate crew, who must have felt safe at this range, because not one of them raised a shield. Not that it would have done them much good. Kellyn aimed for masses of men, and these were no ordinary arrows.

All four struck at the same time, passing with ease through four or five men before either getting stuck in the wood of the pirate ship or falling free into thin air. Kellyn felt a brief pang of loss at the arrows she would never see again, but she had no time to fret. She quickly fired off four more and guided them to the slaughter. Another flight, but this time it was much harder to find multiple targets. The pirates had realized that they faced an unusual enemy, and they'd begun to crouch and take cover.

It wasn't enough. Though each arrow now found only one or at most two targets, she had dozens more in her quiver. The leather bucket that held the arrows—no larger than Kellyn's thigh—contained more than a hundred missiles. With neither fletching nor metal heads to add bulk, the arrows resembled nothing more than sharpened sticks. If any archer not skilled in magic should try to loose these bolts, they'd tumble harmlessly in the air.

Kellyn whooped with glee. She could kill them all! Well, she could if their captain had been willing to let her continue the slaughter. But the enemy ship grew closer, almost directly above the crow's nest, and men began sliding down the ropes. She had time for one last flight of arrows before things got a lot more personal. First, she switched to throwing stars, taking out several more pirates as they slid down the ropes. These weapons, expensive and difficult to replace, Kellyn flew back to her belt for future use. It was time to switch to the sword.

A chunk of steel, undecorated and unnamed, much like the training sword she'd used in her test. A charmed sword could never be truly hers until she had used it in battle. Kellyn and her unnamed sword would soon bond in a relationship closer than any other known to man. The weapon would, after today, become an extension of her body, like a fifth limb, but more than that. It would also become a sixth sense, but one that varied from user to user. Some Brothers called their swords their reason for living.

She had yearned for this day; now she just had to survive it. She'd killed or wounded at least twenty pirates already. Another thirty or so slid down the ropes. She stepped out of the crow's nest, tested her

footing, and pushed time just as the first half-dozen enemies set foot
on Magda.

What happened next would never be entirely clear in Kellyn's
memory. She remembered sprinting to the nearest pirate, moving like
a hawk swooping in for the kill, and the next moment she stood over
four dead bodies. She laughed out loud and allowed time to slow down
to normal. That would allow her enemies to see her. Give them just a
hint that this was not an ordinary foe.

She leapt at the nearest group, seven of them advancing with short
swords and long knives. None of them carried a shield. Kellyn spun
in place, her sword becoming a silver blur, moving slowly toward the
pirates. Suddenly, she sprang at them, her sword slicing cleanly through
two men at once. She noticed with a quiet corner of her mind that she'd
cut through three enemy blades as easily as slicing ripe bananas. Two of
the men facing her turned to run, leaving just three in her immediate
vicinity. She sped time and dispatched them with ease before moving
to the next group.

From group to group, slashing her way through blades and armor
and flesh, screams barely registering in her mind. Only the pure joy
of combat and the complete sense of connection between the blade
and her hand. And, if she were honest, the glee she always felt at the
prospect of death.

The sword jumped in her hand, pulling her toward the rear of the
airhee. Her eyelids grew heavy for a bit, as if she'd drunk too much
wine, but as she gasped for air energy surged through her muscles. A
group of a dozen or more pirates had landed.

Kellyn turned toward the rear without thought, but a high-pitched
scream stopped her.

"Lookee here!" said a male voice. "We gots us a girlie!"

Kellyn turned, dragging the sword with her with a mental effort
akin to pulling a resisting child, in time to see three men surrounding
the crow's nest. Jirra stood there, knife in his left hand, shield in his
right. A long-haired pirate slashed at his undefended back and Jirra
screamed again. A girl's scream, no doubt.

She pushed time and ran for the crow's nest. She hadn't realized just how far the battle had taken her from Magda's mouth.

The urge to attack the larger group hit her hard, like a punch to the gut.

Kellyn stumbled, and almost gave in. "No, Shaethe," she said, "we must save her. There will be time for the others."

She arrived at the crow's nest as one of the men grabbed Jirra and dragged her onto Magda's back. Not until then did Kellyn notice that Jirra had only half of her left leg, but the stump wasn't bleeding. No time for contemplation, though, as she directed Shaethe to kill with maximum speed. In the blink of an eye, all three men lay headless around the crow's nest. She dropped out of fast time.

"Are you hurt, Jirra?"

"It's nothing," she said, her voice now much higher than it had been earlier, eyes flashing. She pointed toward the rear of the airhee. "They're getting away!"

They were, and Kellyn could not stop them. Shaethe assaulted her mind, battering her with the desperate need to kill the men who were even now pulling themselves up the ropes and onto the pirate ship. She knew a moment's temptation to sprint with everything she had and leap for the rope. But even in quick time, there would be time enough for the enemy to cut the rope she chose. Instead, she scanned Magda's back for more pirates. The momentum of the two airships had carried her targets away, and the only pirates atop the *Nighthawk's* airhee were in no condition to offer resistance. Still, perhaps thirty men had rappelled down to Magda's back. Kellyn could see no more than a dozen on the ropes, frantically scrambling up to their ship. She'd killed all the others.

The tip of her blade followed the movement of the pirates of its own volition, but she wanted nothing more now than an end to the fight. The magnitude of what she'd just done hit her with full force. She'd trained to kill for ten years, but not before this day had she actually taken a man's life.

"Let them go, young mage," said Captain Abbatay. "You've done all I hoped you would."

The captain had just arrived, along with Payner and Yuni. "I wanted to kill them all," Kellyn said, her voice suddenly hoarse.

"Better that some of them escape. They'll tell others that an airship flying the flag of Thurn was protected by a warrior mage. And I'll tell the men that this was no accident, that the Brotherhood will be protecting some Thurnish flights from now on. Word will get around. The pirates will think twice about attacking us in the future."

Kellyn looked at the captain, at a loss for words. "But . . . but you know that isn't true."

Abbatay laughed. "Don't worry, mage. These three won't tell. We're family, and this won't be our only secret." Abbatay hugged Jirra and kissed her on the forehead. "You've met my daughter. She's not one for cooking and cleaning, this one. Even with one leg, she's as agile as a squirrel on the ropes, and speaks Airheean like a native."

"You mean the men don't know?" Kellyn said.

"They don't," said Jirra, her voice quite a bit lower now, her eyes once again flashing. Kellyn squinted, wondering if what she was seeing was just anger, or if Jirra's eyes really were different. It might be significant, but she'd have to file that away for later.

"I'm up here most of the time anyway," Jirra continued. "And they all know the captain is my father. That makes them keep their distance a little, too. You won't tell, mage, or I'll make you wish you'd never been born."

Kellyn promised not to tell as the three men laughed. "Now, Jirra," said the Captain, "let's clean that cut on your shoulder. Payner, Yuni, feed Magda. She'll eat well today. Kellyn? I'd say you've earned some rest. Why don't you go below? You can leave your weapons here. We'll take them down."

Yuni and Payner began stripping the pirates and dragging their bodies to Magda's mouth. Kellyn had known a beast this large would need a lot of food to survive, but she hadn't known she'd eat men. She never thought about asking, though, because she had other things on her mind. She left her bow and quiver behind, but not once did she consider letting another handle her sword. She slid it into its scabbard after wiping away the blood and gore, and made her way to the ropes.

"Why did I name you 'Shaethe'?" Kellyn whispered to the sword.

But Shaethe did not answer, and as far as Kellyn knew, the bond between sword and mage never included actual words. But she did feel a chilly wave of rage from the sword, seething that its desire to kill had been thwarted.

More importantly, she had named her sword, or perhaps it had named itself, after an ancient evil spirit. A spirit that drank the souls of the men it killed.

6

Micah slowly blinked his sleepy eyes, then sat up quickly, lost in a moment of panic. *Where am I?* he thought. *Mom!*

But then he remembered and looked around the enormous bedroom with awe. Someone had come in during the night and closed the drapes, and a set of clothes had been laid out on a sofa. First, he had to find the toilet room, since there was no chamber pot under the bed. Should he get dressed first? He decided that would be better.

But even the clothes left him confused. He figured out the under-clothes, but the socks (which he'd never worn before) had odd straps buttoned to them for no obvious reason. The trousers fell to his ankles and he found neither a belt nor a rope to keep them up. One shirt with sleeves and one without: Should he choose one? Or wear both? And what about the long, bright orange cloth? It was all bewildering, and he felt worn out, almost like he needed to go back to sleep.

"Alright, Micah," he whispered while absently stroking Serpent under his nightshirt, "you're supposed to act like a noble now. So what would a noble do?"

Well, for starters, a noble would know how to dress himself. But since he didn't, it seemed obvious that he should pull the servant rope, or whatever they called it. He did, expecting a bell to sound. But nothing happened. Had he pulled it too softly? He pulled again, harder this time. When he let it go, the rope moved smoothly back into place, a knot catching in a golden ring set into the wall. But still nothing happened.

He waited, trying for patience and failing badly. After what seemed forever, Della appeared, pushing a trolley loaded with food. "Your breakfast, my lord."

"I didn't ask for breakfast," Micah said.

"There is a code associated with the call ropes, my lord. One for general service, two for food. Three for an emergency. Shall I send for Chase?"

"Ah, no, that won't be necessary. Just leave the food."

The food was, once again, excellent, consisting of eggs and steamed vegetables and a thick slab of ham, with a cup of watered wine. He could get used to the idea of never being hungry again, but for now he wolfed down all the food on his plate, irrationally afraid that someone might take it away.

Afterward, left with the mystery of the clothes and an increasingly urgent need to visit the privy, he put the socks on, but they caught on the rough calluses on the bottom of his feet; even after he'd gotten them past his hardened worker's feet, they were so loose that they immediately sagged to his ankles. There should have been a ribbon or something to hold them up. The trousers wouldn't stay up either, but that was easy to solve. Whatever the colorful length of cloth was for, it made a decent belt despite being far too long. In fact, the cloth wound completely around his body twice, through wide loops in the waist of the trousers, before he tied it securely. But the socks? He shook his head and discarded them, feeling more at home barefoot.

The two shirts weren't much of a problem. It was too warm for both, so he chose the sleeveless shirt and made his way to the toilet room. After a quick use of the indoor plumbing, he performed the odd ritual of tooth brushing.

But what should he do, with no quarry to dig in, no rock to haul? "I'll explore the palace," he whispered, trying to convince himself that he was thrilled by the notion. He brought Serpent out from under his shirt and laid it on the soft cloth, taking courage from the stone. "And maybe I'll find Mom."

He started with the floor he'd slept on, but found nothing but more bedrooms, toilet rooms, and a few sets of servants' stairs. A single set of stairs at the end of the hall led only down, even though the servants' stairs had led both up and down.

Up, he decided, probably led to the servants' quarters. That's the way it usually worked in town, on those rare occasions he'd been allowed to go with his mother on errands. Usually when she needed something bulky and brought him along to carry it. The shop would be on the first floor, the owner would sleep on the second floor, and the workers would sleep on the third. If the palace was anything like those homes in town, the attic would get awfully hot in the summer, and what noble would want to sweat through the night?

Down the stairs, then. On the floor below, he found no bedrooms, but airy chambers filled with books, or crates, or racks full of bottles, or desks. One large room contained only a couple of tables with strange tools laid out on them. They were sort of like what you'd get if construction tools—like hammers and axes and heavy pliers—were shrunk down to the size of dinner forks. The tables were weird, too, since both were more like shallow tubs than proper tables. They even had drains in the center that led to big ceramic pots underneath.

Micah went back to the stairs. This time, the stairs went straight instead of curving, down to a landing. From there, he could either go up again, possibly to another wing of the palace, or down the widest, grandest set of stairs he'd ever seen. He went down, but stopped halfway to gawk at the floor below.

Every variety of stone he knew could be found in the floor, and many he didn't recognize at all. More importantly, while the marble stairs looked dead to him, with no hint of magical power radiating from the stone, the floor below blazed with diwa. The tiles weren't just thin slabs of polished stone. Each tile must have been least several inches thick, and some of the largest a couple of feet thick. It felt odd to see them that way, but the amount of diwa radiating within each stone proclaimed their thickness, even though they had all been set into the floor so that their polished surfaces were level with each other. The thicker stones positively glowed with power. Here and there, tiny white stones seemed to emit a purplish smoke or mist. No two were exactly the same shape, either. Some were round, though many were square or rectangular, and others irregularly shaped.

Taken together, the tiles formed a mosaic of a face. An oddly familiar face, though he couldn't have said who it resembled. He decided to go closer, but just a few stairs down, the face disappeared.

"What?" Micah whispered. He went back to the landing, and the face reappeared. Just one step down, and it reverted to an unusual collection of randomly shaped tiles. Amazed as he felt, he could gain nothing from staring at a floor, so he continued down the stairs. The circular room at the bottom of the stairs had a ceiling perhaps forty feet high. Opposite the stairs, tall glass windows faced east, with the rays of the rising sun giving everything a golden glow. Arched doorways pierced the walls to either side of the stairs, leading down dark corridors.

Oddly, the round room contained no statues, no paintings, no rugs, no stuffed hunting trophies. Nothing.

So which way to go? One of the halls leading out of the big circular chamber led to floors that must have been beneath his bedroom. That direction led to the kitchen, if he remembered correctly. But his time was his to spend, wasn't it? Why not explore? Even if the unknown left him more fearful with each step. A sudden, nearly overpowering urge to run back to his room struck like a blow. But his mother had to be in the palace somewhere, and he steeled himself to go on despite the hammering in his chest. He chose the hall that led further from his room.

With neither windows nor glowing crystals, the only light came from behind him, and that didn't help much. Dark tiles on the floor of the corridor added to the gloom. Like the stairs, the tiles here held no diwa. Even the walls and ceiling seemed to be tiled in ordinary dark stone. As he walked further, the darkness became absolute, so much so that he bumped into a door he hadn't seen.

Or was it a wall? With neither handle nor hinges that Micah could find, he nearly gave up and turned around. Part of him wanted nothing more. It would be so easy. *Turn around now, and run back to your room, little boy.* He nodded vigorously, before realizing that the voice in his head wasn't his.

"Magic," he whispered. The thought sent a spasm of terror through his bowels, but his mother worked magic. She had to, to change her face, to be Lon's master. He knew she would be on the other side of the door. Besides, he didn't have to hide his abilities anymore. He gripped Serpent with desperate strength.

The obstacle he'd found was definitely a door—he could feel iron bands running horizontally over closely fitted boards, and a tiny gap between the wood and the surrounding stone. He tried pushing the door. He tried grabbing the iron bands with his fingertips and pulling, but he only succeeded in scraping a knuckle. It hurt and it bled quite a bit, but he'd been hurt far worse in the quarry. He sucked his bloody knuckle, knocked with the other hand, pounded hard, but there was no answer.

Finally, he shouted in frustration, "Open, you stupid door!"

The door vanished, but in the darkness he only discovered its absence when he tried to pound on it and stumbled to the floor. Micah hesitated, but the image of his mother propelled him forward. As soon as he was through the doorway, the door reappeared behind him with a whoosh of air, as solid and unmoving as ever, as he found when he tried to retrace his steps. Ahead, he saw light at the end of a long, dark corridor. He walked as casually as he could manage, not wanting anyone to know what a tough time he'd had with the magical door, or how frightened he felt. But the act got harder as he neared the end of the passageway, for with each step he got hungrier.

He'd just eaten, but still the hunger grew, like he hadn't eaten in days, weeks maybe. He tried turning back the way he came, but it made no difference which direction he chose. He thought he'd pass out if he didn't get some food, and fast.

As he came closer to the end of the hall, he heard a voice, but couldn't understand the words. It was Lon, speaking the language of magic, his voice strained and hoarse.

Micah entered another large, circular room, one almost exactly like the one at the bottom of the stairs with the disappearing face in the tiles. The floor looked the same, with a great deal of power emanating from tiles of varying thickness. This room, however, wasn't empty at all. There were several large vases arranged in a circle, each of them large enough to hold a man. Brightly colored ropes had been tied around each vase, each rope a different shade of red. One end of each rope extended from a vase up to a chandelier in the center of the room. Within the circle formed by the vases, two of those odd shallow tub/tables sat end to end. There were straps, pillows, and pads on the tables, and suddenly Micah could see that they were designed to hold a person down. From the position of the pillows, it seemed that two people would lie on the tables with their heads almost touching. He could imagine no benign purpose for any of this equipment and decided he should have heeded the voice.

Between the tables stood Lon, still chanting, painting designs on the tables. Micah slipped Serpent back under his shirt, stepped closer and was about to speak when Lon spun around so quickly that red paint came flying off his paint brush and splattered on the floor.

"Stop!" he whispered. "Micah, come no closer. What are you doing here?"

Micah stumbled a bit, surprised, but also weak with the ever-growing hunger. His eyes widened as he took in the Baron's appearance, for the trim, dapper man had transformed into a skeletally thin wretch, skin wrinkled and spotted, hair mostly gray and thinning considerably. Trying to ignore the sorcerer's physical state, he said, "I'm sorry. I went exploring."

Lon put the paint brush down, muttering, "I'll have to start over, now." He put the paintbrush back into a jar on the table, then took something from a drawer under one of the tables, whispered a few words, then set the object on the floor. It was a thumb-sized beetle, and it immediately scuttled over to the drops of paint and began to devour the red mess. When it was finished, it turned and sped across the floor toward Micah.

"Are you bleeding?" Lon asked.

"Yes. I scraped my knuckle on the door."

Lon tilted his head and looked at Micah like he was seeing him for the first time. "Come . . . no wait, stay there. I'll come to you. Let the beetle do its job; it won't hurt you."

Suddenly, Micah realized that Lon had been painting with blood, but the designs on the tables had vanished. He trembled as the beetle busied itself all around his feet, licking up stray drops, then hurried off down the hallway.

Lon laughed, and it was not a pleasant sound. "Don't worry, young master. You have nothing to fear from me. All of this," he said, sweeping his hands to encompass the room, "is for someone else. Now that person, I must say, does indeed have something to fear."

"Is this for my sister?"

"Perceptive, but no, not really. It's related to her arrival, though."

Micah tried hard to sense the truth of Lon's statement, but he couldn't get a good read on him. It was at times like this that he usually decided that the person speaking was telling some truth, but not all of it. He opened his mouth to speak, but his stomach growled loudly, and he had to grab the edge of one of the big vases to keep from falling over.

Lon was at his side almost instantaneously, taking his hand from the vase, and leading him to the hallway he'd just exited. Near the entrance hung a servants' rope Micah hadn't noticed before. Lon tugged it three times, and soon Chase entered the room through a hidden doorway near the stairs.

"Come with me," Lon said, propping up Micah and leading them down the hallway. "Chase, when we are through to the other side, I will need you to take Micah to his room. I will send a meal. He is to eat all of it, then sleep for as long as he needs. Do not touch the wound on his hand. Do not allow anyone to bandage it. When I am through here, I will attend to it myself."

Micah tried to speak. He mumbled and slurred, then coughed. Eyes bulging and breath coming in shallow gasps, he wondered frantically what was happening.

Lon reached the door, whispered some words, and the door vanished. They crossed the threshold, and Chase carried Micah the rest of the way. Somewhere along the way, they lost Lon, but Micah barely noticed. His head fell against Chase's chest, and the world went black.

Micah woke up after what seemed to be just a few moments but may have been longer. He lay in his bed, wearing nothing but a long nightshirt. The curtains had been closed, but bright sunlight leaked around the edges, so either he hadn't been out for long, or he'd slept an entire day.

"He lives," said Lon. The Baron sat in a heavily padded chair near the door. His appearance had reverted to that of the relatively young man who'd taken Micah and his mother from the quarry. "Feeling better?"

"Yes," he said, after a brief coughing fit. The comforting, warm presence of Serpent formed a lump under his shirt, and he chose a bold response. "What about you? What was wrong with you, before?"

Lon squinted and cocked his head as if listening to some faint sound. "What do you mean?"

"The way you looked. You were old. Now you're young again."

Lon laughed. "I am still old, older than you can imagine. What you see now is a glamour, a simple spell, really, but the work you interrupted yesterday required all my concentration, and so I had to remove my disguise. Few have seen me as I really am. Now, are you still hungry?"

Micah thought about it and remembered how ravenous he'd been. "No, I guess not. Did I eat something?"

"Yes. Though not willingly. It's a foul recipe. But it's what you needed."

"I don't remember it."

Lon stood and walked over to the bed. He sat on the edge and placed his hand on Micah's head. "Cool to the touch. Good." He looked closely at Micah then, staring into his eyes. After several moments, he shook his head and took Micah's hand, running his fingers over the scraped knuckles. "Healing. You gave me quite a fright."

Micah looked down at his hand, surprised to see that what he'd thought was just a scrape had crusted over in dark, greenish scabs. Jet black steaks stained the skin, leading from the wound up his arm and under the sleeve of the night shirt. "What's wrong with me?" he shouted.

"Nothing, now. But you'll need to be more careful the next time you practice magic."

"What? I'm no practitioner."

Lon smiled. "Really? Tell me again about Garron's death."

Micah stared at Lon, unable to speak. Finally, he whispered, "I never told you about that."

"Ah, but you did. Last night, while I attempted to force you to choke down some healing food. Quite a tale. Do you remember it?"

He closed his eyes, not wanting to see the smiling Lon. What had he said? Had he spoken in his sleep? Had he confessed the truth?

"Come now, Micah. Tell me what memories you have of that day in the quarry. And don't worry about silly notions of innocence and guilt. People like us are above such concerns."

Micah remembered two completely different versions of the events. In one, he'd simply been removing quartz, as Garron had ordered. In the other, he'd taken hold of the massive boulder, felt the diwa flowing through him, and heaved several tons of stone with his bare hands, causing the collapse that had killed Garron. Eventually, after much prodding from Lon, he told the baron both stories. As he did so, he began to feel hungry again. Not as bad as the last hunger that had gripped him, but worse than being simply hungry.

Lon must have sensed it. As Micah finished the story, he pulled a servants' rope three times and told the young man who answered to bring a 'healing meal' at once.

"Yes, my lord," the servant answered. "What proportions, my lord?"

"Half and half for the food, but a full measure of the drink." The servant left, and Lon sighed heavily. "Whatever am I to do with you? You clearly possess talent." He seemed about to say something, but instead stroked his pointy beard.

"Lon? Where is my mother? Can I see her?"

"She is very busy making preparations for your sister's arrival."

"I won't get in the way. Really I won't. She used to spend hours polishing prayer stones, and I never bothered her then."

Lon pursed his lips and squinted, and for a moment Micah thought he was considering saying yes, but after a few moments he said, simply, "No."

Micah started to protest, but the food arrived. The servant wheeled it in on a cart, bowed to Lon, and left. Lon lifted the tray off the cart and set it directly on Micah's bed. "I'll expect you to feed yourself this time. And trust me, this will taste horrible. You will want to retch. Your senses will tell you that this is most definitely not food. But eat it you must, for it is the only thing that will heal you."

Micah looked at the 'food.' Small, brown chunks of something that might have been meat swam in a sauce that looked for all the world like thin, yellow vomit. Next to that were several curved bones with tiny scraps of flesh attached randomly. A smell like garbage and urine emanated from the so-called food. A thick, frothy, purple liquid filled a crystal goblet. As he frowned and picked up the goblet, several small creatures began swimming wildly around in the liquid, barely visible, but also unsettling. He set it down.

Lon laughed. "You'll want to suck the marrow out of the bones. The beef cubes aren't really that horrible, but you must have some of the sauce with each bite, and the sauce tastes as wretched as it looks. The drink is the easiest part. I'd suggest you leave it to the end, for though it looks awful, it really has no taste. Well, so long as you don't bite down on any of the wigglers, that is."

"What is it?"

"I'll tell you one day, but not now. It will be difficult enough without knowing where it comes from."

"Will you at least tell me why I can't see my mother while I eat?"

"I suppose it can't hurt, but you must eat. No dallying."

Micah nodded and speared a beef cube, gave it an uncertain look, and popped it in his mouth. He very nearly spit it right out. The taste—a little like spoiled eggs, a little like vomit, bitter, salty—defied accurate description. He coughed.

"Drink a little, but trust me: if you feel something moving in your mouth, swallow it immediately."

Micah drank, and he certainly felt something swimming over his tongue. He swallowed, and some of the awful taste went down with it. "Ugh. I have to eat all of this?"

"Yes, so get busy. Now, as to why you cannot help your mother, I think it should be obvious. You have, within the last few days, accomplished three very difficult feats of magic without seeming to have any idea that you were doing so. First, you moved a boulder weighing several tons with your bare hands. Then, you opened a magically sealed door using nothing but a few drops of your own blood and a simple command. Finally, you have managed to defy a forgetting spell cast by your mother, who is one of the most powerful sorceresses I have ever encountered."

Micah swallowed more of the purple drink, washing down a few chunks of beef. "So? I would think that would make me even more helpful."

"Helpful? Do you think it would be helpful if you were to accidentally upset some arrangement she's made? Without meaning to, you could easily warp a spell."

"So what am I supposed to do?"

Lon started to speak, stopped abruptly. He stroked his beard for a bit, then snapped his fingers. "You truly are dangerous in your current state, completely untrained and unaware of your power. What you need is instruction, and I will shortly have some free time. Your mother is approaching a point in her preparations at which she will not require my assistance. And at any rate, you and I will have to get to know each other eventually. I will train you."

"Thank you, Lon! When?"

Lon laughed. "There are a few things I have to do today, and maybe tomorrow. Perhaps the day after tomorrow, yes?"

Micah nodded, smiling. *I will learn, and become a sorcerer,* he thought. *I'll be powerful like my dad, more powerful than my sister. Mom will see. She'll know I'm better than her.*

7

Kellyn lay in the hammock that was her bed, unable to sleep, trying not to stare at the sheathed sword that lay atop the canvas bag holding her worldly possessions. She should have been putting her stamp on the sword, working her fingers into the steel as if it were a lump of wet clay. She'd never seen it done, but she'd been told about it. It was this decoration of the sword by its owner more than anything else that cemented the bond between the two, this merging, for a few minutes, of steel and flesh.

But she couldn't bring herself to touch the sword, this murderous beast that called itself Shaethe.

Waves of cold emanated from the sword. Kellyn sensed amusement, and a little disgust.

"You think I'm a murderous beast, too, don't you?" she whispered to the sword. Of course it did not respond. "I have to master my love of violence, or I will never become a full member of the Brotherhood."

The enormity of her actions forced her to shy away from the images in her head. She'd trained as a warrior mage for a decade, and of course her father had taught her to fight as a young child. But never before had she killed a real human. Now she had killed several. And loved each bloodstained moment. The sheet that separated her bunk from the men gave her a slim measure of privacy. But each time she parted it, each time she saw the crew, they would see her as she really was: a killer, a monster.

Around her, men snored, talked in their sleep, murmured, coughed and farted, while in the background, the sounds of the ship made a soft accompaniment. Creaks of rope and wood and leather, the slow swishing of Magda's tailfin, the wind whistling through gaps in the hull: there was no silence in the air. She couldn't even find peace in her own mind.

Kellyn's hand moved without conscious control toward the sword. She stopped the movement and clenched her fingers into a fist. The sword wanted them to bond. She resisted, but it was made doubly hard since she also desired the bond.

Magrahim had taught her long ago, when she first began her lessons with the sword, that she would not only have to kill one day, but also live with the killing afterward. She had expected all the emotions he had warned her to anticipate: shame, remorse, disgust. And yet at her core she felt one thing more than any other: a deep sense of satisfaction. She felt as if all her life she'd thought she was one person, only to discover that she was someone else all along.

"No," she whispered. "I can't be a mindless killer." She grabbed her gloves and hat and boots and donned them quickly in the dark before stumbling through the ship and up onto the deck.

But no matter the distance, she felt the tug pulling her back to her bunk.

Kellyn almost turned and ran for her sword, but she fought off the compulsion, walking stiffly for the deckhouse. From there she climbed the center ropes up to the gondola, with the urge to retrace her steps in her mind most of the way. But by the time she reached Magda's underside, she felt like the master of her own body once more. Still, she continued climbing until she reached the topside. She sat heavily on the floor of the crow's nest and tried to calm her breathing.

"What are you doing here?"

Kellyn whipped her head around, saw Jirra sitting up on the floor at the rear of the gondola. "I'm sorry. I didn't know anyone would be here. I just needed a quiet place . . . some time to think."

"You're a weird mage, Kellyn."

"And you're an unusual 'boy,' Jirra."

"Tell no one," she whispered fiercely.

Again, Jirra's eyes flashed in a peculiar way. The kind of flash, she was almost certain, that most people could not see. Kellyn smiled, though Jirra probably couldn't see. There was enough moonlight that she could see Jirra's face, but the mage sat in shadow. Jirra's dark complexion announced her Mohotsan heritage, as did her prominent nose. Now that Kellyn knew this was no boy with a girlish face, she decided she was rather attractive. Kellyn's heart beat a little faster. She'd always preferred girls, but now would not be the time for flirting. "I won't. I promise. I know what it's like, being a girl in a man's world."

Jirra chuckled. "You don't have to hide it, though. And, um, no offense, but Kattenese men aren't usually hairy, right? You could almost pass for a man." She chuckled again, and Kellyn joined her. "So, mage. What brings you up here?"

Kellyn almost told her everything right then, from the failed test to the sword named after an evil spirit. Almost. But she hardly knew this girl who pretended to be a boy. "The pirates . . . I never killed before."

"Seriously? Well, I still never have killed anyone, though I think I stuck one of those bastards pretty good before you lopped his head off. I thought you mages were trained to kill from birth?"

"No," Kellyn whispered. "We . . . we're trained for combat, but killing should never be the first option. I just can't help thinking that I could have avoided the bloodshed yesterday."

"And do what? Talk them into leaving us alone? What would you have said? How 'bout, 'pretty please?'"

They both laughed at that. But an idea came to her then, many hours too late. "I could have flown the arrows in circles around their ship. I could have used my throwing stars to cut some of the ropes of their harness. When they got close enough, I could have pushed time, then ran from one spot to another on Magda's back, slowing down at each new location for a few moments, so that it would look like I was disappearing in one place and magically appearing in another."

"To what end?"

"It would have shown them, quite clearly, that a warrior mage was aboard the *Nighthawk*. Their captain would have fled, then, if he had any sense. And word would still have gotten around that they'd encountered a member of the Brotherhood on a Thurnish ship. There was no need to kill so many."

Jirra said nothing for a few minutes, leaning back against the wall of the gondola. "You're definitely a weird one, mage. But think about this: air pirates are bad folks. They drop on unsuspecting sailing ships at night. They attack villages inland. Even if you scared them away from us and other airships, they would still have been a menace to a lot of innocent people. You might have shown them mercy, but they'd have shown none at all to their next victims. You did the right thing."

Kellyn grunted, neither agreeing nor disagreeing. She was reminded of one of Magrahim's sayings: "The correct action, in any situation, will not always be immediately apparent. Many times, the best path will only reveal itself when it is too late to change course." The intent of the lesson hadn't been to make her overly cautious, for there were times when instant action was the only option. Her teacher had been trying to curb her instinct for violence. When there was no time for thought, work from the ideals of preserving life, and giving mercy when possible. It is better, Magrahim often said, paraphrasing one of the Brotherhood's sayings, to die showing mercy to those who don't deserve it than to live denying it to those who do. But Kellyn had just discovered that in the heat of the moment, she loved killing.

She opened her mouth to speak, but the words caught in her throat. She coughed.

"Spit it out, mage," teased Jirra.

"We are who our parents make us," she blurted. She knew she shouldn't tell her any of this, that she was ruining her already thin cover, but she couldn't help herself. In a voice just a shade above a whisper, she continued, "My parents were evil. They were sorcerers, and they taught me to love violence. They taught me sorcery. When the Brotherhood captured me, I was throwing fireballs. Magrahim said I almost conjured a hell whip before they took me."

"What of it?" Jirra said, flicking a hand, dismissing her words.

"You're a mage now. We *are* who our parents make us, in part. And we are also who we choose to be. My mother, well, you don't need to know anything about her. Just know that I am not like her, not one tiny bit. Because I choose not to be like her. I make myself who I want to be."

"But you can't be everything you want to be, can you? You can't help being a girl. I can't help loving violence. I said I never killed before the pirates attacked us. That's true. I've also never felt so alive as when I killed them. It was . . . ecstasy. The purest joy I've ever known. And I can't wait to feel that joy again. I *want* to kill again, I *must* kill again. I could love death like a drunk loves wine."

Jirra sat silently for what seemed like forever. "What's wrong with you?"

Kellyn laughed harshly, shaking her head and suppressing a spike of anger. Jirra was right to wonder what was wrong with her, but that didn't mean Kellyn wanted to hear it. "I wish I knew. That's why I'm going to Kattenwa. There's a healer there who's supposed to be able to help me."

"What if she can't?"

Kellyn wrapped her arms around her belly as a stab of fear drew an involuntary grunt. "The Brotherhood won't just turn me loose, if I fail. I'm too powerful to be sent away. I could be dangerous. They'd strip my talents first."

She thought about this worst-case scenario. Better that than a monster in human form? No. Better to die.

But she couldn't talk about that. She didn't even want to think about it, so she changed the subject. "Jirra? What will you do, later on? I mean, when you just can't hide your sex anymore?"

Now her eyes really did flash. It might be nothing, or it might be significant. Either way, she was not best suited to judge what she was seeing. Maybe when they arrived at Kattenwa, this Felida woman might be able to tell what, if anything, was different about Jirra.

Jirra remained silent for a long time. When she did speak, she said in a fierce whisper, "My life is no business of yours!"

"I meant no offense. You're a young woman of extraordinary abilities,

Jirra. But men are what they are. You cannot hope to inherit command of this ship from your father. Unfair as it is, the crew would never accept orders from a woman." And then she remembered the very first thing she'd thought about Jirra, before she knew her secret, that the 'boy' had a girlish face. "They have to know. Some of them at least. You can hide up here all you want, but that can only serve to make them wonder why. And when they do see you, however infrequently, they have to see you as you are. It's obvious, and getting more so with each passing day."

Jirra opened her mouth to respond, but remained silent for awhile. When she did speak, Kellyn could barely hear her over the wind. "You sound like my mother. She thinks Father is being cruel, to let me dream of a life aboard the *Nighthawk*. I know he won't live forever, and when he's gone, no other captain will have me. Women on a ship's crew are bad luck; all the men say it. I know."

Kale thought about telling her that there were other alternatives for women aside from the traditional roles of mother and wife, but she really couldn't think of any. Well, besides joining the Sisterhood. But Jirra needed some kind of talent for that, and she had no idea if the girl had even a smidge of magical ability. The Brotherhood wouldn't begin training for one so old, but she didn't know the rules in the Sisterhood. She supposed if Jirra showed some ability, she might be able to train to become a practitioner, but that sort of instruction came with a cost. Would her father pay for magical training? Jirra's predicament distracted her from her own problems, but she really had no solutions for either of them.

"Enjoy it while you can, then, Jirra," she said. "Life has a way of making decisions for you, no matter what you want." She did not respond, but Kellyn thought she appeared more thoughtful than hostile. She tried to think of some reason to stay a little longer, but she was tired from the day's activity, and desperately needed some sleep. She stood to leave, but inspiration struck and she laughed at herself.

"What's so funny, mage?"

"I've just realized how stupid I can be, that's all. Listen, Jirra? I need to lay down here for a few moments. I won't be long."

"Alright."

Kellyn nodded, lay down, touched the time stone in the little pocket on her belt and pushed time to a faster rate than she'd ever tried before. Jirra had been about to say something, but in the relatively slow time she inhabited, her mouth was frozen, just a little bit open. Kellyn closed her eyes, and fell asleep quickly.

She awoke feeling refreshed, her body having experienced several hours of sleep, while the world outside had only moved forward a few seconds. So long as she didn't push herself too much in the next several hours, she might not suffer much more than a little lethargy. She slowed time back to normal, yawning and stretching as she sat up.

" . . . that all about?" Jirra was saying.

"It's a trick I learned from a former classmate of mine. When you desperately need time to sleep, but your schedule won't allow it, you create your own time. I just got a full night's rest. Now I can go back to my bunk and not worry about . . . not being able to sleep down there."

"Uh huh. Well, mage, I don't have that luxury. I have to sleep like a normal person. That's a hint, by the way."

"I'm sorry, I'll be leaving. Um, Jirra? Thanks."

"For what?"

"I don't know. But I feel better, and I think I owe that to you."

"Great. At least one of us got something out of this conversation."

Kellyn left then, and made her way back to her bunk, saddened that she hadn't been able to break through Jirra's sarcastic exterior. She hadn't set out to become her friend, but now that she'd seen just a glimpse of who Jirra really was, she wanted nothing more. She found, too, that she wanted to tell her even more, who her parents were, what they'd done, to unburden herself the way she might have with Magrahim. Well, not exactly. What she needed was not so much a teacher to evaluate her problems. She just needed a friend who would listen without judging, as Jirra had. In all her life, she couldn't remember ever having a friend like that; not even Alonselle. And if she were honest with herself, she wanted more than just friendship with this girl who pretended to be a boy.

The normal routine of an airship in flight reasserted itself after the pirate attack. Kellyn practiced her climbing and became proficient enough that she could get topside almost as fast as the more experienced crewmen. One morning while climbing directly from the ship to topside, bypassing the gondola in favor of the more dangerous outer ropes, she saw Jirra climbing above her. Jirra had strapped a leather and wood contraption with dirty white claws to the stump of her left leg. Her father had described her as 'agile as a squirrel.' Kellyn thought the comparison unfair, for she'd never seen a squirrel move so fast.

She tried to catch up to her, but it was no use. Jirra was up and over the curve of Magda's back before Kellyn was halfway up. "Jirra!" she called. "Wait!"

Her face appeared over the edge of the airhee. "What?"

"I'm supposed . . . to be looking for . . . parasites," she panted. "Can you . . . teach me?"

"I'm on duty shortly. But if you hurry up, I might have a few minutes to spare."

Kellyn grunted with effort. The amulet of strength hung around her neck, but she didn't want to become dependent on it. It was better to let the muscles learn on their own, saving the amulet for desperate situations. The side ropes formed a net, so there were always footholds. But even though she'd made tougher ascents, she still couldn't get accustomed to the thousand-foot drop looming below. After what seemed like far too long, she joined Jirra on Magda's back, breathing deeply. Within moments, her breathing returned to normal.

"You're in better shape than most dirt huggers, mage," Jirra said. "But you're still slow." She looked around, pointed at a spot near the dorsal fin. "Over here, let's go."

Kellyn stood to walk, but Jirra scrambled along on hands and knees faster than she could move on two legs. Jirra's left leg ended at the knee, and she used the artificial claws there like toes on Magda's smooth back. She had another set of artificial claws on her right knee, Kellyn noticed with surprise. By the time she caught up, Jirra was sitting and pointing at a hand-sized brownish scale.

"See this one? Notice how the edge of the scale is slightly darker than the surrounding scales? That's your first sign. Now rub your hand over a nearby scale, and then over that one. What do you notice?"

"A bump?"

"Yes. That bump is a parasite. Most likely a tick. Now, this next part is delicate." She lifted the scale and peered underneath. "Look. See it there? About the size of a grape?"

Kellyn knelt and squinted. "Yeah, I see it."

"Did you bring a knife?"

"Your father gave me this." She held a skinning knife, about ten inches long and tapered to a very narrow point, but the edge was rather dull.

Jirra took it from her, running her thumb along the blade. She nodded. "Good. Now watch closely." She lifted the scale just a little higher and worked the blade up underneath the tick. "You really have to watch this. Here, move closer."

Kellyn did as ordered, until the side of her head rubbed against Jirra's. She squirmed closer until she could see both the tick and the blade. Kellyn's shoulder and elbow touched hers.

"See it?"

Kellyn nodded.

"See how the tick grabs the edge of the blade? Now, as I work the blade up under its body and toward its mouth, it'll start to try to move away from the blade, but the head won't move. See?"

"Yeah."

"Now, just a little further. There! See how it's trying to move sideways? Now you angle the blade up into the tick's body, and pop!" Purplish blood splattered against the underside of the scale, and a little of it got out onto Jirra's hand. "I assume my father gave you some salve?"

Kellyn took a small bottle of yellowish fluid from her pocket and handed it over. As she did so, she moved away, a little conscious now that this was the closest the two of them had been. Thurnish society didn't much care what women did in private, so long as noble women married and had children. Kattenwa tended to be rather less sanguine about women who liked women in that way. She wondered what Mohotsans thought of such relationships.

"No, get back over here," Jirra said. "Look underneath again. First you scrape away the dead bug. Make sure you find the head. Here it is, see? Now put some salve on your index finger."

Kellyn did as ordered, dipping her finger into the bottle of thick, foul-smelling liquid.

"Now reach under the scale. Ticks always attach near the base of the scale, so reach far back and smear it all over. Try to feel for the bite wound. Sometimes it's pretty obvious, but this one was kind of small. Fell anything? A tiny hole?"

"I think so."

"Take your hand out." Jirra reached under the scale, felt around, and smiled. "Good. You are now a fully trained tick hunter. And I'm on duty."

"Thanks," Kellyn said as she crawled away.

"No problem," Jirra said. She was about to say something else but broke down laughing before she could get any words out.

"What's so funny?" asked Kellyn, a crooked smile on her face.

"Oh, nothing. It's just that here we have a brave warrior mage of the Brotherhood aboard. A young woman trained in all the magical arts, deft with weapons, strong and quick footed." Jirra laughed again, ruining the effect of her flowery praise. "And you're hunting ticks!"

Kellyn joined her laughter, though she looked down at her feet in embarrassment. When she looked up again, Jirra was smiling. Jirra gave her a thumbs-up before scrambling forward to the crow's nest. Kellyn shook her head, gathered up the knife and bottle of salve, and went to work.

The *Nighthawk* gained altitude all that day, but from her position lying face down on Magda's back, searching for the signs of ticks,

Kellyn didn't notice. It wasn't until she took a break to stretch that she saw the approaching mountains. She assumed these peaks were the Red Spine Mountains, which formed the northern border of the kingdom. Beyond lay the Principality of Kattenwa, the land of her birth. She sat there, working knots out of muscles sore from hours of unfamiliar work, trying not to think about what those mountains symbolized. The end of her journey. Maybe the end of her attempt to become a member of the Brotherhood. Whatever awaited her, the increased altitude had dropped the temperature while she was working. She shivered despite her warm clothing, thinking longingly about the hat and scarf and gloves that waited in her bunk.

Jirra shook her out of her reverie. "Mage! Come up to the nest," she called. "My father wants to speak to you!"

Kellyn joined Jirra in the crow's nest and took the speaking tube from her with a word of thanks. She put the tube to her ear.

"I'm sending up your weapons," said Abbatay, his voice just barely audible through the tube. "We'll be heading into the mountains to-morrow. I'll want you to stay topside all the time now."

"Why? Ambush?"

"Possibly. You just keep a close eye on anything that moves in the air."

"Yes sir. And, ah, can you send my hat and gloves? It's freezing up here!"

Jirra gave her an odd look as she handed back the tube. Kellyn wanted to ask what was bothering her, but Jirra shook her head and whispered, "Later."

Yuni brought up a leather bag with Kellyn's weapons, some extra clothes, and a welcome basket of food. The three of them ate in silence, Yuni and Jirra exchanging glances the whole time. Yuni left after eating and gave Jirra one last meaningful nod before descending.

"I don't suppose now is later enough?" Kellyn said.

"Have you searched for ticks behind the dorsal fin?" she asked.

"What? Uh, no."

"Alright. Follow me then." Jirra took the skinning knife and salve from her and set them down in the crow's nest, then led the way. They each grabbed a rope attached to the harness and tied it around their waists, then crawled out beyond Magda's body and onto her tailfin. The back-and-forth motion made walking upright impossible, though during the pirate attack Kellyn had walked all over without even thinking about it. Now it was all she could do to hang on.

"This is far enough," she said. "Magda can't hear us here if we're quiet."

Kellyn tried her best to find a comfortable spot to sit and wait for her to spit it out, whatever this secret was that even Magda couldn't be told. Jirra seemed in no hurry to begin, and it was with some surprise that she noticed her brushing tears away from her eyes. "What is it, Jirra?"

"We'll be in the foothills tomorrow. Maybe even in the mountains themselves, depending on how much Father pushes. Some of the passes we'll have to take will be uncomfortably close to the keel."

"He's done this before, I assume."

"Never with a warrior mage on board."

"So?"

"Some . . . some creatures are likely to see us up here. They may come to investigate."

"Flying creatures?"

She nodded. "They look pretty fearsome, but listen to me. They aren't dangerous, do you hear? No matter what Father says, don't try to hurt them."

"What are they?"

"You'll see. Just remember, don't hurt them. They won't hurt us."

Kellyn took a deep breath, not sure if her suspicions were correct, but she had to ask. "These creatures are the ambush your father warned me to look for, aren't they?"

Jirra nodded, not making eye contact.

There was only one possible answer, though Kellyn thought they were extinct, if they'd ever existed at all. "Angels?"

"Yes. Trust me, please. They aren't dangerous. It's just that . . . oh, never mind. Just promise me you won't kill any of them, please?"

"So long as they don't try to harm anyone."

"They won't. Whatever you think you know about them, you're wrong. Believe me."

Kellyn did believe her, but there was something not being said. She'd just have to wait to find out, though, because Jirra started crawling back to the crow's nest. She looked over her shoulder and said, "No more about this."

She saw no angels that day, so she went back to tick hunting. Even that became a fruitless endeavor, since she'd covered most of the easier areas of Magda's back. Her tail, she'd just seen, wasn't an area on which she felt comfortable crawling around. By the time the sun hung low in the sky, she'd gotten really hungry and was about to go down to the ship for something to eat.

Jirra waved to her from the crow's nest, calling her over. She had just finished pulling a canvas basket into the nest. "Food for us," she said. "And blankets for you."

"So your father really meant it when he said I'd be up here all the time now?"

"Yep. I'll be in the gondola. You'll be on your own, so you'll just have to remember everything I've said. Can you do that?"

Kellyn nodded. "There's nothing else you want to say?"

"No." She mouthed the word, 'Later,' and started laying out food: a loaf of bread, dried fruit, and jerky. They shared a leather bag of water, slightly sour with just a hint of alcohol in it to make it safe to drink. The meal was good fuel for the body, if not especially tasty, and they ate with the focused intensity of people accustomed to hard work.

When they'd finished, Jirra sat still, staring at the floor of the nest. Kellyn could think of nothing to say, but Jirra broke the silence first. "I have dreams, sometimes," she said. "Dreams where I have magical power. I see myself transforming lead into gold, making objects float in the air, stuff like that. Do you think I have any talents?"

"I'm not good at judging that kind of thing. I'm not trying to be nice, it's just that evaluating talent is a talent in itself, one that I don't have. But I . . . I'm going to see a woman who's supposed to continue my education. She's a member of the Sisterhood. Maybe she can tell."

Jirra nodded, refusing to look at Kellyn. "I can't stay aboard this ship forever."

"Your father is right about one thing, at least. I can't see you cooking and cleaning. Or taking orders from a man. Well, unless he's an airship captain."

Jirra smiled, but still wouldn't look up. "Even that's a problem. I want to be the captain myself. I'm not very good at following orders." Finally, she did look up, and her eyes narrowed, boring right into hers. "I've defied my captain in telling you some of the things I've told you. I don't do this lightly, understand?"

Kellyn nodded, and shivered. "It's getting colder," she said, grabbing a blanket.

"We're gaining altitude. Father's trying for one of the upper passes. That's where they live. I think he's trying to force an encounter."

Jirra took a blanket herself and moved to sit next to her. Shoulder to shoulder, each wrapped in their own blankets, their own thoughts, there was nothing romantic about the situation, but Kellyn desperately wanted to put her arm around her, to tell her she'd make sure nothing bad happened to the angels, to protect her. Instead, Jirra put her head on her shoulder and whispered, "Hold me."

They sat in comfortable silence for what seemed like far too little time, watching the sunset, wrapped in each other's arms. She tried to work up the nerve to try to kiss Jirra, but she was just so unsure of herself. Jirra probably liked boys, after all.

"I have to get down to the gondola," she said.

"Can't you stay a little longer?"

"No. I'm sorry. I just . . . I'm sorry."

She hurriedly folded the canvas basket and stuck her arms through the handles, wearing it like a backpack. She hopped over the wall of the nest and crawled down to the side nets. Just before she began her descent, she looked back at Kellyn and waved. She waved back, neither of them saying a word.

For the first time since the night of the pirate attack, Shaethe chose that moment to claw at her mind, demanding her full attention.

"What do you want?" Kellyn whispered.

The sword dragged her hands toward the scabbard. She clenched her fists.

"No! I . . . I can't."

But Kellyn knew that she must. Control of her body came back, but her thoughts now swam in strong currents not consciously under her direction. Her memory returned to a lesson on swordsmithing, and she could see where this was heading. She didn't like it at all.

"The form a Brother's sword takes depends partly on the individual wielder," her instructor had said, "and partly on the spirit that inhabits the steel." Vrogan, his name had been. A man whose appearance said 'blacksmith' far more than it said 'mage'. Short, powerfully built, with dark eyes set deep in a round head only partially covered with graying curls. A beard gone almost wholly gray hung on his impressive belly, but solid shoulders and thick arms gave evidence to great strength. "That spirit exists the day the unbound sword is forged, but not in this world. Rather, the spirit exists on millions of versions of our world, every conceivable form of that spirit on every conceivable form of the world, waiting for the moment you draw blood with it. That day, that instant, the spirit floods into the steel, perfectly matched to its wielder."

The memory faded. Perfectly matched. Kellyn and Shaethe, two killers.

But no. There had to be more to her. Magrahim would not have given her a true sword if he believed there was no more to Kellyn than that. Could there be more to Shaethe, as well?

She looked away from the sword, out over the edge of the crow's nest and into the night. Clouds obscured the stars. To the north, the jagged line of peaks formed a deeper black against the dark blue and gray of the sky. They were noticeably closer than the last time she looked. According to Jirra, angels lived there.

"We are not to harm the angels," Kellyn said. "Am I clear?" She felt nothing from the sword.

She took a deep breath, then reached for Shaethe. She drew the sword, set it on the floor of the gondola, and laid her hands upon the blade. Still not entirely convinced, she said the words in a rush before she could change her mind. "Shaethe, my blade, I offer myself to you."

Warmth flooded into her fingers.

The ancient words spoken, matching the wills of the participants, the merging began. It felt to Kellyn like roots were growing out of her fingers, flowing into the steel as if it were fertile soil, while at the same time the steel became soft, like warm butter. Her fingers sank into the blade, and she saw herself, every facet, reflected in Shaethe. She saw compassion, a strong urge to please, and a desperate need to feel good about herself. There was also pride, suspicion, and an ugly sense of superiority. She tried not to flinch from these weaknesses, for they were a part of her.

But she couldn't help shying away from that other side of herself. A thing like a flaming black sphere existed within her, radiating hatred and rage. Almost like a separate being, but she could see little tendrils connecting her to this angry ball. "This is what you saw," she said to Shaethe.

The blade trembled.

Kellyn was gripped by a sudden urge to protect the blade. "Are you well?" Suddenly, this sword that she had feared, that she had almost hated, was the most important thing in her world. She couldn't bear the thought that her twisted love of violence had harmed the sword.

Again, warmth. And comfort.

Kellyn felt herself flowing outward into her sword, melting with Shaethe in a vast forge. She became steel, and her sword became flesh. The merging went on for what seemed like hours, but every time she opened her eyes, darkness still reigned. At some point, she closed her eyes and drifted away.

8

Lon and Chase led Micah deep under the palace, into basements and sub-basements that grew progressively dirtier and less refined. By the time they stopped, there were no carvings, no paintings, no carpets or tapestries, only bare, unfaced stone. And in front of them, a wooden door. Lon opened it, revealing a large room with a low ceiling. The walls and floor and ceiling had been painted black. Three objects dominated the space: a large stone basin filled with water, and two spherical objects on the floor on each side of the basin, covered with black cloth.

"Can you swim, Micah?" Lon asked.

"No." In fact, the only water he could ever have swum in was the green, slime-covered muck that accumulated at the bottom of the quarry. Otherwise, he'd never seen a large body of water. He stared at the basin, wondering at its depth.

"Well, you don't need the ability to swim, but the ability to float would help a great deal. However, I have anticipated this difficulty. The water is extremely salty, and you should be able to float regardless of your inexperience."

Lon had him strip down to his underclothes and step into the basin. The warm water only came up to his knees. Lon handed over two lumps of wax, with instructions to shove them into his ears, but not too deeply. "You'll have to hand me that silly prayer stone."

Micah surrendered Serpent with some trepidation, but he noticed with relief that Chase bundled his stone in a sack with the rest of his clothes. Micah put the wax in his ears.

"Now lie down in the water," Lon continued loudly, "on your back. Try to lie still. Relax."

Micah's breath quickened at first, but Lon was right. He could do it, he could float. He grinned around a poorly stifled giggle.

"Try to concentrate! I know you're only a child, but you are the son of powerful sorcerers. Great things will be expected of you. Now close your eyes. When I seal this chamber, it will become completely dark, but keep your eyes shut anyway and try to remain silent. I want you to try to experience your surroundings with no sensory input."

"What does that mean?"

"It means no sound, no light, nothing to which any of your senses need react."

"How long do I have to stay in here?"

"Until you have had an insight. You will know when you are done, but it may take several hours. Chase will await you outside this room. Call out when you are finished. I have more pressing things on my agenda today, but I will speak to you later."

Lon and Chase left, closing the door behind them and plunging Micah into a deeper black than he'd ever experienced before, darker than night. He didn't fear the dark, however, and he'd been told that this was just the first part of his magical education. So he wouldn't be harmed here. He just wished he knew what was going to happen.

It had to have something to do with those two spheres on the floor, but he couldn't see them from within the basin. He couldn't see *anything*. So just what was he supposed to do? He grasped for Serpent's comforting presence, and swore softly, remembering that the stone had not accompanied him into the basin.

Taking Lon's advice, he relaxed, breathing deeply, surprised to find that he could almost fall asleep. Time seemed to pass very slowly, the moments stretching into hours, until he had no idea how long he'd been floating. It might have been an hour or a day. It was then, only after he had relaxed to the point that he no longer remembered what he was supposed to be doing, that he noticed something about the spheres. They were stones, and very powerful stones at that. Though he couldn't see them, he could sense them. Almost as if he could touch them, feeling the diwa flowing through them and into him. But of course he couldn't touch them, and couldn't have reached if he tried. Moreover, the sensation of touch came from his mind, not his fingertips. He nearly called out to Chase, but stopped himself.

This exercise should have lasted hours, but now he felt sure he'd hardly been floating long at all. There must have been something more, but with nothing else in the room, he focused again on the feel of the stones. The illusion of texture confused him, jumbled and indistinct. As if he were touching something slippery and hard to grasp, yet dry and gritty at the same time. He sensed also a vague sharpness, as though he might cut off a finger if he tried to grab hold of the sensation.

He needed to focus more intently. There were two stones, so might he get a clearer picture if he tried to sense them one at a time? Easier said than done, for diwa permeated the darkness. As if the walls themselves oozed the stuff, creating perhaps the most distracting experience of his life. He shouted at the walls, "Stop it! I can't concentrate!"

But the walls weren't doing anything. They were just there. Still, it made him angry. He wanted to grab them and shake them, the way he moved the boulder in the quarry. Now that had been real power! If only he could feel that again. He tried reaching out to the walls.

Useless. Unless he could touch the stone, he couldn't do anything with its power. He found, however, that by focusing on the walls, he'd forgotten about the stones. One sensation dominated: sharpness. The diwa that flowed through these walls felt dangerously sharp, as if he could cut himself simply by thinking about the feeling. Could he? Could he actually cut with a thought? More importantly, could he cut someone else that way?

He tried focusing hard on the walls, their sharpness, the locations of their edges. The edges were everywhere, unfortunately, but he found that if he imagined them coming together, they formed a massive sword in his imagination. Micah imagined a huge, curved scimitar, the kind Mohotsans from the southern continent were supposed to use in battle. Their ruler, who fancied himself the Emperor of the Sun, seven feet tall and massively muscled, with eyes of pure crimson, carried a sword like that. Or so his mother said once, long ago. That was the blade he imagined, with a single difference: Micah's sword had been carved from stone—highly polished, glossy black obsidian.

The urge to use the sword swelled in his breast. But what could he cut with it? For that matter, could an imaginary sword really cut anything at all? The image suddenly seemed ridiculous, and the blade disappeared like a flame doused with water. He tried to clear his mind of useless fantasies, and instead focused on the stones, one at a time, finding after considerable effort that he could distinguish different textures in the two of them. The one to the left felt slippery, while the one on the right was unpolished. But so what? Who cared if one rock was polished and the other not? But something important danced about, just beyond his grasp, something about the three textures. Could it be so obvious a thing as the very existence of the textures? He thought about calling out to Chase, but a sudden, overpowering urge stopped him cold. He could not tell Lon about the texture of the walls.

He could not, however, have told anyone why not. It made no sense. Maybe because there were only the two spheres in the room? Maybe he was only supposed to sense the spheres? That must have been it. The walls were only there to provide distraction. The test was designed to challenge his ability to focus.

But even that thought felt wrong, even dangerous. He could not tell Lon, couldn't give so much as a hint that he knew anything about the texture of the walls. The time had come to leave this cell. "Chase! I think I'm done."

The door opened, flooding the room with light, though in fact Chase carried only a small candle. "Excellent, Lord Micah. The master has left instructions. You are to return to your rooms, bathe and dine. When you are finished, he will see you."

"Was I in there long?"

"It was midmorning when you entered the chamber. It is now nearly midnight. Not to worry, though. Master Lon keeps late hours."

Micah nodded, noticing for the first time his hunger. He feigned nonchalance as he dried and dressed, but a tinge of anxiety refused to fade until he put Serpent around his neck. He followed Chase up the winding staircase to more familiar levels of the palace, then raced up to his room. He pulled the servants' rope first, ordered a large meal, then bathed thoroughly in the tub down the corridor. A set of clothes had been laid out by the time he returned. He changed into the soft cotton trousers and silk shirt, both a deep red, and waited eagerly for his food. When the meal arrived, he forced himself to take the time to really enjoy it, rather than scarfing it all down as quickly as possible. He'd developed a taste for noodles in a sauce of diced tomatoes and cream, and anyway nobles ate in a serene, dignified manner, or so Chase had said. Though he hadn't ordered any of Lon's healing food, a small dish of meat cubes in vomit sauce sat in one corner of the tray. He ate it quickly, drinking a tall crystal goblet of water afterward to wash away the taste. He'd only just finished when Lon entered his room without knocking.

"Tell me," Lon said abruptly, sitting on the edge of a couch near the windows.

Micah told him all about the spheres, deliberately avoiding all mention of the walls. It was very important to hide that from Lon. Lon asked a few questions about the different textures, and whether or not it had been difficult to tell them apart. "The reason you experience the two spheres as different textures is because they are infused with different diwas. Many think of diwa as one substance, as universally alike as sunlight. We know differently. Different kinds of diwa can be used to accomplish different magical tasks. The fact that you experience the difference through the illusion of texture is unusual, but not rare. I myself experience taste when I distinguish between diwas."

Micah nodded along, his face carefully blank. Lon knew nothing of the walls. But as Micah thought about his secret, Lon smiled.

"You hide it well, Micah. Very well indeed."

"Hide what?"

Lon laughed and clapped his hands together like a child. "The walls, of course! You sensed them, too, I know it. But I charmed the walls, so that you would believe it was extremely important that I remain unaware that you had sensed them. But! Though I know you sensed them, I cannot tell that you are lying. You are extremely talented at deception."

Micah's face remained still, but he worried. Was this a bad thing? Was he supposed to be more honest? He hoped not; he'd never been much good at honesty. There were simply too many things to hide. For that matter, his mother had hidden things from him his entire life. Was that not evidence enough that dishonesty was nothing to be ashamed of?

"I think perhaps—and mind you this is only a theory—I think your life as a bond worker is the reason behind your extraordinary ability to lie undetected. You feared that your abilities would make you a valuable asset for your previous owner to sell, so you taught yourself to hide your thoughts from the world. Ultimately, you feared becoming separated from your mother. True?"

Micah hated the feeling of exposure that came with admitting his fears, but he could think of no good reason to hide such an obvious truth. "Yes," he whispered.

"Well, we will have to test a few things. Deception is valuable, but for you to be a genuine asset to your mother, you must take it a step further. We will need to train you not only to hide the truth in your own speech. You must also be able to prevent others from seeing the truth."

"When do I begin?"

"Soon enough. Your sister will be in Kattenwa shortly, and I suspect I will be rather busy trying to lead her here. But afterward, there will be time."

Micah closed his eyes and wondered what Lon and his mother would do once his sister arrived. Would Lon still teach him? And if so, what then? He could become a sorcerer, but would his life ever again return to the way it used to be?

The way it used to be. Sitting quietly in their one-room shack, listening while his mother told stories about far off lands and times long ago. Never anything about Lon, or his father, or whatever it was that the three of them had done before his birth. But some things were starting to fall into place in Micah's mind. Among them was a growing certainty that the world he once knew would never come back. He wasn't even sure he'd go back if he could.

"Careful, Micah," said Lon, bringing him back to reality. "There are times when your face betrays you. Whatever you were thinking just now, it involved great emotions. Longing, fear, and loss. Not feelings I would ordinarily associate with a ten-year-old boy, but then you are the son of a great man; I suppose I should expect no less. Regardless, you must train yourself to think deep thoughts and experience powerful emotions without letting anyone see them on your face. You're very good at it, but you aren't yet perfect."

Micah nodded.

"Good. As soon as I brought your weakness to your attention, you closed up like a clam. For you to fully develop your talent, you must always be closed. Later, we'll work on projecting false thoughts and feelings, so that it won't be so obvious that you are always hiding something." Lon stood and stretched, yawning. "I still have some work to do before I can rest. You should get some sleep."

Micah watched him leave, then stood and pulled back the curtains to look out onto the palace grounds. At that moment, he wanted nothing more than to sleep in the same room as his mother. Even if it was a huge room like this one, even if he couldn't hear her breathing or feel her warmth, he just wanted to know she was nearby and safe. Would they ever let him see her again? He resolved to find her, with or without Lon's permission, first thing in the morning.

Micah stifled an urge to scream. He'd found the room with the mosaic floor, again. It seemed no matter which hallway he took, whether he tried the grand marble staircases or the servants' stairs, he could only find a few places within the palace: his room and the other rooms on that floor, the kitchen, and this mosaic. Lon must have charmed the entire palace after he'd accidentally found the other room with the mosaic floor, the one with Lon's odd tables and vases. Lon had magically prevented him from finding anything he didn't want him to find. Including his mother.

Thinking of Lon's laboratory, however, made him want to smack his forehead.

He walked confidently up to the doors to the front of the palace, but they would not open. There didn't appear to be any locks on the huge glass doors, but they remained stubbornly closed. Magically closed, he decided. But he knew how to deal with that. He bit the inside of his lower lip and spat blood on the door. "Open," he shouted.

The doors opened. Feeling quite satisfied, he strolled out onto the grounds and around the perimeter of the palace, looking for more entrances. It took about an hour to walk around the entire place. Unfortunately, from the outside, there appeared to be only two entrances: the one he'd just exited, and the servants' entrance by the kitchen. That couldn't be, of course. There had to be other doors, but perhaps they were magically hidden. He thought, briefly, about spitting blood all over the exterior walls, shouting at the doors to reveal themselves, but the notion was silly. He would run out of blood.

Thinking about how he'd opened the doors in the first place made him notice how hungry he'd become. That odd kind of hunger, like the pangs he'd experienced after finding Lon's laboratory. He doubled back to the kitchen and ordered one of Lon's special meals.

"What proportions, milord?" asked the girl whose name he'd never learned.

"Half and half," he replied, though in fact he had no idea what the proper mixture should be. "I'll take my meal by the fountain with the unicorn statue, please."

"Yes, milord."

The hunger got worse before the food arrived, but not so bad as before. Maybe it was a lesser spell that had kept him locked in. At last, the girl arrived and set a tray down upon the edge of the fountain. Micah waved her off and ate the disgusting food. Afterward, he felt the urge to sleep, but decided to fight it. He still wanted to explore, and if the interior of the palace had been sealed off, he could still look around outside.

In the front of the palace, a raised roadway stretched for what seemed a mile or more, arrow straight and lined with trees that formed a canopy over the gravel surface. Broad lawns flanked the road, criss-crossed with paths of crushed stone, and hedges, dotted here and there with benches and statues.

None of it interested him, so he walked back around to the rear of the palace, beyond the stables and barns. He found an enormous stone-lined artificial pond, full of frogs, ducks, and massive golden fish. Dragonflies darted across the surface, and he supposed it must be beautiful, but again, unless he could find his mother sitting on one of the marble benches, he had no interest. But behind the pond stood a hill, and he thought the higher vantage point might give a better view, so he climbed to its summit. There, he wriggled up into the branches of the single oak that stood there, and looked out upon the grounds.

"Much better," he said. There were more outbuildings, the purposes of which he could not begin to guess, but one feature stood out clearly: a cemetery. He climbed down and went to investigate.

The graveyard wasn't easy to find, and several times he stopped to rest, nearly falling asleep each time. But at last he reached the cast iron fence that surrounded the tombstones and mausoleums. A little search-ing revealed the gate, and no magic barred the way. It stood open.

He gained nothing from examining the headstones; he had never learned to read. Some grave markers stood nearly as tall as Micah, adorned with ornate carvings, but uncarved slabs of marble sufficed for most of the graves. All of them—dozens, maybe hundreds—shared one trait: age. The carvings had begun to fade as the rain slowly dissolved decorations and writing. That must have taken decades, centuries even. He rubbed his hands across the stones as he walked by, trying to feel diwa, but these stones were cold and lifeless.

He wondered just how long these stones had sat, ignored, forgot-ten. His mother had said that cut stone rapidly loses its power unless someone works the diwa back in, slowly, with care, over time. She had done that, making prayer stones in their hut. Little carved figurines, or sometimes just polished lumps. Some people used them to bring relief to aching bones. Others with just a hint of talent used them to bring protection to their homes, their loved ones. Or to hurl curses. Her stones had been highly sought after by the locals, back home. The income she brought in should have given them a better station in life, but Garron had taken all of it as his due. He'd owned them, after all.

Thinking of his mother and the life they'd led together brought only pain. He wiped suddenly wet cheeks and stood a little straighter, determined not to show weakness. The cemetery wasn't large, and before too long he'd come to the last row of graves. Some of these looked more recent, but one block of marble, neither older nor newer than those surrounding it, and not particularly fancy, captured his attention. The lettering looked fairly crisp, with just a little softening of the edges to show it had been here for years. He knelt to examine it more closely.

Its ordinary appearance, however, belied its strength, for when he touched the stone it burned his fingers. And when he looked closely, its power glowed like a bonfire. He should have been able to see the stone's diwa with a glance. And when had diwa ever burned before? He sucked throbbing fingertips and squatted on his haunches, peering at the grave marker from just inches away. "It isn't marble at all," he whispered.

The surface appeared grainy, like unpolished granite. A single word adorned its surface, but of course he couldn't read it. Light streamed from the letters themselves, as if the blocky characters contained more diwa than the stone itself. Despite the burns, he reached out to touch it again.

"Don't touch that stone!"

Micah turned, expression carefully neutral, but with a fierce joy in his heart. "Mother."

She walked up a gravel path and stopped several feet from the grave. "Touch nothing. Stand and move away from the stone."

He stood and moved toward her, wanting nothing more at that moment than to run into her embrace, but she had never been free with displays of affection, and he feared that she would either tell him to stop, or just stand there, still as a statue, refusing to return his affection. Instead, he stopped a few feet from her and fought back tears.

"I haven't seen you since the coach ride. Why won't you let me see you?"

"I am very busy. I have been preparing for your sister's return for ten years, and I will not let this opportunity slip away. You must understand, these are very important times for me. For us. Our life will return to the way it once was, the way it should be. I will wear a crown again, and Kattenwa will have its king."

Micah didn't want any of that. Who cared about a king? Who would it even be? Not Micah, certainly.

"Why can't I help? I'm strong. I could carry things for you."

"No. The things I have to do, I have to do by myself. There is powerful magic involved, and you would not be safe. Have I not always kept you safe? For ten years, I have worn this ugly face for you, so that no one recognizes me. If the Prince knew I was still alive, he would hunt me down and kill me. You, too, Micah. No child of Valdis Hittrech would be allowed to live."

Micah watched her face closely, and saw that she was telling the truth, but not all of it. If only he could figure out where she'd omitted something, he might be able to get more of the truth from her. But she excelled at lying. He wondered if she could make others believe her lies, the way Lon wanted him to learn, and assumed she could.

"Please trust me, my son. I have much to do, a crushing burden of work, and only I can do it. You can help me, simply by being patient and waiting for all of this to end. One day soon, you too will be a powerful man in the new kingdom. Can you wait just a little while longer?"

"Yes, mother."

"Good. And one more promise? Do not come to this graveyard again. I do not think you have caused any harm, but if you keep tramping around, you could disturb energies that must remain finely balanced until the time comes for them to be . . . transformed. Promise?"

"I promise."

She smiled then, and Micah could tell it was genuine. He returned the expression, and warmth spread throughout his body. This was almost as good as the embrace he'd originally wanted, and he knew it was probably about all he could have expected. But her eyes drifted to the black headstone, and she stared longingly.

He knew then. "This is my father's grave," he said.

"Yes. He was a great sorcerer in life. He is still powerful, even in death."

"How did he die?"

"He was betrayed. A lesser sorcerer, jealous of his power, told the Prince all your father's plans long before we were ready to strike. We fought anyway, though we were doomed from the start." Her eyes had never left the grave marker. A single tear slid down her cheek. "If I could only feel his touch once more, I would move heaven and earth to do it. But you and your sister are all that I have left of your father."

Micah nodded, staring at the ground. She had left something out, but what she'd said held mostly truth. "Are you and Lon going to start a rebellion again?"

"I hope a full-scale rebellion won't be necessary. I think maybe the first one was a mistake. Give the Prince a nail, and he will call in the Thurnish hammer. This time, we will be more discreet. And more direct."

"Will you kill the Prince?"

She turned to him, a half-smile upon her face. "Yes, but that is only the beginning. Now, my son, I think you had better get some rest. You look very tired. Why don't you run along back to your room now?"

Micah nodded, smiling around a stifled yawn. He'd found her! But soon, his sister would come.

"What is my sister's name?"

"Hmm?" She had resumed staring at the grave. "Oh, her name is Kellyn. You will meet her soon enough."

She smiled then, lost in thought. Micah smiled, too, but his smile lied. He had no smiles for Kellyn.

9

Kellyn awoke, startled, with her sword in her hand. Jirra stood in front of her, her stump on the crow's nest wall, her good leg within the nest. Her mouth hung open and she crouched, eyes narrowed.

"Kellyn?" she whispered.

"Jirra? What is it?"

"Are you well? You look . . . different."

"I . . . I'm fine." And she thought about it, really looked at herself, in the way she had during the merging with Shaethe. She felt well and whole. The black sphere still lurked inside her, but she believed she had more control now. Like she could choose to let the rage engulf her. Or not. Still, she knew that once the blood lust settled over her mind, she'd have no command of it. None at all.

"They're coming."

"The angels?"

"Yes. Remember your promise?"

"Of course." Kellyn sheathed her sword, removed her sword belt and scabbard, and laid them on the floor of the nest. It felt different, and she frowned in confusion for a moment. But then she saw it, a mostly invisible strand of light joining her hand and the hilt of her sword. Not 'Shaethe's hilt,' she noticed. Shaethe no longer inhabited the sword alone. They were, in many ways, one being now. The sword was just a sword. Only when she held the sword in her hand would it be capable of anything extraordinary. Even another member of the

Brotherhood couldn't expect anything magical from this sword. Just as Kellyn couldn't effectively wield another Brother's sword.

"I have to go. I wasn't here, yes?"

Kellyn nodded, smiling. "Deal, but only if you kiss me."

Jirra blinked, a slight smile upon her lips. Kellyn was a little surprised herself. She hadn't intended to be so bold and wondered if this were a result of merging with Shaethe. Had she pressed too far, too soon?

"Hey, I was just joking," Kellyn said hurriedly.

"Remember your promise."

With that, Jirra left, glancing back only once, when she was about to grab hold of the top of the side net. She nodded, a stiff breeze tousling her short, black hair, and scrambled over the edge.

Stupid, Kellyn scolded herself. *Should have kept my mouth shut.* But soon all thoughts of romance soon left her head, as she caught her first sight of the angels. A flock of them approached in a V formation, more than two dozen. She found it hard to judge their size when the only references were the mountains in the distance, and the valley below. Still, she'd never seen larger birds. Distance, too, she found hard to estimate —they might have been miles away, or only a few hundred yards. She couldn't tell until they came closer, at which point she decided her first thought had been correct—nothing save airhees outsized them in the air. The angels split up near the *Nighthawk*, flying in complex patterns that formed a living net all around the airship.

Several flew by her within an arm's length. She noticed their wing-span first, easily ten feet across, maybe fifteen. They might have been huge white eagles except for a few details that emerged upon closer inspection. Underneath the wings, a second set of bird's legs sprouted, though the talons were arrayed more like a human hand than a bird foot. Any resemblance to ordinary birds ended at the face. A face very nearly human in its features and proportions adorned the angels' heads. Large eyes set wide and on the front of the head, not the sides, a small and upturned nose, and a wide, full lipped mouth, set in an expression much like a smile. She could see why they'd been named angels, for their strange, otherworldly beauty.

Until one of them noticed her. It unleashed a high-pitched scream, but not like a child. More like a wounded horse, mixed with something much more human. The sound undulated, rising and falling, setting Kellyn's teeth on edge. Its cry grated on her, and other angels joined the audible assault, their faces transformed into terrifying masks of rage. Their wide mouths split in snarls, too large to look human. Within those bright red mouths laid multiple rows of triangular teeth, more like a shark's gaping maw than anything else. She wanted to kill them all, the force of her reaction shocking the breath from her lungs.

The urge to snatch up her sword and attack came with a force like a gale wind. She knew in that instant that she could call the weapon to her hand with a thought. Kellyn shook her head. She'd seen Magrahim do just that, bringing his sword into his hand from several yards away.

"FRIENDS!" boomed a voice, loud as thunder. Magda. "DO NOT HURT MY FRIENDS!"

Kellyn looked down, saw that she had snatched her sword up off the floor without even realizing it. Had the airhee sensed it somehow? She bent to place the weapon on the floor again, and heard, just barely, Abbatay's voice in the speaking tube. "Kill them!" he said, in a strained, maniacal voice. "Kellyn, if you can hear me, I order you to kill them!"

"NOOOOOOO!" bellowed Magda.

"You don't understand, my sweet," said Abbatay, and Kellyn frowned until she realized the captain was speaking to the airhee. "They want to take you from me. Don't listen to them! They would take you up into their mountains, high up where humans cannot breathe. We will all die if you go with them! Do you want to see me die?"

Magda responded this time with a blast of sound, a discordant symphony of song and trumpets and thunder. The angels seemed to shudder in the air before resuming their aerial ballet. Each time one passed Kellyn's position, snarling and screaming, she felt the urge to comply with the captain's orders. It wasn't the sword this time, nor some malevolent spirit. Had it ever been? No, it was that thing within her, that orb of violence, demanding to be fed with blood. It would be so easy. They were so close. The bow, the stars, a nice stable fighting platform beneath her feet. She could litter the ground below with their corpses.

"No," she whispered. But refusing the urge would not be easy. She felt her hands reaching for her weapons and decided she would just hold the sword. What harm could that do? The angels weren't coming very close anymore. Had Magda warned them? At any rate, Kellyn couldn't reach them with the blade, so she drew it, hoping the feel of the wood and leather grip would calm the beast within her.

For the first time that day, she took a good look at her sword. She hadn't thought to see what kind of design she'd worked into the steel, and now that she saw, she wished she hadn't. On one side she saw the fine tracery of black and silver known was Woteen steel, for the remote region of the southern continent where the technique originated. The flowing, multilayered pattern of black lines alternating with silver covered every inch of the blade. The sword had not merely changed its appearance. A dishonest swordsmith might etch the Woteen patterns with acid on ordinary steel. This sword had not been merely decorated. The steel itself had changed, becoming not just Woteen in look, but Woteen in fact. The idea that she could produce this with her bare hands astonished her.

The other side of the sword stopped her heart for a moment. Lacking designs or lettering, it felt like a completely different sword when she looked at this side. She knew little about the significance of most sword designs, but she knew enough that this bizarre blade should not be able to exist. On impulse, she looked at the blade edge on, and it was as if there were two separate swords, one plain, one Woteen. Turn it a little one way, and the other sword would disappear. Turn it back, and the process would reverse.

If only Alonselle could see this. His master, Sister Pau, the instrumentor, might be able to tell what was so wrong about this blade. How it had happened, what it all meant. Sister Pau was hundreds of miles away by now. For that matter, she was beyond anyone's help until she reached Felida Uffgold.

"Magrahim, what have I done?" she said aloud. "How is this possible? Shaethe? Are you with me?"

Kellyn felt a distinct sense of unease coming from her sword.

Magda lurched beneath her feet. Her nose now turned sharply upward, gaining altitude quickly. Had Abbatay told the truth? Were the angels really trying to lure the airhee up to where the air thinned so much the humans on board the ship would suffocate? She looked out in front of the ship, and saw that whatever Magda's intentions, she needed altitude badly. Mountains loomed far too closely, and a strong current of air was forcing them toward a pass that looked far too high for Magda to clear. Kellyn wondered just how long she'd been lost in the beauty and confusion of her impossible sword.

Magda swerved to the left, either trying to get out of this current or simply stalling for time as she flew higher in the sky. The *Nighthawk* needed altitude, and she was giving it all she had. Kellyn felt more than heard a rumble from the rear of the airhee and knew she'd just vented water. The sudden loss of ballast made the ship jump higher in the air, but it didn't look like they'd make it. They were going to crash.

But she still hadn't gotten accustomed to judging distance in the air, and the *Nighthawk* had some ways to go as Magda struggled. Kellyn stared at the onrushing line of jagged rock and snow. Snow! She'd never seen snow in summer before, and the sight made her shiver despite the fur-lined parka and leggings she wore over her clothes. She was warm enough, though she wouldn't be if they crashed. If they became stranded in these mountains, they would all surely freeze to death.

A blur of white streaked through her field of vision. She looked behind her and saw four angels landing on Magda's back, their feet grasping harness ropes. She leapt out of the crow's nest, sword in hand and murder on her mind. Something white and heavy slammed into her side and she fell, sliding along the airhee's back until her frantically scrabbling left hand caught on a rope. The rage was close now, like a physical object resting just over her shoulder. She could give in to it, let it consume her, guide her to the slaughter of these filthy creatures.

The four angels grasping the harness flapped their wings, pulling the harness up into the air. "They're trying to help," Kellyn whispered, but the rage nearly had her, so close that she couldn't move, could barely breathe. Her right hand twitched, and the sword stabbed up at the air. An eagerness seeped into her mind, tingeing her vision red, bringing the taste of copper to her mouth, and the scent of iron to her nostrils. The hilt of her sword began to feel sticky, and her heartbeat hammered in her ears. She closed her eyes. It would be so easy.

But it didn't look like the angels meant the ship harm. She knew that they could free Magda from her harness, and she'd be safe, but they were also trying to save the humans and their fragile ship. It made no sense, for the angels of legend were supposed to be ferocious fighters who hated mankind. Magda had called the angels her friends. Her bond with the captain wouldn't allow her to let the ship be destroyed, or so Kellyn believed. "Help me, Shaethe. I don't want to kill them, but you have to help."

The urge to kill began to subside, but she still didn't trust herself enough to move from her position, so she stood and stared. How much could four angels possibly help? And what were the males doing? Could Marshall and Spot possibly inflate themselves enough to help Magda? Or had they simply detached to get rid of their extra weight?

As she watched, more angels appeared, grabbing the drag ropes she and Jirra had tied around their waists for their private talk on the airhee's tail. They lifted the ropes into the air, flying high and slightly in front of Magda's dorsal fin. They strained, pumping their wings frantically. Finally, Kellyn wrenched her eyes away and looked to the front. It looked as if they'd make it after all, but the ship hung below Magda. Was there enough clearance?

One of the peaks passed to the right, and she started to sigh in relief, but the breath caught in her throat as a sudden tug sent her stumbling forward onto her knees. A muffled crunching sound came from below, and faint screams. Their forward progress almost came to a halt, but finally the drag of the pass they had crashed into let go, and Magda flew free. The angels had all disappeared. Magda let loose a heart wrenching wail, and though Kellyn couldn't understand any of her song, tears sprang forth from her eyes.

The only question remaining was one she was terrified to ask. Was the *Nighthawk* still attached? There was only one way to find out. She sheathed her sword and retrieved her other weapons from the crow's nest, placed them in a leather bag which she slung over her head and diagonally across her back. She made her way to the side ropes and noticed with relief that they were taut. Of course, that didn't necessarily mean that the ship remained attached to the bottom of the ropes. Maybe it was only wreckage dangling below the airhee. But as she climbed downward, the ropes didn't sway. She couldn't look down, but she felt certain there was a ship below her.

Voices registered in Kellyn's ears. Shouts, urgent and loud, but not panicked. Finally, as she was about to reach for the rail, Abbatay called her name. "Kellyn! You're alive! Did you drive them off?"

She stepped onto the deck and took a few deep, calming breaths. A crazy glint in the captain's eyes gave her pause, and she held up a hand, pretending to catch her breath as she decided what to say. "No, sir. I was about to attack them when several of them started trying to help Magda."

"Help?"

A small crowd gathered around her. "Yes. They grabbed her harness and ropes and tried to lift her. I don't know if they made any difference, but I didn't want to take the chance."

The captain's face went pale and very still. After a few tense minutes, he whispered, "They were probably trying to cut the harness with their talons." He paused. "They hurt you."

Kellyn frowned, noticed for the first time the blood trickling down her neck from a gash in her left earlobe. "It's nothing," she said.

"I'll go check the harness," Jirra said. She wouldn't look in Kellyn's direction, and for a moment she wondered if Jirra was angry. She didn't get the chance to ask, for Jirra was up on the side ropes and climbing faster than she'd ever seen her move.

"How bad is the damage, sir?" Kellyn asked. Belatedly, she added, "Did anyone get hurt?"

Payner was just coming up from below the deck. "Well, Mr. Payner?" said Abbatay. "How bad is it?"

"Sir. There's a great gaping hole just to the left of the keel. In the floor of the storeroom. We've lost most of our food, and a fair amount of trade goods. And I can't find Big Red." Big Red, a tiny man whose mostly gray hair he claimed had once been flaming red, was widely acknowledged as one of the best climbers aboard, though Kellyn had only seen the man once. "Last I heard, he said he was going down below, looking for some tool or another."

"Or a drink," someone whispered. No one laughed.

"Have one of the males go back and search the pass," Abbatay said. "In the meantime, are we airworthy?"

"The *Nighthawk* won't break up, but with that hole, and some wreckage hanging out of it, she ain't exactly sailing smooth. Lotta wind drag; that'll slow us down some."

Abbatay nodded. "Priorities! Clear away the wreckage from the hole. Keep anything that might help make repairs and jettison the rest. We'll cover the hole with sailcloth as soon as Magda finds some calm air for us to work in. We'll all be on short rations, so eat sparingly. First village we see, we set down."

"What about the angels?" Kellyn asked. "Won't they come back?"

"They didn't cross the pass. They're very territorial. Maybe the pass is a dividing line between two flocks. Who knows? But you should be back up there, just in case. And Kellyn? If there is a next time, don't hesitate. Kill them."

Kellyn nodded, but she wasn't sure of her feelings. Had the angels not distracted Magda, they wouldn't have been in any trouble to begin with. But then, had they really meant trouble, they could have made things much worse. The cut on her ear was still bleeding, and she'd need to take a look at it. But that had been an accident, hadn't it? She climbed back up to the crow's nest, but she couldn't see Jirra anywhere.

"Jirra!" she called. "Are you up here?"

"Over here," she called, from beyond the dorsal fin.

Kellyn dumped her weapons and joined Jirra, tying a rope around her waist. "Please believe me, Jirra. I had no intention of harming them. I—"

"Quiet. I don't have much time. Father will expect me on deck with a report soon." She beckoned Kellyn to join her further down Magda's back, very near her tail. She reached to touch her wounded ear, frowning deeply. "Something strange is going on here, Kellyn."

"What do you mean?"

"The angels never act that way. They would never endanger an airhee like that."

"Then why does your father hate them so?"

Jirra sighed. "All airship captains are jealous of the angels. They know that given the choice, any airhee would rather bond with an angel than a man. But my father isn't acting right. I can't figure out what's going on here, but he's doing something to antagonize the angels, I'm sure of it."

Kellyn stared at her for a moment, then asked, "Have you been through these mountains before? And at this exact spot?"

"Hard to tell. But we airmen talk a lot amongst each other. On land, you know? When we get leave, there's a lot of shop talk in the taverns and such. Airhees and angels are a favorite topic, and I've never heard of anything like this. I do know one thing, though. My father is far more obsessed with angels than any captain I've ever encountered. You should know this: the harness is fine. They never meant to harm us."

Kellyn wanted to ask more questions, but Jirra quickly scrambled away from her, untied her rope and disappeared on the other side of the dorsal fin. Kellyn followed more slowly, and Jirra was already gone by the time she untied her rope. She sat in the crow's nest and prepared for a long day and night.

They made landfall at a village called Toruumby four days later. They'd passed a few tiny hamlets among the mountains and foothills, but nothing large enough to provision an airship. Kellyn was awfully hungry by the time they'd tied up at a massive oak near the center of town. With no proper air dock, they'd had to haul supplies up to the ship with nothing but muscles, ropes and pulleys. She had pulled a ten-hour shift on the ropes, leaning heavily on the amulet of strength before the day was over, and though she was now more tired that she could ever remember, she decided to take her leave dirtside. Jirra had agreed to join her.

She and Jirra walked down Toruumby's main street toward the town's only tavern, a tiny place made temporarily rich with the crew's gold, and Kellyn looked forward to adding to the total. Jirra, however, scowled the whole time, limping along with a wooden peg attached to her stump and a cane in her hand.

"I hate coming down," she said. "On the *Nighthawk*, I'm agile and strong and as valued as any man aboard. Down here, I'm just a cripple."

Kellyn wanted to comfort her, put an arm around her shoulders and tell her she didn't care, but that wouldn't sit well with the "airman's" disguise, and from their position a hundred feet up in the air, any man looking down would see them. Would it matter though? If they knew Jirra's secret, they might assume nothing more than a little feminine friendship. She shook her head, too tired to worry. Weariness seeped right through her muscles and into the bones. Using the amulet of strength as much as she had for last few days had done more to weaken her than she would have thought. Food, rest, and a respite from magic: that's what she needed. "Well, just remember," she said, "I am no one special. Just hired muscle."

"Why so cautious? We've never had trouble in Kattenwa before," she said.

"It's just about ten years since the rebellion. If there are a lot of people here who hate Thurn, they might want to commemorate the anniversary. I don't know if the fighting stretched this far south, but it's best to assume the locals are not friendly toward their Thurnish overlords. And from what I understand, the Brotherhood did most of the fighting. I especially would be unpopular." She did not add that the rebellion's leader had been her father.

They entered the tavern, saw that they were the only crewmen in the place, and sat at a table near the door. An older woman approached and tried to take their orders in bad Thurnic but got a pleasant surprise. "I speak Kattenese," Kellyn said. "I was born here," she added, unnecessarily. With her looks, she could be nothing but Kattenese.

"Here?" the waitress asked. "In Toruumby?"

"No, up north in a little place called Verring, near the capitol." Kellyn ordered them a hearty lunch and two mugs of chikka, a bitter herbal tea popular in Kattenwa.

The waitress looked like she was about to say something else but narrowed her eyes at Jirra and walked away.

"I don't think she likes me," whispered Jirra in Thurnic.

"Yeah, you're too dark to be Kattenese. Anybody different here is assumed to be Thurnish. Doesn't look like we're getting too many dirty looks, though. So, what did you want to talk about?"

Jirra checked their surroundings one last time. "It's about my father's boss. You know, your patron?"

Kellyn nodded; she meant First Minister Nigh. "Don't use his title or his name."

"I didn't, did I? Anyway, I think he's the reason for some strange things on this voyage." Jirra paused when the waitress brought out the chikka, took a drink and made a face. "Who could like this stuff? It's terrible!"

Kellyn laughed. "It's supposed to have healing qualities. Anyway, you were saying?"

"Look, I've heard dozens of stories about angels, maybe hundreds. I know normal angel behavior. For that matter, I know when my father is acting like he should. Nothing about this trip has been right."

Kellyn nodded, sipping her chikka. It really was awful.

"My father went to meet the boss. This was about a month before we left. When he came back, he had this mad sparkle in his eye, said we'd have a special passenger. That must have been you."

"Impossible. I didn't even know I'd be going until a couple of days before we left."

Jirra smiled lopsidedly. "So you've never noticed how the boss knows things before other people do? That's how he stays in power. He uses information like a weapon." She stopped suddenly. "I hope I'm not offending you. Father says you're really close to the boss."

Kellyn shook her head. "He takes a special interest in orphans." An insight struck her just then, and she couldn't believe she'd never seen it before. "What better way to stay in power than to have friends among the graduates of my school?"

"Sounds like the boss. So after this meeting, my father was unusually happy. He's been friendlier to you than to any other passenger we've ever had. He's not usually at ease among your kind, if you know what I mean. And that whole business with the angels, well, that was bizarre. He hates them, he's very jealous of them, but you just don't kill them! Everyone knows that."

"Why not?"

"Because, though they're territorial, different flocks will always help each other when they're attacked. An airship wouldn't dare take on a whole flock, even with someone like you aboard. And I'm not the only one who's noticed. There's lots of whispers. We're a superstitious lot, we airmen. The men heard my father yelling at you to kill them, and then we lost Red and took damage. The crewmen have connected those events, even if one didn't necessarily cause the other."

Their food arrived then, and they sat in silence as they ate their stew and bread. They'd been eating very little for the last few days, and working very hard; they ate with single minded attention to their food. The pause in conversation gave Kellyn time to think. *Abbatay meets with Nigh,* she thought. *Nigh gives him a mission, involving me. Nigh wanted me on board the* Nighthawk *to complete this mission, which for some reason involves me killing angels. Me specifically, since the crew wouldn't have killed them. Options? One: he really wanted angels dead, and it didn't matter who killed them. Two: he really wanted me specifically to kill the angels. Why?*

She was about to give voice to a few of these unasked questions when three crewmen entered the tavern. The three men pushed a table next to theirs and sat, somber nods all around.

"We'll have what they're havin'," one of the men said to the waitress.

"Except I don't think they'll be having chikka," said Jirra.

"Gods, no! Beer and lots of it! We're here to mourn the loss of a friend, and you can't do that with a belly full of tea!"

Kellyn stood. "I'll leave you to it then. I didn't know Big Red, and it wouldn't be right for me to intrude."

"Stay if you like," said the crewman, but it was clear he wasn't unhappy to see the mage leave.

"I'll see you all back on the ship." She tried to make eye contact with Jirra, but she wouldn't look her way. Maybe that was best. After all, there was a lot to think about, and she didn't need distractions just then.

I O

Micah, Chase, and Lon stood in the same basement chamber in which Micah had floated earlier. Lon was dressed, not in his usual finery, but in undyed homespun garments, three-quarter length breeches and a short-sleeved tunic: peasant's clothes. His face had changed, too: the flesh hung off his bones, like the sagging skin of a man considerably older than Lon usually appeared to be. His chin sported several days' worth of stubble, and his usually well-groomed pointy beard and mustache had been inexpertly hacked away. His teeth were brown, with several missing entirely. And he smelled. Micah couldn't tell how much of his appearance was a glamour spell, and how much a real, physical change.

Either way, he couldn't have been more excited. "You will witness today a very powerful act of sorcery," Lon had said earlier. He and Chase had appeared late at night, rousing Micah from a deep and dreamless sleep. "I want you to witness it, that you may feel the energies flowing through my body as I transport myself two-hundred miles to Roccobin in an instant."

Micah stripped down to his underclothes and stepped into the salty water of the basin. Lon leaned against the wall, hands spread at his side to touch the stone behind him. "These walls are cut from the bedrock," he said. "They are directly connected to stone that goes all the way down into the center of the world. Unimaginable energies exist down there, and these walls are constantly refreshed. No matter how much energy I drain from them, they are always as strong as they were when I first began building this palace thirty years ago."

"How are you going to do it?" asked Micah, eagerly.

"Patience. And remember, you will see more with your eyes closed. Relax. Feel the walls, the texture of their diwa. Try to spot the spike of energies that occurs as I prepare the spell."

Micah did as he was told, able to isolate the texture of the walls from the stone spheres with ease this time. The familiarity of the room offset the absence of the comforting presence of Serpent, which once again had been bundled with his clothes. He was able to relax much more than he'd been able to during his previous dip in the basin. Lon was right, the walls were not only filled with diwa, but growing ever more so with each passing heartbeat. He felt the increase in power like that massive Mohotsan sword being sharpened and growing bigger at the same time. Once again, the urge to see if he could cut something with that sword almost overwhelmed him, and though the notion didn't seem quite so ridiculous this time, he managed to hold himself back. He also remained silent, despite a strong desire to ask Lon if the sword was real.

The diwa surged, and now Micah became aware of Lon, like a living statue of water clinging to the blade in his mind. The water-Lon grew hotter, glowing bright orange in its center, until it began to boil from within. Jets of steam escaped, painfully loud. The hissing grew louder still, merging with another sound that gradually took over: the sound of a man screaming in agony.

He wondered if he should help Lon, but as soon as the thought occurred, Lon disappeared. Or rather, he moved from one place to another in a highly unconventional way. His spell had folded the world in such a manner that for a moment, in just this one location, the basement of the palace was physically in the heart of Roccobin. Lon then spoke a few more words, opening a gateway between the two places, and stepped through.

For a heartbeat, that gateway stood open, and Micah knew he could walk through it, too. He'd have to say the words, and he hadn't heard them very well. Lon had mumbled, and the wax plugs that kept the water out of his ears did a pretty good job of keeping out sound, too. But he had felt the words, their shape, their texture. A picture of them existed in his mind, or rather a kind of sculpture. By thinking about that three-dimensional image, he could mentally caress it, causing it to vibrate like the strings of a guitar. As he touched the sculpture in his mind, it made a sound. The syllables reverberated in his head.

Micah whispered the words, and the rapidly closing gateway swung back open a little. He could see Lon's back, moving impossibly fast, far away from the basement under the palace. Meanwhile, energies surged in the walls, up through the water in the basin and into Micah's body. He began to feel warm, then hot, then scalding, as if something within his chest had burst into flames. The water, too, heated, flashing into steam. He screamed, then leapt from the basin and toward the gateway. Somewhere, another man screamed, too.

As he entered the gateway, the sensation of heat vanished, and he slid sideways, as if he were caught between two perfectly smooth, slippery surfaces. With a sound like a stone dropped in a bowl of water, he slid out onto a roadway under a moonlit sky. He stumbled and fell, feeling weak and cold. Still, he grinned fiercely.

He stood on wobbly legs, looking around in panic. The pale stone and dust of the roadway poorly lit by a half moon obscured by clouds; to either side of the road, fields and hedgerows marked cultivated land. In one direction, the road led on into the farmland. In the other, he could see lights. Roccobin? He assumed so and trudged in that direction, picking wax out of his ears as he walked. As he approached a stone bridge over a small stream, he saw three people coming in his direction and resolved to ask directions.

"Will you look at this, my boyos!" said one approaching stranger. The strangers resolved into three youths, townsmen in appearance, not peasants, dressed as they were in bright, tight fitting clothes. The largest of the three grabbed Micah by the undershirt.

"Soaking wet, 'e is! What's a matter, boyo? Wet the bed?"

The three laughed loudly, and Micah could smell alcohol on the breath of the man holding him. He could also see that all three men were armed, one of them casually cleaning the dirt from underneath his fingernails with a dagger. "We got us a lordling," the knife wielder said. "Look 'ow clean 'e is. I wonder, little lord, what you is doin' out 'ere late at night?"

"Think 'e gots any money?" asked the third.

"Naw, look at 'im," said the large one. "Musta fell outta the bath. Got nothin' on 'im but 'is under things. Maybe we'll just have to take those silkies off 'is hands."

"I'm a sorcerer's apprentice," Micah said through clenched teeth, hands shaking at his sides. The image of the sword hovered on the edge of sight, and though a part of him longed to use it against these idiots, he needed to find Lon. "Please don't make me hurt you."

"Oh! A magic boy! Well, magic boy, let's see something! Do us some magics, pretty please?"

The large man laughed as he spoke, and shoved Micah to the dirt. The other two gathered around him, shoving him back down each time he tried to regain his feet, cursing at him, spitting on him. Micah felt energy building within him, and clearly saw the blade in his mind. He held out his hand, grasping the imaginary hilt. It felt real, heavy, and quite deadly, though he couldn't see the scimitar with his eyes.

"You want magic?" he asked. He kept his eyes closed, but he saw through his eyelids, his tormentors glowing pale silver and green while their surroundings remained dark. He swung the blade and felt it make contact. One of his assailants grunted. Another pulled a knife from his waistband, the metal gleaming in the moonlight. Micah slashed the man's hand, and he shrieked. The third tackled Micah from behind, but he, too, was soon reduced to a howling, writhing mess. Two of the three fled, but the man who'd tackled him, the big man, it turned out, lay on his side all curled up around a gut wound, moaning loudly.

Micah opened his eyes, and he could see the man wouldn't live long. A pool of blood, slick and black in the moonlight, spread around him. His moans became softer. Diwa seeped from his body as fast as the blood. Micah knelt to touch the blood soaking into the dirt, and felt a shock as the dying man's diwa shot into his fingertips, an effect like nothing he'd experienced. He reached out and touched the man's neck, and the last of his diwa fled into Micah. The nameless attacker died.

Micah stood on wobbly legs, catching his breath. "I'm lost," he whispered. "I've just killed a man. And I'm wearing nothing but wet underclothes." The weakness he felt came from the sorcery he'd used. The dead man's diwa helped some, but not nearly enough. Each time his thoughts drifted toward the body at his feet, he flinched. He'd fallen into a deep well of trouble.

Unless no one found out. Lon said he lied well. Time now to hide some very troubling truths. He stripped the dead man and put his clothes on. They were too large, and sticky with blood, but the stream under the bridge should suffice to wash it away. Touching the still warm corpse sent shivers of disgust through Micah, but what choice did he have? As for the body itself? The best alternative seemed to be to drag it off the road and into the bushes. Still, he remained well and truly lost. He wasn't in a town, but there were some buildings just barely visible down the road. His attackers hadn't been peasants out for a midnight stroll, so there must be some kind of settlement nearby. At least a tavern. He hid the body and bathed as best he could.

He walked toward the buildings, farmhouses as it turned out. Had anyone heard the screams? Would they investigate? He heard no dogs barking and took that for a good sign. He hoped for a well, at least, that he might fill his empty belly with water, if nothing else. At a slight sound, he turned to find an old man holding a pitchfork like a weapon.

"Explain yerself," the man croaked, eyes wide and the pitchfork trembling in his hands.

For once, honesty seemed the best alternative. Or at least partial honesty. "I'm lost. I became separated from my master in the night. We were headed for Roccobin. I was attacked by some men on the road."

That seemed to calm the man, though he didn't lower his pitchfork. "Ya hurt?"

"I don't think so, but I hurt one of them."

"With what? Ya ain't got no weapons."

"I'm a sorcerer's apprentice. I don't need weapons."

Now the farmer's eyes went wide again, and his trembling resumed. He dropped the pitchfork. "I don't want no trouble, mister. Just please leave my family alone."

"You point me on the road to Roccobin, and forget I was ever here, and I won't trouble you at all."

"Where'd ya turn off the turnpike?"

"I wasn't on the turnpike. I transported myself here with magic."

The farmer laughed nervously, then coughed. "Um, yes. Well, ya go down this road a far piece. Maybe six, seven miles? You'll get to a wooden bridge. On the other side of the creek, there's a fork. Take a right turn. That road runs into the turnpike. And once yer on the turnpike, it's only about another ten or twelve miles to town."

"How far, total?"

"What? Oh, yeah. From the bridge to the turnpike, that's another five or six miles. Uh, my figurin' ain't so good. What's it add up to, maybe twenty-five, thirty miles?"

Micah scowled. He was still in great shape from all the years working at the quarry, but he wasn't prepared for a long-distance hike just now. "You have a horse, or at least a donkey, don't you? And a wagon?"

"I got a donkey, mister. But she's all I got. Fever took my ox last winter. Ya take my Bessie, my family'd starve."

"I won't take her. Hitch her to a wagon. You're taking me to Roccobin."

"Now, hold on there—"

Micah turned on the farmer, grabbed his magical sword, quite visible to him now, even with his eyes open, but of course the farmer couldn't see it. He pressed the blade against the farmer's chest, not quite hard enough to draw blood, and smiled. "You're going to take me to Roccobin, or I'll kill you and take the animal myself. Which would you prefer? At least if you take me, you can come back home, none the worse for wear."

The farmer stared at his chest, clearly bewildered as to how Micah was stabbing him with nothing but thin air. He nodded jerkily, stumbled backwards and turned toward a small barn. There he hitched his wagon to his lone beast of burden. "Only room for me up front," the farmer said. "Ya want I should put some straw in the back for ya to lay on?"

Micah nodded with a smile. "Yes," he said aloud, in case the man hadn't seen his nod in the dark. Soon, they were on their way, Micah stretched in the back, feeling exhausted, a little disoriented, and, he had to admit, exhilarated. He'd transported here with a spell, and the sword in his head truly existed. He glanced guiltily at the farmer, but what choice did he have? He had no idea if he'd die without Lon's healing food, but he knew quite well that he needed it desperately. He moaned as a hunger pang punched him in the gut.

"Serpent," he whispered, but of course he'd left the prayer stone behind.

"What's a matter back there?" called the farmer. "Are ya sick?"

Micah tried to answer but his mouth refused to cooperate. He reached for the farmer, wanting nothing but to steal the man's diwa, but his hand dropped to his side. He was so weak. Despite the jouncing ride of an unsprung wagon on rutted country roads, he slept.

"Your eyes are open, but I don't think you're seeing anything just yet, are you?"

Micah blinked, but the woman's voice refused to match up with the blurry vision hovering above him. "Hnnh?" he managed.

She laughed. "I know you speak Kattenese. The farmer told me everything you told him. So, young sorcerer's apprentice, attacked on the road and forced to defend yourself magically, what brings you to Roccobin?"

He squeezed his eyes shut and tried to wipe away the sticky stuff that gummed up his eyelids, but his hands were tied to the bed on which he lay, as were his feet. "Wha?"

"Oh, my. This may be worse than I thought," the woman said.

Micah focused on her, and she slowly resolved from a brown blur into a middle-aged woman, thin, dark-skinned, dressed in loose-fitting brown robes, her graying black hair braided into thick, ropes tied and dangling over her right shoulder. Bracelets and rings adorned her wrists and hands. Various bits of jewelry pierced her face and hung around her neck. Micah closed his eyes and tried to see her magically, and was unsurprised to find that diwa steamed from her body, especially from all those metal and crystal trinkets that adorned her. A mage, most certainly.

"Not talking, eh? Well then, I'll talk. I like to talk anyway." She laughed again, moving quickly about the room, mixing various liquids and powders into different bowls, adding a feather here, a lizard's foot there. Sometimes a sizzling sound accompanied the different mixtures, sometimes a puff of colored smoke. "I am Felida Uffgold, and you, mystery boy, are extremely lucky. I am not the only healer in Roccobin, but I am the only one who could have helped you. My reputation pre-ceeds me, however, and though the farmer took you first to that idiot Barrinola, at least he had the sense to see your condition was beyond his feeble abilities. He knew I was the one to whom you should be brought. Had you arrived a few weeks later, I would almost certainly not be here, since I will shortly have business to attend to which will require me to travel out of town."

"Am I . . . a prisoner?"

"Don't be silly. I am a mage of the Sisterhood. I heal regardless of innocence or guilt, political affiliation, race, or ability to pay for services rendered. Hence this hovel I call my home. Now, what sort of sorcery, specifically, were you engaged in? This is important, youngster, because while I can make you feel better temporarily, I cannot cure you of the diwa sickness that infects you unless I know exactly what spells you were using."

Micah carefully shut down his reactions. If he could get out of here and find Lon, the sorcerer could heal him better than this crazy old woman. He said nothing.

"I won't turn you in. You are not my prisoner. You are tied down to keep you from harming anyone, most especially me. I have also placed a few charms around your body to keep you from trying to use that sorcerer's sword you poked the poor farmer with. Hmmm. Still no answer? Well then, let me tell you what I think happened, and who I think you are. Keep in mind that you may interrupt me anytime you wish. The longer this takes, the worse you will feel, and the closer you will come to experiencing permanent damage, even death."

Micah looked away from Felida. She already knew about the sword. But she didn't know he'd absorbed a dying man's diwa. Would she turn him in for that? What about Lon and the transporting spell? He knew that no matter what, he couldn't mention Lon or his mother. Whatever their plans—rebellion, assassination—he couldn't let anyone know about them.

"Stubborn," she continued. "And foolish. You're engaged in dangerous work, work you clearly don't understand well enough to see the peril all around you. The people you call your friends do not love you, else they would never have set you on this course."

Micah glared at her with pure hatred for a moment before he clamped down. He clenched his hands into fists and wished he could caress Serpent to calm himself.

"Hah! I got through to you after all! And all I did was speak the truth. So, to begin with, you killed the man who wore that bright red jacket you were wearing, and you did it with a sorcerer's sword. You tried to wash the jacket out in a pond or stream, but neglected to check the pockets, where some blood had accumulated, along with three water bugs and a leech. The blood in the jacket does not match your blood. I took the liberty of pricking your finger while you slept so I could check. Now, if I had some highly specialized crystals, or the time to acquire them, I could see exactly what sickness you have. I don't however, since this sleepy little outpost hasn't seen a sorcerer since Hittrech's Rebellion."

Micah yawned. He needed Lon's special food, and soon.

"Glad to see you're so enthralled. Moving on, then. You are a former slave. Well, bond worker, technically, but there's really no difference. Someone recently removed your bond mark, leaving a curiously diwa-free patch of skin on your neck right here." She reached out and flicked a patch of skin on Micah's neck.

"Don't touch me!" Micah frowned at his outburst, confused by his reaction. Much as he didn't want to admit it, he knew that she only wanted to help.

Felida grinned, crinkling her eyes like a child deliberately getting into trouble. "You have the body of a well-muscled sixteen-year-old, but the face of a much younger child. Your muscles are hard and frequently used, which matches your hands, so heavily calloused and scarred. Clearly, someone caused you to grow much faster than a normal boy, but no slave owner would bother with the expense merely to get a stronger slave. That will have to remain a mystery for now. I—"

"I grew myself," Micah boasted.

Felida blinked, a sly grin teasing one side of her mouth. "Really? One as untrained as yourself might have managed to grow a little without help, but you'd most likely sprout extra arms, or blind eyes on stalks emerging from your ears. No, I'm afraid you couldn't have done what you clearly believe you did. Evidently someone wants you to think you accomplished this extraordinary feat without assistance. Now, why would that be? What purpose could your masters have for creating a boy in a man's body?"

Micah gritted his teeth, determined to remain silent rather than respond to this mage's lies.

"To continue: you are now clean in that way that only nobles and wealthy merchants ever get, so I can also assume that your status in life has recently changed quite dramatically. Someone saw your talent. You were apprenticed to a sorcerer recently. I say recently, because you display a curious mix of shocking ineptitude and raw ability. A sorcerer's sword is not something I'd expect an apprentice to wield so effectively. But then, only an apprentice would casually snap off dangerous spells without preparing for the inevitable diwa sickness."

Micah felt the room growing dark and his eyelids drooping. "I need food," he said.

The smile disappeared from Felida's face. "You'll get none. I know what kinds of sustenance you're talking about, and I'll have no part in that. Which brand of dark sorcery does your master use to heal himself? Tell me that much at least, and I'll have a better chance at healing you."

Micah remained silent, though he wanted to tell her, if only to get whatever medicine she had to give. Had Lon cursed him?

"Such arrogance," she whispered. She shook her head, frowning deeply, then continued mixing ingredients. Finally, she set a cup of some fizzing, smoking liquid on a low table near the bed on which he lay. "This will make you feel better, but only for an hour or two. Once again, I implore you to tell me more of your master and his methods. It is at least possible that I can heal you completely, if you would but speak."

Micah saw nothing but truth in her light brown eyes. This woman hadn't lied once, or even attempted to hide anything. Maybe he could tell her a few things. He didn't need to be completely honest after all. Just enough to get the potion and get out of here.

"I transported myself here from miles away," he said. "I used a sorcerer's sword, but you know that already. That's it. No other spells."

"What was the name of the transporting spell? There are several, you know."

Micah didn't know. Would telling her the words reveal more than he wished? He had an inspiration. If he could whisper the words to the spell, perhaps he could transport himself back to the palace.

"Careful, youngster. I see devious thoughts moving around in your head. Thinking of escape? Or signaling your master? Neither will work. But you're welcome to try."

Micah whispered the words. Nothing happened.

"Well, now, how did that feel? Telling the truth, I mean. No answer? Thought so. Well, helpful as I am sure you thought you were being, the words of the spell aren't nearly as important as the name of the spell. All you did was say, 'Fly me to the place of my heart's desire,' in an ancient, rarely used language."

"I don't know the name of the spell," he said.

Felida stared at him for awhile, until finally she reached for the cup and held it to his lips. "A little at a time. Don't gulp. There. Now lay here for a bit, it'll take time to work."

Micah gave a small grin of triumph and noticed that he was feeling better already. Not quite satisfied, but not ravenously hungry, either. "Can I leave now?"

"We mages avoid direct contact with diwa," she said, ignoring his question. "Yes, it means our spells are less powerful, but this frees us from the more damaging aspects of diwa. You see, young sorcerer, diwa will corrupt you; it corrupts everyone who touches it. Even the mages who make the magical objects I and my sisters use to heal are corrupted by it. The worst aspects of your character will come to the fore, the longer you practice sorcery. And since your life has been one filled with fear—fear of being sold, fear of punishment, death, the activation of your bond mark—your soul has been indelibly marked. You can overcome your upbringing, and learn to trust, or you can move further and further away from the light. You will fear and distrust everyone, and it is not so long a step from fear to hatred. As your power grows, so too will your urge to dominate and destroy those you fear. You will never love anyone, and no one will ever love you. Or you can turn away now. You have talents—anyone can see that. Let me put you in touch with people trained to help children like yourself, and your future could be quite bright indeed."

Micah blinked, shocked at the sudden burning behind his eyelids, as if he might weep. Her words were lies, they had to be, and yet he sensed nothing but truth in her speech. "You're just saying that! You're just jealous of sorcerers' powers."

"I have seen diwa corrupt good people with my own eyes. A woman I have known since childhood, when she and I were both initiates, has but one talent: the ability to infuse diwa into ordinary objects. She is one of those who create the various trinkets and treasures we mages use to manipulate diwa without suffering infection. What she does is a form of sorcery, but her warden watches her closely, healing her as she does her work. Yet it is not enough. She was always a little vain, and loved playing pranks when we were children. At the heart of every prank is a hint of cruelty. Now her cruelty and vanity are all anyone can see in her. She's my age, just forty-three. And yet she will not live beyond fifty, if she makes it that far. Fifty might sound quite old to you, but a mage should see eighty or ninety summers. Diwa, they say, is a cruel mistress. This is the path that has been chosen for you."

Micah had heard enough. "Then your friend is a poor sorceress. My . . . teachers are in good health. They'll live a long time, you'll see."

"Perhaps. It is ever a goal of sorcerers to find some easy road to immortality. And the most powerful among them do live a long time. But as slaves to their infection, not as free men and women." Felida started to say more, then shook her head. She waved her hands over the table and the knots tying him down unraveled at once. "Feel free to return if you can't find your master. Or if you have a sudden urge to be honest."

"Not likely."

She opened her mouth, thought better of it, and instead opened the front door. "The path you're on is a dangerous one, and this master of yours means you no good. Come back to me, or any healer mage, if you should decide to change course. Remember, you have at most an hour or so before you begin to sicken again, and this time it will be worse."

Micah stared at her as he left, wondering if she really meant what she said. He was greeted by a bright, sunny day and a crowded street full of carts, people, horses, donkeys. He wondered what happened to the farmer. The man had saved his life, even though he'd threatened him with violence. And Felida seemed to care what happened to him.

She's wrong, he thought. *My mother is different. She loves me.* But what if Felida wasn't wrong after all? What if his mother didn't see the danger? He had nearly decided to turn back when a voice sounded in his ear.

"Don't turn around. Keep walking. Don't speak until I tell you to."

Lon! Micah smiled, heaving a great sigh of relief. He noticed something in his ear, like a stone or a crystal, and reached to remove it.

"Don't! That's how I'm speaking to you. Now listen carefully: take the next right, then go three streets until you find the Street of Doves. It is marked with a sign."

"I can't read," Micah whispered.

Lon said nothing for several minutes, waiting until Micah had made the first turn before speaking again. "I'm in front of you. See me four or five storefronts ahead, to your left?"

"Yes."

"Good. Follow, but at a distance. Say 'wait' if you lose sight of me. Understand?"

"Yes."

Lon turned and hobbled on, and Micah wondered if he'd been injured, but he decided it must be a part of his disguise. He kept up easily, but he had to remind himself several times not to get too close.

"Now, see that tavern on the left? The one with the carving of a one-eyed woman? That's where we will meet. Go in and ask to sit at the Widow's Table. They'll take you to a small room in back. I'll meet you there."

Lon hobbled passed the tavern, and Micah entered to do as he was told. The bartender gave him an odd look, but said nothing, merely nodded and led the way to a small, dimly lit room, just as Lon had said. He sat at the one table and waited, wondering when Lon would make his entrance.

He didn't have long to wait, as a thin bar of light appeared across the room. Lon slid sideways out of the light, and Micah heard the same stone-dropped-in-water sound he'd heard when he transported. Lon grunted, scowled and sat.

"So you followed me? That was extremely foolish."

"I couldn't stop myself. It was so easy."

"How did you end up in Uffgold's house?"

Micah explained everything, leaving out no detail he could remember. When he finished, Lon's scowl had grown deeper. "We just have to hope Chase didn't panic. So long as he keeps to the plan, we can salvage this operation."

"What's next, then?"

"We have to assume she questioned you while you were sleeping, and now knows everything you know. Fortunately, that isn't a great deal. She will have followed you here, but she can't have seen me enter, and never saw us together. The question is whether she'll alert the Prince first or go straight to the Brotherhood."

"I don't think she'll do anything. She acted like she didn't care about anything but healing."

"Of course she did. But how much did she seem to know about you? And how do you think she got that information? Was it merely her awesome powers of deduction? Ask yourself this: what would you do in her place?"

Micah frowned. Of course, he would go straight to the authorities. "What do we do?"

"We go ahead as planned. I'll transport back to the palace to make sure Chase is still on course, then return quickly. How are you feeling?"

"Not so good. I'm hungry."

"I'll bring back something for you. Meanwhile, I'll get us a room here. This time, you will stay put and do nothing until I return. Am I perfectly clear?"

Micah nodded, staring at the surface of the table. When he looked up, Lon had vanished.

11

Far from the elegant, stone cradle in which the *Nighthawk* lay when Kellyn first set eyes on her, the air dock in the town of Destrona looked feeble, a cobbled together tangle of pine logs and rope, with wool-filled leather bags as padding. The ship sat in the dock just six feet off the ground, its keel and the gaping hole exposed. Workers had hastily removed the temporary sail cloth patch, whistling at the extent of the damage. Abbatay motioned Kellyn over.

"What do you see?"

Kellyn examined the wood closely, especially the keel. The damage to the central beam of the hull consisted mostly of surface cracking, though she suspected the full extent remained hidden. She searched for accumulations of diwa, and found damage the dockmaster couldn't.

"You can see this crack, the one that starts just a little in front of the hole in the hull," Kellyn explained. "It's about finger-wide here, but narrows down until it rejoins the grain of the wood over here. What, fourteen feet long? It goes right through the keel to the inside of the hull from here to here, maybe three or four feet. I don't see any other damage beyond the surface. And the ruined cladding, of course." The thin, overlapping boards nailed to the ribs of the ship, hadn't fared well, nor had several of the ribs.

Abbatay made a face like he'd just smelled something awful. "How long?"

The dockmaster pinched his lips, pacing back and forth under the keel for a few minutes before pronouncing, "We'll have to remove the hull cladding from here to here," he said, marking the wood with chalk. "Then we sweat iron bands around the keel, once between each rib, repairing or replacing this rib, this one, and this one, then attach fresh cladding. Six days."

Abbatay nodded, and the two began to haggle over price. Kellyn shouldered her bag and turned away, surprised that Jirra stood so close behind her. Jirra inclined her head to one side and hobbled down Destrona's main street without looking to see if Kellyn followed. She did. Not until they'd turned off onto a fairly busy side street did Jirra turn to speak to her.

"What will you do now?"

Kellyn checked the position of the sun; it was late afternoon, early evening. A young man had followed them from the dock, but that might have been a coincidence. She didn't believe it. "We're only about sixty miles from Roccobin, so I'll walk the rest of the way. Too late to leave now, though."

"The crew's staying at a place called The Traveler's Haven," Jirra said.

"Yeah, but you've seen the looks they've been giving me. You're a superstitious lot, you airmen. You said so yourself. I think they blame me."

"I'm sure you're right. There's other inns."

They walked awhile in silence, Kellyn's boldness from the other day completely forgotten. She searched frantically for something to say, but kept coming up empty. Jirra hadn't broached the subject, but neither had she kept her distance. Finally, Kellyn said, "I wanted you to meet Felida."

"She's in Roccobin, you said? I can't stump along for sixty miles."

"No, I guess not. But remember the town and her name, alright? I'll tell her about you, tell her to watch for you. Maybe if you ever get near there, you two can meet."

"Long odds against it, Kellyn. But I appreciate it."

"I wish I could do more." The silence returned for a while. Their follower was still back there.

Jirra nodded. "Take care of yourself. I, uh . . .." She looked like she wanted to say something more, but she settled for, "See you, mage."

Likewise, Kellyn could think of nothing better to say. "See you, airman."

She walked alone onto the main street, searching for a messenger service, deliberately not looking back for one last glimpse of Jirra.

A town this size probably boasted one or two messenger services, but for her purposes, Kellyn needed something a touch more discreet, to see if the boy really was spying on her. She asked people on the street and found that the town did indeed boast a "more discreet" messenger service, but its location was in an unsavory tavern called the Empty Head.

The old man who told her about the place eyed Kellyn's sword. "Dey don' letcha bring weapons inna da Head," he pronounced with a strong rustic accent. "But dose men in dere, dey is armed, ya better believe."

Kellyn handed the old guy a few coppers and made her way to the Empty Head. She couldn't mistake the place. A drunk had passed out on the street in front of the tavern's half-open door. There were two windows in front of the building, neither with glass; one sported a broken shutter. Inside, someone mangled a song, accompanied by a lyre. The singer couldn't have held a tune in a stout bag, and the musician clearly possessed only the most passing familiarity with his or her instrument. From the cheers of the patrons inside, however, no one seemed to care. And the boy still tailed her, pretending to look at a blacksmith's wares laid out on a table.

A large man held out an arm to stop her as she entered. "Ya wants a room, or jus' a drink?"

"Both."

"Yer weapons stay in yer room. It's fifteen decs a night."

"That's highway robbery."

"So? Take yer fancy butt someplace else, then."

Kellyn smiled. "Worth a shot. So, fifteen? I assume I'll have to pay up front?"

"Whatcha think? I look like I trust people?"

She chuckled, handing over the money. "I hear you have a messenger service here."

"Yeah. He ain't in yet. Probably still sleepin'."

"I'll wait." She dug some more coins out of her pocket and handed them over. "Send him to me when he arrives, will you?"

The big man smiled for the first time, and it was a hideous sight, full of brown and broken teeth. "Pleasure, ma'am."

Kellyn found her room, little more than a closet, with a filthy straw-stuffed mattress taking up most of the floor. She laid her weapons down and searched through a little suede bag she kept tied to her belt. From within she retrieved a small green stone and a larger chunk of carved wood. She exited the room, closed its flimsy door and pressed the wooden piece into the handle. The door and the carving merged, meshing together until you couldn't tell where one left off and the other began. The door was now quite effectively locked, as only another warrior mage could possibly open it. Of course, any reasonably strong person might smash the thin panel and step through the wreckage, but at least she'd secured the room from casual intrusion.

Downstairs, she bought a mug of chikka, chose a table near the rear of the room, and sat with her back to the door. Opposite, she laid the green stone upon the table, then closed her eyes. She saw through the stone, much as she had with the dragonfly, but she could not move this stone. She needed only its eyes, though. Her shadow had taken a seat with a few men at a table near the door. She supposed the men and boy thought they were being subtle, the way they sat still, saying little and not looking at anyone at any other table. Their actions shouted their intentions, and Kellyn guessed them amateurs at best.

She sipped her chikka, and had just settled in for a long wait when a fat man in dusty gray robes arrived. Kellyn closed her eyes and watched through the stone as the new arrival spoke to the bouncer, who pointed toward her and said something she couldn't quite hear. Kellyn opened her eyes and retrieved the stone.

"I hear . . . you want to send . . . a message," the old man said. He took a seat opposite her without asking, and wiped sweat from his brow. He breathed heavily, likely unaccustomed to much in the way of exercise. He was stooped, nearly bald, and had a lazy eye.

"Yes, and I want everything you have in the way of shielding. I don't want anyone reading this message, understand?"

The old man smiled. "That's why people . . . come to me, young lady. Leteek the Gray, at your service. But, ah, my services aren't cheap. Discreet, but not cheap."

They haggled, and Kellyn spent more for one message than she had for one night at the inn. "Very well," said Leteek. "What is your message?"

"What, here?" said Kellyn, pretending to be shocked that such a thing didn't require more secrecy.

Leteek laughed. "I've already activated several layers of protection. No one will hear you, or be able to read your lips. Give me the message, and it will be on its way in moments."

"Very well. Um, it's this. I'll be leaving for Roccobin tomorrow. I'll probably be there three days from now. Do you need my name?"

Leteek smiled, as if dealing with a not very bright child. "Yes, and the name of the recipient as well."

"Sorry. It's going to Felida Uffgold in Roccobin. My name is Kellyn."

"No other identifiers? The recipient will know you by that name?"

"Yes. She's expecting me. I'll be delayed, is all."

Leteek closed his eyes, cupped his hands in front of his mouth, and mumbled a spell. Not a particularly effective message spell, and the so-called security placed upon it forced Kellyn to suppress a laugh. Anyone with even a beginner's ability at message cracking could know the contents within a heartbeat. Exactly as she had planned. "It is done," Leteek said. "My pigeons fly out of a secret location, and they will deliver your message very shortly. You have nothing to worry about, miss."

"Good. Now if you'll excuse me, Mister Leteek, I have to get some rest. I plan on being on the road at sunrise." Kellyn went back to her room and laid down on the vermin infested mattress, pushed time, and got a few hours of sleep. Then, still pushing time, she gathered her weapons and left the Empty Head through a back stairwell. If she continued to move in fast time, she could arrive in Roccobin not long after the message pigeon. By then, the boy spy would have delivered the contents of the message to his employers.

She considered one last goodbye with Jirra, but rejected it. "No, it has to be this way," she whispered. She could always send a message to her after she reached Felida Uffgold.

Kellyn arrived in Roccobin in the small hours of the morning, before the birds awoke. She had stopped along the road to sleep in fast time again, and had pushed herself very hard. Travelling that far, that fast, while pushing time, stressed her more than any training exercise she could remember, but she hoped to have time to rest once she reached Felida.

She made her way as stealthily as possible, through the streets of the third largest city in Kattenwa. She moved in fast time, and now that she had merged with Shaethe, she found that she possessed a sixth sense with which to observe her surroundings. Twice, she felt the presence of prying eyes, the kind that might see her despite her abilities. And once they'd arrived in Felida's neighborhood, her new sense directed her to the rear of the healer's home, noting that at least one set of eyes watched the front door.

Thank you, Shaethe, she thought, grasping the hilt firmly. In response, a feeling of warmth spread into her belly, almost enough to help her stifle a yawn.

She reached for a window ledge in the rear of Felida's home, felt the stout shutters, and knocked quietly. "I come as a friend," she whispered in an ancient language.

An opening appeared in the blank wall in front of her, and she slipped in as silently as a cat. The opening vanished, and light flooded a small storeroom.

"Kellyn, I presume?" said a small, dark woman.

"Yes. I apologize for my method of entry. You are Felida Uffgold?"

"I am. Come, you need some rest and a little food. You look terrible."

"I've pushed all the way from Destrona."

Felida hummed tunelessly as she moved through her small home, preparing a mug of restorative tea and a small plate of roadtack, a hard, tasteless bread that would do more to restore her strength than a seven course meal. "I assume you have a reason for such foolish overexertion?"

Kellyn told her about the boy who'd spied on her in Destrona, everything that had happened on the *Nighthawk*, omitting only her struggles with Shaethe. "I assumed the boy intercepted the message and got word back to his master that I won't arrive for another couple of days. I wanted to get inside their decision cycle."

"Well, you do sound like Magrahim. 'Desicision cycle,' indeed! However, if you're correct, you've done exactly what you should have. You are now where they do not expect you to be, if there actually is a 'they.' Tell me, what do you suppose these mysterious conspirators want with you?"

Kellyn ate her small meal, relating her instructor's plan to flush out the Kattenese who might—or might not—have been waiting for her return. The food helped take the edge off her exhaustion, but the only real cure for the bone deep lethargy she now felt was to sleep in normal time. She yawned.

"Let's assume you're onto something, Kellyn. You go to sleep, and I will begin by examining your sword."

Kellyn blinked, holding her breath. She didn't dare speak.

"Oh?" Felida said, one eyebrow raised. "Something you don't want me to see? Hand over the sword. Now!"

Kellyn felt the magical command Felida had placed in her words and handed her the sword, still sheathed.

Felida pulled the sword free and examined the rippling surface on one side, then turned it over. She nearly dropped the blade, cursing softly in several languages. She replaced the sword in its scabbard and cleared a pile of books from a low table. She began drawing magical symbols on the table with chalk, symbols that glowed when she was finished. "Get up on the table. Lie down on your back. Do not speak until I direct you to do so."

Kellyn complied, barely daring to breathe. Her hands trembled, but a feeling of calm settled over her, a feeling she suspected came from Shaethe. Meanwhile, Felida placed candles and small stones around her, sprinkled powder upon her face and chest, and snapped her fingers. The powder flashed brightly, and the candles lit all at once.

She leaned over the table, looking deeply into Kellyn's eyes. Felida said something in a language she didn't recognize, and she heard herself responding in words that sounded quite similar. The conversation went on for several minutes before Felida clapped her hands, causing the candles to go out. Only a lamp in the corner remained lit. Felida walked to a chair and slumped into it.

"What is it?" Kellyn asked. "What did you see?"

"Nothing I can speak about. I'm afraid of an associative reaction."

Kellyn sucked in her breath. An associative reaction came from the activation of a latent spell. Talking about the spell, even reading about it, could set it off. Only the person who'd cast the spell knew what would happen next. Had her parents turned her into some sort of spy for their doomed cause? Would she go berserk and kill everyone around her? It had to be that black sphere in her breast. If only there were some way to communicate that to Felida, but she couldn't. She wondered if even thinking about that mysterious spell might set off a reaction.

"You and I together, Kellyn, could probably fight off the spell if we knew exactly what kind of curse had been laid upon you. But I can't tell you what it is, and I'm fairly sure you don't know what it is."

"But you do?"

"Careful! If you knew, you would be a great deal more afraid than you appear to be." Felida stood and paced. "From what I have seen," she continued, waving at Kellyn's chest, "and from an encounter I had with a sorcerer's apprentice just hours ago, I have a good idea of what we face. But you need sleep, and I need to meditate. Right now there are too many alternatives rattling around in my head. I need clarity."

She directed Kellyn to a small bed, forbade her to push time, and gave her a small cup of a reddish-brown liquid. She drank it without question soon drifted off to sleep.

When Kellyn awoke, sunlight and the sounds of a bustling city came through the windows. She sat up, noticed that everything had been placed neatly on shelves and in cupboards, the slightly cluttered look of Felida's home replaced with strict order. Two leather backpacks sat on the floor, and the smell of cooking wafted through the air.

"You're awake. Good," said Felida. "Come. Eat. We leave as soon as you are finished."

"Where are we going?" she asked as she sat at a small round table piled with fruit, bread, bacon and eggs. And more chikka. She could learn to hate chikka.

"D'Arrune."

"The capitol? Why? We're two-hundred miles from there."

"We need help, and the closest brother or sister is there. Captain Zang of the Prince's Auxiliary Guard, to be specific."

"Never heard of him," Kellyn said around a mouthful of food.

"He's a talented mage, even if he is a pig and a slimy politician. Unfortunately, we cannot handle your problem by ourselves."

Kellyn nodded, but there was another problem, one they hadn't yet discussed. "Felida? What about my other problem? I was sent here because I can't control my love of violence. It's holding me back from completing my training."

Felida said nothing. Her eyes looked calm, but she rubbed the hem of her sleeve between the fingers of her left hand. She opened her mouth, closed it, and finally sighed. "I believe," she began, slowly and deliberately, "that your two problems are closely related. Further, I believe that the solution to one is also the solution to the other."

Kellyn smiled. That had been her thought on the matter as well. The black sphere wasn't her dual nature, though it had fooled Shaethe for a time. No, the black sphere was the latent spell. It radiated hatred and violence. It prevented her from passing the test. If they could find a way to get rid of it, she would be herself.

"Are you full?" Felida asked, clearing away her plate and mug. "We will both need our strength."

"I feel great."

"Good, though I caution you not to entertain the thought that you're cured just yet. You will need time and rest, but you should be able to travel. We won't be able to push time, in part because you're not well enough yet, in part because I don't have that talent." Felida paused and examined the tops of her shoes for a few moments before continuing. "Now, there's something I need to say. Your . . . problem is a very . . . sophisticated one. It has remained undetected for your entire stay in the Brotherhood's school. Only your weapon's unconventional appearance prompted me to look for it, and no ordinary examination could have found what I found." She stopped talking, and Kellyn wondered if she were finished or merely trying to find a way to say something without triggering the spell. "I may not be strong enough to help you. I am a healer, and we may have more need of a fighter before all is done."

"I can fight well enough."

"I'm counting on it. I . . . I may have no choice but to do something very . . . unpleasant . . . to thwart the plans of those who seek you. You won't like it. You'll curse me. You'll think I've betrayed you. But please trust me. If the worst comes to pass, the alternative I'm considering may be the only way to save you. Or, more to the point, for you to save yourself."

Kellyn nodded, her mouth suddenly dry.

"Come. Take the smaller pack. We need to get on the road."

12

The room at One Eyed Jane's, though barely big enough for the small mattress, table, and two chairs that filled it to bursting, brought a faint smile to Micah's face. The shack he'd shared with his mother had been no larger, and of course their home's walls had never seen plaster, nor did it possess a floor fancier than packed dirt. This room boasted wooden floors. Splintered and stained, to be sure, but wood nonetheless. And the cracked and discolored plaster formed interesting patterns. He imagined that the cracks were rivers on the surface of a room-sized world, the yellows and browns and greens, even the few relatively clean white patches, were all regions of differing vegetation.

No matter how closely he examined his surroundings, however, he could not long distract himself from his raging hunger. Where was Lon? He'd been gone for hours. The day had faded into evening, and soon it would be dark. He needed that special recipe, and soon. His hands trembled, and he could barely keep his eyes open. But when he tried to sleep, he found that he could only keep his eyes shut for a few moments at a time. It was maddening. So much so that he failed to notice when Lon reappeared in the room.

"Sit up," Lon said.

Micah jumped and shouted in alarm.

"I have what you need, but in a less refined state."

From within his shirt, Lon retrieved a small bag. Something within it moved, something about the size of one of Micah's massive hands curled into a fist. He felt a sense of dread that made him queasy and dizzy. Or was that the diwa infection?

Lon opened the bag and held out a beating heart.

Micah stepped back. "Is that . . . ? Am I supposed to . . . ?"

The heart continued to beat, though no blood poured forth from the fleshy tubes that exited it from the top. Nor was Lon's hand bloody, or even wet. He smiled. "You won't have to eat it, though it might do you some good. You merely have to drink its contents. I warn you that this liquid is far viler than anything you have previously tasted."

"What is it?"

Lon shook his head and handed the heart to Micah. He felt bile rising in his throat, but the weakness and hunger drove him, and he put his mouth over one of the tubes. Immediately, fluid rushed into his mouth and he swallowed reflexively. The thick liquid moved slowly down his throat, burning every inch of the way to his stomach, where it sat like a ball of molten lava. He burped, and the taste returned with a vengeance.

"Finish it."

Micah fought back the urge to vomit, and drank another mouthful, and another. His knees shook, and he fell to the floor. Lon did not move to help. Gradually, however, he began to feel stronger. The hunger subsided, leaving only a craving for solid food. He crawled to the wall and sat with his back to one of the cracked, discolored patches.

"If you're still hungry," Lon said, "you can eat the rest. It would be good for you."

"Is it . . . ?"

"It's not human, if that's what you're asking."

"I . . . I can't."

Lon gave Micah a withering glare. "Give it to me," he snapped, tucking the heart back into its bag and tossing a few coins Micah's way. "Go downstairs and get something to eat then. Bring it back up to the room."

Micah left, returning a little later with a wooden platter of eggs and toast, which he ate with his fingers as he walked. He sat at the rickety table opposite Lon, whose scowl had mellowed into a look of boredom. He could have eaten more, but he felt well again.

"I am continually amazed at how ill-informed you are. Did your mother teach you nothing of sorcery?"

Micah shook his head.

"Hm. Well, you were in hiding back then, and I suppose it would have blown your cover had you suddenly started casting spells. Unfortunately, I have never had an apprentice before, and I don't really know where to begin. So let's start with this: the superiority of sorcery over magic."

"I thought they were the same thing," Micah said.

Lon nodded. "Most people do. Some even refer to magic as 'lower sorcery.' They are incorrect. Diwa can be used in either practice, but mages do not handle it directly. We sorcerers do, and we pay a great price for it. As you have now seen, on a couple of occasions."

"So what do the others do?" Micah asked, but he knew; Felida had told him that much. He answered his own question. "Mages use magical objects infused with diwa so they don't have to touch it directly, right?"

Lon nodded. "Of course, they are hypocrites, since the individuals they employ to make those magical objects are practicing a form of sorcery. In this way they avoid direct contact with the diwa, but this weakens them. Their spells are weaker; their weapons, while fearsome, are inferior to ours."

"Like a sorcerer's sword," said Micah, grinning.

Lon seemed less amused. "Yes, like your sword. But again, handling the diwa directly comes at a cost. Unless you replenish your energy using . . . unique foods and drinks, or, in special circumstances, by ingesting another being's diwa, you will soon find yourself so weak that you cannot even think straight, much less defend yourself. Again, as you have discovered. Incidentally, you have practiced some very powerful sorcery already. Some of the less powerful spells do not require an immediate recovery. As you will find in time."

Suddenly, Micah realized that he had inadvertently omitted one detail of his journey from the palace to Roccobin: that he had soaked up some of the diwa from the man he'd killed. He decided not to bring it up now. "When do I begin?"

"Not yet. We have work to do. I spoke with Chase. He's on the way. Never varied from the plan. He will be here in two days, about the same time as your sister."

"Two days? To travel two-hundred miles?"

Lon smiled. "Chase's talents are quite limited. He is a lesser sort of practitioner, and cannot handle diwa at all. But he is good with animals, and I have enchanted the horses. The coach, as well."

"So what do we do now?"

"Now? We go back to the home of that Felida woman."

Micah narrowed his eyes. "And we kill her, right?" His hand began to tremble, but he clenched it into a fist before Lon could see. He had mixed feelings about the mage. She had seemed to truly care about his well-being, but as Lon had said, she must have spied on his memories while he was unconscious. She'd lied about it, of course, but still, she didn't deserve death for so little provocation.

"Not right away. I'll need to study her for awhile, so that I can change not only my appearance, but my behavior, to match hers."

"You'll take her place, then."

Lon stood and stretched. "Yes. I'll need to become her so that when your sister arrives, she'll trust me and get aboard the coach willingly, without a struggle. That is the plan, at any rate. It would be best if she arrives at the palace unhurt."

Micah kept his face carefully neutral, but Lon was perceptive enough to see the suddenly blank look.

"You're jealous of your sister, aren't you?" he said, gently. "No need for that, believe me. What your mother has planned for her . . . granted I don't know the exact details. But I wouldn't be too concerned that all the spoils will go to her. There will be plenty left for you."

Micah tried on a slight smile, then, trying to do that one thing he hadn't yet succeeded at: presenting not just an unreadable face, but a false one. Lon smiled a little in response, and Micah felt a tiny surge of triumph.

"Good," said Lon. "I knew you'd see that this will all be to your benefit, too. Now, sleep a little. We'll move against the healer as soon as you
are ready."

Micah tried to keep Lon's shadow in sight, for that was all he could
see of the sorcerer. On this cloudless night, moon- and starlight were
more than adequate to see, but Lon wore a special kind of cloak that
made him nearly invisible. He'd told Micah that he couldn't render himself truly invisible, because Felida would almost certainly have sentinels
watching for intruders, especially of the magical kind. The cloak each of
them wore, however, was of the kind often used by thieves. She wouldn't
react to the appearance of common thieves, or so Lon assured him.

He'd thought Lon would try to move around to the back of Felida's
home, a tiny, thatch roofed square amidst a cluster of poor, small dwell-
ings. Many shared walls, but not hers. They would, he had thought,
at least move to the narrow walkway between her house and another.
Instead, Lon walked directly up to her front door and knocked. He still
wore his thief's cloak, but he hadn't signaled for Micah to join him, so
he stopped a few houses away and loitered in a doorway. Lon knocked
again. Still, nothing. Lon signaled for Micah to join him.

"She'll have defenses in place, even if she isn't home," Lon said. He
knocked again. Still, no response from the darkened home. "Close your
eyes," said Lon, as he turned and reached for the door latch. Micah
squeezed his eyes shut, but a bright light shone red through his eyelids.
"You can open your eyes now."

He did, and inhaled in shock at the sight of Lon's right hand: the
skin had blackened and shriveled, and bones showed through weeping rents.

"That," said Lon, "hurt." He took a deep breath and released it slowly
before continuing. "And it was completely unnecessary." Lon grasped
the doorknob, again with his right hand, which although apparently
ruined, functioned normally. This time, however, the door opened. Inside, the place was much as Micah remembered it.

Except that Felida wasn't there, and the little home appeared far less cluttered than before.

Lon prowled around the place, touching books, chairs, the table, bottles, wooden crates, virtually everything, with his left hand. Every once in a while, he stooped to sniff something, and once even licked a spoon. "She's gone," he announced. "But she isn't alone. There's a young woman with her. They left less than an hour ago. There are no signs of struggle, so we must assume they left together and willingly."

"My sister?"

"Probably. I get a slight whiff of a time-pushing spell. Your sister must have known she was being watched, and deliberately led my spy to believe that she would be arriving in two days, then pushed time to get here in a few hours instead." Lon paced around the little room, pinching his lower lip. He stopped. "Give me your hand."

Micah obeyed. Lon withdrew a narrow knife from his belt and slit Micah's finger. Lon cupped his good hand under the finger and gathered the blood, then told him to find a bandage and clean up the wound. While Micah went looking for bandages, a bright light flashed. He turned to find Lon holding his left hand outstretched. The knife floated above his hand, its point aimed directly at Micah. Lon whispered a few magical words, and the knife spun around, finally settling, still afloat, but with the point aimed north.

"What is that?" Micah said.

"A blood compass. You and your sister have almost identical blood." Lon walked quickly out of the front door. "Come along! The range is only a few miles. We must not fall too far behind. We'll just have to hope she's pushed herself too hard and has to move at a normal pace for a few days while she recovers."

Micah blinked, trying to keep up. "What about Chase?"

Lon stopped, reached within his cloak and retrieved a handful of coins. "Go back to the inn, wake the keeper. Give him the money and a message for Chase: 'Our quarry has fled. Meet us at Bel Denlo at the Inn of the Dragon's Heart.' Then, Micah, come back to me. I'll be on the Turnpike, headed north. Go!"

Micah did as he was told, though the innkeeper fumed at his interrupted sleep. His anger eased somewhat at the sight of the money, but Micah didn't care. After delivering the message, he ran back out to the Turnpike, a road he knew only because it was the only road with a gate and a toll taker. As a pedestrian, he would pay nothing, but he remembered his cloak at the last second and removed it before coming into the little circle of light surrounding the lantern at the toll gate. He'd look too much like a thief slinking around half-invisible in the middle of the night.

He needn't have worried—the toll taker snored at his post. He pushed himself then, walking briskly, then jogging for a bit, then slowing to a walk, then jogging again. He'd never done much long-distance walking—his strength lay in standing in one place and shoveling stone. His breath came raggedly by the time he heard Lon's whisper.

"Stop, Micah!" Lon emerged from behind a tree. He, too, had removed his cloak. "You make an awful racket, but not to worry. They are at least a mile ahead of us." He consulted the compass once again, nodded, and put it away.

Micah noticed that Lon's left hand was clean. "Don't you . . . need my blood . . . to make it work?" he panted.

"No. Only to teach the blade what to look for. Come along now. They're moving quickly, but there's no need to run."

Micah walked alongside Lon for a while in silence, until he got his breath back. "Lon? Something I've been meaning to ask you. How did you find my mother in the first place? I mean, after Garron's death."

"Your mother and I had a system in place to signal one another. Each of us chose a person and cursed that individual. Neither of us was to know the identity of the person chosen, but we knew the curse intimately. Should that person die suddenly, the curse would send a signal that only I or your mother could detect."

"So you thought my mother killed Garron as a signal to you?"

"Yes. Imagine my surprise when I found that a boy had killed Garron."

Lon fell silent, but Micah had a feeling that this might be his last chance to get a few questions answered.

"What happened? Back then, with my father's rebellion?"

Lon looked at him for several moments, and Micah wondered if he would answer. Finally, Lon pursed his lips and nodded. "Yes, I suppose it's time you heard about some of that. Kattenwa was once an independent kingdom, with a Kattenese king. The last man to wear the iron crown was Victor III, more commonly known as The Traitor. The Traitor married a Thurnish noblewoman, whom most believe was a sorcerer of some talent. She would not bear him a son, giving instead only daughters."

"People can do that? I thought babies were whatever they were, boy or girl. You know, randomly."

"Usually, but as I said, she was a sorcerer, like your mother. Now, please do not interrupt."

Lon checked the blood compass again and nodded. "Victor was enthralled with his wife and his daughters, most likely under a spell. He ignored the laws and customs of our land and declared his eldest daughter heir to the throne. Now, in Thurn they might choose to live under the reign of a woman from time to time, but no Kattenese man will stomach female rule. The nobles rebelled, and would have won had not The Traitor called upon his wife's uncle for aid. That man was Mikkel, a younger prince of Thurn. Mikkel crushed the rebels, murdered Victor, and claimed Kattenwa as a principality of Thurn. So we have remained ever since, for a hundred and sixty years."

As he spoke, Lon flexed his charred right hand, and Micah was surprised to see that it had mostly healed. The few bits of blackened skin had spread to cover most of the charred ruin. Bright red cracks covered the hand like a spider web, but they did not bleed.

"Your father planned to return Kattenwa to its glory days," Lon continued. "Valdis would have been our king, with an army of ten-thousand highly trained soldiers, led by a core of a thousand sorcerers. We would have been invincible, if he'd had the time to complete his work."

"What happened?" said Micah, though he remembered that his

mother had told him about a betrayal. It couldn't hurt to hold a little back, to see if either of them lied.

"We were betrayed. Or, rather, one of his sorcerers was on his way to betray us."

"Huh?"

Lon smiled. "I was a spy for your father. In my capacity as the Prince's private diviner, I practiced deep and dangerous sorcery, looking into the future. I saw a great many things in the future that I never reported to the Prince. But one thing I had to report. One of your father's sorcerers, a man named Khadiah, was jealous of some of the others, their power and prestige. He felt he wasn't getting his due, so he decided to betray your father in the hopes of rising high in the Prince's service."

Lon consulted the compass again, and signaled for a halt. "They've stopped. We don't want to get too close." He pulled a small bag out of a pocket, and Micah feared he'd now have to eat the heart from earlier. Instead, the bag contained nuts and dried berries. They munched in silence for a bit.

"Your parents and I had a plan for such a problem. Khadiah was too far from any of us for one of us to silence him before he could speak. We didn't know his exact location, either, so we couldn't teleport there. So, I went to the Prince and 'betrayed' Khadiah. I told the Prince that Khadiah was part of a rebellion, and for good measure I named a few of our less powerful and less reliable sorcerers and commanders. Prince Johann apprehended these men and tortured confessions out of them. And I, his loyal servant, was awarded with power and money. Enough of each to finish the palace at Engvar."

"But you betrayed the rebellion!"

"A planned betrayal, ordered and endorsed by both of your parents. Had Khadiah remained loyal, I would never have acted. The knowledge that the betrayal was coming allowed your father get many of his people into hiding. Some of them are still alive to this very day, waiting for the time when we rise to throw off the rule of the Prince and proclaim our own king once more."

Micah thought about Lon's story for a while. One question kept nagging. "How did my father die?"

Lon looked at Micah then, and placed his good hand on his shoulder. "The Prince called in the Brotherhood. No matter where your father hid, they tracked him down. He ran from one end of Kattenwa to the other, concealing himself in mountains, swamps, cities, and forests. They ran him to ground on the Plains of Ogol. He fought a furious battle there, calling upon energies those petty little monks could never dream of controlling! He was doomed, of course, vastly outnumbered as he was. But he killed dozens of them before suffering a mortal wound."

The sorcerer gazed up at the stars then, sighing. "I wish I could have been there. But I was with your mother; we were formulating our plans for her survival, and preparing your father's grave, just in case. Your mother sensed that he was dying, and we teleported to his side. We were too late--the wounds he suffered were magical in nature, and we could not save him."

"He died then?"

Lon sighed. "Not really. You will know this eventually: a part of your father survived, and we hope to bring him back fully. But we need your sister for that."

Micah frowned. So his mother had lied to him, again.

"Exactly why we need her is one of your mother's many secrets. Kellyn cannot rule. So once your father lives again, he will be our king. But unless he tries to have another son, you are his only heir." Lon smiled. "Your mother and father planned something . . . grand. Something never before seen in the history of sorcery. I could guess, but I won't." A smile spread across his face. "Frankly, I can't wait to see what will happen."

"The cemetery," Micah said. "At your palace. You kept the part that lived there? In the grave marked with a black stone?"

"You've seen that?" Lon asked, evidently shocked.

"Yes. My mother was there. His gravestone was concealed, or disguised. But I saw through it."

Lon shook his head. "When you are fully trained, you will be a powerful sorcerer, Micah. Already you possess abilities that terrify me. But

I suspect the part of your father that survived was hidden somewhere else—his grave was too obvious a choice, no matter how well concealed the tomb." He checked the compass again, and stood abruptly. "They're moving."

"Wait. Lon, you said you could see the future. Can't you just see where they're going and teleport there?"

Lon chuckled. "It's not that easy, Micah, or every sorcerer would do it. I would have to devote all of my energy to the task, and remain in the basin in the basement of the palace for weeks on end. Getting even a single vision is an exhausting, and often dangerous task. And even then, I would see not 'the' future, but many possible futures. Only when the overwhelming majority of possible futures all look substantially identical can one accurately predict the future."

"Can you teach me how to do it?"

"You wouldn't want it. Being a diviner is as close to slavery as a sorcerer will ever come. I did it for the Prince, but only because your father asked it. You would not choose to do it, not willingly. At best, you might choose to see in the limited way in which mage-diviners see. But their visions are far less reliable than those of a sorcerer. Moreover, mages tend to see movements, but not motivations."

They trudged on in dogged pursuit, hour after hour. Finally, as the sky began to brighten, Lon called a halt. Felida and Micah's sister had stopped in a tiny village just a mile or so ahead of them. "We'll take turns sleeping under those trees," Lon said, indicating a grove of apple trees to the left of the road. "You first."

Micah nodded, grateful for the rest. He was exhausted, and once they stopped and sat, he realized just how sore his feet and legs had become. Lon, however, seemed unaffected, so he said nothing. But he felt hope, for the first time. He was his father's only heir. Kellyn could never wear the crown—Lon had said so himself. He laid down with his head on the root of a tree with a grin on his face, and quickly fell into a deep sleep.

13

Kellyn sat heavily on the ground, stifling a yawn. They'd been travelling for three days now, and they'd fallen off their first day pace of twenty-seven miles quite a bit. The second day, they'd only made about eighteen miles. Today they'd be lucky to make ten. Granted, the pouring rain had slowed them some, but they'd covered only about eight miles so far and it was nearly dark.

"At this rate . . . it'll take a week . . . to reach D'Arrune," she said. She found it hard to catch her breath, and speech came with difficulty.

Felida pursed her lips. "The ability to push time for long periods must be built up gradually. You still need rest, and the harder we push ourselves, the worse you will feel. A mage like Magrahim might be able to do what you did without ill effects. But he's had many years of practice."

"How well do . . . you know Magrahim?"

"Not so well as I would like," Felida answered with a sly smile.

Kellyn's eyes went wide.

Felida laughed. "Must it be shocking that your elders can also dream of romance? I was just finishing my third year of coursework when he began his first. Keep in mind, it takes many more years of school to learn to heal someone than it does to learn to kill. I'm a bit older than your instructor. Still, even as a five-year-old, it was clear that he would make a great mage one day."

Kellyn nodded, smiling a little at the thought of Magrahim as a child. And the thought of him as being . . . involved with a woman struck her as either absurd or shocking. Magrahim had always been an instructor, and for the last five years, Kellyn's instructor only. "I miss him."

"You'll see him again. Now, let me examine you." Kellyn sat still, opening her mouth and turning her head and breathing deeply, and generally performing all the odd movements healers required of their patients. "The physical exhaustion you feel is a manifestation of the psychic stress you're experiencing. Each body, each mind, is different. You should feel lucky; some people react to such stress with memory loss, blurry vision, or uncontrollable muscle spasms. Pushing time is harder on some than on others. Your suffering isn't much worse than average. Unfortunately, time is the only cure for what ails you. As is so often the case." Felida looked up, sniffing the air like a dog on the hunt. "They're getting closer," she said.

"The people behind us?" She'd caught her breath. It was so frustrating, being so limited physically. As one of the older students, she'd become accustomed to dominating any physical challenge.

"Yes. I just wish I could tell if they were following us or if it's just a coincidence that their pace is almost exactly the same as ours."

If only Alonselle were here, Kellyn thought. He'd have one of his master's instruments, something to let them see who their followers were. With a start, she realized she had an instrument of her own. She rummaged through the bag tied to her belt and fished out the green stone, wishing it were the dragonfly. "What if I position this so I get a clear view of the road, then leave it there when we move out? I could get a good look at them, at least."

"What's your range?"

"I can do at least six hundred yards."

"They're between seven hundred and eight hundred yards behind us, give or take. I can't be more accurate than that, unfortunately. They're at the very edge of my perception as it is."

"Why don't we do it now? I can certainly walk another thousand yards."

Felida took her time answering, but eventually she nodded. She helped Kellyn to her feet and offered her arm. "Don't overdo it. Take your time. There's a town up ahead. Maybe another mile or two. Bel Denlo, I think it's called."

"I feel ridiculous. I'm not a child."

"A little caution never hurt anybody. Incidentally, I remember Magrahim as a very cautious young man."

Kellyn smiled. "He still is. Cautious, I mean. Not young."

She placed the stone on a fence post bordering the turnpike, closed her eyes and adjusted the view until it was perfect. No one coming up that road could possibly get by unobserved. After walking about five hundred yards, Felida ordered her to close her eyes and test her connection with the stone. She could see the road clearly. "Good. Now keep your eyes closed. I'll guide you."

Minutes later, two people walked into Kellyn's view. In the lead was a tall, thin man who might have been fifty or sixty years of age. He walked confidently, briskly. Behind him walked a much younger man. She opened her eyes and described both to Felida.

"That's our sorcerer's apprentice. I'd say the older man is his master."

Kellyn closed her eyes again. "Wait, Felida. There's something else. Ah, he just walked out of my line of sight, but I think he was using a blood compass."

Felida's step faltered. "You know how they work, don't you?"

"I've never used one, but I know the basics."

"Somehow, they have obtained a sample of either my blood or yours."

Kellyn's hand flew to her ear. "Jirra," she whispered. An overwhelming sense of betrayal flooded her, and she would have fallen had it not been for Felida's steadying hand.

"Don't assume it was your friend. That gash must have bled quite a bit, and likely left drops all over the airship. Any member of the crew could have taken a sample. For that matter, a talented sorcerer could have scraped some dried blood off the wood hours or even days after you were injured. It's conceivable that the sample was taken by someone at one of those villages where the ship landed before you came to me."

Kellyn nodded, and quickly mastered her emotions. *Emotions,* she thought, paraphrasing one of the lessons of the Brotherhood, *are not to* be trusted. *Even thoughts must be examined in the cold light of rationality.* She took a deep breath before speaking. "We cannot rule anyone out as a suspect just yet. Even Jirra. I was unguarded with my feelings around her."

Felida smiled. "Fifteen is a difficult age, Kellyn. Had you graduated at age ten, as you should have, mastering the problem within you would have been a little easier. Assuming that someone was able to identify the problem." Her gaze shifted to Kellyn's sword. "That blade very likely saved your life. I would never have thought to look for . . . what I looked for, without that extraordinary chunk of steel hanging at your hip."

Kellyn gripped the hilt of her sword. "I treated Shaethe unfairly aboard the ship. He frightened me."

"But now?"

"Shaethe is . . . a part of me. I trust him like I trust my own right arm." Again, warmth spread into her belly as she praised the sword. She smiled.

Felida shook her head. "We healers have nothing like a warrior's bond with a sword. I would almost be envious, except that so much bloodshed usually accompanies such a bond."

Kellyn smiled, but she agreed a little. The battle against the pirates had been a slaughter, and her savage joy at killing had sickened her then. It still did. She stumbled.

"Are you well enough to continue?" Felida asked. "We could make camp here, but I would rather get you out of the rain."

Now was not the time for a silly display of courage, and Kellyn examined herself critically. She was about to conclude that she lacked the strength to continue when Shaethe poured strength into her legs.

You can do that? thought Kellyn.

A sense of satisfaction radiated from the sword.

Thank you. To Felida, she said, "I can keep going." With a small but detectable surge of energy, she covered the last mile or so to Bel Denlo, where they found an inn with a room overlooking a stone bridge over the river. Kellyn washed her face with a clean cloth and a bowl of cold water while Felida looked out the narrow window, tapping her lip.

"Let's see how well our followers adapt," she said, almost to herself.

"What do you mean?"

"We're a little over halfway to D'Arrune. We'll hire a boat tomorrow. That will take us to within seventy miles of the capitol, and about twenty miles west of the turnpike. The roads aren't as good from there, but I think we'll hire a wagon for the last leg of the journey anyway. I don't want you walking any more than you have to. Should our followers catch up to us, you'll need your strength."

Felida forced Kellyn to eat a small meal and another draft of the reddish-brown liquid before going to bed, and she fell soundly asleep shortly thereafter.

Sometime during the night, she dreamt of smoke, shouting and pain. She almost woke up, struggling at the edge of sleep, but exhaustion won out.

Lon had been jumpy ever since they had arrived in Bel Denlo. The sleepy river town boasted a garrison of five hundred soldiers, and their presence was much in evidence. At the gates, on the street corners, in the market, and, especially, in the taverns. Rumor had it that the Prince had decided upon a show of strength to overawe the residents, many of whom had supported Valdis Hittrech's revolt.

"We've no time to waste," Lon told Micah. "As soon as Chase arrives, we move against them." The sorcerer's discreet inquiries produced the name of an inn at which two mages had arrived just a few hours earlier. Lon's blood compass confirmed the information.

Micah thought it would be safer to take them on the road, away from the Prince's soldiers and the narrow, twisting streets of Bel Denlo, but he held his tongue. Jumpy as the sorcerer appeared, his own nerves were stretched rather thin. He knew Lon intended to kill the woman, and no matter how necessary her death might be, he couldn't shake the feeling of wrongness at the thought of murdering Felida.

Chase arrived well before daylight, his face and hands bandaged from Micah's clumsy attempt to follow Lon. Apparently, when the diwa had flowed through Micah's body, the terrible energies had boiled the water in the basin back at Engvar House, and the steam had caught Chase before he could escape the dark chamber. Micah tried to apologize, but Lon's man had shrugged it off.

"Serving a sorcerer is not a safe way to make a living," he responded. "You can't see, but I'm grinning underneath these bandages."

Lon, who had left to scout the inn where Felida and Kellyn slept, returned just before sunrise. "Now," he said. "Follow me."

Chase drove them in Lon's fantastic coach, to a dark, narrow alley behind the inn, a three story wooden structure crammed cheek and jowl among other tall, wooden buildings. As with many of the neighboring tenements, the inn featured a rickety wooden staircase attached to the back of the building. Their arrival sparked interest from the sort of folk who prowled around dark alleys while the rest of the city slept. Three shadowy figures approached the coach.

Chase drew his sword and spoke in low tones, "You'll be wanting to move along now, boys. Or you'll be wishing you had. Your choice." The shadows drifted away, but not very far.

"Chase, you wait here," said Lon. "If you must kill those scum, do it quickly and quietly. We will be back shortly. Micah, with me." Lon led the way up the staircase, barely pausing outside the door to the top floor. For a moment, Micah feared the door handle would burn him as Felida's had, but nothing more than a loud squeak announced their presence. A narrow hallway greeted them, lit only by cloud-obscured moonlight from the open door behind them. More than enough light, however, to reveal a small person standing in their way.

"Murder in the middle of the night, is it?" Felida asked.

"Not murder, my lady," said Lon, as a bright red explosion rocked the building. Micah fell to the floor, temporarily blinded. "This way, fool!"

Micah blinked purple afterimages from his vision and followed Lon, who let the blood compass lead them to one of the rooms. This time, Lon clapped his hands together above his head and uttered a dark incantation. Bolts of lightning flew from his fingertips and shattered the door. The sorcerer then tossed something small into the room. The object emitted a sharp *'crack!'* and a great quantity of foul-smelling smoke.

"Wait for the smoke to clear, or I'll be carrying you out."

Micah obeyed Lon's orders, awed by the display of magic. If he'd had powers like that, Felida would never have been able to tie him to her table. Thinking of the healer, though, brought a lump to his throat.

Lon strode into the room, threw open the curtains, and placed his hand on the forehead of a body lying on the straw-stuffed mattress. "She's alive. Carry her down to the coach. I'll handle the healer."

Back in the alley, Chase leaned against the coach, clutching his ribs. Moonlight revealed a dark stain beneath his fingers. "Chase!" Micah shouted. "Are you well?"

"Well enough. Damned thugs. They jumped me."

Chase tried to help him with Kellyn, but Micah waved him off. "Save your strength."

"You!" came a shout from further up the alley. "Halt!"

Two forms came striding toward them. Lon appeared then, Felida held in his arms as if she were a sleeping child. Micah had just finished dumping Kellyn in the coach; he took the healer from Lon as the sorcerer turned to face the two strangers.

"I told you to stop, ye daft buggers!"

Again Lon muttered a curse and clapped his hands above his head. Micah watched with fascination and envy as Lon pointed at the men. Lightening leapt from his fingers, striking one of the men square in the chest. That one fell moaning. The other fled. Lon ran to the stricken man and knelt at his side. The moaning abruptly ceased.

Several people had seen them, as curious and fearful faces peered out of open windows. At the sight of the deadly lightning, most of the shutters above the street slammed shut, but some people not only continued to watch, they began shouting for the militia. Lon ran for the coach, said some more words and sprinkled drops from a small glass vial on the wheels. "Go!" he shouted to Chase as the bleeding driver struggled with the reins.

The horses bolted once they were all aboard, taking the coach down the main road of the town at a speed so frightening they only noticed the gates as a brief series of shouts that faded quickly behind them with distance. Well beyond the gates of Bel Denlo, Chase stopped the coach and Lon hopped down from the bench and went inside. As Micah and Chase waited patiently outside, Lon threw a sword and a small bag onto the road. Then they heard him shouting, and Felida shouting back. Gradually, their conversation quieted down. After about an hour, Felida emerged. Or so Micah thought.

"It's me, Chase," Felida said, with Lon's voice. "I'll be impersonating her at least until we get back to Engvar."

Micah had blinked in confusion, but Chase caught on immediately. "What about the healer?"

Lon/Felida looked from Chase to Micah. "She's still alive; I may need to study her more to perfect my disguise. Once I'm finished, we'll dispose of her."

"Why do you need her at all?" Chase asked. Micah thought it an excellent question.

"I can't keep Kellyn unconscious all that way back to Engvar—she'll suffer from too much of the drug, and the spell I would use could cause some unfortunate side effects. From what my informants have told me over the years, she's a formidable fighter, and I'd rather she came along peacefully. If she thinks I'm Felida, she'll trust me completely."

Kellyn awoke to swaying, soft cushions and silk sheets. Stray shafts of sunlight brightened the gloom now and then. She was about to congratulate Felida on finding such a luxurious boat when she noticed the 'clip clop' of horses' hooves. "Felida? Are you there?"

"Relax, Kellyn," Felida answered from somewhere outside of the coach in which Kellyn lay. "Lie back and try to sleep some more."

"I take it you've changed your mind about the boat."

"Hmmm? Oh, yes. There weren't any available." Felida opened a sliding panel and looked in. The sudden bright sunshine made Kellyn squint, and she could barely make out the healer's face. "I'm going to stay up front with the drivers. We should be in the capitol late tonight."

"Tonight? Sixty miles in a single day?"

"Hmm? No, silly. You slept all day yesterday. I gave you something to help you sleep. Don't you remember?"

Kellyn's eyes went wide. How badly must she have hurt herself by pushing time? But there was something else more important, and her fuzzy thoughts were slow and disorganized. What was it? "Oh," she whispered as comprehension dawned. "What about our followers?"

"Our what?"

"The people following us?"

"Oh, sorry! I almost forgot. We gave them the slip. It wasn't really that difficult."

Something felt wrong. Felida could be chatty, but now she seemed almost giddy. If Kellyn could just order her thoughts and work it out. Maybe Shaethe could help. She thought Shaethe's name, but felt no response. But that was impossible, because Shaethe was a part of her. That would be like trying to pick up a cup of water and finding that her arm had disappeared. She felt for her sword, and found that her sword belt had been removed. As had her bag of amulets and talismans. She tried to calm herself, but the fuzziness in her mind would not go away. *I'll figure it out after a little nap*, she thought.

Or perhaps she'd said it out loud, because Felida said, "Excellent. You really do need more sleep."

Micah watched Lon out of the corner of his eye as the sorcerer silently mouthed words and made signs in the air. Lon clapped his hands and sat back heavily upon the driver's bench.

"She can't hear us now," Lon said. "So, Micah, how well am I impersonating Felida?"

Micah stared at the sorcerer. He really did look exactly like the healer, even down to her short stature. His voice sounded correct, too. But there was something not quite right. "She was always so sure of herself. You hesitate too much."

Lon pursed his lips and waved a hand at Micah. "There are bound to be things I don't know about the woman. But Kellyn hasn't known her long. She won't question any mistakes."

Micah nodded, and tried to make eye contact with Chase, but the driver merely flicked the reins to urge the horses on a little faster. Bumps in the road brought grunts of pain from Lon's man, but he gave no other complaints. The three men they'd encountered in the alley behind the hotel had proven to be nearly more than Chase could handle. Two had died, and another fled with terrible wounds, but Chase himself had not escaped unharmed. Lon had patched him up a little, but they didn't dare stop long enough for a proper and complete healing. Broken ribs and a few cuts, the sorcerer had said, wouldn't stop them.

"Before long," Lon continued, "Kellyn won't be able to tell the difference. I was afraid this bit of improvisation would miscarry, but everything will work out. You'll see."

Now Chase did make eye contact, squinting and shaking his head. Micah wondered if Lon believed what he said. His planning had shown more confidence than ability, as Micah saw it.

He wondered how much longer Lon would keep the healer alive, bundled unconscious in a trunk strapped to the rear of the coach. His impersonation got better with each round of questioning. But soon enough Lon would declare her usefulness at an end. Micah couldn't wait much longer. If Lon were to find the time to heal Chase completely, the driver would receive the order to kill the healer.

Micah swallowed hard. "How much longer 'til you kill her?" he asked.

Lon squinted at him. "Why do you care?"

Micah studied his shoes for a few heartbeats before answering. "I hate her," he whispered. "She . . . ." He shook his head, not sure where he was going with this.

Lon laid a hand on Micah's shoulder. "When the time comes, do you want to do the deed?"

Micah nodded, still not daring to make eye contact.

"Very well. We'll start looking for a likely place, then, someplace where we can hide the body. Now that I think of it, it's probably better that you do it. If I were to kill her, any competent mage would be able to tell a sorcerer had committed the murder, even if I didn't use any sorcery at all. It would be best if Chase did it, since he has even less ability than you, but I wouldn't want to risk further injury to him. He has several broken ribs, I believe. And you do seem eager."

"Yes," Micah whispered, with more feeling than he'd expected.

Lon chuckled. Before long, Lon declared their location suitable and ordered Chase to pull off the road and up a small rise in a pasture. "We can see for more than a mile in any direction from here. I'll question her one last time, then you'll take her across the road into that copse." He handed Micah a knife. "Use this, and no sorcery. Cut her throat from ear to ear, right down to the neck bones. Healers are notoriously hard to kill. Even unconscious, she can heal herself of all but the most severe wounds."

Micah took the knife and put it through his belt, nodding. Lon hopped off the coach and made his way to the trunk, humming merrily.

"Are you sure you can do it?" Chase asked Micah quietly. "If you carry her for me, I can do the deed."

"No. I'll be fine. Don't want you to hurt yourself."

The sounds of another shouting match between Lon and Felida emerged from the rear of the coach, an argument that lasted only a few minutes. Silence stretched for several heartbeats before Lon said in a conversational tone, "Time, Micah. Kill her."

Micah hopped off the driver's bench and joined Lon at the trunk. The lid stood open, and within Felida lay as if sleeping, looking peaceful and innocent.

"*Now, boy.*"

Micah hauled the healer out onto the ground, heaved her up over his shoulder, and easily carried her light frame over to the little stand of trees. Saplings and undergrowth slowed him, but he dragged her as far into the copse as possible, setting her down where the shade of the leaves overhead kept undergrowth to a minimum. He could not see the coach from there, and so neither could Lon or Chase see him.

He tested the weight of the knife and pressed it to her throat with a shaking hand. A tiny bead of blood formed where the point penetrated her skin. Immediately upon removal of the knife, the skin closed, the bleeding stopped. He pushed the knife into her throat again, deeper, and removed it once more. Again, the wound closed, but more slowly, and some blood seeped into the ground before she had healed herself. This time, he pressed the knifepoint far into her neck, finger depth, before removing it. More blood flowed, and he made sure to get some of it on his hands. Again, though, her body healed itself. One last cut, this one from ear to ear across her throat, but quite shallow. One end of the cut had healed before he reached the other end.

"I don't know if you can hear me, Felida," he whispered, "but I want you to know who did this, who saved you. My name is Micah. I'm . . . I'm sorry." His own actions confused him. Why should he care?

With one last look at her unconscious form, he left the copse, wondering at his motivations. No, she didn't deserve to die, and she'd seemed a decent enough person. But more lurked beneath the surface. His mother had lied. Lon, too, hid something important, he was sure of it. Only the healer seemed to care. Maybe it was only self-interest, keeping someone alive who might not lie, might not use him.

"What took so long?" Lon asked when he returned to the coach.

"I had to be sure."

"Well?"

"From ear to ear, right across the throat, all the way down to the spine."

"Good." And then Lon noticed the blood on Micah's hands. "Idiot! Take some water from the jug and clean your hands. We'll have to burn your clothes, as well. But not here. Couldn't you have been a little more careful?"

"You didn't say anything about the blood. How was I supposed to know there'd be so much?"

The baron shook his head and sighed. "Be quick about it."

Micah obeyed without another word, but a fierce joy lit a fire in his breast. He'd fooled the sorcerer and saved the healer. As he dipped a ladle into the clay water jar on the back of the coach, he noticed that the utensil had a letter embossed on its handle. Maybe it was the first letter of Engvar, whatever that might be. He thought about throwing it into the grass, but Lon would notice a missing water dipper. He started looking for something else to throw onto the road, when Lon barked at him to hurry. Nor was he entirely convinced that signaling their destination to Felida was a good idea. If only he knew more.

Back on the driver's bench between Lon and Chase, he worried that his ruse might be discovered. Something of his thoughts must have found its way onto his face, because Chase squeezed his shoulder. "First time with a blade, eh?"

Micah nodded jerkily, unable to trust his mouth.

"Different, isn't it? I'm no sorcerer myself, but the baron once gave me an enchanted arrow to shoot a man with. It turned to a shaft of pure crimson light when I shot it, and it leapt from my bow to the man's heart faster than the blink of an eye. Didn't feel real at all. But killing with a blade in your hand, feeling the steel piercing flesh, that's a . . . unique experience."

Micah looked for some sign that the talk of killing troubled Chase, but he spoke about killing the way Micah might have spoken to another boy at the quarry about hauling rock. Just a job that needed doing. The sort of job he'd have to do to prove his worth to his mother.

But did he want that? Did he care whether their mad rebellion succeeded? He blinked in surprise at his conclusion: he *did* care, and wanted them to fail. He wanted everything to go back the way it had been before his sister came back. Let his father remain dead, let his sister become a mage. He wanted only a shack to share with his mother, but that dream faded further with each clop of the horses' hooves.

14

"I gave her another vial of sleeping potion," Lon said. The coach sat in a warehouse near the shore of Lake Arrune, the body of water that gave the capitol its name, D'Arrune. The place stank of the oily fish that usually hung on drying racks inside the warehouse. Chase stood near the broad doors, watering and feeding the horses. Lon had healed the worst of his injuries, but claimed he didn't have all the necessary supplies to give his assistant a complete recovery.

"Kellyn doesn't suspect anything?" Micah asked. "What about her weapons and things?"

"Not at all. I told her I placed her sword in a null box so no evil sorcerer could detect it, and she believed me without question."

Micah nodded, but he wondered if the sorcerer wasn't being over-confident. After all, Micah lied to the sorcerer undetected. Why couldn't Kellyn?

Chase returned. "We'll kill the horses if we keep up this pace."

"Horses can be replaced," snapped Lon.

"My Lord, I am afraid that they will not last long enough to get us back home. They need rest. Barring that, we should replace them now."

"Fine. Go out and buy four new horses. We'll sell these to a butcher."

"How long will you keep up the disguise?" Micah asked Lon.

Lon, who still looked exactly like Felida, answered in her voice, "Until we are safely back in the palace. It isn't easy, maintaining her shape, but it's easier than going back and forth between this and my true shape."

Lon looked at the horses, and Micah saw a look of longing on the sorcerer's face. He made eye contact with Lon, then looked at the horses.

"I need more diwa," Lon said quietly.

"You'll consume it directly from the horses?"

"All living things produce diwa. That from a horse is far more powerful than what you would get from a tree, but also far less powerful than what you'd get from a man."

Micah squinted, nodded. "That guard you killed, back in Bel Denlo. Did you consume his diwa?"

"Very observant. It is not the ideal solution. I have found the best cure for diwa infection lies in the special meals you've eaten. Constantly consuming diwa directly leads to a form of addiction. And, of course, the infection never really goes away until you eat the meals."

"Didn't you bring any of the food with us?"

Lon scowled at him. "Do you think I am a fool? Of course I did! But I can't eat any of it now. I'd have to drop my disguise, for the food only works when you aren't enacting powerful spells. Just a little while longer, and I'll be able to be myself instead of this woman."

Micah watched Lon surreptitiously. The sorcerer's eyes never strayed too far from the horses. After what must have been half an hour, Lon stood abruptly, walked over to the horses and laid his hands upon one of them. The animal died instantly, falling over and nearly crushing Lon in the process. The other three animals whinnied and shied, backing away from the sorcerer as much as they could. But that wasn't far, for their reins were tied to the same support beam. Lon backed away, smiling slightly, eyes glassy and unfocused.

"Better?" Micah asked.

"Hmmm? Ah, yes, that is, for now." Lon stumbled a bit as he went to the coach, climbed up and stretched out on the driver's bench. He was asleep within a few heartbeats. With nothing to do and no one to talk to, Micah wandered around the warehouse, found an office full of papers that he couldn't read, and a desperately needed privy. He even found a small kitchen, and helped himself to a little stale bread and dry, crumbly cheese. The contents of an earthenware jug smelled like alcohol, so he put the cork back in and continued to search. There was water back at the coach, but he didn't want to go back there.

A sudden thought came to him: *I could kill Kellyn.* No one could stop him, but Lon lay stretched out on the bench, and he had no idea how soundly the sorcerer slept. And besides, where would he go then? He had no doubt that his parentage wouldn't matter if he killed his sister and Lon found out about it. Whatever plan his mother and Lon had for Kellyn, it didn't involve her dying just yet.

Someone stirred near the coach. The door opened, and Kellyn stepped down to the dirt floor of the warehouse. Micah walked steadily toward her, noticing that the sorcerer did not stir. Indeed, he snored.

His sister. There could be no doubt. Micah had seen few mirrors in his life, but he had a sense of his appearance. Kellyn was taller than him, thinner too. But her eyes, hair, skin tone, the shape of her face: she looked like him. Would she recognize the similarities?

Kellyn noticed Micah and stopped, staring. She blinked a few times, then smiled. A fake smile, Micah noted. His sister clearly didn't lie often or well. He wondered if she'd somehow managed to spit out the sleeping potion without Lon's knowledge.

"You must be the son of that healer Felida told me about," Kellyn said. "Janeh, her name was, I think. You'd be Niko, right?"

Micah smiled and nodded. "Yes, that's me."

"Where is Felida now?"

Micah pointed to the coach. "Up there. She's exhausted."

"Well, I won't wake her, then. Is there a privy around here? I really need to go."

Micah pointed his sister toward the little stall with its bucket for waste. No sooner had Kellyn closed the door behind her than Chase burst through the door to the warehouse. Micah spun and placed a finger on his lips, shaking his head and pointing toward the privy. Chase seemed to understand for he asked, "Where's Felida?"

"On the coach."

Chase ran to the coach. "Felida! You have to wake up now!" He clapped his hands loudly. Lon awoke, but before he could speak, Chase continued. "Kellyn is awake, in the privy." He jumped up onto the bench and whispered something in Lon's ear, but Micah couldn't hear it.

"Kellyn!" Lon called with Felida's voice. "Where are you? We have a problem."

Kellyn emerged from the privy. "What is it, Felida?"

"Chase tells me the Prince's men are on the lookout for us. They have a good description of us, but no drawings. They want you in particular, and I think we both know it isn't for any reason you'd wish to experience."

"How did they know we were coming?" Kellyn asked. "I thought you said we could trust the healer to whom you sent the message."

Micah jumped. "My mother is completely reliable!" he said. "I am Niko, son of Janeh the healer, and I will not hear anyone slander my mother!"

Kellyn looked down at the dirt floor and said, "Sorry, Niko. I meant no offense."

Micah nodded, but he'd seen just the hint of a smile upon his sister's face as she apologized. A poor liar indeed. But what was the correct path for Micah now? Perhaps he should be helping Kellyn escape. Well, there would be time for that later.

"Enough," said Lon. "Chase, were you able to find fresh horses?"

"I'm sorry, Felida. There was no time."

"That is unfortunate. One of the horses has died. We'll just have to make do. How did you find out they were looking for us?"

"I saw soldiers pasting a broadsheet on a message pillar. They had a pretty good description of you, Felida. Also of Kellyn, but not, ah, Niko here or myself. Perhaps he and I can move about freely."

Lon ran a hand through his hair, but his fingers got caught in the complex braids he'd adopted as part of his Felida disguise. "Go back out there, but alone. Niko is too inexperienced. Get us fresh horses, but be discreet. We'll just have to try to slip out of town."

"How will we do that?" Kellyn asked as Chase left to do Lon's bidding. "Surely they'll be searching every wagon and coach that tries to leave town."

"Haven't you noticed that wealthy people are almost always exempt from the law? This coach obviously belongs to a wealthy man. So I will disguise myself as a wealthy man. You will have to hide; this coach has a hidden compartment that should do well enough. For now, though, there's nothing to do but wait for Chase."

Kellyn started walking toward the horses. "What about these three?"

"Don't go near them!" Lon shouted. "They're jittery beasts. I wouldn't want you getting hurt. Not when we may need you at your best, should we have to fight our way out."

"You'll give me my sword back, then? And my bag of amulets?"

"Not just yet. A blade like yours would stand out like a beacon to those with eyes trained to see."

"Of course. I understand completely."

Micah saw quite clearly that Kellyn really did understand. She wasn't fooled at all by Lon. Likely the whole story about 'Janeh' and 'Niko' was just a lie she'd made up. When Micah had played along with the lie, she'd have seen instantly the danger around her.

Lon, however, apparently believed that he'd fooled Kellyn. Micah could think of no way to communicate this to the sorcerer, nor was he entirely sure he should say anything at all, and so remained silent. Lon climbed into the coach, asking for some privacy to work on his 'disguise.'

Meanwhile, Kellyn went through a series of exercises. She ran around the perimeter of the warehouse, shimmied up one of the support beams and leapt back and forth among the rafters. Micah had to admit, his sister was quite formidable, physically at least.

"What are you doing up there?" called Micah.

"I've been cooped up too long. I need to stretch my legs and work my muscles. After all, we may be in combat at any moment, yes?"

Or maybe she swung about up among the rafters just to look for a way out. There were no windows among the rafters, and Lon soon emerged from the coach, wearing his true form. Whatever his sister had been doing, she played along now.

"That's quite a disguise," said Kellyn, as she slid down to the floor from a rope that hung from the rafters. "You've even changed your height! How is that possible?"

"We healers know many things we don't tell the Brotherhood," Lon said.

"What shall I call you, then? Now that you're a man."

"How about 'Lon'? I've always liked that name."

"Pleased to meet you, Lon. And what is our story, should the Prince's men not respect the obvious wealth of this wonderful coach?"

Lon stared at Kellyn for a few seconds, and Micah wondered if he'd finally figured out that she knew that all was not as it seemed. "I'll say that Niko here is my son, and Chase our servant. You, of course, won't need to worry, since you'll be in hiding."

"Right. I forgot. So, what about—"

Chase came back just then, and as he opened the door, they could hear shouting outside. "They're here! They've found us. I don't know how, but they've found us."

"Check the other exits, Chase," said Lon. "Find us a way out."

Chase ran to the rear of the warehouse and opened a small door. There was a scuffling sound, and Chase slammed the door shut. When he turned to face the rest of them, there was an arrow sticking out of his left shoulder.

"Well," he said through gritted teeth, "we won't be using that exit." He barred the door, staggered to the next one, but he was much more careful this time. "I think we're surrounded."

"My weapons," Kellyn said.

Lon stared at her for a few heartbeats before climbing onto the rear of the coach. He retrieved a sword belt and handed it to Kellyn. Micah noticed that he didn't give her back the little bag, but his sister made no comment. "Don't draw the blade just yet," Lon said. "I don't want them to know what they're up against."

"Of course," Kellyn said, tightening the belt around her trousers. "What about you, Niko? Have you any weapons?"

"He can defend himself well enough," Lon said. He walked over to Micah and placed his hands on his shoulders. "Do everything you can to defend yourself, do you hear? Now, all of you, listen! This warehouse belongs to a friend of mine. He is a wealthy baron in the service of the Prince, but he is loyal to our cause. If we become separated, we will meet in another of his properties, a small tavern near the docks called the Bloody Noose. Kellyn, you especially must avoid capture by the Prince's men at all costs. They know who you are and will not bother trying to find out why you're here in Kattenwa. They'll just kill you, understand?"

Kellyn nodded.

A loud knock came from the two large sliding doors at the front of the warehouse. "Come out with your hands in the air!" said a man outside. "Surrender and no one will be hurt! You have a quarter of an hour to comply, or we will break the doors down."

"Fifteen minutes. Good," whispered Lon. "That gives us a little time to prepare a surprise for them."

But the man outside had lied. After just a few seconds, the two big doors flew off their supports with a thunderous bang, sending smoke, splinters, and debris everywhere. One chunk caught Micah in the belly and knocked the wind out of him. He fell to the floor. He wasn't dying, or even badly hurt. Still, he found it hard to concentrate when he couldn't breathe. He heard shouting and saw a flash of light, but couldn't really tell what was happening through the smoke that filled the interior of the building. Slowly, painfully, his wind came back.

Whichever side he might want to win here, survival demanded he fight. He reached within for his sorcerer's sword, drew it and advanced toward the sound of combat. The smoke had begun to clear, and he found Chase locked hand to hand with a man clad in steel armor. Micah brought his blade down on the guard's shoulder, and the steel plate parted like warm butter, leaving the guard gaping at the blood pumping out of the place where his arm used to be.

Micah laughed, dizzy with power. He advanced on a group of men armed with ordinary swords and spears. With a single mighty slash, he cut off the tips of three swords, and reduced two spears to stubs. A couple of the men facing him turned and ran, but the rest fought on. He slashed and thrusted, littering the floor with broken weapons, bits of armor, body parts and blood.

But there were too many of them. He felt a sharp pain in his left arm, looked at it and saw blood leaking steadily from a wound in his biceps. The pause allowed another soldier to get within striking distance, and quite suddenly Micah was bleeding from another wound, this one on his right hip.

He staggered away from the fight, waving his invisible sword back and forth. Occasionally, an enemy soldier would get too close and suffer for their mistake, but they knew they'd hurt him, and so they were content to surround him, gradually forcing him back against a wall. Blood loss weakened him. The sword began to fade from Micah's vision.

A blast of blue-white lightening lanced through three of the soldiers surrounding Micah. The gap widened as a few of the surviving men fled. Micah took the opportunity to run in the direction of the coach, hoping to find Lon within the thick clouds of glowing smoke. Someone grabbed his shoulder, and he would have stabbed blindly with his sword, but it no longer existed.

A good thing, too, because the man was Lon. "Get into the coach!" the sorcerer shouted. Micah nodded and stumbled to where he thought the coach was parked. It wasn't there, but he found it after a few minutes of searching blindly through smoke that seemed suddenly thicker and more colorful than before. He opened the door and found Chase inside, groaning and clutching his shoulder.

"Chase! Are you alright?"

But Chase didn't answer. Shortly afterward, Micah collapsed next to him on the padded bench. Light began to filter through the curtains covering the coach's windows, bright, eerily colored. Louds bangs, screams, and shouted orders came through as well. The screams got louder as the coach started rolling. No sound of horses' hooves accompanied the movement, nor had there been time to hitch the animals.

Micah wanted to peek through the coach's windows. What had become of Kellyn? And Lon, for that matter. His questions would have to wait, because he could barely keep his eyes open. He sat back on the cushions and passed out.

Kellyn supposed that Lon had intended her to defend herself. May, in fact, have been counting on that. Instead, as the Prince's men approached, she took her hands from her sword belt and held them high. "I'm not with these people," she shouted. "I've been drugged and kidnapped."

She glanced down at her sword belt, wishing she could feel anything emanating from Shaethe. Even frustration at not being allowed to draw blood would be an improvement over the sword's unresponsiveness. Lon had clearly done something to the blade, but she couldn't imagine what. Was it possible to kill the spirit that inhabited a sword? She didn't think so, not without completely destroying the blade. Even then, some remnant of the spirit should survive in the mage to whom the sword was bonded. Only the death of the swordbearer and the destruction of the blade should be enough to finally kill the spirit. So where was Shaethe? She tried not to let her agitation show, projecting an aura of innocence.

The soldiers she faced did not look reassured, but at least they didn't try to kill her. They merely gestured with their spears and swords towards the open doors, and Kellyn willingly obliged. Outside the warehouse, she was greeted by bright sunshine and a man in gleaming plate armor. One of the soldiers guarding Kellyn saluted the man and spoke in low tones.

"Are you Kellyn Hittrech?" the armored man asked.

Kellyn knew that admitting to be a Hittrech in Kattenwa was a bad idea, but it stunned her that this man knew her identity. She had assumed Lon was lying to keep her compliant. "No. My name is Kellyn, but I am an orphan."

"Then you'll come along with us peacefully?"

"Of course," she said, but she began to worry. This didn't feel like a rescue. The officer led, with a soldier on either side of her and another behind. They marched to a horse drawn cart, where a soldier ordered her to sit between two escorts while another tied her hands behind her back and bound her feet together. The officer removed Kellyn's sword, unsheathed it, and swore softly. "Am I under arrest?"

The officer answered by hitting Kellyn with the flat of his sword, across the knees. "You will not speak, traitor! Gag her!" The man who'd bound her quickly tied a cloth over her mouth.

Kellyn sat still and bided her time, wondering who had charged her with treason, and against whom. There were no answers, of course, not now. The cart rumbled along the city's cobbled streets, in the general direction of the castle. When they arrived, the soldiers stripped and searched her quite thoroughly, not at all shy about touching her naked body. She glared, but could do no more. They gave her fresh clothes, and led her to a cell in a tower near the main gate. The door closed behind her, and a heavy bar slotted into place, locking her in. There was one window, very narrow and heavily barred, allowing a tiny amount of sunlight into the cramped room. At least her hands and feet were free, and they'd removed her gag.

The officer who'd arrested her spoke through a grate in the door. "You'll be guarded by a man specially trained to resist sorcery. Any attempt to break out of your cell or use magic in any way will land you in a much less pleasant cell. Do you understand?"

"I am not a sorcerer. I am a member of the Brotherhood, a novice—"

"Silence! You will not speak unless spoken to! Do you understand?"

"Yes."

The officer stomped away. With nothing to do but worry, Kellyn sat on the bare stone floor of her cell and tried to meditate. If she could clear her mind, focus on complete inner peace, slow her breathing and heartbeat, she might find a way out of this mess, and find a way to get Shaethe back. But no, that's not the way Magrahim would have done it.

"Meditation," her teacher had said on many occasions, "is not a means to an end. It is its own purpose. If you try to find peace for any purpose other than finding peace, your mind will not be able to let go of the material world."

Kellyn smiled at the memory, and at the thought of her many failed attempts at meditating. One thing at a time, then. She breathed deeply, willing her heartbeat to slow. She bowed her head, let her hands fall limply to the floor, and focused on sitting still. Not still like a coiled snake, ready to strike, but still like a pile of rags, unmoving, inert. "I cannot control my environment," she whispered softly. "I can only control myself. Relax. Breathe. Simply exist."

For the first time ever, she achieved the state of complete still-ness Magrahim had always tried to get her to reach. Thoughts stopped flowing, and she slipped into a state of semiconsciousness much like sleep, from which she'd been taught she would emerge feeling refreshed and keenly aware. She embraced it, so much so that when the door to her cell opened, she was surprised to note the night sky outside her window.

Kellyn stood in one fluid motion and turned to face the door. A man entered, and the door closed behind him. Tall, probably a hair over six feet, and thickly muscled, clean shaven, with short, curly auburn hair fading to gray at the temples, a hard face full of angles, pale even by Kattenese standards. He might have been of Khedrish descent, since his eyes lacked the epicanthic fold common to Kattenese. He wore black robes that hung to the floor, leather-and-rope sandals, a sword in an undecorated scabbard, and air of complete calm. He had to be a warrior mage.

He bowed slightly and said, "Kellyn Hittrech, you are a prisoner of Prince Johann of Kattenwa. You are charged with treason, and will be executed as soon as the Prince returns from his hunting trip. How do you respond to this charge?"

"I'm not a Hittrech. But does it matter? You've already decided I'm guilty, and the sentence has been handed out. Not the way the law is supposed to work, as I recall."

The man ignored her comments. "You are guilty because you are a Hittrech. All of his direct descendants, known and unknown, were convicted ten years ago."

"What about you? You're clearly a Brother. Does your loyalty to our order stop where the Prince's law begins? Will I even be given a chance to prove I am not who you say I am?"

The man smiled then. "I am Captain Albertus Zang, of the Prince's Auxiliary Guard. And you are Kellyn Hittrech. You look exactly like your father, and you do not lie well. So please drop the pretense."

Neither admitting nor denying Zang's accusation, Kellyn said, "What happens now?"

"Johann has a very specific standing order. When a Hittrech is found, he wants to witness the execution. Just as he was forced to watch the execution of his parents, sisters and two of his brothers. The prince would have been next, had not a special combat team of mages burst through a window and rescued him. You will have the honor of being the first Hittrech found since the end of the rebellion."

"Send a message to the Elders," said Kellyn, trying to sound calm. "They will get the king to order Johann to cease and desist."

Zang sighed. "Perhaps. And perhaps such an order would arrive before Johann returns. But it doesn't matter. He would defy that order, leaving the king in an uncomfortable position. Should he forgive an act of defiance from a previously loyal vassal? Or should he punish him as an example to others? I know which way I would bet."

Kellyn lost the cool composure she'd felt after meditation. "This is ridiculous! I was five when my father died! What crime can I possibly have committed?"

"Sit, please," said Zang. When Kellyn complied, he joined her on the bare floor. "A better question would be: why is Captain Zang not willing to let me go, claiming that the prisoner was not a Hittrech after all?"

She blinked. "Yes, that is a better question. Well?"

"I saw your father die. I wasn't supposed to, mind you. No one with magical ability was supposed to witness his death, I'm sure of that. I was recuperating from serious wounds in a field hospital when a grass fire forced us to relocate. I was able to walk by then, and I decided to rejoin my company. I had just found them when your father and a handful of his diehard loyalists attacked."

Zang placed his hand on Kellyn's shoulder, and gave her a look that sparked just a hint of hope.

"Your father was already dead. Oh, his body was still alive, but there was no light behind his eyes. He didn't use sorcery, he never spoke. He used an ordinary sword. The soldiers around me hacked through his loyalists and cut your father down. I tried to get them to capture him alive, but they were in a frenzy, and cut him to pieces."

Zang stood, walked to the door, and said, "I saw his eyes before he died. There is more to a man than a body, and that element was missing. I read Felida Uffgold's message asking for my help with your 'associative reaction' problem. And now I've seen your sword. I know what lies within you, and I think now you do, too. Were it not for your problem, I would indeed let you go." He pointed at her chest. "But there is something truly dangerous in there. If it weren't for the Prince's desire to see you die, I would have you executed immediately."

Zang left the cell, but Kellyn hardly noticed. She sat with her mouth hanging open, finally understanding. Her love of violence. Her failure in the test. Shaethe's bizarre decoration. The black ball of hatred within her: it was her father's soul.

Somehow, in the closing days of the rebellion, when it must have been clear to everyone that the fight was all but over, her father's soul had been implanted in Kellyn's body. Some other sorcerer had controlled her father's body like a marionette, attacked against hopeless odds, just to make sure the Thurnish forces believed Valdis Hittrech was dead.

But he isn't dead, thought Kellyn. *His soul lives within me, waiting to emerge.*

She had little doubt what would happen next. Though she didn't know much about possession, she knew that if she somehow escaped, Lon would try to recapture her to make sure her father's soul would take control of her body. And that Kellyn would die.

15

Micah carried a large sack of supplies, his wounds still a little sore despite Lon's healing efforts. The bag contained most of what they had been able to salvage from the ruins of Lon's once-fabulous carriage. It now sat behind a warehouse near the city wall, and looked nothing like the sleek, black coach he remembered from outside the shack he had shared with his mother for most of his life. The paint had peeled off completely, leaving bare wood, gray with age, splintered and riddled with worm holes. The iron bands that had held the wheels tightly together had rusted and snapped, while the wheels themselves sported broken spokes, or they wobbled, or in the case of the front left wheel, had fallen off.

It was as if the coach had aged a hundred years in the last hour. "Is that a disguise?" he asked Lon.

Lon carried only two things: a clay jar, and a small, leather sack, and he cradled each as though it were his most valuable possession. "No. That, unfortunately, is reality. The coach was enveloped in several layers of magic. Most of that was as a last-ditch defense, in case I should ever need to escape quickly, with or without horses. If the guards hadn't chased us, or if they hadn't shot fire arrows at us as we fled, I might have gotten away with using less of its power. As it is, the coach now has no diwa left in it. Within a few days, it will crumble into dust."

Micah's step faltered, and he nearly dropped his sack. He was tired, hungrier than he had ever been, and he trembled all over. Ahead, Chase limped along, carrying little besides himself, which he barely managed. "We need rest."

"Soon, curse you! I told you, we are heading for the Bloody Noose! When we arrive, we will be among friends."

Micah narrowed his eyes, wondering briefly if he could simply kill Lon. Now would be the perfect time. He could draw the sorcerer's blade, kill both Lon and Chase with a single swipe, then heal himself with the contents of that jar. It had to be the healing food. But what then? Go back to Engvar? He wasn't even sure where that was.

A sudden thought made him stumble again. Did he even want to go back? What had his mother given him since Lon found them, since she discovered that her darling Kellyn had returned?

"Nothing," he muttered.

"What?" snapped Lon.

"Nothing," Micah repeated, nodding. No one owned his allegiance now. He tried to summon the image of the sword, and succeeded briefly, but his hands were full. He couldn't grasp the blade without dropping the sack. He thought about telling Lon he needed to rest, but as soon as he stopped concentrating on the sword, it vanished. And after that, he couldn't make it reappear. He succeeded only in making himself hungrier and weaker. So he trudged on, for what felt like hours, until at last Lon led them to a door behind piles of rubbish. The sorcerer arranged the jar and sack in one hand, then knocked, a complex pattern of fast, light raps with his knuckles and fingers.

The door opened. Lon led the way in, followed by Chase and Micah. In the gloom, they found a woman holding a candle and a cane. "My Lord Baron," said the woman in a dry raspy voice, "it is a great pleasure to be at your service."

"Enough, Anna! We need a large room, immediately! My men are near death."

Anna, a wizened woman stooped with age, turned without a word and led them down a flight of stairs to a storeroom crowded with casks, strings of sausage, nets full of onions, and a dozen other items, all smelling of food and spice.

"We will need an open space," Lon said. He pointed to a large trestle table loaded with jars and wooden crates. "And clear that table."

Anna dropped her cane, set the candle on a table, and straightened her posture. She bowed her head, mumbled a few words, and extended her hand. Barrels, casks, crates and sacks slid away from her, first to the left, then to the right. Finally, ahead of and behind her, until she'd cleared a square patch of bare, wooden floor twenty feet on a side. The tabletop she cleared the old-fashioned way, with surprising strength for one as small and frail as she initially appeared. "Will this be sufficient, Lord?" Her voice didn't sound as subservient as her words. Almost as if she were mocking Lon.

"Fine. Tend to Chase's wounds, then leave us." Chase slumped to the floor, clutching his left arm. Anna immediately knelt by his side and laid her hands upon his shoulder. She whispered and sang softly, and soon Chase was asleep, snoring. Lon laid his two items gently on the table near the candle, motioning Micah to join him. "Put the sack on the floor, Micah. Now step back." He rummaged through the sack, removing a few items, putting some of them on the table, and some on the floor.

Micah thought he'd never get a better chance to kill Lon and make his escape, but he couldn't summon the image of the sword. He swayed and nearly fell.

"Sit down!" said Lon. "If you fall and break something important, so help me you will suffer!"

Micah obeyed, and had to admit that he had little strength to stand anyway. He began to tremble as soon as his butt hit the floor, and immediately began shaking like a leaf caught in a stiff breeze. He laid his head on the floor and tried to sleep, but he was kept awake by the shivering, chattering, convulsing cold. The dark room, lit only by the single candle, blurred until he could sense only vague shapes, areas of dark and slightly less dark. Pain stabbed through his guts.

Lon's face appeared in his field of vision. Everything else was a blur. He put something in Micah's mouth. "Eat! It's all I have left."

Micah chewed, and managed do not to vomit the healing food. He needed it badly, but would the tiny morsel in his mouth, a chunk no larger than a grape, really be enough to cure him? The convulsions stopped, and the shaking subsided, mostly. Still, he was hungry, tired, and cold, very cold. A memory from the fight in the warehouse intruded on his consciousness: Lon had told the group to meet at this inn, should they become separated. Surely they would have questioned Kellyn, if she survived. They would know about the Bloody Noose.

Lon crouched near Chase. He patted Chase's good shoulder, stood and approached Micah. "Stand up! We both need the food, and I will need your help making more."

Standing seemed like a terrible idea, but Micah did manage to wobble to a standing position, though he leaned heavily against the table. Lon handed him a knife. The same knife that he'd use to pretend to kill Felida.

"I'm going to bring something back to life. When it assumes a human form, stab it. Keep stabbing it until it changes to something else. I can't tell you exactly what it will look like when it changes. Every one of them is a little different, but it should revert to its original form—a fish."

"What is it?" Micah asked in a raspy voice.

Lon removed what looked like a leather mask from the sack. It had holes where eyes, nostrils and mouth would be. There was no hair on the mask, and no way to fasten it to a person's head. It was also too small for a grown man, and its edges were ragged. "It's a face," Lon said.

"A real, human face?"

"Yes. Quiet now."

Lon mumbled a few words while caressing the jar. He pulled a piece of chalk from the little sack and drew a roughly human shape around the jar. Lon placed the jar in the center of the chalk outlined body and laid the face on the head. He reached for the cork that sealed the jar, but turned to Micah before opening it. "Do not trust your eyes. What you are about to see is not human. If you do not kill it, it will certainly kill you."

He pulled the cork out of the jar with a twist. Immediately, tendrils of fog began seeping out of the jar and sliding along the table. When the fog reached the chalk outline, it curled in upon itself before sending out more tendrils, always seeking to escape, it seemed, and always thwarted by the chalk.

"Have you heard of a fish called a raven gar?" Lon asked as he hefted the jar and poured the remainder of its smoky contents onto the table.

Micah shook his head, too weak for speech but jolted into focused awareness by Lon's description of the danger they would soon confront.

"It's a massive river fish, up to eight feet long and weighing a couple of hundred pounds. It gets its name from its jet black scales. They're common in Kattenwa."

By this time the fog had taken the shape of a man, but flat, and no more than an inch thick. It began to rise, and thicken, until it resembled a three-dimensional sculpture of smoke.

"Raven gars can be possessed by an aquatic spirit most common in Kattenwa, though they can be found all over the world in fresh water. The spirit is called a face stealer. It possesses a raven gar and begins patrolling the riverbanks in thick reeds, searching for a woman. If it finds a lone woman, it will attack, tear her face from her head, devour her body, and assume human form. The face stealer will then take the identity of the dead woman, wearing her face, and return to her home with no one the wiser."

"Why?"

Lon did not answer immediately. He spoke more words in the language of magic, moving his hands along the surface of the smoke sculpture. The smoke thickened further, becoming liquid, then solid. It began to take on the color of pale, Kattenese flesh.

"Soon. Be ready. As to why? The newly made woman will return home and immediately mate with her husband, if she has one. Or with the first available man, if she does not. She becomes pregnant, and when she is about to give birth, she goes to the river's edge and resumes the form of a raven gar, leaving the human face behind. As the gar, she will give birth not to a human or a fish, but to dozens of tiny wigglers, each home to a newborn face stealer spirit."

"Is that what I drank? Those pollywog-looking things?"

"Yes. There are a few different ways to produce healing food from face stealers. The wigglers themselves are a good source, but hard to find. I maintain a breeding population of face stealers at the palace, but they don't travel well. Also—ah! Soon now!"

The shape on the table was now clearly female, and Micah tried to look away and stare at the same time. The face looked nearly alive now. Only the lack of eyes ruined the effect.

"Raise the knife! Be ready!"

Fog began leaking up toward the ceiling from the holes in the face. The not-quite-woman made a choking sound, and her naked chest began heaving for air. Micah blinked and tried not to stare. She inhaled sharply, sucking all the fog above her face back into her body, and suddenly Micah was gazing into a pair of bright green eyes. The woman on the table smiled. "Please," she said. "Come to me."

"Now, Micah! Now!"

Micah raised the knife, but the woman continued to smile. "You don't want to hurt me, do you? I don't want to hurt you. Come, kiss me."

"Now, Micah, kill it!"

He stabbed, but lightly, encountering little resistance as the knife penetrated the skin of her belly. The knife sank to its hilt, and he yanked it out. Not blood, but fog trailed the knife as he brought it up above his head. The woman who wasn't really a woman screamed piteously, crying out, begging Micah to stop.

"Again, Micah! Don't stop now!"

He stabbed again, and again, trying to make the screaming stop as Lon chanted louder and louder. Micah's cries joined the face stealer's, great wracking sobs wrenched from his body. He could hardly breathe, but he kept stabbing. Her cries grew fainter, and suddenly she wasn't human at all. Now a great, black fish flopped and squirmed on the table. Micah froze, his arm raised.

"Keep stabbing!"

Micah stabbed again, this time in fear of razor sharp, three-inch long teeth in a snapping, elongated mouth. The fish was as long as a man was tall, and as thick as a grown man's thigh. It writhed and jumped on the table, but the chalk outline kept it from escaping. Gradually, it ceased struggling, and it began to melt. Thick, yellowish liquid dripped out of the fish and puddled on the table, but like the fog it could not pass the line of chalk. Before long, the fish was gone, leaving only a human shaped puddle three inches deep.

"My, my!" breathed Lon. "She was a strong one."

Micah wiped his face, covered in tears, sweat and mucus, and tried to catch his breath. "What now?"

"Anna! Come down! Now, Anna and I will refine this mess and make more food. This substance is called gris. Its magical properties have been known for centuries. But only I have discovered how to harvest it reliably, and refine it into a cure for diwa infection."

Two women joined them then, Anna and a younger woman who might have been a decades-younger version of the crone. Anna drew two lines on the table with chalk, from the edge of the human shape to the edge of the table, while the younger woman heaved an iron pot halfway under the table, directly under the two lines. Anna then erased a bit of the human outline between the two lines with her finger, allowing the liquid to flow over the edge of the table, and into the pot.

"You've done this before?" Micah asked.

"Yes," Anna answered. "My husband makes a habit of this morbid procedure."

The younger woman chuckled. "My great-great-grandmother Anna is an odd sorceress," the girl said, "to be moved to pity for a creature that murders innocent women in order to breed."

Lon placed his arm around Anna's waist. "Will you be young again for me, my wife?"

"Will you act your age, for me, husband?"

They both laughed. "I thought not," Lon said. "Perryn, take this pot upstairs for me. You know the procedure; get it started. Anna and I have planning to do."

The young woman bowed her head. She was short, and slightly built, and not what anyone would call pretty. Still, her flaming red hair, pale skin, bright blue eyes and a spray of orange freckles across her nose rendered her striking. He'd heard of people with such hair before, but he'd never seen one. She pointed at Micah, and motioned for him to join her. "Come along. I'll need some help. I'm Perryn. You?"

"Micah."

"Are you well?"

"No. I'm weak. I need food."

"Soon enough." Perryn easily lifted the pot, which must have weighed quite a bit, and walked slowly up the stairs. "I'll go easy on you. Nothing too strenuous, I promise."

Upstairs, in what must have been the kitchen for the tavern, she placed the pot on an iron stove. There were a few girls around, preparing typical tavern food for the customers in the front of the building. The workers avoided Perryn and Micah, casting nervous glances at them. Perryn ignored them as if they didn't exist.

"Our servants, Micah. Face stealers, all of them. They've been altered, and cannot mate with a human man. Not yet. If they're good, Anna releases them. If they're naughty, it's into the pot!"

Micah gaped, horrified.

Perryn laughed. "I'm teasing! Of course they aren't face stealers. These are just ordinary girls. Saved from a short life of dreary poverty in exchange for their work here and their cooperation in some of Anna's . . . experiments." She threw some wood into the stove and lit it with a small, red-tipped stick, which she scraped against the stove until it burst into flame. He'd never seen anything like it.

Perryn saw him watching her, smiled and held up the now blackened stump of the fire-starting stick. "Not magic. Just a clever invention, one of Anna's. She calls these tinder-sparks. She could make a fortune selling them, but she doesn't want to put the flint sellers out of business. Like I said, she's odd. Soft in the heart, until you cross her. Then she's like a cornered badger."

Perryn moved briskly about the kitchen, adding ingredients to the pot. The liquid began to boil, emitting a foul odor. She spoke a few magical words and lit a candle, and immediately a mouthwatering scent of roasting beef filled the kitchen. "The smell of boiling gris would drive off the customers. And draw unwanted attention."

Micah sat heavily in a chair by a desk stacked with papers and books. "How long?" he asked.

"An hour, maybe a little less. Touch anything, and I mean any single thing, on Anna's desk and you won't have to worry about diwa infection. Got it?"

Micah looked up, wide eyed, but Perryn was smiling. She added a few more ingredients, mostly powders, then stirred the pot with a large wooden spoon. Her lips were moving, but he couldn't hear any words. Finally, she covered the pot and pulled a stool over to Micah.

"So, who are you, Micah?"

He glanced nervously at the serving girls who continued to bustle about.

"Don't worry about them," Perryn said. "They've been charmed. Not only won't they talk about what they see in here, they won't even remember anything out of the ordinary once they leave the Bloody Noose."

Micah nodded, and told Perryn just about everything. Excepting certain things, specifically that he'd allowed Felida to live and had been actively considering killing Lon, or at least running away.

"Great-great-grandpa Lon, with an apprentice?" she squealed. "Ha! This should be rich. He has all the patience of a starving fox in a hen house."

Micah smiled weakly. "I've noticed."

"Seriously, though. He should really think about letting someone else train you. I don't think he's ever had an apprentice before."

"How old is he? You said he's your great-great-grandfather?"

"How old is Lon? How old is dirt! He's ancient. He and Anna have had about a hundred kids."

Micah blinked, a slight smile on his face, but saw that Perryn was absolutely serious. And she seemed to be telling the truth. At the very least, she truly believed what she was saying.

"They should have thousands of descendants by now, then."

"You really are ignorant, aren't you? Ignorant as in uninformed; no offense. Sorcerers have a difficult time having children. Those they do produce tend to be either lacking in magical talent or dangerously unstable. Something to do with the generational impact of too much diwa infection. I don't know. And it gets worse with succeeding generations, so that their first descendants have a harder time having children, and it's even harder for the next generation. And so on, and so on."

"So you're saying that you're a rare exception?"

Perryn laughed. "Rare? I'm a fifth generation sorceress of considerable power, and I'm not crazy. I'm not just rare; I'm the only one of my kind, as far as anyone knows. I don't know if I can have children yet, 'cause I haven't tried. I'm in no hurry, and no, you may not convince me otherwise, tempting as that might be."

It took Micah a few beats to figure out what she was talking about, at which point he blushed furiously, embarrassed into silence.

Perryn smiled at him, but the look on her face was odd. She looked . . . incredulous, as if she couldn't believe what she was seeing. She pointed at him. "You're . . . the younger son of Valdis Hittrech? His older daughter was Kellyn. I knew her when she was little. But you said you never met your father? Was he dead before you were born?"

Micah nodded.

"Oh. Oh! You . . . you're ten years old? Ten! I've been flirting with a ten-year-old? Uggh!"

Micah stared at the floor. "I told you everything I know," he said, quietly. "It isn't my fault you weren't paying attention."

Perryn shook her head. "Fine. Just sit there, then, little boy. I'll let you know when it's ready."

Micah sat, staring at the piles of papers, wondering if he could really kill Lon, and if he might have to get rid of Perryn, too. Gradually, he mastered his anger and tried to focus on something else. Every sheet of paper he could see had writing on it, most of it in the letters he'd seen on signs and papers all his life, letters he'd come to think of as Kattenese, rounded, loopy letters with dots inside and above most of them. Other letters looked remarkably different, angular, more like tiny pictures than letters. Some looked like the symbols Lon had written on the floor of the palace, in the hidden room with the mosaic tile floor. The style of those letters was the same as those that had been on the coach. Magical. If only he could read. If only someone would teach him. Perhaps the girl could be useful.

He waited a bit, watching the girl until she finally glanced in his direction. "Perryn? I'm sorry."

She sighed heavily. "My fault, too. You're right, I didn't really listen. You look a lot older than ten, is all. Your parents are sorcerers, and I think three of your grandparents, too. So you act older than a non-magical kid would. And you're cute. I don't meet too many sorcerers my age, you know? And now that I think of it, ten isn't really that much younger than me. Maybe in seven or eight years, I'll flirt with you again."

Micah looked up, sure she was making fun of him, but she flashed a warm and genuine smile. He smiled back. "Can you teach me to read?"

Perryn's eyes went wide and the smile dropped off her face. "Your mom never taught you?"

"No."

Perryn's mouth closed tightly, her lips forming a thin, straight line. "I'll do better than teach you," Perryn said, quietly. "When you're feeling better, I'll help you enact a knowledge spell. You'll be able to read in minutes."

"Really? Any language?"

"One at a time, and you need to let each new language settle into your mind for several days before trying a new one. Thurnic first, because you can't be educated without it. I hate to say it, but it's true: most of the world's knowledge is available only in Thurnic. Then Ancient Magic, for obvious reasons. Maybe follow it up with Kattenese? It'd be a nice touch, considering your parentage. Not that there's anything especially useful about Kattenese."

"It's really that easy?"

"Who said anything about easy? No, it's actually very difficult. That settling process is harder than it sounds. In fact, I better talk to Lon first. You'll be the next best thing to useless while you're learning a new language. If he needs you to help rescue Kellyn, we better not start right away."

Micah nodded, but he'd rather be useless. If the Prince's men executed Kellyn, his mother's plans would come to naught, wouldn't they?

Not long after, Lon and Anna joined them in the kitchen. Lon checked the gris, and complimented Perryn's work. Lon, though he spoke in the light tones of a man without a care, moved stiffly, muscles taut and face set in a painted-on smile. Micah looked closely at Anna, whose face was splotchy and wet, as if she'd been weeping.

Perryn must sensed something, too, because she kept sneaking glances at her great-great-grandmother. Anna would not look at her. Finally, Perryn cleared her throat. "Lon? I need to ask you a question."

"Yes?"

"I'd like to take over some of Micah's education. Beginning with reading. May I?"

Lon pressed his lips together and narrowed his eyes. Anna turned to stare at her husband. "So he doesn't know how to read, eh?" she asked, glaring at Lon. "Not in any language? Sarah never taught him? Now, why would that be, I wonder?"

Perryn and Micah exchanged glances. Lon would not meet anyone's eyes. "No," he said quietly. "We are going to need Micah's ability to move stone. I can't have him lost in a learning spell."

"That's it, then?" asked Anna. Her shoulders slumped, and she looked like she was about to cry again. "Nothing else matters?"

"We have discussed this," Lon said, quietly. "Will you help, or won't you?"

"What choice do I have? But think about what I said earlier. I meant every word."

Lon nodded, but still wouldn't look her in the eye.

Whatever had just occurred, Micah felt sure something momentous had passed between the elder sorcerers. A glance at Perryn told him she'd seen it as well, though the glare with which she impaled Lon made it clear she'd chosen sides.

"Perryn, prepare meals for all of us, and we should all get some rest," Lon said. "Tomorrow, we attack the castle to free Kellyn."

16

Kellyn found that her impending death brought a measure of calm. With no way out of the cell, Captain Zang firmly ensconced in the Prince's camp, and her father's soul waiting to possess her body, she would die, likely soon. Either Prince Johann would return from his hunting trip to enjoy his revenge, or Lon would 'rescue' her only to draw her father's soul out into the open. Felida, as evidenced by Lon's impersonation of her, must surely be dead.

But why hadn't Lon enacted the latent spell when he had Kellyn under his control? There was clearly more going on here, information she didn't have, and likely never would. Reviewing what she knew about possession didn't take very long. It wasn't a subject a young mage would ever delve into with any depth. Magrahim had covered it only briefly. So, what was there?

First, two souls could not permanently inhabit the same body. One of the souls must perish. Second, a soul could only permanently inhabit the body it was born into, which seriously reduced the effectiveness of possessing another person. Third, a body without a soul could only be preserved for a matter of days, maybe weeks. And yet her father's soul had lain hidden within her for ten years.

If her father's soul were to possess her, Kellyn's soul or her father's must flee to the afterlife within days, weeks at the most. Her father's soul could not long remain in her body, and his body had been dead for a decade. So far as she knew, it was not possible to bring a dead body back to life. Necromancy might reanimate the dead, but in no sense were such creatures alive.

So, what had her father hoped to accomplish? Kellyn could only wish for more knowledge, and wishes had a habit of remaining unfulfilled. And so she deliberately turned her mind from the manner of her approaching death, and wondered instead what death would be like. Many people thought of the Brotherhood as a kind of religious order, but it was nothing of the sort. Mages from all over the world, many with beliefs completely at odds with worship of the Thurnic pantheon, worked side by side regardless of which god or gods they worshipped. They all had their own beliefs about the afterlife. In fact, the only thing upon which they agreed was the existence of some form of life after death.

But Kellyn didn't have a religion. She thought she believed in something, but she could not have said what it was. Had her parents ever tried to teach her about religion? If so, she couldn't remember. Magrahim worshipped the Mohotsan sun god, but he would not allow Kellyn to join him when he prayed. The sun god would only bestow favors on his chosen people, the Mohotsans. The thought of choosing a god to worship at this point felt both desperate and dishonest. Perhaps it had been easier in ancient times, when the gods walked the earth. The god or goddess that ruled your land, in those times, owned your soul.

Her thoughts were interrupted by noise outside her barred window. Above the sounds of a city just awakening, she could hear shouting, the clash of weapons, and the sharp crack of nearby thunder. "That's odd," she said. "There's not a cloud in the sky."

But then she knew. Someone was practicing some very powerful sorcery out there. And the sounds were getting closer. Perhaps she wouldn't be executed after all. Perhaps, instead, she would be possessed, if the sorcerer hurling lightning bolts were Lon, coming to break her out of this prison and bring her father back to life. She turned to face the door, certain that at any moment Lon would come bursting through.

"Kellyn!"

She spun around, and saw something she never thought she'd live to see again: Jirra! Her face was pressed up against the bars of the cell window, and she snaked a hand through. Kellyn ran to the window and grasped her hand. Any thoughts she might have had that Jirra had betrayed her to Lon and 'Niko' were instantly dispelled. "How? I mean, what are you doing here?"

"We don't have much time. Felida sent me."

"Felida? She's alive?"

"Yes. It's a long story, and I hope I have time to share it with you one day. But right now, there's a sorcerer and a small army battering their way through to the castle. Felida thinks they're coming for you, and we can't think of a way to stop them." She took her hand away, and fed the end of a length of rope through the bars. "Your hands are both free. Tie this to the bars. Tightly!"

Kellyn had a thousand questions, but as Jirra said, they had no time. She tied the strongest knot she could think of, then brought Jirra's hand to her lips and kissed her battered and dusty fingers. She must have free-climbed the tower from the street below. Kellyn longed to hold her in her arms. Jirra smiled back at her, but tears welled in her eyes.

"I'm so sorry, Kellyn. Felida says it's the only way."

"What do you mean?"

Jirra pulled her hand away. "Step into the center of the cell, please. Do you remember, Felida once told you that she might have to do something very unpleasant in order to save you?"

Kellyn nodded, and moved to the center of the room. She had a terrible suspicion that she knew what was coming next.

"I'm so sorry," said Jirra. "I wish it didn't have to be me. But Felida couldn't make the climb."

"Don't worry. Do what you have to do." Kellyn spread her arms wide. She thought she should close her eyes, but she couldn't drag her eyes away from Jirra. "Once this is done, you'll need to get away very quickly. I don't think you'll like who I am about to become."

"Felida warned me. I'll slide down the rope. It won't take a minute." She was weeping softly, tears falling silently down her boyish face. "I'm sorry," she repeated.

"Don't be. We'll see each other again. I swear it."

Jirra nodded. She took a few breaths, gathering herself, then looked into Kellyn's eyes and said, "Valdis Hittrech, come forth! I summon thee, possess this body, take life!"

Kellyn was smiling at her as it happened. The black ball within her split open, and what waited inside poured forth like water over a broken dam. It swept over everything before it, drowning Kellyn in her own body. She felt control slipping. Limbs, breathing, speech, everything falling away as her father's soul took command. She thought she would simply let it happen, but the flood crept into her mouth and down her throat, into nostrils and lungs. Panic welled within her, the sensation of drowning close to overwhelming, but she found she still had some control. She could move her head and see through her eyes, though only with great effort. She fought savagely for her eyes, so that her last sight might be Jirra. But she had already let go of the bars and slid out of view.

And then sight left her. A dim awareness of her body came to her as she slumped to the floor. Something else tried to control her movements then, but she jerked and spasmed painfully. She felt like a marionette in the hands of an unskilled puppeteer. The puppet master seized control more firmly, violating Kellyn in a way no physical abuse could imitate. A burning sensation, the kind one only experienced with extreme cold, crept over her, and a vile, oily viscosity replaced the sense of drowning. An urge to vomit took her, but she had no throat, no stomach, no body at all. Whatever she was, at that moment, it seemed distant, impossibly remote, the oily, sticky sludge congealing into a prison that prevented her from sensing the world around her. She tried to gasp for air, but no longer had lungs with which to breathe. Panic finally overcame her—she screamed in silence.

Perryn laughed out loud as she wielded a weapon far more fearsome than Micah's invisible sword. He cringed and flinched, though he was in no danger. She swung the fire whip in a loop above her head, snapping it forward. When she did, the whip shot ahead of them in a streak of flames, engulfing three of the Prince's soldiers. When the whip cracked and jerked back, the men exploded. Most soldiers who witnessed her attacks fled like frightened children; Micah could sympathize, as he also felt the urge to run.

The narrow street between rows of townhomes filled with a shrieking mass of people, most of them townsfolk caught up in a fight from which they desperately sought to flee, but the buildings crowded so close upon one another that no one could escape. From the direction of the castle, more of the Prince's men tried to force their way through the civilians, but there weren't enough of them. Thanks to Anna, most of the Prince's soldiers were dealing with a violent demonstration on the other side of town.

At an intersection, the crowd split and ran to the right or left, and it took Micah a few heartbeats to discover why: a solid phalanx of armored soldiers blocked their path. The enemy lowered steel-tipped spears over the tops of their shields and advanced to the beat of a drum, slow and steady. They looked like death personified, and Micah felt his feet getting heavier. He thought about allowing Lon and Perryn and their tiny handful of supporters go on ahead of him, but the press of bodies forced him to the front.

The Prince's forces, however, weren't numerous, a phalanx only two men deep, and twenty across. Lon shouted, and Micah felt the hairs on the back of his neck stand up. The ancient sorcerer raised his hands in the air, and between them a ball of lightning began to form, jagged spikes of energy spilling out in all directions as Lon mumbled the words that kept the spell alive. Suddenly, the ball of lightning burst, sending Lon, Perryn, and Micah, as well as several of their supporters, sprawling in all directions.

"They've got a mage!" Perryn shouted as she staggered back to her feet. Some of the ordinary men who'd come with them began to edge away, ready to flee at any moment. Anna had gathered their supporters, men who'd fought in Valdis Hittrech's rebellion and had hidden ever since, sending them to Lon with whatever weapons they found at hand, often no more than pitchforks or clubs. These men hadn't fought or trained in years, and the professional killers in plate steel advancing toward them brought them to the edge of flight.

"There!" Perryn pointed at a man in dark robes at the center of the oncoming phalanx. "There! Concentrate on the mage!"

Perryn and Lon both attacked the mage, and he could do little against two sorcerers besides defend himself and the soldiers nearby. That still left a few dozen soldiers coming at them, and swords and spears could kill just as effectively as spells. Micah crouched and placed one hand on the surface of the road, drawing diwa from the stones, as Perryn had planned with him earlier. Each grapefruit sized stone contained only a little diwa, but there were thousands of them on the road, and he drew the power to him in a growing web of energy. He held the strands of the web in his hands, and as the advancing soldiers stepped on new stones, he felt their booted feet like tiny points of pressure.

He focused and tried not to think about the fact that he'd never done anything like this before. The feel of all those booted feet gave him a target, as Perryn had predicted. "Do you think you can do it?" she had asked. Micah had said he could, but his confidence seeped away now that the moment had come.

He reached out, grabbed hundreds of gossamer thin strands of diwa in his hands, and shoved, hard. The cobblestones tore loose from the road and flew at the soldiers. Some of the stones underneath the soldiers flew away as well, so that even those men who weren't hit by the flying stones found their footing suddenly giving way beneath them. More importantly, the mage in the center of the phalanx fell with a soldier on top of him, and that was all the opening Lon and Perryn needed. With lightning and flame, they slaughtered most of the Prince's men. Perryn snapped her whip at the center of the disintegrated phalanx, and the resulting explosion sent bits of armor—and bits of unfortunate men—flying. Lon formed the ball of energy above his head once more and lashed out with several bolts of lightning at once. Men died less spectacularly when hit by the bolts, but they died just the same. When only a few remained standing and unhurt, the survivors, as well as their officer-mage, turned to run.

"Let them go!" Lon shouted. "To the gates!"

They ran for the nearest entrance to the castle, each of them gagging down little packets of Lon's healing food. The gates, fortunately, stood open. And why not? Until just minutes ago, there had been no reason to bar them. Now it was too late. They stormed through, intent on the tower that held Kellyn. For all that Micah didn't want to rescue her, he ran with as much enthusiasm as anyone else. This was what true power felt like!

They reached the base of the tower, then fought their way up a stairway to find an entrance along the castle wall. The men standing before them presented no serious threat, just garrison soldiers, too old or too young to do any real fighting, and badly shaken as they were by bolts of lightning and sheets of flame, most of them ran without trying to defend themselves.

Perryn reached an undefended door and blasted it to splinters while Lon created a shield of solidified air to protect them from the concussion and shrapnel. The three of them ran up the stairs while their friends stopped to hold off any soldiers foolish enough to try to follow. Lon stopped at a landing, pulled out his blood compass and whispered a few words. "Up," he said. Four more flights, until they were almost at the top, where he cried, "Stop! This way."

He led them away from the stairway, where a lone soldier attacked. Lon was first, and concentrating so much on the compass that he didn't have time to defend himself. The soldier stabbed Lon in the chest before Perryn or Micah could react. Perryn screamed in rage, but Micah recovered first, cutting the soldier in half at the waist with his sorcerer's sword.

Perryn raised an eyebrow in Micah's direction. "Nice. I'll tend to Lon, you find your sister."

Micah stared at the body for a second or two, then shook himself and looked around. There were three doors, all of them barred. He cut through the bars with his sorcerer's sword and checked the rooms, one by one. In the third, Kellyn lay on the floor, asleep or dead. Micah entered. "Kellyn? Are you alive? We're here to rescue you."

Kellyn blinked, slowly focused on Micah. "Wha?"

"Hurry! We need to get out of here before the Prince's men realize what we're up to!" She didn't move, and though Micah really didn't want to touch her, he reached down and hauled his sister to her feet. "Get moving! Now!"

He turned, roughly yanking his sister along, to find Perryn trying to stop the bleeding from a nasty looking gash in the center of Lon's chest. Lon looked gray. He grimaced, tried to speak, and instead moaned. Blood pumped out of the wound, and Micah wondered if he would die. He wondered, too, if he could kill the three of them. Perhaps, but how then would he escape the castle?

"Step . . . aside," said Kellyn. "Lon, can . . . can you hear me? It's me, Valdis."

Micah stopped to look at Kellyn, noticing for the first time that his 'sister' looked terrible, older somehow, less coordinated. She shoved Micah to the floor. "I said, step aside!" Kellyn, or Valdis, or whoever, stumbled a bit, knelt by Lon's side and placed her hands over the wound. She mouthed some words silently, and plunged her fingers into the gash. Lon shrieked, and Perryn backed away, her eyes wide and fixed upon Kellyn/Valdis.

"Who are you?" Micah asked.

"I am V-Valdis Hittrech, now . . . be silent! If I am to . . . save Lon, I m-must concentrate!" Valdis continued to work on Lon, and slowly withdrew her fingers. The skin closed around the wound, but blood still seeped from a jagged, red line. Valdis frowned and swore, drew her palm over the line, again and again, and it faded from red to pink, finally leaving nothing but a white scar.

Valdis slumped to her side. "I assume y-you . . . brought Lon's wonder-food along," she croaked. She began to tremble all over.

Perryn acted first, stuffing a little ball of food into Valdis' mouth, and then the same for Lon. "Are either of you well enough to move?"

she asked. The sounds of shouting and running feet came from the stairwell. "Quickly, now. The Prince's men approach!"

Lon tried and failed to raise his head. Valdis stood shakily. "Plan?" she asked.

"Lon was to create a protective shell for us. Can you do that?"

"In my old body . . . yes. In this one, I'm not sure. Who . . . whose body do I wear?"

Perryn glanced from Micah to Valdis before answering. "Your daughter's. Kellyn Hittrech."

Valdis covered her eyes with her hands, shook her head violently as she snapped off a string of curses in a language Micah didn't speak. Finally, she regained her composure, and breathed deeply. "I-I can, but not for long . . . and not while moving. I'm not used to this b-body, but it does feel slightly . . . familiar. Now?"

The sounds of shouting came closer. "Yes, Lord Hittrech. Now."

Valdis raised her hands, clapped them together and shouted. A sphere of energy formed around them, encompassing the section of floor on which they stood, knelt, and laid. Sounds still penetrated; they could hear booted feet running up the stairs. Micah knelt and pushed his hands slowly through the protective shell so he could touch the stone of the tower walls. Perryn had said that only slow-moving objects could penetrate the shell. He reached deep within the stones, thousands of them, like the cobblestones, but much more massive. And the further down he went, the larger the stones became, until he reached the massive blocks at the tower's base, each a cube five feet on a side. Cumulatively, more diwa than he had ever felt resided in these stones, though the granite boulders back in the quarry had been more powerful individually.

Gathering all that power, from all those different sources, nearly overwhelmed him, and he felt his grasp beginning to slip. Soon, it wouldn't matter. He began pulling and pushing, but the stone blocks had been set and mortared perfectly, and they were extremely difficult to move.

"Hurry, Micah," Perryn said. "Is something wrong?"

"No! Quiet!" Finally, the blocks began to shift, crushing the mortar between them to dust. He pushed harder, using more diwa than ever before. Their protective sphere shifted and started to roll. A circular section of floor came with them, still intact and sliding around on the inner surface of the spherical shell. Micah ignored it all, reaching for the biggest blocks with the most diwa. After what seemed like an hour, but was probably no more than a few minutes, the tower leaned drunkenly, and with a sudden roar, the entire structure gave way, collapsing to the ground in a shower of massive stone blocks and a noise like the end of the world.

Micah tried to snatch his hands back through the layer of energy, but found his fingers stuck. He remembered then to pull them in slowly, despite the fear that his fingers would be sheared off as the tower fell. Valdis' sphere held. Stones falling from above bounced away, and they found themselves rolling among a vast field of debris that had taken down not only the tower, but a fair length of the castle wall, as well. Valdis released the shell, and Micah and Perryn hauled Lon between them while Valdis stumbled after.

"To the safe house," Perryn said. They made it a couple of blocks, through awed and mostly silent crowds of people staring at the empty place where a section of castle had stood only moments before. A woman approached and offered to help, but Perryn said, "We're well enough. Go to the tower! All of you! There are people buried in the rubble. They need help!"

Several townsfolk ran to help, though many melted away from the street. Buoyed as he was by his success, Micah began to fade. "I need rest and food," he said to Perryn. "Valdis, too."

"Not long."

It wasn't. A few more blocks brought them to an apothecary's shop, full of herbs and powders and liquids, most of them completely useless, the sort of stuff that people who couldn't afford magical healing bought to ward off disease. The proprietor of the dusty shop, a stooped old man with cloudy eyes and a pronounced limp, led them to a back room. Without a word, the man left, closing the door behind him.

When they had settled in, eaten Lon's food, washed, and tried to find a comfortable position in which to sleep, Perryn asked the question on Micah's mind. "What now?"

Lon had lost consciousness, and Valdis wasn't in much better shape. Still, she answered. "We need to get to Lon's palace. I assume h-he still has Engvar?" Micah nodded. "Good. We're in D'Arrune, yes? I thought I . . . recognized the castle."

"Yes, D'Arrune," Perryn said.

Valdis shook her head. "A hundred miles? More, I think. We need to get word to Lon's man Chase as soon as possible. But we'll . . . need disguises. They'll have d-descriptions of all of us. If we can get to the palace safely, none of that will matter. We'll work out a way to solve this little problem," she said, touching her chest, "and all will be well."

Valdis paced the little room then, shuffling and muttering to herself in a language Micah couldn't understand. Lon hadn't moved, and might have been a corpse if not for a barely detectable rising and falling of his chest. When Micah looked at Perryn, he found her staring at him. They made eye contact, but she looked away quickly. He wanted to ask her a hundred questions, and his father/sister a million more, but neither one of them looked in his direction, and he couldn't think of anything to say. Nor was he strong enough to ponder his situation much longer. He slept.

17

A featureless gray void, like being trapped in the thickest fog bank any sailor had ever seen. But where was the ship under her feet, the creak of rope and wood and leather?

Am I dead? she thought. The words felt strange. She had tried to speak aloud, but she had no mouth with which to speak, no ears to hear. Even thoughts felt odd, muffled somehow, like the whole world was pressing. *Pressing in on . . . me? Who am I?*

No body, no memory, no world around her. She felt panic bubbling up from within. *Within me? It can't be. I don't have a form. I'm just a . . . a something. But what?*

There was a word for what she was, a word she could almost see, even feel its shape, but she became distracted by the first external sensation: thunder! The world made a sound, and she heard it!

But was it really thunder? It might have been the angry shouting of a giant, a being with a voice like the biggest storm the world had ever known. It certainly sounded angry. If she concentrated, the noise became words, but not words in any language she knew. For a while she was certain the sound was the ranting of an angry god, that she truly was dead. But if she were dead, then she must at some point have been alive. Alive, with a body under her control.

There was something there, just at the edge of perception, something about having no body. It felt wrong. She did have a body, only . . . someone or something else controlled it. More sound penetrated her foggy awareness. Words, still angry, but in a language she recognized. And a voice that felt familiar.

"I can, but not for long, and not while moving. I'm not used to this body, but it does feel slightly familiar. Now?"

And another voice, softer, female, unfamiliar. "Yes, Lord Hittrech. Now."

Lord Hittrech? she thought. *That's me! I am . . . Kellyn Hittrech! Wait, 'Lord'? Shouldn't that be 'Lady'?* Her joy at remembering dampened a little, though, by her inability to control her body, even to sense anything beyond the dimly heard words. A new sensation began to creep into her awareness. Something flowing through her body, into her fingers, a powerful force, and oddly familiar.

"Hurry, Micah. Is something wrong?" A female voice. She had spoken before. She called Kellyn, 'Lord Hittrech'.

"No! Quiet!" A new voice. Male, young, and afraid. Micah? She couldn't place names to either voice, but the boy sounded familiar. Time passed, but she had no way of measuring it. Then thunder again, but different this time. Not as sharp. More like a bunch of very large stones tumbling down a hill. Beyond the sound, other senses began to report. She was falling, bouncing. She could smell dust and needed to sneeze. Finally, she stopped moving, and the power that flowed through her body ceased at once.

Diwa, she thought. *That was diwa. But that's wrong. It wouldn't flow through me like that. Only sorcerers do that. I'm not a sorcerer. I'm a . . . I'm a mage!*

Memories began to come back, then, little by little, and in no particular order. She felt hampered by the exhaustion that overtook her body, a body someone else controlled, using diwa in a way strictly forbidden. She felt hungry, like she hadn't eaten in days, and began to tremble. Her body moved, and there were more sounds, more words. There were four of them. A man named Lon was with them, too, and they were moving as quickly as they could to a safe house. A safe house in D'Arrune. They were waiting for a man named Chase to take them to

Lon's palace. Her body ate something foul tasting, and the exhaustion began to fade.

None of the words made any sense. If only she could see. If only her memories would return in full.

If only her body was hers to control.

If only she hadn't been . . . possessed. Possessed by Valdis Hittrech.

It was coming back now, all of it. Valdis lay down, and just before he closed Kellyn's eyes, she caught a glimpse of the room they were in. A dusty storeroom of some kind, full of jars and bottles, the smell of medicinal herbs strong in the air. The other three people were visible, but only for a moment. It was difficult, looking through eyes controlled by someone else. She wanted to focus on the faces, but Valdis wasn't really paying attention to them. She thought she recognized Micah, but he'd gone by a different name. Niko? And Lon was definitely the same man who impersonated, and likely killed, Felida.

Yes, it was all coming back, but suddenly Kellyn wished it hadn't. All seemed lost, until she remembered Jirra. She remembered seeing her outside the bars of her cell window. She had released Valdis to possess Kellyn's body. Why? Because Felida told her to. And Felida had said she might have to do something horrible in order to save her. *Felida's still alive, and I'm not lost yet. There's a way out of this. I just have to find it.*

They moved at night, from one safe house to another, under assumed names, speaking to no one, if possible. Like scared mice, scurrying about the kitchen, afraid of getting caught by the cat.

The Prince's soldiers swarmed the city; no one moved without their permission. Officially, anyway. They'd been on the move for a week now, and had yet to encounter any soldiers. Evidently, the Prince's net had wide gaps. But they would eventually run out of hiding places; they needed a way out of the city. To Micah's way of thinking, they were doomed. The basement of an inn was their current refuge. They lay among stacks of crates and barrels and bushels, secure in the knowledge that the owner was yet another of Lon's many friends. He hadn't told the owner about Valdis, though. There was a reward for the return of

'Kellyn,' a reward that might double or more, if they were to find out that his sister was now Valdis.

Footsteps on the trapdoor above their heads. Two fast knocks, three slow, and two more fast. The door opened, spilling dust and daylight into their hiding place. A ladder slid into the basement, and Chase climbed down. Lon stood and clapped his servant on the shoulder. Chase grunted; that was his bad shoulder, the one that had been per- forated by an arrow just a week ago. But he used the arm without too much obvious pain.

Valdis stayed seated against a wall with his legs splayed out in front of him. Or her. It was weird, thinking of his sister as a man now. Even weirder that she was now his father. She still looked female, though she really wasn't very feminine. From certain angles she looked just like a man. Micah shrugged. Valdis looked terrible, red-rimmed eyes half closed, face pale, hands trembling. Every time they had to move it seemed to take more out of him. Or her. Micah thought perhaps his father/sister might die. So many problems would solve themselves if the two of them were to be removed.

"What news?" Lon asked. He had improved dramatically since his wounding at the castle. Valdis had gotten worse.

"The gates are sealed, and they've put a temporary wall where the tower used to be," Chase said. "No one in or out. But I've found an escape route. The old postern gate."

"What's that?" Micah asked quietly.

Perryn, seated next to him on the floor, answered, "It's a secret way out of a castle or a walled town. Usually a tunnel with a barred and carefully disguised exit well beyond the wall."

"They aren't . . . watching the postern gate?" Valdis said in a hoarse whisper, clearly skeptical.

Chase smiled. "There are two postern gates. The newer one is being watched, but the original collapsed in an earthquake thirty years ago. The entrance inside the walls was sealed up, but the exit was left alone."

"But it's collapsed, you say?" Lon asked.

"A section of it has been secretly restored. It's used chiefly by smugglers, now. The Prince must not know about it, or it would be guarded as well. I had to bribe heavily and often to learn of its existence. They'll demand more to allow us to use it."

"Why wouldn't they turn us in for the reward?" Micah asked.

Lon sneered. "Because we know about their operation. If they turn us in, we'll turn them in. The best kinds of business deals are those in which each party holds a knife to the other's throat."

"When d-do we move?" asked Valdis.

"Tonight." Chase left with the promise to return when all was arranged. While he was gone, there was little to do. They ate. Perryn prepared little packets of gris-food. They slept. Lon tried to talk to Valdis, but the man wearing Kellyn's body only grunted in response. The scowl on his face might have been etched in stone. Eventually, Lon gave up and settled in for a nap.

The possession of his sister by his father's soul had started to make the girl look masculine. She even looked older, now. He wondered if she were actually becoming a man. When Perryn had finished pre- paring what little they would take with them, she sat next to Micah and sighed.

"I hate waiting," she said.

"Me, too. So, what happens after?"

Perryn looked away. "You mean once we get out of the city?"

Micah shook his head. "Once we get to Engvar. It seems like things are kind of messed up."

"Not sure what you mean."

Micah smiled. Perryn was lying. He decided to do something he rarely did: reveal something about himself. "Perryn, I can always tell when someone is lying. You know what happens once we get back to the palace, but you're hiding it from me. Why?" Micah stared at Perryn, but he could see movement out of the corner of his eye. Valdis watched them.

"Honestly, Micah, I don't know. I have some guesses, but no more than that. What is your truth sense telling you now?"

Micah nodded. "True so far."

"Good. You've figured out that Valdis possessed your sister's body, and that Valdis is your father. Somehow, he and Lon and your mother conjured up a way to preserve Valdis' soul within your sister's body for ten years. I don't know how, and I'm desperate to hear that tale, but it may remain a sorcerer's secret. Valdis hasn't told anyone how it came to be that he has possessed his daughter, or why, or any other details. But I know that wasn't the plan." She turned to Valdis and said, "Was it, my lord?"

Valdis stared at Perryn, and it seemed he wouldn't answer. Eventually, he sighed and said, "There was a girl. When I first took over . . . this body, her face was outside the bars of the cell I was in. She was only there for an instant, and then she dr-dropped out of view. She released me from . . . my self-imposed captivity."

"How do you know it was her?" Perryn asked.

Valdis shook his head, still frowning deeply. "The method we created, Sarah and I . . . is a new thing in the world. We didn't know how the soul would react to confinement, or to a sudden release. I feel an . . . . uncomfortable bond with the girl who freed me. It wasn't supposed to happen this w-way."

"You were supposed to revive your old body, yes?" said Perryn. She was looking at Valdis, but he was staring blankly, eyes unfocused. Perryn shifted her gaze to Micah, an intent look on her face, like she was trying to tell him something without saying it out loud. He had no idea what she was trying to communicate.

"Sarah had contacts," Valdis continued. "She said she'd be able to retrieve my remains. No matter how . . . little was left, it would have worked. We'd prepared for this. She drained some of my blood before I . . . left. Took a lock of my . . . my hair. We made other preparations. Lon's palace was to be the sight of my r-rebirth. Sarah was supposed to remove my soul from Kellyn's body without freeing it from its prison, implant it in my new body, and then call me forth. I would have awoken in my . . . own body, and Kellyn would still be alive."

No one spoke for a while. "But she is still alive," Perryn whispered.

"For now."

"Why can't you transport yourself, like Lon?" Micah asked.

Valdis did not look in his direction. "I can't"

"Few sorcerers can do that," Perryn said. "Lon is quite powerful. Your mother can do it, too, but I don't know of anyone else alive who can."

"I did it," said Micah. They both looked at him. "I told you, Perryn. When I said I followed Lon, I meant it literally. He opened a doorway and stepped through. I stepped in, too."

Perryn stared at him. "I guess I didn't appreciate what you were telling me. So how did the two of you become separated?"

"I don't know. I suppose he closed the doorway when he arrived. I was a step behind, so maybe when the door closed, the passage collapsed? I wasn't all the way through, so I only made it part way. I guess."

"Makes sense. Except for the part about you following him. That's not supposed to be possible," she said, the look on her face halfway between skepticism and awe.

Valdis turned away from them and lay down. "Let me rest."

Micah had more questions, but Perryn shook her head and settled in to sleep. He thought there was no way he could sleep. Nor should he: there were things not being said. He felt sure that he could work it out, if he could only keep the two of them talking. But soon enough, the only sounds were the heavy breathing of three people, and Micah found his breathing slowing to match their rhythm. His eyes began to droop.

###

Kellyn didn't seem to get tired anymore. It was strange, since she'd felt exhaustion at first, but as time wore on, she felt less and less of what her body was doing. That couldn't be good. How long before she couldn't even hear what was going on around her? She had no body, no mind for her thoughts to flow through, no need for a constant supply of energy. So why would she feel fatigue? That was a plus, at least. Valdis, however, using this unfamiliar body, seemed to be worn out. He slept, but only in fits and starts. When his eyes would flutter open, Kellyn could see through them. She could hear as well, but only when Valdis was awake. When he slept, it was as if a thick fog covered the world, the only other sensation a sound like rain on a cobbled road.

Kellyn's thoughts kept coming back to her predicament, and the fact that she couldn't see a way out. She tried not thinking about it, and failed miserably. She tried to meditate, but with no body to calm, she found it impossible to focus. She had her thoughts, and the noise. It was soft, kind of like rain, but also like a room full of people whispering.

Rain. Whispering. A room full of whispering people, rain falling on the roof. She tried to focus on individual raindrops, and found that she couldn't. There were no raindrops. But when she focused on the whispering, words emerged. Her father's memories? Words spoken in that other body, the one that had died, the one her mother wanted to revive.

She didn't want to think about that, about a mother and father who'd used their little girl as a means of hiding the soul of Valdis Hittrech. Never mind that Kellyn would have died if Prince Johann had gotten his hands on her. They had used her, the way one might use a tool. She'd known for a long time now what a monster her father had been, but she'd somehow managed to convince herself that her mother was different. Mothers were supposed to be different, weren't they? Not Sarah Hittrech, though. She was every bit the monster her husband was. Is. Whatever. It would be so easy to give up, to sink into a black despair and await her fate.

The words began to separate from the other noise. Memories, or a dream? Her father was speaking to someone, a woman. He was whispering to her, professing his love. She spoke back, frantic, passionate. Kellyn wanted the dream to stop; she couldn't eavesdrop on her parents making love. As soon as she wished the dream/memory to stop, it faded away.

There were other words, other conversations. She focused on them, one by one. Some were the grunts, curses, and magical words shouted in combat. Some were orders given, subordinates praised or punished. Some were boring, or bored. She sifted through them for what seemed like days, though every time her father woke, it seemed that hardly any time had passed at all. She found other conversations between her parents. Conversations that felt old, much older than she believed her parents to be. She listened, but the words blurred together. When she grew disinterested, the words would fade, and she would focus in another direction, find another remembered discussion, monologue, debate, fight. Always she searched for memories of her mother, irrationally desperate for some evidence that her mother's soul had not been as devoid of value as her father's.

She listened to dozens of conversations. Once she found what must have been a terrifying incident in Valdis' childhood, when he had inadvertently used sorcery for the first time. But the next memory came from many years later. She found her parents first encounter, in some secret meeting between sorcerers planning some outrageous bit of magic. They argued, a lot. Kellyn found herself as a young girl, asking her father how to make a fireball. After what seemed like forever, she found another memory of a conversation between her parents. There was no intimacy involved, but there was certainly passion. They were yelling at each other. She focused on this one exclusively, concentrating hard on the words, which began to emerge, distinct, definable.

" . . . another way, I would do it," Valdis said.

"You ask too much of me!" her mother shouted back. "I can bear you another child, a son if you wish. But you cannot ask this of me!"

"I ask nothing! I am telling you!"

They were silent for a time. Finally, she pleaded with him. "Don't, Valdis. Please don't. We can preserve your soul. You could possess anyone once it's safe to come out of hiding."

"We have been over this. I will not jump from one body to another. I'd have no more than a few weeks before I would have to move to another body. Where would we find such a string of victims without attracting attention? And more to the point, I could not do what you suggest indefinitely. The soul is damaged with each possession. It would become so degraded that I would no longer really be myself after a few years."

"Then we would have a few years. Give me that. Give your daughter those years, that she may know and remember you. She will avenge your death."

There was silence again, and Kellyn nearly moved on to another memory before her mother spoke again.

"This thing you speak of . . ."

"Will give me life again! In a body young and strong, free of the ravages that have weakened me to the point that I cannot even stand against the mages. With the strength of youth, and the lessons of my experience, I will be the strongest sorcerer the world has ever known! And Kellyn will live, to fight at my side. What more could we want?"

"But the cost! You would have me bear a son, raise him, and sacrifice him so that you can live again! Don't you hear what you're saying? I don't . . . I can't do it."

"Do you not love me, Sarah?"

Her mother sobbed fiercely. "Don't say that! How can you do this?"

"No more argument! I command you!" Her father's voice, even in memory, had a power that Kellyn had only read about. When he wanted, her father could force others to do his bidding with words alone. Felida had shown that she had a bit of that talent, but it paled in comparison to her father's ability.

More importantly, the actual meaning of her parents' argument had finally sunk in. Valdis had forced Sarah to have another child, one they would sacrifice to bring her father back to life. That child was Micah, Kellyn saw with sudden and absolute certainty. But why had they brought her brother along for such a dangerous mission? Micah had said he'd followed Lon. Had Lon not known about that?

Whatever Lon knew, Kellyn saw with perfect clarity that Micah did not know their plan. She had to warn her brother. If Micah could get away, Valdis could not live again.

Yes, her father was evil. And her mother, to an extent. But she had resisted. She had wanted no part in this inhuman plan. There might be something redeemable left in her after all. But for her father? Nothing.

The move came well past midnight. Micah yawned, but excitement soon dispelled his sleepiness. They had eaten, and each sorcerer in their band carried gris-food in one or more pockets. Chase led them first into an alley, and then down a deserted street. They ran one at a time along moonlit streets, from shuttered storefronts to temple awnings, and finally to the deep shadows along the wall of a granary. They had seen nothing moving save a cat.

"Where is he?" Lon whispered.

"He'll be here," Chase said.

Finally, a small man darted out of the shadows of a nearby building and motioned them to follow. His head never seemed to stop moving, swiveling back and forth. He would run a few paces, stop, hold up a hand, then scurry forward again, starting and stopping for all the world like a squirrel caught between trees, hoping to avoid the notice of a hawk overhead. Their escort never straightened from his hunched posture until he reached an inconspicuous stairwell that led into the basement of what appeared to be a modest townhome. All at once, the little man relaxed and stood straight. "Down there," he said, and pointed. "Don't knock; they're expecting you."

Chase stepped aside, allowing the sorcerers to lead the way. Micah went down the stairs just ahead of Chase, and ducked to pass through an oddly short doorway. Once inside, a woman's voice commanded them to close the door. What little moonlight had penetrated the basement vanished, and they were plunged into total darkness.

"Where is your messenger?" the woman asked.

"I'm here," said Chase.

"And the money?"

"With me. Five hundred in gold, as we agreed."

Perryn gasped next to Micah. He thought it sounded like a fantastic amount of money, but he couldn't imagine what that sum would buy. A house? A mansion? A noble title? Who knew?

"And the vows?"

Chase explained to the sorcerers. "We cannot pass unless we each state a magical contract, promising not to reveal what we know of this passage."

"Who will judge the vows?" Lon asked.

"I will," said the woman.

"Then you must be a sorceress," Lon said.

"Ask no more about me, or we will refuse passage."

"I promise not to reveal the existence of this passage to anyone, at any time, or my life is forfeit," said Chase.

Valdis followed suit, though he mumbled and stuttered, then Lon and Perryn, and finally Micah. A door slid open, revealing a tunnel lit by torches at intervals of thirty feet or so.

"Pass freely then," the woman said. "I have your vows, and no one—"

Her voice cut off in a gurgling rasp. In the light from the tunnel, Micah could see her, a woman of indeterminate age, leaning against the wall in a corner of the room. Her hands clutched her throat, strangling herself. But why? How? He looked around and saw Valdis, his hands extended toward the woman, strangling the air in front of him. With eyes blazing, face contorted as he mumbled some words, trembling violently, Valdis looked more like a man now than at any time since possessing Kellyn. Micah wondered again if he were somehow changing his sister's body into that of a man. The woman collapsed to her knees, still strangling herself, fell over and died.

"No one will . . . extort vows from me," whispered Valdis.

"Ah, we'd better, ah, better be going," Chase stammered. He led the way as if he knew which direction was correct, and everyone followed. Lon stared at Valdis, frowning.

The tunnel walls dripped brown slime, and stagnant water stood a few inches deep on the floor. They moved quickly, splashing along with little care for stealth. The murder of the woman almost assuredly wouldn't go unnoticed, and Micah thought they'd need to be as far away as possible by the time someone discovered her body. He couldn't imagine what had possessed his father to kill the woman, and he had started to believe that killing Valdis would be his best bet.

Perryn stopped suddenly, and Micah bumped into her. "Stop," she whispered. "Everyone, listen!"

There was a sound coming from behind them, a scurrying sound. "Just rats," Lon said.

The sound got louder, like splashing, and claws on stone. A lot of claws. "I don't think so," said Perryn. She turned to face back the way they'd come, and Micah turned, too. Little glowing eyes shined from deep in the tunnel, hundreds of them.

"We'd better get out of here," Chase whispered, turning away.

"No!" said Lon. "If we run, they'll take us from behind. These aren't just rats. They're a tunnel guardian. We have to stand and fight."

Lon arranged them in the narrow confines, where no more than two people could stand side to side. Perryn and Lon would face the beast first, since their weapons had the greatest range, then Micah and Valdis, who possessed weapons with a much more sharply limited reach. Chase would be last, since he could use only sharpened steel.

"Keep your spacing!" Lon shouted. "Careful you don't hurt each other! We can defeat the guardian, but only if we all stand together."

Whatever a tunnel guardian was, Micah couldn't see it, because as it came, it snuffed out the torches it passed, so that the tunnel behind them kept getting darker. Still, the tiny red eyes kept coming, too many to count. Either Lon was wrong and this really was a horde of little creatures coming for them, or the guardian was covered in hundreds of eyes.

Lon lifted his arms and formed a ball of lightening, then lashed out with dozens of bolts. The shrieking that emerged from the tunnel caused Micah to cover his ears, but Lon slapped his hands away. "Keep your hands free! They want you to cover your ears!"

Perryn struck with her fire whip, and the explosion at the furthest extent of her range lit up the tunnel for all to see. Micah wished it hadn't. The tunnel guardian was indeed comprised of hundreds of rat-like creatures, each sporting a face like a bat, all fangs and ears and nostrils; four legs, each with nasty, blood red claws; and a foot long, whip-like tail that slashed the air around it.

"There's too many of them!" Perryn screamed as she lashed the on-coming horde. Every time she blew a dozen or more of them to bits, more came rushing from behind to fill the gap.

"They're a single entity!" Lon shouted back. "Many bodies, but only one controlling intelligence! Keep killing!"

They had come within range of Micah's sword. He slashed back and forth with the invisible blade as fast as he could, but there were too many of them. They climbed up the walls, even across the ceiling, coming at him from every conceivable angle. It wasn't long before a few managed to attach themselves to his body, raking his flesh with their claws and sinking their teeth into any uncovered bit of skin. He lost his concentration, and the sword vanished. Good thing, too, because he was now flailing his arms around wildly in a desperate bid to keep them from his face.

It wasn't working. More and more of them climbed up his legs, dropping onto his shoulders from above, shredding his clothes and biting him, until it felt like every surface of his skin would be one massive, bleeding gash. He opened his mouth to scream, but closed it again immediately as some of the beasts tried to get their claws between his lips. He covered his face with his hands, screwing his eyes shut as tightly as he could manage. Despite the creatures clinging to his legs, Micah tried to run, though with his eyes closed he had no idea which direction would bring safety.

All around him, the sensations of combat continued. Perryn's whip kept blasting away. Lon's lightning crackled through the air. Valdis' weapon, whatever it was, made no noise, but waves of freezing air came from his direction. Micah wondered how Chase was fairing, but there was no time to help. He had to get out.

He stumbled, regained his balance for a heartbeat, and fell. Immediately, the creatures covered him in a living blanket of shrieking, biting tormenters. *Die!* he shouted in his mind. He grabbed one of the creatures. *Die, damn you!*

The furry ball of death collapsed in his hands, and as it died, its diwa flowed into Micah's hand. He felt a surge of strength, and knew what he must do. He grabbed another, took its diwa, and another and another. Each creature he touched died instantly, and Micah was beginning to feel like he could simply float away from the guardian. He killed dozens that way, many more than he could count, and the diwa surged through

224 - TODD WOODMAN

him. It felt so good, in fact, that he risked opening his eyes, and was greeted with a gruesome sight.

Tiny bodies littered the tunnel. They'd been burned, blown up, and torn to shreds. More, possibly hundreds, simply lay dead. The living retreated down the tunnel, leaving their dead and dying behind. Micah stood, and nearly fell again. They'd carpeted the tunnel floor with the bodies of their attackers, many of which hadn't quite died yet. And the filthy water had been churned into a frothy, reddish-brown sludge. The stench—sewage, blood, and burnt fur—was overwhelming.

"All alive?" Lon croaked, holding a glowing blue crystal. "Call out, everyone!"

"I'm still here," said Perryn.

Chase grunted. Micah made eye contact with Lon and nodded, unable to speak.

"Where's Valdis?" Lon asked, panicky.

Valdis was nowhere to be seen. "Did they take him?" Perryn asked.

"Check the floor," said Chase. There were drifts of bodies, a few large enough to conceal a human form. The three of them searched frantically, until finally Perryn cried out wordlessly. She grabbed something beneath the muck and heaved. Micah stepped over furry bodies to help, shoving aside the dead and dying creatures. Underneath, he found Valdis and pulled him free. He was pale, unresponsive. He had fallen face down in the ooze, and must have drowned.

Micah and Chase dragged Valdis along, until they found a portion of the tunnel that sloped up enough that the floor was mostly dry. They set him down, and Perryn went to her knees at his side, feeling for a pulse, placing her ear directly on his chest, listening for any sign of breath.

Perryn turned Valdis over and placed her arms around his middle. She squeezed, lifting him to a nearly standing position. Red-brown sludge emerged from Valdis' mouth and nose. She laid him down and listened to his chest. She slumped back against the tunnel wall. "Lon? Do you think you can make a tiny bolt of lightning? Strong enough to hurt, but not enough to kill?"

"What? I suppose, but why?"

"Just do it. Aim for Valdis' heart. Now."

Lon formed the requested ball of energy, but a very small one. Lightning lashed out at Valdis and his body convulsed, arching up until only his head and heels touched the floor. Perryn put her head to his chest, shook it and commanded, "Again!"

Lon struck with lightning again, and again, six times in all, before an ever more desperate Perryn shouted in triumph, "Yes! A heartbeat! He's breathing. He'll live."

Chase lifted Valdis over his shoulder. "Come, my lords. We need to get out of here."

Micah brought up the rear, silently cursing. His father had been so close to death. So close.

18

"He's weak," Perryn said.

Kellyn had learned their names. She could see them, occasionally, when her father opened his eyes. Her eyes? No, it was better to think of the body she couldn't control as his. She shied away from the thought of what shape she'd be in if she ever regained control. Their shared near-death experience had so weakened her father that Valdis exercised only intermittent control. Too weak to walk, the other three carried him.

If Valdis had possessed enough control, not just over Kellyn's body, but over his own actions, maybe the ugly scene in the tunnel wouldn't have happened. Or maybe he was simply that sort of person: vicious, violent, and prone to spur of the moment decisions like whether or not to murder someone over some slight provocation. Kellyn had learned to despise her father.

"Not much further," Lon said. "We should find the Mendrion River shortly. We'll hire a boat there. Another couple of days should see us in Engvar."

They'd been carrying Valdis for days now, and Kellyn could feel her father's control slipping more and more each day. Occasionally, she would try to move a hand or open an eye. At first, Valdis would easily shut her down, but the more she persisted, the harder it became to stop her. Valdis' companions had asked once or twice if anything was wrong, but her prickly father would only snap at them in return for their concern.

Kellyn had even taken to forcing her way back into her body

whenever her father tried to sleep. At first, Valdis would jerk awake after just a heartbeat or two, reassert his control, and then drift off to sleep. Each time she interrupted Valdis' sleep, he grew weaker, and Kellyn maintained control for longer periods of time. Almost time for the final effort.

Micah set Valdis down on a soft patch of grass near the riverbank. Valdis didn't stir from his sleep. It really was creepy how much Kellyn looked like an angry man while their father possessed her body. Even creepier was how old she looked after the experience in the tunnel, like she'd aged ten years, maybe twenty. He almost felt bad for what he was about to do. Chase had gone off to gather wood, while Lon and Perryn scouted the area for a boat to hire or steal. He and his father/sister were alone.

Micah moved Valdis closer to the edge of the bank. There was a steep drop there, but not a long one. Maybe a yard down to the river's surface. And the depth? Hard to tell, but Valdis had almost drowned in just a few inches of sludge back in the tunnel. He placed his hands on Valdis' side, but his father didn't react at all. Micah's heart hammered in his chest, breath coming in rapid, sharp gasps. Decision crystallized, and he shoved his father/sister over the edge and into the water.

No one reacted. There'd been a loud splash, but the noise of the rushing river was all around them. Micah looked briefly over the edge, but couldn't see the body. He moved away and started looking for firewood, or a decent place to make camp, or anything to get away from the river.

His most pressing question now was, should he run or should he stay? He could plausibly say that his father had simply rolled over the edge in his sleep, but would there be evidence? Would there be signs that he'd been pushed? Marks in the turf where his heel had dug in, or something like that?

A splashing sound came from the river, obviously someone struggling for the shore. Micah ran back to the bank, where he found Valdis struggling in the mud, barely keeping his head above water, gasping and calling feebly for help. He lowered himself into the river and splashed over to his struggling father, intent on murder.

Valdis looked up at him and held his hand out. "Micah!" he croaked. "It's me, Kellyn, your sister. Help!"

Now that Kellyn had control, she looked feminine again, though only her expression had changed. Micah stopped and blinked, his mouth hanging open stupidly. He shook his head, closed the distance between them and grabbed Kellyn by the shirt. But while it had been so easy to push a sleeping man over the edge of the bank, he found he couldn't look his sister in the eyes and shove her under. He held her above the surface, cursing himself for a coward and a fool.

"They're going to kill you," Kellyn whispered.

Micah froze. "What did you say?"

"I can't control this body much longer. He's going to kill you so he can revive his old body. You have to—"

Valdis' face, or Kellyn's, whatever, contorted into a mask of rage for an instant, then went blank, suddenly very male again. Micah stared, still holding him by the shirt, wondering if Kellyn's warning could be believed. He started lowering Kellyn/Valdis into the swirling brown water.

"Micah!" Perryn shouted. She splashed down into the water. "What happened?"

"I don't know," Micah said. "I left him for a second and the next thing I know I heard a splash. Help me."

Between the two of them, they wrestled Valdis out of the river and onto the same stretch of grassy bank Micah had just pushed him off. Perryn checked his pulse and breathing, closed her eyes and ran her hands through her hair. "Can anything else go wrong?" she wondered aloud.

Lon returned. "We've got a boat," he said with a smile. But as he took in the scene on the riverbank, the smile faded away. "What happened here?"

Micah told the same story he'd given Perryn. Lon watched him carefully, and Micah wondered if he'd somehow given anything away. But the sorcerer merely nodded as he knelt by Valdis' side. He passed his hands over Valdis' temples, tracing designs with his fingers.

"He needs rest," Perryn said.

"And I need answers."

"Do you doubt Micah?"

"I need to know how Valdis ended up in the water. No more or less."

Valdis' eyes fluttered open. Lon leaned close, whispering words that sounded like magical incantations. Finally, he sat back and said, "Valdis? Are you awake?"

"Yes," Valdis whispered.

"What happened to you, Valdis? You nearly drowned."

Micah's father sat up straight, but his head lolled back and forth. "She tried . . . to take over. She pushed me aside. She said—" Valdis took a sharp breath. "What . . . what d-did she say to you, Micah? Answer me!"

Micah knew this would have to be his best performance. He took a deep breath. "I think it was Kellyn. The voice sounded different. But I couldn't understand him. Her, I guess."

"What do you mean?" asked Lon.

"Does Kellyn speak another language?" asked Micah, gambling that his weakened father wouldn't be able to tell what language she had spoken. Or that he knew perfectly well what words were said—if Kellyn were telling the truth, Valdis might try to hide it. "She was saying something, but it didn't sound like Kattenese. I think I heard my name, and hers—Kellyn's you know."

"Kellyn took her body back," said Perryn. "She might have slipped into the language she's spoken most of her life."

"That would be Thurnish," Lon said. "Did it sound like this?" Lon then said something, presumably in Thurnish.

Micah recognized his name, and 'Kellyn.' "Could be," he said. "I'm not really sure. She seemed desperate. Like she was begging for help or something. Probably was, you know? She was drowning, after all."

Lon stared at Micah for a few moments longer, and he was certain the sorcerer had detected the lie. He began to envision the sword in his mind, ready to slash out if necessary. But Lon, whatever he may have suspected, apparently wasn't ready to accuse him of trying to murder his father.

"Valdis?" he said, turning away from Micah. "Are you still with us? Can you tell us more?"

"It's as Micah said. I . . . thought I heard her s-saying something in . . . in Thurnish. She fights me . . . every waking moment."

Micah kept his face very still, but emotions waged war under the surface. His father did know what Kellyn had said, but he couldn't admit it aloud. Which meant his sister had been telling the truth, had in fact been trying to save him.

"We need to get you to the palace," Perryn said. "I say we go right now. Let's not wait for morning."

Lon nodded. "You're right. We need Sarah's help as soon as possible. I just don't know what to do to stabilize Valdis. She will."

Micah nodded along with the others, but he knew one thing: the last place he could afford to be was at the palace. But how to escape them?

"What about Chase?" he asked.

"He should return soon," Lon said.

"I think I saw him just before Valdis fell in the river," Micah said. "He was a ways off. Why don't I go fetch him? If we wait, he might go off hunting up some dinner and we'd waste what daylight we have left."

"Good idea," said Perryn. "I'll help Lon with the boat."

Micah trotted off toward the south, upstream from the little band, back the way they'd come. He hadn't been lying about Chase. He really had seen the man, but off to the north. He had no intention of finding him, or of being found. As soon as he was out of sight of the river, he broke into a run, found the road, and skirted along the edge of the woods that flanked the rutted, dusty farmers' track, so that anyone looking down that road would not be able to see him. It was slow going at first, trying to run and stay hidden at the same time. But not far off, maybe a mile or so, he spied a low line of hills. Once among the hills, he could use the road, make better time.

Beyond that, though, he had no concept of a plan. Get away quickly, put as much distance between himself and the palace as possible. Once he was safely beyond their reach, he'd think about whatever came next. "Maybe I can find work in a quarry," he said. But even as he thought it, he knew he could never go back to that life. "No, I'll become a great sorcerer! I'll become so powerful even my parents will fear me."

He stopped suddenly. "The blood compass," he whispered. "They can find me." But hadn't Lon said something about the compass having only so much range? And they wouldn't yet know he'd run. "So get running, Micah!"

Whatever spell Lon had used on Valdis had given him strength for a while. Kellyn had been shut down completely and hadn't been able to hear what was going on around her. She'd been blind for a time, too. But gradually, Valdis' newfound strength ebbed, and before too long he was just as weak as ever. Kellyn could hear again, and see through her own eyes whatever Valdis looked at.

The band of sorcerers argued. They sounded desperate, and maybe a little afraid. Night had fallen, and two of their group were nowhere to be seen.

"There's nothing else we can do," Perryn said, calmly.

"She'll be furious at the interruption," Lon said. "And what she should be working on now is quite delicate. If she had to stop, even for a few hours, she might have to begin her preparations anew. Timing is quite important just now. I say we keep going. Get Valdis to the palace as quickly as we can, and leave Sarah to her work."

"If Sarah knew the situation, she might decide the delay was worth the risk. But if you keep her in the dark, you're taking away her options."

"No! I will not go back alone. Not yet. Not until we have no other choice."

Perryn sighed. "Fine. But we still have to retrieve Micah. That oaf is lost, and Chase is probably in the next village, scaring up supplies. We're losing an entire day!"

"Time is pressing, as you say. So why don't you leave now? Go track down the boy. I'll get Valdis in the boat. Chase will know what to do when he comes back and finds no one here. I'll leave you with the blood compass. You go find Micah and join us at Engvar later."

"We . . . need him . . . now," Valdis said in a voice just barely audible. "I grow . . . weak."

Valdis had been staring at the ground. When he spoke, he looked not at Perryn, but at Lon. Yes, they needed Micah, but Kellyn wondered who besides Valdis knew the reason. She also wondered what Felida and Jirra were doing right now. Were they trailing this desperate little band? Would they be able to defeat them? She felt certain she could defeat her father's tenuous grip on her body, but what then? Without Valdis, they might simply kill her. And though she wouldn't shrink from self-sacrifice, she didn't want to die just yet.

"Listen to him, Lon!" said Perryn. "He's worsening. If we don't get Sarah to have a look at him, he'll lose his grip on Kellyn's body. Even a few hours might make the difference."

Kellyn waited, sure that Lon would eventually see the wisdom of Perryn's idea, but any delay suited her well. She didn't dare interfere just yet. Anything she might do could spook them into some drastic action. Better to bide her time, then strike at Valdis with everything she had.

Finally, Lon shook his head jerkily, looking unsure. He reached within a pocket and retrieved a dagger, which he handed to Perryn. She held the dagger, whispered an incantation, and the blade floated over her palm. The knife pointed directly at Valdis, and Kellyn finally understood how they'd gotten a blood sample. She and Micah shared their parents' blood, and so any compass that could find Micah could also find Kellyn. The relief that she felt then at finally dispelling the idea that Jirra might have had anything to do with these sorcerers surprised her a little.

"We'll do it my way, and that's final. Go find Micah. I'll take Valdis in the boat. If his condition gets worse, I'll transport myself back to the palace and get Sarah. If he remains stable, I'll stay with him. And I'll leave a note here for Chase."

Perryn said a few more words, and the blade swung to the south. "Well at least he's not too far. He's still in range, anyway."

"The blood used to calibrate the compass was Micah's," Lon said. "So its range will be greater. He might be several miles away and you'd still get a reading."

"Then I'd better not dally." Perryn left.

The only question Kellyn had now concerned Micah's motives. Had her brother believed her, or was he merely lost?

Micah had passed a couple of farmhouses, and a small village, but out here in the countryside, there'd be no one out and about at night. No taverns, no walled towns, no castles full of lords and soldiers. He had only his thoughts for company, and those weren't exactly comforting. At least he'd gotten a clearer picture of what was really going on.

Anna had been angry at Lon, upset at something he planned to do. Was she upset that they were planning to sacrifice Micah to revive his father? Something about that felt true, and Micah wondered if his ability to sniff out lies could also be used to tell the difference between ideas that were right and those that were not lies at all, just incorrect.

Anna had also been upset that he'd never been taught to read. Well, why would you teach a child to read if you intended to kill him? Especially Micah. He clearly had magical talent. If he'd learned to read, he might have learned how to better control his powers. He might have become so powerful that they couldn't kill him even if they tried.

And what about the time when Perryn had seemed to be trying to tell him something when he'd asked her what would happen once they reached the palace? Maybe she hadn't known, exactly, but she knew something unpleasant was in store. Perhaps she'd tried to warn him without giving herself away? She had been so quick to believe Micah's story about Valdis' 'accident' by the river. Maybe she wanted to deflect suspicion away from him.

"Too many maybes," he whispered. He trudged on, moving from a walk to a jog, then to a flat out run for a bit, then back down to a walk. He had trouble catching his breath, and the warm, humid summer night did little to help. With no water since leaving the river, doubts compounded his fears. But not quite an hour later, he came upon a farm and left the road. Rutted tracks led to a barn and a thatch roofed home. He found a well, and lowered the bucket down on its rope, heard the splash below, and hauled it back up. The cool water was reasonably clean, certainly better than anything he'd had back at the quarry. He sat with his back against the stone of the well, catching his breath.

If only he'd brought some food, aside from the few scraps of gris-food left in his pocket, but that was for emergencies only. He'd just about worked up the nerve to steal a chicken from the barn when a voice stopped him.

"What are you doing on my land?"

He turned and saw just the dim outline of a man, darker than the surrounding shadows. His accent had been that of an educated man, not some peasant. And had he said, 'my land'? As in land that belonged to him, not to some lord in a distant castle? This might not be some easily frightened peasant. Perhaps a little truth telling was in order.

"Sir? I'm on the run from a band of sorcerers. They were going to kill me, but I slipped away from them. I've been running for hours. I just need some water."

"Sorcerers? And just why would I believe that?"

"Please, sir, you have to believe me. I found them by the river, the Mendrion. They had a girl with them down by the riverbank. I think they were trying to lure a face stealer out of the water. I must have made a noise, and they saw me. They chased after me."

The stranger stepped forward, and in the dim moonlight Micah saw a tall, broad-shouldered man carrying an unsheathed sword. Definitely a noble then, but on a farm out in the middle of nowhere? Probably a very minor noble. The man motioned with the blade toward the house.

"Come inside then, fugitive. I'll know the truth of your story soon enough."

Or not, Micah thought, as he conjured the sorcerer's sword in his mind. He leapt forward, aiming to disembowel the man, but he was faster than Micah and leapt aside. The tip of the man's sword was no longer attached to the rest of his blade, but Micah had missed his target.

"Liar! You're a sorcerer yourself!"

"I never said I wasn't. But I am on the run from other sorcerers. And I can't afford to waste my time with you."

The man backed away, twirling his sword in the air. He clearly knew how to use it. "You won't find me easy to kill, magic man. I've fought against blades like yours before and lived to tell the tale."

"I'll be on my way, then. I've taken nothing from you but a bucket of water."

"You've ruined my sword. This blade was my father's, and his father's before him. You'll answer for that."

The stranger lunged forward then, quick as a cat. Micah brought his blade up, but he wasn't nearly fast enough. Fortunately, the man's sword now lacked its point, and the shortened blade punched him hard in the ribs but penetrated no more than a finger's width. The cut hurt, but at least he didn't have a foot of steel through his heart.

The stranger danced sideways as Micah tried to slash with his blade. He found nothing but empty air.

"Hah! You sorcerers think your fancy weapons make you immune to common steel. But you use that invisible sword like a peasant with a pitchfork! Idiot! I'll watch you bleed out before this night is over."

Micah looked around, hoping to find a handy stone. There was nothing besides the mortared blocks that made up the well. And the stranger was between him and the well, anyway. He knew, suddenly, that he could not defeat this man.

"Think on this then. The sorcerers on my tail want me alive, as a sacrifice. If you kill me, they'll have to find a substitute. I doubt your blade would be much good against lightning. Or a fire whip. For that matter, you're good with a blade, but their man Chase is at least your equal."

The swordsman was no longer boasting, nor was he advancing for the kill. He wasn't exactly backing down yet, though.

"Do you have a family in your little home? A wife, perhaps some children? How well do you think they'll fare once the sorcerers are through with you? And don't think they won't know it was you. They're tracking me with a blood compass. They'll know exactly where I died, and it won't be too difficult for them to figure out who did it."

The stranger let the shortened tip of his sword drop to the ground. "Leave, then, you cursed sorcerer! You've no honor, to threaten a man's family! I hope your friends do find you, and kill you slowly. I hear they can make a man's death last a very long time."

"Turn around and go back into your home, sir. I'll be gone and it'll be like none of this ever happened."

Without another word, the swordsman did as he was told, and Micah walked gingerly back to the road. The cut in his ribs hurt, a lot. He tried jogging, but the stabbing pain brought him up short. "Walking it is," he whispered. But how much time had he lost? And how much slower would he be now? Between the energy already expended, the wound, and the use of his sorcerer's sword, he was tired.

He took out the little bit of gris-food and took a small bite. Foul taste filled his mouth; there was simply no getting used to it. But some of the bone-deep exhaustion went away, if not all of it. If only there were some way to tell if they were chasing after him. And if so, who was doing the chasing? Surely not all of them. They'd need to keep Valdis safe, and get him to the palace as soon as possible.

But without me, they're out of luck, he thought with a smile.

The boat wasn't much, just a little rowboat, really. Kellyn wondered whether they'd bought it or stole it, and hoped for the latter. Anything to make Lon a little more desperate, anything that might put someone else on his tail, maybe cause him to make a few more mistakes, however insignificant. And in the meantime, she worked on Valdis, temporarily taking back various portions of her body, popping back out before Valdis could shut her down, waiting for her father to drop his guard again, and repeating the process all over. It was almost fun.

But only almost. Lon had alternated between rowing and simply steering the boat along with the current through the night. When it was finally light enough to see, Kellyn took complete control of her body for a few seconds, just long enough to check her physical condition. She looked at her hands, and was shocked to see how gray and loose her skin had become. Her fingernails had yellowed, and a couple of them had split. She trembled. The overall effect was that of decades worth of aging in just a couple of weeks. How much worse would she be if Valdis' possession of her body were to continue for much longer?

Valdis shoved his way back into Kellyn's body, clamping down hard. But the effort so exhausted him that he passed out immediately afterward. She could simply drown the both of them now. Take control of her body, dive in and push hard for the river bottom. But would that work? If Lon tried to save Valdis, if he were in physical contact with Kellyn's body at the time of its death, might her father's soul simply jump to Lon's body instead? Would Valdis feel any loyalty to his servant? Probably not. That might only result in Kellyn's death and her father's continued survival. Not yet then. But if she could worsen Valdis so much that Lon found it necessary to transport himself to the palace, she might have some time alone. She could then kill herself, destroying her father's soul as well.

As plans went, it seemed one with a fair chance of success, if a bit grim. It floundered on one supposition, however: she hadn't counted on Chase's return. Toward noon of the first day on the river, Chase hailed Lon from the shore, mounted on a horse, waving. Lon, who'd let the boat drift along with the current for a couple of hours, dipped the oars in the water and pulled hard for shore.

"Any word from Perryn?" Lon asked, once Chase had tied the boat to a tree on the bank.

"Not yet, my lord." Chase removed saddlebags from the horse and threw them into the boat. "Food." He removed the saddle and tossed the blanket from under it into the boat as well. "In case it's too cool at night."

Kellyn watched what Valdis watched, wondering why he was so focused on the horse.

"Bring me . . . to . . . the horse," croaked Valdis. "I need . . . "

"Yes, of course!" said Lon. "Help me, Chase!" Together, they lifted Valdis and hauled him out of the boat. They propped him up and placed Valdis' hands on the horse.

The horse died, and Chase gave it a hard shove to control its fall.

Kellyn felt its diwa flowing through her body, a great shock that traveled from her fingertips up into her torso, and then back out again to every extremity of her body. Valdis inhaled sharply, suddenly stronger, and shoved Kellyn down further. Sight was denied her, though she could still hear what Valdis heard.

"Better, my lord?" Lon asked.

"Yes . . . a little."

"There's no time to waste. Come, Chase, let's get him into the boat. Are you fresh enough to row for awhile? I need sleep."

"Of course, my lord. Sleep as long as you wish."

Kellyn sank into despair. The diwa flowing through her had been exhilarating and nauseating at the same time. Her body had been subjected to extreme abuse by her battles with her father. Diwa infection spread like a wasting disease.

Valdis began to tremble, but Lon handed him a chunk of gris-food. As he chewed, he grew stronger still. "I feel almost . . . human again."

"Excellent, my lord," said Chase.

Lon said nothing. Indeed, his breathing was so deep Kellyn assumed he was already sleeping. Soon, Valdis slept as well. She tried to interrupt his rest, but with the influx of diwa from the horse, and the vile food, her father could fight back without conscious thought. Kellyn cursed. She'd have to wait for Valdis to weaken again. But how long would that take? And would he simply kill another horse, or worse yet a person, to strengthen himself?

A sudden stab of guilt rocked her—she hadn't thought about Shaethe since the sorcerers broke her out of the tower. Her sword was probably still with Zang. Or perhaps it had been in the tower when it fell. She imagined the blade broken, its spirit destroyed or imprisoned. Whatever fate Shaethe had suffered, it seemed Kellyn would not be far behind.

19

Micah was no judge of distance. He'd run and walked and jogged through the night, doing his best to ignore the pain of his wounds as he stumbled along the road. He hadn't encountered anyone else since leaving the noble's little farm, but that couldn't last forever. The sun had just begun to come up over the tops of the trees and surrounding hills, its light obscured by thick cloud cover. He hoped for rain. A good storm might help cover his tracks, even if they were using a blood compass.

And he had to assume they were coming. Perhaps Kellyn had lied, but could he take the chance? No, her warning felt true. In the meantime, he could do nothing but put one foot in front of the other, as quickly as possible. If only he were a better runner.

Perhaps he could make himself a better runner. After all, he'd made himself bigger, hadn't he? But Felida had said that someone else had done it for him. He hadn't sniffed out any lies from the healer, but why would his mother want him physically larger? Just to make him more valuable to Garron? Or did it have something to do with Micah's fate: to be the sacrifice that brought his father back to life? Tears leaked down his cheeks. "I don't need her," he ground out through clenched teeth.

He increased his pace from a fast walk to a slow jog. "Breathe. Take deep breaths. I can do this."

The jog gradually became a run. Maybe, just maybe, he was a tiny bit faster now. Or perhaps that was his imagination. Either way, the pace was too much to keep up. He lost his breath easily, and the cut in his side burned like a brand. The injuries from the tunnel guardian burned as sweat and effort reopened a few of the deeper cuts. Against his better judgement, he ate the last of the gris-food and waited for it to have an effect. His stamina improved quickly, and he continued to jog.

Micah rounded a bend . . . and found the noble he'd left behind standing in the middle of the rutted road.

"I challenge you to single combat, sorcerer," he said quietly. He wasn't a particularly big man, but he stood with a poise and grace that looked dangerous, sword straight up in the air, its point held perfectly still. He had long, graying hair, and a sparse beard streaked with white. His face sported a crooked scar that ran from the bridge of his nose down to his left cheek and up to the ear on that side. He didn't appear to be wearing armor, but that didn't seem to make him any less deadly. Everything about the man, including his reflexes during their brief combat the previous night, screamed 'warrior.'

But how had he repaired his sword? The noble must have noticed him staring at the blade. "What? Did you think me so poor I had but one sword? Unfortunate for you that I didn't find this blade first, last night. I might not have pursued you had you broken this. But it will do well enough. And now that we no longer stand on my land, your sorcerer friends will not connect your death with me. Now! Fight, or die like a dog!"

He leapt, his sword held high for an overhead slash. Micah frantically recalled the sorcerer's sword in his mind and brought it up to counter the attack, but no sooner had he moved than his opponent was no longer there. He'd slipped off to Micah's right and brought his sword down on Micah's unprotected shoulder.

Pain seared through his arm. He screamed wordlessly, and the invisible sword vanished just as quickly as it had appeared. His opponent kicked his wounded shoulder, hard. Micah sprawled in the dirt, moaning. He tried to roll away, but stopped short with the tip of his enemy's sword pricking the skin under his jaw.

"You may recall your magic sword, little sorcerer," the man said, a savage grin on his face, "and you may even be fast enough to cut me down with it. But not before I'd slash your throat."

"What do you want from me?" Micah asked, trying to choke back a sob, suddenly feeling small, and very alone.

"Excellent question," said a woman. He knew the voice. From behind, someone slipped a leather thong over his head. A stone hung from the thong, cold and heavy. The stone rested on the skin of his chest. It couldn't have been larger than his thumb, but it felt as heavy as a large man.

Micah groaned. "Get it off," he wheezed.

Felida stepped into his field of vision, and a younger woman, girl really, whom he'd never seen before. The younger one limped along on a peg leg, and Felida looked her way. "Good work, Jirra. I knew you could do it."

The girl, Jirra he supposed, nodded. "Thank you. I just wish I'd known I had this talent a few weeks ago. Maybe I could have stopped all this."

"Don't beat yourself up, dear. There is still time for us to succeed." Felida squatted near Micah and grinned. "And you, little sorcerer, what are we to do with you? As I said, you asked a good question. What do I want? What do any of us want? We'll start with the good knight here. Sir Lambeth, what do you desire?"

Lambeth's sword had not moved a fraction of an inch. Nor had his eyes strayed from Micah's. "I want revenge for my grandfather's sword."

"Ah," said Felida, smiling broadly, "but what if I were to bring the sword to a mage who could restore it to its original condition? Would you still want revenge?"

Lambeth shrugged. "My honor would be satisfied. Or it would be, if this swine would apologize."

"I'm sorry! Spirits and demons, I'm sorry! Get it off!"

Felida's eyes crinkled in amusement. He wanted to scream at her, but as he opened his mouth to say something especially pungent, the weight eased off. After a few ragged breaths, the stone felt like it weighed no more than a couple of pounds. Far more than a stone that size should have weighed, but quite bearable. "What have you done to me?"

"That," Felida said, pointing at the stone, "is a fail-spell amulet. As long as you wear it, you cannot enact any spells or use any magical objects. And you won't be able to remove it. Only I can."

Micah tried frantically to remove the stone, but it seemed glued to his flesh. Pulling at it did not hurt, especially, but neither did it move. To think that he had saved this woman.

"Didn't I just tell you it wouldn't come off? Now, getting back to satisfying everyone's wants. Lambeth will let it all go, but only if I can convince my mage friend to fix his sword. Jirra and I want the same thing: Kellyn. We want her unharmed, and in control of her body. I will not help Sir Lambeth unless I get what I want."

She knelt beside him, probing the gash on his shoulder with her fingers. Pain shot up and down his arm and he gasped involuntarily. "Which brings us to you. What do you want?"

"Leave me alone!"

Felida beamed. "He wants to be left alone! I take it that means you want to live? And earlier, did you not request the removal of a certain amulet?"

"Yes, please! Get it off!"

"So, you want me to remove the amulet, and you want to live. It would seem, therefore, that we can all help each other achieve our goals. First, you help Jirra and I retrieve Kellyn, then I will make sure Sir Lambeth's sword is made whole again, and you will live, free of the amulet. Are we all in agreement?"

Lambeth said, "I agree. And I, too, will assist in saving the mage apprentice Kellyn. If she dies, sorcerer, you die."

"I agree," said Jirra. "But if Kellyn comes to harm, I may wish to bargain with Sir Lambeth for the right to kill this wretch."

"Tsk, tsk, novice Jirra. If you are to become a healer, you must resist the urge to harm others. I will, of course, overlook any infractions until you have been officially entered into the rolls of the Sisterhood." Felida removed a small leather bag from her shoulder and sprinkled some white powder on Micah's wound. It burned, but not unbearably. "And I, too, agree to this proposal. And what of you, young sorcerer? Do you agree?"

Micah stared at the healer, loathing the sight of her. But he had no choice. And anyway, what validity did an oath have if the alternative was death? "I agree."

"Excellent. Sir Lambeth? Jirra? Please patrol the area while I treat this child's injuries. I would not want to be caught off guard when his friends show up to retrieve him." From her bag, she brought out a needle and thread. "This will hurt. And don't think me a fool; I rather doubt you'll be faithful to your oath."

The stitches did hurt, but with a little forewarning, he was able to grit his teeth and get through the ordeal with spirit enough to taunt her. "You won't defeat them, you know. Three of them are powerful sorcerers. I've seen them do amazing things. Two healers and a swordsman? You've got no chance." Rational thought crept back to his mind, though, and there was no profit in making her angry. "Please, our only hope is to run. I helped you. Lon wanted you dead. I said I'd do it, but I only cut you a little, and you healed yourself. I told him you were dead."

"For which I thank you. But my gratitude knows some limits." Felida looked around before continuing. She lowered her voice. "Now, let's be honest, shall we? I know who you are. You are Valdis Hittrech's son. You were conceived as part of a long-term plan to bring your father back from the dead. Your mother helped transfer your father's soul into Kellyn's body, but in such a way that it remained hidden and dormant for all these years. They did this when their rebellion was in its final death throes, and they knew that your father would not be allowed to run away from defeat. Especially after what they did to the Prince's family."

Micah stared at her. How could she know all this? Ah, but there was a better question: "Then why has my father possessed Kellyn now?"

"He didn't want to, but Jirra and I released his soul before their plan was ready. He had no choice but to possess Kellyn. He'll be weak, confused, unstable. Without you to complete their plan, he'll have no choice but to possess another body, and soon."

A picture of his parents' plan was beginning to emerge. "So why couldn't he just hop into another body, then use Kellyn's body as the sacrifice to remake his body?"

Felida smiled, a very unpleasant expression. "Because he doesn't want to kill Kellyn, for one. I'm not sure how he'll react when he learns that Kellyn wants nothing to do with her sorcerer father. But more pragmatically, Kellyn is a woman. Making a new body for your father to inhabit will be hard enough to accomplish without the added difficulty of changing the sex of the donor body."

The words hit Micah like a bucket of cold water. The final pieces had fallen into place. If Kellyn had been a boy, likely Micah would never have been born.

"Should we fail, by the way, I have taken steps to assure that the Prince gets a full report. He'll know another Hittrech lives, and he'll stop at nothing to see you dead."

Micah knew a sharp stab of fear, but he stifled it and rolled his eyes at the threat. "So why has Kellyn lived all these years?"

Felida smirked. "Because her identity has remained a secret within the Brotherhood. Some very powerful mages saw the potential within your sister and made her disappear. Prince Johann must have thought she died during the rebellion. Otherwise, he would have pursued her no matter what the Brotherhood said. He is rather single minded when it comes to your family."

Felida finished attending to Micah's wounds. "So, remember this little chat, yes? One word from me, and Lambeth will know who you are. Honorable as he is, I doubt he'd be able to resist the lure of the fantastic reward he'd receive from the Prince for turning you in."

Micah sneered at her. "I don't care what you do."

"Ah, but you do. You found out what your sorcerer friends had planned for you, somehow. Else why did you run? I'll help make sure their plans fail, but only if you help me. Do we understand each other? You really have no one else."

Micah didn't answer; he didn't trust his voice. Felida had put words to the fear that had been growing in his belly. He had no one. His mother had never really cared for him, had planned his death from before he'd been born. She'd been the stable anchor in his life, the one person he'd do anything to protect. The one person, he had believed, who would do anything to protect him, as well.

It was all a lie, he thought.

Felida put a hand on his good shoulder, and he was shocked to see tears in her eyes.

"I don't read minds, young one. But I am an empath; I read feelings. Now that you can't shield yourself from me with magic, I can see your feelings on your face. Especially the powerful ones. The fear, the betrayal. No child, no matter the contents of his character, should ever have to learn the things you know. I am sorry, truly I am. I promise you this, and I expect nothing from you in return: when this is over, I will do whatever I can to heal your heart."

Micah squeezed his eyes shut, furious at his tears. "Leave me alone," he whispered fiercely. "I don't need you. I don't need anybody."

"You're wrong, little one. You do need someone. We all do."

Kellyn rejoiced. Micah had believed her and made a run for it. Maybe it wouldn't work, but he'd tried. Even if her brother could only succeed in delaying the murderous ceremony that their parents had planned, it might be enough to keep Valdis from coming back to life. And after that? Once she'd thwarted her father's plan, then what? These sorcerers would never let her go. She'd die then, almost assuredly.

But what of Micah? They might let him live. After all, he'd been on their side until he found out he was to be the sacrificial bull. Kellyn found herself rooting for Micah's survival. The thought that she had a brother made her irrationally happy.

More to distract herself than anything else, she focused on Valdis. Her father was weak, but not so weak that she could assume control. She tried anyway, and her father shut her down immediately. She tried again soon afterward, but the wall Valdis had put up still held. She slammed into the wall, repeatedly, thinking that if she forced her father to keep a constant watch on his defenses, it might weaken him further. Perhaps it would, but it had no obvious effect right away. Still, she wasn't tiring, so she kept hammering.

Eventually Valdis grew tired enough that Kellyn was able to see out of her eyes again. They were on a small boat, not much more than a one-man rowing boat, but they didn't need much more than that. Lon sat at the front, eyes closed, right hand held straight out, index finger pointing north. The little craft sped along the river much faster than the current, and Kellyn wondered how long the sorcerer could keep up the pace.

Valdis must have wondered, too. "Don't kill . . . yourself, Lon," he said. "It won't m-matter anyway."

"Please, my lord, don't speak such nonsense. We'll be safe in Engvar House soon. Sarah will know what to do."

A strangled sound escaped Valdis' throat then, and it took Kellyn a few moments to realize that the sound was laughter. "And if . . . they can't r-retrieve Micah? What will my wife do then?"

The boat slowed, and Lon turned to face Valdis. "I don't understand. Why is this so hard? You should be able to control Kellyn for at least several more weeks."

"She . . . she fights me. She is so st-strong. I would . . . be proud of her, if she . . . she weren't k-killing me."

Lon stared at him for a few heartbeats before turning his attention back to the boat. "We'll be in Engvar soon," he repeated.

Micah trudged along, torn between hope and despair, dutifully following Felida and her little band as they marched quickly south and west. The road they travelled was little more than a goat track, but his captors must have known the way. They had a particular destination in mind, supposedly not far off. It didn't matter, though.

"You don't have a prayer," he said to Felida, for perhaps the tenth time.

"Shut up," snapped Jirra.

Micah glanced her way, a little impressed that the cripple wasn't slowing them down at all. She stumped along with her peg leg and a walking staff as fast as any of them.

"What will you do when Perryn and Lon catch up to us? If it's just Chase, I have no doubt our good knight here will be able to take him out. But how's he going to counter a fire whip? Or lightning? And I still don't know what, uh, what the other guy is capable of." He'd almost slipped and said, 'my father.' Felida had scared him when she revealed that she knew his true identity. That business about the Prince's desire for revenge against the Hittrechs was . . . disturbing. What had his father done all those years ago? How could he still be so hated and feared?

"I told you to shut up," said Jirra. "We have a plan, and you'll find out about it soon enough."

"If you told me what it was and took this stupid stone off my chest, I could help."

"I trust you like I trust a viper."

Micah shook his head. "Are you an idiot? You think I want to go back to those people? They're planning to kill me! I don't much like you or your boss, but at least you folks don't want me dead."

Jirra looked at him then, the kind of look you might give something disgusting stuck to the bottom of your shoe. "I want Kellyn back. What happens to you doesn't mean a thing to me."

"Enough, Jirra," said Felida. "Focus. Do you see anything?"

Jirra stopped walking and closed her eyes. "Just what I told you before. There's a tower, that's all. It's as I described earlier."

"That should be the tower I'm thinking of; we'll be there soon. And I've activated our half of the crystal, so they'll know where we are."

"Wait! We can't go there! I see a girl, with red hair. She's already at the tower!"

Felida took Jirra's hands in hers. "No, dear, she isn't. She will be, but not yet. It's confusing at first, but you'll get used to thinking about your visions as things that haven't happened yet."

Jirra nodded and opened her eyes. "You said I only see possible futures. So she might not find us, right?"

"She has a blood compass," Micah said. "She'll find us." He did his best to sound bored, but he couldn't help but feel a little awed that this crippled girl could see the future. It seemed so easy for her, but hadn't Lon said divining the future meant slavery for a sorcerer? Maybe he lied. Perhaps she'd find a way for them to succeed. He saw a tiny glimmer of hope, and almost allowed himself to smile. He knew where Lon and Valdis were taking Kellyn, but hadn't told them yet. If they knew that much, they might kill him. Well, Felida probably wouldn't, but Jirra and Sir Lambeth didn't seem to care much if he lived or died.

Jirra ignored him and resumed walking. "I don't see how I never knew. I don't remember having visions or dreams about the future or anything like that when I was little. Shouldn't there have been some hint that I had this ability?"

Felida sighed. "Each case is different, and I can't see the future myself, so I can't really say what's normal and what isn't. From what I do know, however, there should indeed have been something like that: visions, dreams, at the very least, some confusion concerning present reality and the myriad branches of the future."

Felida looked at Jirra, cocked her head to one side and opened her mouth to speak. But she shook her head and closed her lips with an exasperated sigh.

"What?" said Jirra.

"Nothing. Or probably nothing."

"You can't leave a statement like that hanging!"

Felida shook her head again, but she relented. "Very well. Do you . . . were there any magical practitioners aboard your father's ship?"

"No. A couple of the crew may have had a smidge of talent. Big Red's ability to climb seemed magical, but he may have been just really athletic. Not that it helped; he's dead now."

"Any magical passengers? Aside from Kellyn, that is?"

"Not that I know of. Why?"

"Most talents show signs of their potential, even when a child is too young to use them," Felida said.

She was carefully looking forward, and Micah saw the lie forming on her face. Maybe the stone around his neck prevented him from lying very effectively, but he'd had a lot of practice in sniffing out lies in others. Maybe that talent wasn't magical after all.

"Your experience," Felida continued, "makes me suspect that some-one . . . suppressed your talent. Kellyn saw something in your eyes that made her suspect magical ability, but nothing obvious. By the time you came to me, your talent was there for anyone to see. And of course, by then you weren't aboard your father's ship."

Micah could see the truth in her words, but clearly she'd left some-thing unsaid. He would have bet anything that she believed she knew who the prime suspect was.

"So if there was someone suppressing my ability aboard the ship, I would have been far from him when I found you."

"Think of this: how did you find me in the first place? You said your father gave you his permission to seek my guidance, but you knew nothing of me save my name and the town I live in. You went there, and found my home without questioning anyone. You then followed my path to the side of the road, where I lay recovering from a botched murder attempt. How did you follow me?"

Jirra frowned. "I don't know. I mean, it felt like the direction I was going was . . . correct, that's all."

"Your ability was finally free of suppression. It's quite powerful, and though you don't use any magical objects to enhance your ability, you are still remarkably free of diwa infection. Ask our young sorcerer here how it feels to handle diwa directly. Great while it lasts, but terrible afterward. Correct, youngster?"

Micah pursed his lips and remained silent.

Felida started to say something more, but Jirra held out her hands, her eyes wide and her mouth hanging open. "She's near," she whispered. "The one with the fire whip: she'll catch us soon!"

"Anyone else?" Felida said, sounding calm and focused.

"Just her."

"Well, Sir Lambeth? You fought against Hittrech's Rebellion. Have you ever faced a fire whip?"

Lambeth had been leading their four-person column. He slowed and called over his shoulder, "I've seen that weapon in action, but I've never faced it. I think I can beat the girl, though."

"She's fast," Micah said. He hadn't intended to help, but he also didn't want to go back to Lon and Valdis. "If the whip catches you, you're as cooked as a roasted pigeon."

"I thank you for the advice, young sorcerer—"

"Micah. I'm Micah."

All three of his captors looked at him at once. "Very well, Micah," continued Lambeth. "I thank you. But still, I believe she cannot best me."

"Let's move," said Felida. "The tower is just a little ahead. We should see it soon."

The 'road' curved through stands of pine, and ran generally straight only through cultivated fields. As they neared another forested area, the road curved around a low hill. It wasn't until they'd pushed through the trees that they saw the tower.

"That's it?" Micah asked. "It looks like it'll fall down in a stiff breeze." The derelict square tower had once sported surrounding walls, but those had mostly fallen. Micah wondered how much diwa the stones contained, but he couldn't see anything. No light, no power. Either the amulet around his neck had robbed him of that ability, as well, or this place was truly dead. Lon had said that cut stone loses its diwa eventually, but the kind of large blocks that made up most fortifications should retain their power for centuries. How old must this tumbled ruin have been?

"Well, Jirra," said Felida. "Is that the place?"

Jirra nodded vigorously.

"And when you saw the sorceress here, what time of day did it appear to be?"

"It was dark, definitely."

"Good. We have about an hour of daylight left. Let's get to the top of the tower."

Jirra pulled a pink orb from a pouch hanging from her belt and whispered a few words. The ball began to glow. "My father will know exactly where we are now," she said. "He'll be moving at top speed to join us."

Lambeth turned around slowly, searching for threats. "Let me lead, ladies, Micah. If we are the first here, you three go to the top. I'll remain behind to see what I can do about the sorceress."

They were indeed alone. Inside, they found a stone floor littered with debris and dust, loose stones, weeds, even a few stunted trees thrust up between the pavers. Two wooden floors above them had partially collapsed, and fire had blackened much of what remained. The roof of the tower was open to the sky, and Micah could plainly see that the stone staircase along the interior of the tower had collapsed perhaps two-thirds of the way to the roof. To make matters worse, the clouds that had been gathering all day chose that moment to release their burden of rain.

"And how will we get to the roof?" he said, pointing.

Jirra grinned, an expression nearly pleasant, removing a coil of rope from her pack. "I'll see what I can do. I may have to haul you up." She unstrapped her peg leg, attached some sort of fake claws to her stump and the knee of her good leg, and scrambled up the stairs. When she reached the collapsed section, she scurried up the intact portion of the wall like a spider. Micah gaped.

"She is impressive," Felida said with a chuckle. "Come. Let's—"

A loud 'crack' filled the air, and a blast of hot air sent them sprawling, courtesy of a red-haired girl twirling a flaming whip over her head. Perryn had caught up to them earlier than anticipated. Apparently, Jirra's visions weren't entirely reliable.

Lambeth hurled a rock in her direction, but Perryn avoided the projectile with ease. She stood straight, exuding confidence. Drops of rain struck her whip, hissing into steam like a pit of vipers. "Give me the boy and I'll let you live," she said, her voice loud and clear, yet also soft, alluring. Micah turned toward her voice, wanting only to please her.

"Easy, Micah," said Felida, her hand upon his shoulder. "She's got a bit of the Command in her voice. She'll try to make you do what she wants, and make you believe it was your idea in the first place. Come."

With a shake of his head, Micah followed Felida to the stairs. The stairs were broad enough that he could climb and still watch the combat below. Sorceress and swordsman circled each other warily, but Micah didn't see how Lambeth could survive. Perryn lashed out with her whip, but Lambeth dove to safety, landing in a roll that brought him back to his feet.

Perryn again sent her whip at the swordsman, but this time he stood his ground and slashed at the flames. A length of the whip dropped to the floor, smoking and writhing like a wounded snake. Perryn cried out.

"Come, little girl," said Lambeth, "finish me off! I'm no sorcerer, just a man with a sword."

Perryn snarled, but stopped herself from charging with a visible effort. Instead, she stalked Lambeth, gradually forcing him into a corner with short bursts of flame. Though her weapon no longer appeared as fearsome as before, it looked as if she had the situation well in hand.

"Perryn, look out!" Micah shouted.

The sorceress fell for the ruse and dove to her right, allowing Lambeth to escape to the other side of the tower to stand guard at the base of the stairs. He looked up at Micah and gave a slight nod.

Felida shook Micah's shoulder. "You're too big for Jirra to haul up by herself," she whispered, tying the rope that dangled from the roof around her chest just under her armpits. "I'll go up first, and between us we'll get you to the roof."

Micah nodded, and returned his attention to the battle. Lambeth crouched near a pile of fallen stones and kept up a barrage of missiles that Perryn dodged nimbly, closing the gap between them. Just as Micah thought she'd have the swordsman cornered again, he at last found the mark, striking her on the side of her head. She fell with a grunt of pain, and Lambeth landed a few more stones as she fought to regain her feet.

Micah looked frantically for something to throw at her, but there seemed to be no stones small enough for him to lift. If only Felida had removed the fail-spell amulet from his chest. Another cry from the floor of the tower brought his attention back to the duel, but this time it was Lambeth's turn to suffer. The swordsman groaned, but Micah couldn't see him.

"Time's up, Micah!" shouted Perryn. "Rejoin us now, and I may let your new friends live. If you make me come up after you, they will die."

Micah cringed, whispering, "No, please. Please stop." Whatever power she had, it made him tremble, torn between running away and leaping to obey her, though he found it helped a little to know that it was a spell, not his own desire. Regardless, he had nowhere left to turn. Perryn mounted the stairs.

Lambeth charged her at that moment, tackling the sorceress from behind. The two combatants went down in a heap on the stairs, cursing and grunting as they fought. Lambeth had the advantages of both weight and reach, but he was also more severely injured, his face a charred mask of ruined flesh.

Micah jumped as something struck him in the back, but when he turned to confront the new danger, he found a rope dangling from above. Felida motioned for him to grab the rope. He did, clinging with all his strength as the two slightly built women hauled him up to the roof.

Screams echoed from the interior of the tower as Micah finally gained the stair landing at the collapsed roof. Felida, who had been chanting something, fell back against the floor. "I don't think I'll have the strength to haul myself up again," she said.

"Where do we go from here?" Micah asked. "We're trapped."

Jirra peered down into the tower, then out at the sky. "The wind is light," she said. "But they won't be able to remain on station here. Not with a firewhip down there. If this light rain would unleash a downpour, maybe. They'll have to hang ropes."

"Is Lambeth still alive?" Felida asked.

"He was," Micah said. He started to recount the swordsman's bravery, but the words caught in his throat as he thought about the burns on his face. More screams came from below, more like wordless howls of rage than shrieks of pain. "It doesn't matter. We can't get away."

"You mean you haven't figured it out, yet?" Felida said.

Jirra stood then, tied her rope to an upthrust stone that may once have been a crenellation, and pulled to test its strength.

"What are you doing?" asked Felida.

Jirra grabbed the rope and jumped, rappelling down into the lower levels of the tower.

"Damn her. Get ready, Micah. Jirra's father should be here soon. He's an airship captain."

Micah nodded, frantically scanning the sky for any sign of the ship. He'd seen one once, floating by over the quarry. He'd been so excited that day and couldn't wait to tell his mother. She'd brushed aside his energetic description, scoffing at his stated desire to fly one day. If the ship arrived in time, he would fly today.

More screams sounded. The firewhip cracked again and again. But when he glanced behind him, Micah couldn't see who was winning. Nor could he see the crippled girl.

"There!" Felida said, pointing to the west. An airship floated toward them just above the treetops. "Jirra! Lambeth! Time!"

Micah's eyes went wide as he watched the airship approach. The enormous bulk of the floating fish above the relatively tiny ship made him take a step back. Something that big had to be dangerous. Two dark shapes detached from the blimp and unfolded their wings. Whatever they were, they flew directly toward the tower. He crouched low, pointing at the flying creatures with a trembling hand.

"Easy," said Felida, laying a hand on his shoulder. "Those are the airhee's mates." At Micah's confused look, she added, "They're on our side."

But Felida didn't look relaxed at all. Her brow furrowed in worry, she kept glancing back down into the interior as the airhee's mates began circling overhead. After a few passes, both of the creatures dove into the tower through the broken roof. Both emerged seconds later, one of them trailing smoke. That one also had Jirra grasped firmly in its claws. Micah thought they were rescuing her, but the one that held her threw her up into the air as it executed a back flip. Micah gasped as she flew through the air, only to be grabbed by the other mate and flown on up to the airship, which was now just a few dozen yards from the tower roof and closing fast.

"Up!" Felida said. "We'll only have one chance to grab a rope."

From the staircase came laughter, harsh, almost maniacal. "Your man was good," said Perryn from somewhere down below. "But not good enough. Come with me, Micah. It's over."

"Soon," Felida whispered. "Ignore her, the ropes are almost upon us."

But Micah couldn't ignore Perryn. He could see her now, limping up the stairs, her face covered in blood, a fierce grin of triumph giving her features a demonic cast. Their eyes met, and she opened her mouth to speak.

Her eyes widened. Something dark and immense flew past Micah trailing smoke and flames, nearly bowling him over. One of the mates slammed into Perryn just as she tried to raise her whip.

"Micah!" Felida screamed.

He turned from the spectacle on the stairs to find a handful of ropes swinging toward him. He grabbed frantically, caught two of them, and was dragged from the rooftop. He screamed as he tried to get his legs wrapped around one of the ropes. Just as he thought he might not fall to his death, an explosion shook the tower. He gained altitude. After minutes that felt like hours, he found himself on the deck of the airship.

"What happened?" he said to Felida.

Felida didn't answer. The deck was crowded with crewmen. None of them spoke. A dark, bearded man embraced Jirra, but there were no smiles, no welcomes. Only Jirra's sobbing broke the silence.

Finally, the man holding Jirra broke away. "I have to go to her," he said. His voice cracked, and in the last dying light of the day Micah saw tears on the man's cheeks. "I have to tell Magda that Marshall is dead."

20

Kellyn looked out of eyes being controlled by her father, into her mother's eyes. She hadn't seen her in ten years, and her memories of that time were spotty at best. But her face—she remembered that. The broad, soft peasant's face into which she now gazed failed to match up with the angular beauty of the woman she recalled. Her mother had gone pale, sweating with the exertion of trying to find a way out of the jam into which her husband had gotten.

The palace in which they stood resembled nothing in Kellyn's memory. Engvar, Lon's home, headquarters of the reborn rebellion. Or so the plan went. Unless she could find a way to thwart them.

Her mother held Valdis' hands, and neither of them had spoken a word. How long would this go on? Kellyn had no way of knowing, but they must have held this pose for more than an hour already. In all that time, Kellyn had tried not to give any hint that she lived on inside her body. It felt like a game of hide and seek, but with much higher stakes than bragging rights among children. Her mother was searching for Kellyn's soul, but she could hide simply by not resisting her father's control. Or so she thought.

Finally, her mother relented, squeezing her eyes shut and releasing her hands. "Enough," she croaked. "She's in there, watching me, listening to us. But she won't act."

"You will find . . . a way," Valdis said.

"Not without Micah."

Valdis reached out to touch Sarah's hair, but she slapped his hand away. "No!" she said. "Do not touch me in our daughter's body! Not like that."

"I have longed to h-hold you for years," Valdis said. "Please, just . . . let me put my arms around you."

Sarah shook her head. "You ask too much. You always have." She stepped away and stretched. "There is only one way to handle this."

"I won't go back. N-never again! Ten . . . years confined to that prison, it's too much for anyone."

"Unless Perryn returns with Micah soon, there will be no other way."

"Then I'll possess . . . someone else. Someone w-weaker."

Sarah slashed the air with her hands. "Do you not understand? It can't work, not anymore. She's battled you for too long. Your soul is degraded. Far more than it should have been after so little time. If you try to possess another body, you may not make it. Even a weak person, drugged and under my supervision, would resist. All souls resist possession; my research proved that decades ago."

"You said . . . only that I may . . . not make it, not that I can't p-possibly—"

Kellyn chose that moment to strike with all her might; Valdis' words cut off and he fell to the floor. For a few precious seconds, Kellyn had complete control. She lashed out with her foot, catching her mother in the side of the knee. Sarah crumpled to the floor, and Kellyn should have been able to crush her undefended throat with a backhand punch, but she hesitated at the last possible instant, unwilling, or unable, to kill her mother. Her father regained enough composure to weaken Kellyn's control. She clutched her chest, suddenly having a great deal of trouble breathing.

"I will fight you to the end, Father," Kellyn said, grinding out each word. "And I will win." Then she fell back before her father's onslaught, trapped again behind the wall in her mind.

Valdis panted. "Do you see? We . . . must act . . . now!"

Sarah rolled to her side, clutching her left knee, her face a mask of rage, bright red and sweating profusely. She scooted across the floor on her bottom, taking several deep breaths before she spoke again. "You stand at best an even chance of making the jump to another body, even if we do everything right. If you will agree to go back into the prison we designed, I can preserve you indefinitely. Micah cannot hide from us forever."

Valdis shook his head. Suddenly, he laughed. "I have a . . . better idea. Much better." He crawled across the floor toward Sarah. "Lon! Come in . . . here. Hurry!"

Sarah whipped her head back and forth, from Lon to Valdis. "What are you doing, Valdis? Tell me!"

But Valdis wouldn't speak to her. "Hold . . . my body, Lon. Be p-prepared to . . . render it unconscious."

"No!" Sarah screamed. "Valdis, you cannot do this!"

She continued to scream. Like a puppet whose strings have been cut, Sarah slumped to the floor, her screams stopped, and Kellyn knew a heartbeat's release, as control of her body came flowing back with the force of lightning. And then blackness.

Micah stared out at the ground, hundreds of feet below the airship. The sun had just begun to rise, and so there wasn't much to see, details obscured in the near dark. He saw the course of a river outlined as the water reflected the dawn, its banks dark and forested. He felt safe from Lon and his father up here. Beyond their reach, beyond Perryn's. Well, Perryn couldn't reach anybody now. The other male blimp thing, Spot, had flown back to the tower to confirm that Marshall was dead. It had reported two human bodies within the tower as well, one male and one female.

Perryn. He hadn't known her that well, but it felt like he'd lost someone very important. His mother hadn't loved him, and indeed no one ever had. Perryn had been the closest thing to a friend he'd ever known. Felida . . . well, he didn't think she wanted him dead, may even have wanted to save him from the life of a sorcerer. While he no longer wanted to return to his mother, the craving for a life of power hadn't left him yet.

He tried not to think about Lambeth. The knight had sacrificed himself, holding Perryn off just long enough for the rest of them to escape. He remembered that brief moment when he'd locked eyes with the swordsman. "He knew," Micah whispered. He had no chance of escaping, and yet he'd fought on. He scowled, shaking off the melancholy that kept trying to envelop him.

The ship's crew reflected the black mood of Jirra and her father. They'd lost one of the airhee's mates, one of the males. So what? Who could care that much about an animal? They acted weirder around Jirra. Her father had embraced her, as had a couple of the others who might have been her cousins. But everyone else acted like there was something wrong with her. "Aside from being a witch," he said aloud.

"Who's a witch, now?" Felida asked.

Micah turned slowly. He hadn't heard her coming, but there was no reason to give her the satisfaction of knowing she'd startled him. "I wasn't talking about you."

Felida had been smiling, but the expression left her face all at once. "You haven't told us where we're going, but I think I've figured it out. Lon is Baron Ypreille, isn't he?"

Micah tried not to respond, but a grin crept onto Felida's lips. "Not such a good liar, after all. Not without magic. The Baron was supposedly a spy for the Prince during the rebellion, but I never believed that. I always thought he was secretly working for Hittrech. Now that I see his present company, my suspicions are confirmed."

"Engvar House won't be easy to attack. You'll have a hard time even getting through the doors."

"You've been there, I take it. We'll need to discuss what you've seen. And there's no point in lying, now. I'll know when you're telling the truth, and Jirra can tell us much of what you don't know. In fact, I think I'll put you under. You'll remember more that way."

Micah turned away from her, staring out at the sky just beginning to brighten. "Do whatever you want."

"Come along, then. The captain has agreed to let us use his cabin."

Micah followed Felida below decks to a relatively grand cabin at the rear of the ship. He'd been allowed free run of the *Nighthawk*, though a crewman usually accompanied him, but this was one place he'd never seen. The captain's cabin might have been cramped by the standards of Engvar House, but he had a bed, not a hammock like everyone else. He also had a writing desk and a small table and chair, a single bookcase packed with well-worn books, each row held in place with a rope tied tightly across the books' spines. Glass windows looked out on an amazing skyscape. Sunrise among the clouds, painted various pastel shades, awed him.

Sunrise. He frowned. "Wait a minute. If the rear of the ship is facing the rising sun, then we're going west, right?"

Felida joined him at the window. "And Engvar is to the north, yes. We're picking up another passenger. It won't delay us much. In fact, I believe we've begun our descent already. Please, Micah, lie down on the captain's bed."

Micah did as he was asked, wondering why there was no one else around. Did she think he was no longer a threat? Well, without magic, maybe he wasn't. He lay down on a bed that wasn't particularly soft or large, not after what he'd experienced at Lon's palace. Felida knelt at his side and dabbed his face with various powders and oils. She massaged his temples and sang in a low, soft voice. He couldn't understand the words, but knew he was being put under and didn't bother resisting.

When he opened his eyes, a single candle lit the cabin. Beyond the window, the sky was dark. Micah whipped his head around, suddenly feeling another's presence in the room. A man sat at the small desk, making notes on a large piece of parchment. "Captain?" Micah said. "How long have I been asleep?"

The man turned, and Micah shouted in blind panic. It was the mage, the man they'd fought outside the castle in D'Arrune. The mage held up his hands. "Not to worry, Micah. Felida has told me everything. I am Albertus Zang, a mage of the Brotherhood, formerly captain of Prince Johann's guard. I have joined this mad quest, even though I believe the result will be the death of us all."

Micah tried to slow his breathing, and gradually a degree of calm came over him. "You were holding Kellyn prisoner. Why are you willing to help us now?"

"Us, you say? So I'm not the only one who's changed sides. Well, two reasons. First, the Prince wanted my head after what you and your former friends did to his castle. Ah, and the fact that I'd let a Hittrech get away."

Micah tried to present as bland a face as possible. What would Zang do if he knew there was another Hittrech in the same room?

Zang looked at him with bored disinterest for a few heartbeats, then continued. "The second reason is simply that I must help defeat Valdis Hittrech. He cannot be allowed to walk the earth again. I say this to you as one who fought him ten years ago. I know what he is capable of."

"Why does everyone hate him so much? What did he do?"

"Aside from the rebellion, you mean? Aside from killing every member of the royal family except Johann? And believe me, they very nearly succeeded in killing the Prince, as well. He was quite lucky to survive. Well, aside from all that, Valdis Hittrech was too powerful. He delved deeper into the nature of magical essence than anyone ever has. He found ways to kill and control others that we in the Brotherhood never dreamt of. If we hadn't gotten wind of his plans when we did, he probably would have won."

Micah thought back to the waves of bone-chilling cold coming from his father during their escape in the postern gate tunnel. It didn't seem especially powerful or deadly, but maybe that was because he wasn't in his true body.

"And? Kattenwa's nothing compared to Thurn. It's not even a kingdom."

Zang smiled without humor. "If allowed free rein, in control of an entire country, no matter how small, there's no limit to the trouble he could have caused. I was part of a small force composed entirely of mages at one point. We assaulted a castle where he was doing research into necromancy." At Micah's blank stare, he continued, "The raising and controlling of the dead. You've no idea how hard it is to kill a reanimated corpse. Nothing short of cremation can completely stop the undead. What's worse, even if a soldier is only injured by one of those things, the wound invariably gets horribly infected and they die. At which time, they're under the direction of the controlling sorcerer, and begin attacking their former friends. Now, imagine an entire country under the control of such a man, raising the dead in every cemetery in Kattenwa. How many thousands of nearly indestructible soldiers would he have at his disposal? And as each new war would bring thousands more corpses under his sway, who could stand against such an army? He'd conquer the entire world."

Micah listened to Zang, torn between horror and awe. His father had done that? No wonder people feared him. Could he ever be that powerful?

Zang stood, shaking his head and sneering at Micah. "Only another sorcerer could hear that tale and not be repulsed. You're jealous of his power, aren't you? You disgust me. When this is all over, if any of us are still alive, I will recommend we permanently strip you of your powers. And seeing that you're a Hittrech yourself, they might just let me do it."

Micah's mouth hung open.

"Oh, yes. I know who you are. It was a guess, to be honest, but your reactions confirm it. And we *will* strip you, if you're allowed to live. It doesn't happen often, and the Elders must approve before it can be done. But I think you've earned it. I challenge you to prove me wrong."

Micah said nothing, trying not to show Zang how much he hated him right that instant.

"Come along," Zang said. "Jirra should be finished soon." He sprinkled sand on the parchment, rolled it up, and led the way out of the captain's cabin.

They went down to the cargo hold, where they found Jirra, Felida, several crewmen and the ship's captain. A makeshift table had been set up in the hold, and a miniature landscape sat atop the table. There were trees and buildings, but the scene was dominated by a large white structure in the center. It had columns in front, and a stone barn behind it. Micah blinked. "That's Engvar," he said.

Felida nodded to Micah. "As accurate as I can make it. Your memories were quite vivid, but the details were not the sort of set-in-stone accuracy you get with someone intimately familiar with a location. Jirra's visions have filled in some of the gaps." She lifted her gaze from the sorcerer's apprentice and spun slowly around, making eye contact with each person in the room. "We've a good deal of work to do, people." She took a metal rod from her pocket and waved it at a section of the miniature mansion. Walls and roof vanished, revealing the circular room with the mosaic floor. Tables and vases stood in the center, next to a miniature Lon. Brightly colored cloth connected each vase to a chandelier that hung from a long chain. The chain hung in midair, the ceiling having disappeared. "The ceremony will take place here. Without Micah, they will have to sacrifice Kellyn." A tiny Kellyn appeared on one of the tables. "I believe that in order to do this properly, Valdis will have to possess another body. They will murder his daughter, reform her remains into an exact rendition of Valdis' body, and at that point Valdis will move from whatever body he has possessed into what had previously been Kellyn."

"Will he do that?" Abbatay asked as he put his arm around Jirra's shoulders. "Will he murder his own child?"

"He'll stop at nothing," Zang said. "You've no idea what this monster is capable of."

"He's right," Felida said. "Listen, all of you. I want to save Kellyn. But her survival is secondary to preventing Valdis Hittrech from returning to the world. I'm going to give each of you an amulet that should give you added strength in resisting possession, should Valdis try to take over your body. It isn't a perfect defense, but it may give you a narrow window of time to strike at him." She brought a leather bag from the folds of her robe and passed it around. Each person withdrew a stone attached to a leather necklace and put it around his or her neck. When it came to Micah, the bag was empty.

"I don't get one?" he asked.

"You're the bait," Jirra said.

"You could have phrased that with just a tad more compassion,"

Felida said. "No matter, she's correct. Micah, your parents had planned to sacrifice you. As long as we arrive before they kill Kellyn, they will still try to use you to make Valdis' new body. They'll sense your arrival and try to take you alive. Until you are positioned here," she said, pointing at the tables in the center of the room, "they dare not harm you."

"Your dear old daddy won't focus on anyone but you," Jirra said. "We can't have Valdis sensing these amulets before we strike, so you go in unprotected." Her smile was unpleasant, to say the least.

Felida cleared her throat, frowning at Jirra. "While they're preoccupied with Micah, we strike. Destroy those tables, break the vases, kill anyone who tries to resist. But please, do not destroy any body before I've had a chance to examine it. Valdis Hittrech got away from us once by playing dead. Let's not make that mistake again."

"Unless he's still powerful enough to raise the dead," said Zang. "If he sends reanimated corpses after us, there's little we can do but destroy them."

"No," Felida said. "Cut them up. Each constituent part will continue to come after you, but once the limbs have been hacked off, there's little to fear. Until we're absolutely sure Valdis is dead, we take no chances."

Zang scowled, but offered no objections. He did, however, take over the rest of the planning session. "We have one chief disadvantage: Valdis will know all of us, but only as well as Kellyn knew us."

"You think the girl's cooperatin' with her dad?" one of the crewmen asked.

"Not at all. But Valdis has spent a great deal of time in Kellyn's body. He's had access to her memories all that time, and in the past he has shown great skill at sifting through other people's memories to find important details. One good thing is that he won't know who's coming, but as soon as he sees one of us, he'll know everything Kellyn knew about that person."

"But only what the girl knows, right? Nothin' else?"

"Exactly," Zang said. "And that's an advantage for us, slim though it might be. For instance, he'll know Jirra might have some magical talent, but he won't know what it is, since the last time Kellyn saw her even she didn't know what talents she might have. Moreover, Jirra sees the future, or rather she sees possible futures. Lon also has that ability, and he's better at it. But when two seers are trying to see the same future, they tend to reduce each other's accuracy. Lon won't know that he's facing another seer, and so won't have any reason to doubt his visions."

"Lon told me he won't look into the future anymore," Micah said. "He said what he had to go through to see the future was like slavery."

Zang inclined his head. "Let us hope you're correct." He stood next to the simulation and pointed at the two corridors leading out of the mosaic room. "When we had Valdis cornered in the Bostic Mountains, he took refuge in a cave. It was a large cave, but he made it all the more difficult to find him by magically creating false passages, making it appear that the cave was many times larger than it really was. He may do the same here, by creating many false corridors. He'll use his knowledge of each of us to craft lures in each false corridor to trap a specific individual. So if that is what he's done, if there are many false corridors, we should each avoid any corridor that feels right. We'll also stick together. Valdis escaped us last time. Not again."

"What about the sword?" Felida asked.

Zang nodded slowly. He was wearing two scabbards. From one of them, he withdrew a strange weapon. It was a sword, but unlike any Micah had ever seen. One side was undecorated steel, the other with flowing, swirling black and silver lines. Seen edge on, it looked like a sword with two blades impossibly close together, but that never quite touched.

"This is Kellyn's sword. It's a mage's sword, which means it is also a spirit. Kellyn is bonded to this weapon, but one of the sorcerers has silenced it. I don't think what they did to the blade is permanent, but no one save Kellyn can communicate with this sword. Felida and I have done our best to remove the curses placed upon the blade, so that when we find Kellyn her touch should reawaken it. I'm told she is quite formidable with this weapon."

The crewmen gave low whistles, nodding. "You don't know the half of it, boyo," said one.

"And Felida has done her best to assemble a collection of amulets and talismans that Kellyn should be able to use." Zang held up a small leather bag. "We'll keep the bag and the sword separate, in case we get split up. Who'll carry these, then?"

"I'll carry the sword," said Jirra.

"Are you sure?" her father asked.

"Yes. I've seen myself wearing that blade on my hip as I encounter Kellyn."

"Remember," said Felida, "that Lon may be trying to see the same future."

"I don't see anyone else with the sword in any of my other visions."

Zang unbuckled the scabbard and handed it to Jirra. "I'll keep the bag for myself. Even if I don't meet up with Kellyn, at least I will know how to use some of these objects." He cleared his throat and looked at each person in the room for a heartbeat. "We stay together. No matter how many false corridors we have to check out, we do not split up. If anyone does get separated, try to make your way back to the mosaic room. Now, are we all clear? Good. Eat, rest, limber up. We still have a couple of hours of left. We strike at midnight."

"You warned him, didn't you?" Lon asked.

Kellyn lay on a stone bench in her prison cell, her shackled hands connected by a thick chain to an iron ring in the wall. Another set of shackles weighed down her feet. Her joy at regaining control over her body had been short lived. She felt weak, aged well beyond her years, aches and pains torturing her every movement. But she lived, and Micah had escaped.

"That's one of the things I'll never understood about sorcerers," Kellyn said. "None of you have any loyalty to each other, and yet you're continually surprised when one of your so-called friends betrays you."

Lon sighed and shook his head. "You could have been the heir to a kingdom that will one day encompass the entire globe. And you threw it all away to save that nasty little brother of yours? Foolish. Perhaps it's better this way. Your soft-hearted friends won't kill Micah as they should, and we'll get him back in the end. The Brothers and Sisters will think he's just a child and try to save him. Exactly as they tried to save you. And how well did that work out?"

Kellyn smiled. "But they did save me. Even if you succeed, and I die, I am uncorrupted by my parents' evil. I'll go to whatever afterlife awaits me with a clear conscience. I doubt you can say the same."

"Tsk, tsk. The last resort of the righteous. You know you can't win, but you take comfort in knowing that you will have died well. I, personally, don't intend to die. Moreover, I don't actually want you to die, either."

Kellyn watched the sorcerer as he paced around the tiny cell, waiting for him to get into range. She had very limited freedom of movement with the chains, but if Lon would come just a few feet closer, she felt certain she could get in a few kicks or punches. She tried not to let her frustration show as Lon remained stubbornly just out of harm's way.

"Your mother wants you to live," Lon continued. "Even your father knows that it would be best if you lived. Sarah won't willingly stand by his side if he allows you to die."

"More of that famous sorcerer loyalty, I see. So, what do I have to do to live? Whom do I have to betray? Or do I need to murder some innocent bystander? Come, Lon! Tell me just what a worthless, evil piece of slime I have to be to earn my life back!"

"You don't have to do anything. If we get Micah back in time, you will live, whether you want to or not. In time, you'll see the error of your ways."

"Never."

Lon chuckled. "Never is a very long time, young mage. Your father will rule the world one day. He doesn't intend to die, either. If it takes a thousand years, he'll conquer everything in his path. And he'll keep you alive all that time so you can watch it happen. Do you think you can resist for a thousand years?"

Now it was Kellyn's turn to laugh. "You haven't even found Micah yet. I'm betting you won't."

"So we don't find him. What of it? Your father will still come back to life; he'll still conquer the world. And you? You'll be nothing more than another mage who failed to defeat him. I suspect that gives you very little comfort."

Kellyn did not respond. Lon had given voice to the scenario she feared was most likely to play out. The sorcerer left the cell without ever coming close enough for her to strike.

Abbatay stood alone at the front of the ship, hands clasped behind his back. With his eyes closed, it looked for all the world as if he'd fallen asleep standing up. Micah sat with his back against the rail just a little to the left of the ship's bow, trying not to feel miserable and afraid. These people cared little for him. He might just as well have been a bond worker once again.

Just for a moment, he became lost in the fantasy that none of this had ever happened, that he *was* still a bond worker, that he and his mother still lived in a little shack near the quarry. He smiled for that moment, but the image vanished all too quickly. He could have cried then, and why shouldn't he? Hadn't he been through enough? "I'm just a kid," he whispered.

"A kid with extraordinary abilities," the captain of the airship said.

Micah didn't bother hiding how startled he was that the captain had heard him. "And if I couldn't do the things I can do, I wouldn't even be here. I'd probably be dead." He reached for Serpent, forgetting that he'd left the prayer stone behind when he'd followed Lon to Roccobin. At least Felida had removed the fail-spell amulet.

Abbatay strolled over and squatted next to Micah. He folded his arms and rested them on his knees. "Then be glad you have those abilities. Not all of us are so fortunate."

Micah blinked. That wasn't quite a lie, but the captain was trying to make him believe a lie without coming out and saying it. And all at once, he figured it out.

"It was you," Micah said. "You're the one who repressed Jirra's magical talents."

Abbatay looked at Micah, then looked away. He sighed heavily. "She is my only child. When she was very small, I took her aboard the *Nighthawk* for her first flight. There was an accident at the dock, a rope snapped, and a load of cargo fell to the deck all at once. A barrel of salt cod rolled over her leg. The healer said she was lucky to live."

Micah said nothing, trying hard to examine the captain's face: crafty, and sly. He had the look of a man who showed only those emotions he needed to show, which was probably a good trait in a ship's captain. He knew instantly the man had some ulterior motive for showing Micah his pain.

"Her mother didn't take it well. We tried to have another child, but we couldn't. Childbirth had been very difficult for my wife, and the healer said she'd likely never have another; she was right. She cried every time she saw her daughter hobbling along with a crutch. So Vendalyn kept coming up with more reasons why I should take Jirra on voyages with me. She was a rough girl, and many in the crew assumed her to be a boy. I encouraged that."

Micah could see the scene, now. The protective father, alarmed when his daughter began to have frightening dreams about the future, when she knew things no child should ever know. "You thought you were protecting her," he said.

Abbatay nodded slowly. "I shouldn't have. I should have taken her to the Sisterhood. But I couldn't. How could I send my little girl away, after what I allowed to happen to her? So yes, it was me. I suppressed her gift. Now, I'm glad she's had some time away from me. Now she can embrace it and become the woman she was meant to be." He stood, looking down at Micah with a crooked smile. "Do you think I'm a bad father?"

Micah shook his head. "I think I know a little about bad fathers. Having you as a father would have been easy."

"I don't have much in the way of magical gifts, Micah. I'm nothing at all like you or your sister. I can prevent magic from happening around me, and not much else."

"That wouldn't be so bad. I have all these abilities, and the only people who don't hate me for what I've done are the ones who want to kill me."

"I have nothing against you," said Abbatay. "I don't judge you according to what your parents have done, or even much of what you yourself have done. After all, you're just a child." The captain paused then, gazing up at the stars. "When this is all over, I would like to introduce you to a man I know. A man who searches out children like you."

"Who?"

"Patience. Just know that I was once like you. A boy with . . . particularly awful parents. A boy with magical talents, though not nearly at your level of power. This man took me in, trained me, and gave me this position. I think—rather, I know—that he will want to meet you."

Micah frowned. Abbatay was telling the truth, but that didn't make him feel safe, or even hopeful. "Zang thinks they're going to strip my powers from me. If I live through this, anyway."

"Zang is one man. Felida won't side with him. And if you perform well, that will put a few notes on the positive side of your personal ledger." Abbatay reached out to squeeze Micah's shoulder. "Think about what I've said. Things aren't so bleak as you think. And there is a future for you, a future considerably brighter than your past."

"You can't know that."

"But I can. Magical talents run along bloodlines, you know. And usually similar talents. I can see a little of the future, too."

"Won't that interfere?"

"I think not. I've been suppressing my gifts since I found out about my daughter's ability. But I have seen you, in the future, meeting my patron."

"So I live through this?"

"Most likely. But as with Jirra, I see only possibilities."

"What if you don't live to make the introduction?"

"I've already sent a messenger pigeon. If you live through this, he'll seek you out, whether I live or die."

Micah cast a suspicious glance at the captain, and yet he wanted to trust Abbatay. After all, the captain was the only person who'd seemed interested in helping him instead of using him.

21

The strange harness chafed Micah's armpits and pinched his groin, but it saved him from a fifty-foot drop. Aboard the *Nighthawk*, crewmen lowered him to the roof of Engvar House. He knew they were up there, but when he looked, only a darker area of a very dark sky gave away the ship. All around him, other members of the assault team hung from similar harnesses, waiting for Micah to finish his part, but he could barely see them.

When his boots hit the roof, he yipped in surprise. The others hung back, each now about ten feet from the roof if all had gone according to plan. Micah knelt and placed his bare hands on the roof. He was above the mosaic room. The domed roof, constructed of poured concrete, contained only tiny pebbles mixed in with the sand and cement. Zang had warned him that the roof itself possessed very little diwa. No matter: he walked to the edge of the roof and placed his hands on the exposed stone that formed the walls. Plenty of diwa there, and he brought the tendrils of power into his hands. With the fail-spell amulet removed, he could work magic again, and his mood had improved dramatically. When he'd gathered all the tendrils he could, he pushed hard.

Nothing happened. He pulled, then pushed, then pulled again. The blocks of marble began to shift. With one mighty push, the wall began to flex. The portion he'd been working on gave way, massive blocks tumbling to the ground, followed quickly by tons of concrete in massive, jagged chunks. He fell a few feet before the rope went taut, jerking him back to hang suspended in air. The roar of the collapsing building rivaled that of the tower in D'Arrune, and the choking dust that plumed upward coated him in grit.

When the last of the blocks settled, the crewmen began lowering Micah and the rest of the attackers down into the tumbled ruins.

"Your friends are here," said Kellyn's mother, or rather her body.

Kellyn had a difficult time thinking of her as her mother, especially as she was pretty sure that her body had been possessed by Valdis. He had to have gone somewhere when he released Kellyn from possession, and he'd been weak. He would have needed a body that would know how not to resist. If Valdis really did possess her now, he sounded stronger, more certain.

The sorcerers had chained Kellyn to a table in the center of a vast circular room. Vases surrounded her table and another like it. "You don't seem concerned," she said.

"I'm not. That brutal destruction of the palace can only have been Micah's work—you may yet live through this day. What do you say, Lon? Can you retrieve him for me?"

Lon frowned deeply, nodding but refusing to look in Sarah's direction. "We'll need Kellyn off the table. Shall I unchain her?"

"Not just yet. Just in case those people are smart enough to keep Micah safely out of my reach. Now hurry along. Bring Chase if you need to."

"What about our, ah, our soldiers?"

"They'll be along. Don't worry; they won't attack you. Now go!"

Lon left at a run, Chase dutifully following in his wake. Sarah/Valdis smiled at Kellyn. "I've left recognition spells throughout the palace. When your friends pass near them, I'll receive a vision. Thanks to your memories, I'll know them, their strengths and weaknesses. And of course, the palace won't look like it did when Micah was here last. They'll be lost, isolated, confused. Easy prey, my daughter."

She knew, then, that her father had indeed possessed her mother's body, and she did her best to ignore the monster. Now that she knew, her mother even looked a little less like herself, more like the man who had possessed her. She tried to focus on the memory she'd seen of her parents arguing. Her mother had resisted, refusing to bear Valdis a son. She'd only complied when forced to do so, compelled by powerful magic. She hadn't seen all her father's memories, though, so she had no idea what other compulsions he might have placed upon her mother. Kellyn looked up at the chandelier, trying to figure out what all the brightly colored cloth was for, and if she could possibly find a way to help whoever had come for her. But the shackles around her ankles and wrists were tight enough that she could never wriggle her way free.

"I don't expect you to join me," Valdis said through Sarah's mouth, "not willingly. Not at first, anyway. So don't bother trying to fool me into thinking you've suddenly switched sides. I know you'll hate me for a long time. Years, certainly, perhaps centuries. But you will relent in time."

Kellyn tried to focus on her father's words. Did he really believe that? And if so, was there any way to use his arrogance against him?

A sound like chunks of metal hitting a tile floor interrupted her thoughts. There was a tinkling of breaking glass, and a crunch of falling stone. A shout followed, and then an explosion. Sarah's eyes went wide for a moment. She grabbed the edge of the other table.

"What's the matter?" Kellyn said. "Getting worried?"

Micah unhooked his harness and looked around for the others. Things weren't going very well so far, and they seemed to be getting a lot worse: he was alone. As soon as his feet had touched the pile of rubble, the rope connecting him to the *Nighthawk* had come tumbling to the floor, much of it landing on Micah's head and shoulders. Alarmingly, the mosaic room had been restored to its former glory. Pink crystals in golden sconces along the walls lit the room, the roof and walls suddenly intact. The restored mosaic chamber unnerved him enough. The absence of the others terrified him, but he tried to think rationally.

Zang thought there'd be extra corridors leading to traps. Instead, the room itself was the trap. Had everyone fallen into their own trap-rooms? Regardless, he had to be the first to find them. No one else would try to spare his mother.

There were two corridors, exactly as he remembered. The corridor to his right had previously led to the other version of this room, the version equipped with all the things his parents needed to complete the rebirth of Valdis Hittrech. He'd never explored the other.

Muffled footsteps sounded from the corridor to his right. He had to hide. Under the stairs? Too obvious. He ran for the other corridor, dragging the rope, went in just far enough to get out of the light, and crouched by the wall. As he waited, that familiar hunger clawed at his belly.

Micah heard Lon whisper, "He's got to be in here somewhere. This is the only exit." Then the soft metallic slither of a sword leaving its scabbard. Chase, most likely.

Micah placed his hands on the floor, gathering strands of diwa. He didn't dare bring the walls down again, but there had to be something he could do. He felt a pair of feet exerting pressure on the stones, but he couldn't just fling stones at whoever it was. The stones were of varying thickness and he'd have to carefully work them free of each other before he could use them as weapons. He saw no options in his hiding place and he dared not enter the room. Too much light.

With sudden inspiration, Micah released the tendrils from the floor and reached instead for the walls. Once he identified the stones holding the sconces, he simply popped the brass fixtures out of the wall one at a time, starting with those furthest from his hiding place. As the crystals hit the floor, they shattered and their light went out.

"Clever boy!" called Lon. "Do you really think that'll be enough to save you?"

Micah ignored the taunt, focusing instead on the floor. The voice seemed to be coming from further away than the person walking into the center of the mosaic room. He gathered the tendrils once again, located what was most likely Chase—moving under the staircase at that moment—and began slowly working a good-sized stone free of the floor. It was granite, his favorite stone, square, maybe two feet on a side, and at least a foot thick. With exquisite care, he wriggled the stone free, moving it only when Lon and Chase were themselves making noise. When he had it out of the floor, he held it easily in one hand, though it must have weighed a couple of hundred pounds. With his free hand, he felt the tendrils for Chase's location. He stood on the staircase, but must have decided against it. He turned and stepped down onto the floor. Micah hurled the granite.

Micah heard a meaty thud and the sound of the granite crashing to the floor. Chase shouted, an incoherent cry of pain. At that moment, a lance of lightning stabbed through the darkened room. It struck the wall several feet from Micah's position, where it did something different. Instead of fizzling out as it had when Lon used it to kill the Prince's soldiers, the bolt of lightning caused a stretch of wall of explode into the room, showering the floor with jagged chunks of stone.

Micah wiggled out of his harness and left his hiding place, running over to the pile of rubble and ducking behind the largest pieces. He winced as pain shot through his side: a chunk of stone must have grazed his ribs. Warm wetness spread through his clothing, but there was nothing he could do about it then. To his left, Chase continued to moan. He reached for the floor, gathered the tendrils again, and felt for Lon.

"You can't hide forever, little Micah!" Lon said. "Why not make this easier on yourself? Give up, rejoin us. Soon your sister will be dead, her body reformed into a proper host for your father. He'll have need of an heir."

Micah felt the pull of Lon's words. They were lies, of course, but something within them urged him to obey. As with Perryn, the knowledge that he was being manipulated with magic robbed the spell of some of its power. He shook his head and placed his hands on the floor once more. It took a few frantic seconds to relocate Lon in the darkness. The sorcerer walked slowly, along the walls, away from the staircase, toward Micah. Not far from Lon, a sconce lay directly in his path.

He'll stumble, Micah thought, a plan forming in his mind. He hefted a chunk of stone no larger than his fist. He'd gotten lucky with Chase.

That wouldn't happen again. With his other hand, he used the remaining magical diwa from the destroyed wall to lift a jagged stone larger than his body.

Sarah/Valdis paced the room in circles, muttering. "There is still time."

Kellyn watched her mother's body closely. It walked stiffly, and at times the hands shook. At other times, the arms gesticulated wildly, as if in a silent conversation.

"Lon won't fail me!" Valdis/Sarah shouted. "He's our most reliable servant. Give him time. When he returns, with or without Micah, everything will progress as planned."

Sarah's body stood still then, little gasps and groans escaping her lips. Sarah/Valdis shook her head violently.

"Silence! I won't abandon the plan! I won't go back!"

Apparently, Valdis got the silence he wanted. It was confusing, watching her. Him. Them. Kellyn wondered if her mother resisted possession as she had, however briefly, or if she simply let it happen. After all, Sarah and Valdis were supposedly working toward the same end. But were they still?

And why were they waiting? Clearly, something had gone wrong. The smart thing to do would be to start the process of forming a new body for Valdis so he could jump into it and escape. But there were two tables here. Obviously, they needed another person on the other table to complete the spell. That could be Sarah's body. But then who would enact the spell? They weren't waiting because they wanted to. They couldn't proceed. She laughed.

"You find something amusing?" her father said.

"There's not enough bodies to go around, are there?" Kellyn said with a smile.

Sarah/Valdis turned away from her.

"This is wonderful. You need either me or Micah to make a new body, but there's more. You need a second sorcerer to complete the spell. How amazingly arrogant you people are. You always assume your opposition isn't strong enough, or ruthless enough, or whatever. Were you this surprised when your stupid little rebellion failed ten years ago?"

"Silence!"

The room echoed with Valdis' shout. Kellyn shut her mouth. She didn't want to goad her father into something rash. He'd killed that woman in the tunnel under D'Arrune with less provocation.

"I said there was enough time," Valdis/Sarah shouted, her voice cracking with effort and strain. "I'll just cancel the replication spell. It won't take them long to find this room, and we'll put one of them on the table. Very well! I'll go back to my prison, but only for as long as it takes you to make me a new body. No! Not yet."

Micah held perfectly still, barely breathing, listening as Lon crunched across the rubble strewn floor. He tossed the smaller stone underhanded so that it landed behind Lon. The sorcerer spun and unleashed a barrage of lightning at the spot of floor where the stone hit. With the sorcerer silhouetted against the ensuing explosions, Micah threw the much larger chunk of wall with his other hand. He must have been growing weaker, though, because instead of crushing Lon's head as intended, the stone slapped him on the back, hard. Lon sprawled across the floor, moaning, but otherwise quite still. Micah approached cautiously. He needed to be sure.

Strong arms grabbed Micah from behind. He screamed and struggled, but to no avail. The arms were too strong.

"I have him, Master," said the man holding him.

It was Chase, but he sounded wrong. With no inflection in his voice, and the arms around Micah emanating cold like chunks of ice, he knew at once that Zang had been right to fear his father—Chase had died and been reanimated.

He continued to struggle, but the reanimated corpse was far too strong, and Micah grew weaker with each passing breath.

"Master?" the corpse said. "Are you well?"

Lon gasped. "Chase," he croaked. "Take me to Valdis. I'm hurt."

Chase stood still, unable to lift Lon without putting Micah down first. Even if Chase did drop him, though, Micah feared he wouldn't be strong enough to fight again. He needed gris food, and soon. *Or diwa.*

Micah waited for Chase to put him down, then pressed his hand against the corpse's bare arm. He felt for diwa, and found it. Not the same diwa as in stone; it had a different texture. Not rough, or smooth, or sharp. It felt oily, and cold. Regardless, he drank in the magical essence, and Chase collapsed.

Immediately, Micah felt better. Not perfect. Not even good. But better.

"Chase?" Lon said, his voice now no more than a hoarse whisper. "What's wrong?"

"What's wrong?" Micah said. "Nothing at all." He reached for Lon, touched the sorcerer's face, and drank his diwa in an instant. He exhaled, feeling better still, but shaky, dizzy. At almost the same moment, a sound like a giant bringing his hands together in a single, thunderous clap drove him to his knees. He was back in the original version of the room, undamaged and lit by the pink crystals. He blinked, breathed deeply, and stood slowly. All around him other members of the assault team popped into existence.

Felida was at his side almost immediately, holding him up and looking into his eyes. "Are you well?"

He nodded. "I think so."

"Sound off," said Zang. "We need to know who made it. Zang."

"Felida."

"Jirra."

"Abbatay."

"Payner."

"Micah."

"That's it?" Jirra said. "There were fifteen of us. Oh, Daddy, I'm so sorry."

Abbatay embraced her, but it was clear he was favoring his left side.

"What's wrong?" Jirra said. "Where are you hurt?"

"Don't touch the wound!" Zang shouted. "Captain Abbatay, you're bleeding. How were you wounded?"

"One of those things got me. Those walking corpses."

"Did it bite you?"

"I'm afraid so."

Zang took Jirra's shoulders and pulled her away.

"No one touch the captain," said Zang. "Felida, examine Jirra to make sure none of her father's blood is on her. If it is, and she's cut anywhere on her body, make sure his blood doesn't touch hers."

"Wait!" Jirra said. "What about my father?"

"I'm still alive, and I can still fight," said Abbatay. "You may as well use me for the most dangerous jobs from here on out. I won't live to tell the tale anyway."

Jirra lowered her head and sobbed as Felida examined her.

"My sweet daughter, I'm so sorry. For everything. Now let's go find Kellyn. Time for mourning later."

Micah wobbled a bit as he led the way down the corridor that led to the other version of the room, the one with the tables and vases. The diwa failed to keep the hunger at bay and he almost fell, but Zang supported him with a hand around his shoulder. With his other hand, the mage activated a glowing crystal.

At the door without a handle, Micah bit the inside of his lip and spat bloody saliva on the door. But as he was about to open it, Jirra whispered, "Stop!"

"What is it?" Zang asked.

"I have to go first," she said, sniffling away the last of her tears.

"Why?"

"Please, you have to trust me. If I don't go first, this will all end very badly."

Jirra moved to the front of their little column. Micah, leaning against the wall, shouted, "Open!"

Jirra moved through before anyone could act.

And just as quickly, someone grabbed her and dragged her down the corridor, faster than any human should be able to move. Micah tried to move, but his legs felt too heavy. He fell to the floor as the others sprinted after whatever had taken Jirra. All except Felida, who pulled Micah to his feet and helped him forward.

When he and Felida stumbled into the room, they found his mother holding Jirra's left arm behind her back and Kellyn's sword to her throat.

"That's far enough," she said as she dragged Jirra toward the tables. When she reached the center of the room, she threw Jirra to the floor and held the sword just a fraction of an inch from Kellyn's neck. "No one moves or Kellyn dies. Give me Micah, and you can all leave unharmed."

"No deal," Zang said.

"Micah," his mother said, looking into his eyes, "I know you don't trust me right now, but I need you. I'll need another sorcerer to complete the spell. Lon's dead, isn't he? I need you, my son. Join me!"

Micah tried to obey. At that moment, he wanted nothing more. But he was too weak to move. Had Felida not held him up, he'd have collapsed again.

"Mother!" he whimpered.

On the table, Kellyn was staring at the sword held near her throat. She jerked her neck toward the blade.

The world vanished. Kellyn had been in the room where she was supposed to die, surrounded by her would-be rescuers, her own sword poised to kill her. Her mother held the sword, but her body was being controlled by Valdis' soul.

Then darkness, absolute black. Until a tiny orange light appeared in the distance. It grew into an immense, silent flame. Not a bonfire, though. This flame had arms and legs. It came closer. It also had a head and a face. The face was not human. It had a pointed snout, like a wolf, and fangs that overlapped its gums from both top and bottom. Its ears were like bat wings, and there were several pairs of enormous horns sprouting from all over its skull. Even those features, however, were made of living flame.

"Kellyn," the fire thing said. "Do you not know your own sword?"

"Shaethe?"

"It is I, in my true form. No mage should ever see her sword like this. It is a sign that we are in terrible danger. We must move quickly."

"I'm chained to a table and my parents—my father, at any rate—he'll cut my throat if he has to."

"There's a way out, but you won't like it. We'll have to fight your parents as only we can."

"What do you mean?"

"We will possess your mother's body and kill both of their souls."

Kellyn stood very still. "Shaethe, you're proposing darkest sorcery. I would rather die."

"Would you? Would you rather let all your friends die, too? Would you rather take the chance that your father will find a way out of this mess, that he'll still find a way to remake his body and conquer the world?"

"He's surrounded."

"Remember the vases, Kellyn? What do you think is inside each of them? I'll tell you: my brethren are in there. Spirits just like me, only they won't be called into existence to bond with a mage and a sword. I'd wager their destiny is to provide the diwa your parents need to remake your father's body. But if they have no other option, they will release the spirits from the vases. Then my brothers and sisters will kill everything in the palace. Maybe everything within a thousand miles, before their rage is spent."

Kellyn thought for a few moments. "Wouldn't they kill him, too?"

"When I first sensed your father's soul, when I thought it was just another part of you, I examined it carefully. It was a sort of shell, totally unbreakable. He could retreat into that shell, after releasing my brethren. Everyone within range of their fury would die, but he would survive, I believe. His soul could last like that indefinitely. Or we could kill him now."

Kellyn couldn't respond, torn between wonder that she was actually speaking to her sword, and revulsion at what Shaethe suggested.

"You would sacrifice your life to kill him, wouldn't you?" Shaethe said.

Kellyn nodded.

"Then how much of a sacrifice would it be to commit this one act of sorcery?"

"Possessing someone . . . that's an unforgivable offense."

"So what would the Brotherhood do to you? Kill you? You've already decided to throw your life away. At least make your death accomplish something worthwhile."

She stood very still for what seemed a long, long time. Finally, she whispered, "I'll do it."

Shaethe disappeared, then reappeared at her side. The spirit held out a hand, and she took it. A sensation of movement came over her, though they didn't appear to be going anywhere at all. The sensation stopped, and they stood before a vast, smooth wall. Very much like the wall that had held Kellyn prisoner within her own body. Shaethe reached out to touch the wall, and it crumbled like a paper-thin sheet of dust. Behind it, two figures stood. One was clearly her mother, small, thin, and weak looking. Her face now looked exactly as she remembered it from ten years ago. The other, her father, immense, impossibly well-muscled, and glowing with red-hot hatred. His blazing white eyes focused on Kellyn.

"Ah, my daughter! I see you've met my old friend, Shaethe."

Kellyn felt her eyes go wide as she looked back and forth between her father and her bonded sword. "Please, Shaethe, tell me he's lying."

Shaethe stood motionless. "No, Kellyn. He speaks the truth. I'm sorry. I didn't remember until this very instant."

"Did you think me so short-sighted, girl? I knew the Brotherhood would take you, and try to make you one of them. I knew one day they'd give you a sword, so I made one for myself and called Shaethe into existence. I picked his name especially for you—I remember as a young girl you used to love the stories of the spirit who first took the name, Shaethe Soul-Drinker."

Kellyn closed her mouth with an effort, thinking frantically as her father laughed. She looked to her mother, but she stood mute, arms hanging limp, eyes downcast. "Afterwards," Kellyn asked, "you sent him back where he came from?"

"Yes, but he'd already bonded with me, and the presence of my soul in your body would allow no other spirit to inhabit your sword. Shaethe cannot harm me now, for killing me would be like killing half of himself. Isn't that right, old friend?"

"Half of me is bonded with Kellyn. The bond I felt with you is diminished, and I am no friend of yours. But you have the right of it. I cannot harm either of you without harming myself."

Valdis laughed again. All the while, though, Kellyn had been thinking, and planning. This place—no place, really—wasn't real. The four of them existed in her mother's mind, where anything any of them could imagine might become real. Only the power of the mind doing the imagining limited the possible. She thought she might have ended all this days ago if she'd had this insight earlier.

Kellyn pulled a bow from the air, loosing dozens of arrows at a time. When she'd exhausted the quiver, she threw stars again and again. Unlike the physical world, here she could control an almost unlimited number of missiles in flight, and all of them struck her father's immense body.

Strike they did, but most simply glanced harmlessly off his naked skin. Most, but not all. Some penetrated, and once she heard her father grunt in response. No wound appeared where the missiles hit, and no blood flowed, but Valdis' body seemed to shrink. Or had she imagined that? Either way, the smile fell from her father's face and he roared, a sound so huge and deafening Kellyn thought her ears might rupture. A blast of wind struck her shortly after the awful bellow began, flinging her backward.

She landed awkwardly, bones in her left arm and both legs snapping audibly. Breathing hurt terribly; she'd have wagered most of her ribs had been broken. *It isn't real*, she thought, and suddenly the bones mended perfectly, as if she'd never been injured at all. She stood with a crooked grin on her face.

Kellyn sprinted toward her father, running faster than any human ever did in the real world, swinging a sword half again as long as her body. She leapt to assault her father, who may have been thirty feet tall. Her wicked, serrated sword bit into Valdis' arm as he raised it to defend himself. The blade passed effortlessly through first the arm, then through ribs and lungs before lodging in the spine.

Valdis laughed. He grabbed the blade and yanked it out of Kellyn's hands, then ripped it free of his body. The steel crumbled like thin, rusted iron. But it had done what Kellyn intended: Valdis had shrunk again, visibly this time. Whereas he had been a mountain of a man before, now he was at most twice her height. Kellyn barely paused, imagining a spear twelve feet long, which she thrust toward her father's belly. But the wooden shaft burst into flames which engulfed her hands. She hopped backwards, extinguishing the flames and healing her burns.

"I don't actually want you dead, girl. A thought from me and your friends will die. Go back to your body and they may live, if they will yield."

He's negotiating. I've hurt him.

Kellyn stood straight and turned toward her still-silent mother. "And what of you, Mother? I watched Father's memories. I saw you resist this terrible plan. You only cooperated because he forced you. Is this what you want, as well?"

"You don't know how it is," she said, barely above a whisper. "I . . . we have no choice, Kellyn."

"But we do. Anything we can imagine can happen here. There are no limitations at all. His compulsion carries no power here, unless you choose to let it. Your mind is yours."

Sarah shook her head and lowered her eyes.

A massive hand fell upon Kellyn's shoulder. Her father stood just inches from her now, a smell like rotting corpses and burning flesh filling the air. He was now just a little taller than a very tall man, maybe seven feet. "Your mother cannot help you, and neither can Shaethe. You cannot defeat me. Even if you could slay me, I have already taken steps to assure that my army will be waiting for you outside the palace. Only one path allows your friends to live. Choose."

Kellyn looked at her hands, shaking her head. Out of the corner of her eye she saw a bright, reddish orange shape moving toward them.

There was only one thing she could imagine that might prevent her father from thinking the command to open the vases and unleashing the sword spirits. One thing her father feared and hated above all others.

Her hands became red-black hemispheres, growing from the size of her palms to immense shells ten feet tall in the blink of an eye. She slammed the two halves shut over her father, an instant after Shaethe slammed into Valdis from behind. Her hands emerged from the sphere, and she struggled to keep it closed. The shell, as she dreamed it, consisted of layers of steel and rock and molten lava, but the battle raging within released such energies that the light from Shaethe penetrated the shell and cast her father's shadow through the solid surface. Kellyn groaned with the effort of keeping the shells together.

"Mother, help me! If he breaks free all is lost!"

Sarah looked at her, a sad smile upon her face. "I never wanted to hurt you," she whispered.

For an instant, Kellyn's fears materialized, the shell halves splitting apart. Within, Shaethe and her father grappled, hands around each other's throats, engulfed in flames and smoke. A sound like a landslide pummeled her ears as she fought desperately to reclose the sphere.

"Help me. Or I'll die. As will you. As will Micah. Only Father will survive." She closed the sphere, but it opened again, revealing the dueling pair rolling over each other like wrestlers. Her father leaked copious amounts of blood; smoke poured from a dozen wounds in Shaethe's body.

"Do you think your friends will let me live? After all I've done?" Sarah said.

"I'll tell them the truth. You had no choice. But you have one now." Kellyn's arms trembled, her voice grew thick. She could almost seal the hemispheres, but the energies within kept forcing her hands apart. "Quickly! Help me!"

Sarah stood behind her, placed her hands over Kellyn's and pushed. What little strength she added, however, mattered little. The pressure of her mother's face, nuzzled between Kellyn's shoulder blades, gave her more strength than she'd dared hope. "I love you, Kellyn. I love both of my children. Tell Micah for me, promise you will."

"You're going to live, Mother. Tell him yourself."

Sarah said nothing, but Kellyn could hear her sniffling. In front of her, Valdis stood over the sword spirit, a massive blade of white-hot steel chopping down toward Shaethe's unprotected head. Kellyn pressed the shell together, the pressure combining with the heat of the titanic struggle within to melt the two halves together. She continued to push, and the sphere shrank. Her mother's hands radiated heat, power, and something she chose to identify as love. The sphere shrank to no larger than a child's kickball and continued to diminish until she had to kneel to keep her hands pressed to its sides.

A rumbling sound emerged from the ball, now no larger than an orange, and red-black fissures appeared on its pebbly exterior. Light erupted from the cracks and the tiny ball forced Kellyn's hands apart. For an instant the sphere hung free in the air. Suddenly Shaethe stood beside her.

"It is done," the spirit said in a voice like water hissing over a hot stone. "He is dead."

The sphere crumbled in Kellyn's hands, falling to the ground between her fingers like sand through an hourglass. She grinned triumphantly, turning first to her mother, and then to Shaethe. Her expression faltered.

Shaethe slumped to his knees, his fires nearly extinguished. Between the sparse squirts of flame, his body consisted of smoke and ash, some of it red hot, but most of it cooling to white like logs in a fireplace.

"I told the truth, Kellyn. I could not harm you or your father without harming myself."

"I thank you, Shaethe. I can never repay your sacrifice." She reached to clasp hands with the spirit, but when they touched, Shaethe's fingers dissolved into drifting flakes of pale ash.

"You may yet repay me, Kellyn," Shaethe said as he died. "My brethren . . ."

Sarah once again embraced her.

"I must leave, Mother. I have to go back to my body. I'll try to stop them from harming you. Perhaps if you—"

Kellyn never finished the thought. Her mother cried out in pain, and she flew backward, away from Kellyn's reaching hands. Kellyn fell down a tunnel that narrowed along the way, her mother lost in a bright light.

Kellyn's neck broke contact with the blade, and at that instant Sarah began to fall, the sword slipping harmlessly out of her hands. Micah tried to summon the last of his energy to run to her side, but Zang was there first, sword in hand. He ran her through, his sword penetrating her gut just under the rib cage. She slumped against the blade, then slid limply to the floor. Micah screamed.

On the table, Kellyn took a shuddering breath. Zang withdrew his bloody sword from Sarah's body and held it against Kellyn's cheek. "Who are you?" he said.

"Kellyn," his sister croaked.

"Felida, come examine her. Check her mother's body as well. We have to be sure Valdis did not escape."

Micah tried to crawl to his mother's side, but he was too tired. He no longer felt hungry, but that wasn't exactly a blessing. Everything hurt. He felt as if death hovered just over his shoulder, and he welcomed the thought.

"These two are clean," Felida announced. "Everyone else, one at a time. Brother Zang, you'll have to examine me yourself." They were all clean. Zang announced that Felida was clean, too, as far as he could tell.

Kellyn was whispering something to Jirra. She nodded and called for everyone's attention. "Kellyn says the vases contain imprisoned sword spirits. She says if we break them the spirits will kill all of us."

"Demons!" Zang exclaimed. "She's right. My sword senses them. They're enraged. We don't dare move the vases. We need to get out of here."

Kellyn grabbed Jirra's arm and spoke urgently, though Micah

couldn't make out the words. Jirra paled and swallowed. "She also says her father's army will be waiting for us."

"The undead," said Zang. He looked to Micah. "How many servants did your sorcerer-baron have?"

"I don't know," said Micah through his sobs. "But there's a cemetery out back. There's dozens of graves, maybe more than a hundred."

Zang closed his eyes briefly. He looked at each of the surviving members of the assault team before continuing. "Without a controlling intelligence, the undead will attack anything that lives. Anyone injured by them will become infected and die. Those killed by the undead will become undead themselves. Even so few as a hundred of them will expand their numbers exponentially, until an unstoppable horde of thousands roams the countryside. We have but one chance to stop them, though it may cost all of our lives."

22

After warning Jirra, Kellyn kept her mouth shut. What was there to say, anyway? Her parents, Shaethe, all dead. And now her friends, likely about to die soon, as well. The pit in her stomach reminded her of the absence she'd felt from her sword when Lon had silenced Shaethe, only worse, like waking up one day to find someone had amputated your right hand in the middle of the night. And murdered your best friend. And cut out a chunk of your brain while they were at it.

And more: she had committed an act or sorcery. Hadn't she? Now that she looked at her memories, she wasn't quite so sure. Shaethe had led her. Shaethe had broken the wall that had separated her parents from the rest of the world. It hadn't felt like possession at all. It had felt, in fact, like no one at all was in control of her mother's body. Whatever had happened, three of the four souls that had briefly occupied one body were now dead. And Kellyn, the lone survivor, felt dead herself. Even seeing Jirra once again gave her no joy.

Zang cut the chains that held her down with ease, his magical sword slicing through the irons like they were made of cheese. Kellyn was too weak to move unsupported, so Zang put an arm around her shoulders and they stumbled along the corridor. Payner held up Micah, and dragged him ahead of the rest of the little group. She heard Micah whisper 'open' and they continued down the corridor into a room just like the one they'd left, except that in this one the vases and tables were gone.

"Which way now?" asked Payner.

"We need to find something for Micah," Felida said.

"What are you saying?" Zang asked.

"He's done us a great service. Lon must have kept some sort of sorcerous food on hand to restore his health from time to time."

"The substances you speak of are abominations!"

"It's already been made. It's not as if we'd have to make it ourselves."

"It's an abomination," Zang repeated. Kellyn watched the two mages face off in silence, wondering if Micah were really suffering that much, and if she really cared. They were all going to die.

Felida nodded. "Yes, it is. But if you refuse to let us look for it, you may as well kill Micah right now. He'd suffer less."

"Whatever the case," Jirra said, "we must find our way to the roof, and quickly."

"Where do they keep it, Micah?" Felida asked.

"Kitchen, I think," mumbled Micah, barely audible. "It's called gris."

"His memories showed only one way to the kitchen," Felida said. "Up these stairs, down a hallway, then down the servants' stairs. Or I suppose we could exit this room through the windows and make our way around to the back of the palace."

"No," Jirra said, pointing through the windows. "Look."

Just visible on the lawns outside were several figures walking around, seemingly aimlessly. They stumbled and shambled, and occasionally bumped into one another. In the faint starlight, most of them appeared to be in their nightclothes. Many of them had dark stains on their chests.

"Servants," Micah whispered. "Lon's people. I think that one's Della. Killed them all and brought them back."

"I don't see any that look like they've been buried. These things look recently dead."

"The cemetery is further back," Micah said in a hoarse, quiet voice. "Maybe they haven't reached this far yet."

"Then we go up the stairs," Felida said. She activated a small blue crystal, which gave off just enough light that they could see. "With Valdis dead, those things don't have anyone telling them what to do. That won't make them any less dangerous, though."

Felida took Kellyn's arm, allowing Zang to lead the way. As she led her, she fed Kellyn little bits of food and drops of oil, and placed an amulet on her chest. It stuck there as if it had been glued on. The effects of her aid soon gave her the strength to walk, but she still felt miserable.

They made their way to the kitchen without incident, but there they found the doors wide open and a crowd of walking corpses milling about just outside. Zang whispered in Jirra's ear, and she closed her eyes. After a few heartbeats, she pointed at a cupboard. Zang tiptoed over to the cupboard and found a glass jar full of pale liquid. But as soon as he removed the jar from its shelf, it slipped through his hands and shattered on the floor.

Everyone froze. Outside, the walking corpses turned their heads toward the kitchen and advanced.

"Up!" Zang said, slamming the kitchen door. "We need to get to the roof!" They ran.

"What was that all about?" said Felida. "Am I supposed to believe that was an accident?"

"It was a trap," Zang said. "As soon as I took it down from its shelf, it became as slippery as an eel. I couldn't hold it."

To her credit, Felida didn't question his explanation. "There'll be other traps, then."

"How would they have had time to set traps?" Kellyn asked. Her strength had continued to improve, and suddenly she felt the need to survive this, or at least try.

"Contingency snares," said Zang. "In the event that the palace was attacked, certain magical entrapments were activated. Damn me, I should have foreseen this! It was a favorite trick of the rebels ten years ago."

The undead servants banged on the kitchen door. Kellyn and Felida shoved a table against the door, but another servant smashed an arm through a window. "Zang!" Felida shouted, "What's the plan?"

"Go!" Zang said, ignoring her question. He stood at the door to the servants' stairs as they retreated, but the corpses were already coming through the broken window. Before the last of them exited of the kitchen, the outer door splintered and several more pushed their way in.

"My sword," Kellyn said. Payner had picked it up; he handed it over. Kellyn joined Zang, who passed her a leather bag. She found a time stone, fingered it and pushed time, wondering why Zang wasn't doing the same. She pushed the thought from her mind and stepped toward the nearest corpse and aimed an overhead slash at its shoulder. Her sword sliced into the dead man's shoulder, but there it stuck.

"What?" she shouted, bewildered for a moment. But then she remembered. Shaethe was dead. This sword no longer housed a spirit, was now in fact just another length of sharpened steel. She yanked the sword free, hacked again and again before managing to sever one arm from one corpse. This wasn't going to work. She slowed back to normal time and staggered, nearly bowling Zang over as she fought to keep her feet.

"Zang! My sword is dead! Why aren't you pushing time?"

"Not all of us have that talent. At any rate, you're too weak to push time now. Let me cover our retreat. Go with the others!"

"You can't stand against them alone." With no time to argue, the two mages stood their ground. Kellyn overturned a table and between the two of them, they managed to wedge it into the doorway to the kitchen. "That won't hold for long."

"We need fire," Zang said. He motioned with a nod—firewood and flint lay stacked in the kitchen, beyond their flimsy barrier. "Find candles, paper, draperies, anything. I'll hold them here." Zang severed the limbs from any reanimated corpse that tried to climb over the table, but there were simply too many of them. Had he been able to push time, he might have held them as long as the table held. After no more than a few minutes, however, the boards of the tabletop had begun to crack. "Hurry, Kellyn!"

She searched the corridor, opening doors, rifling through cupboards, cursing Lon's extravagant display of his power in lighting his entire palace with glowing crystals. Finally, she came upon a candle in a pewter holder. When she reached into her bag of amulets, however, she found nothing with which to start a fire. "I don't have a firestarter crystal!"

Zang hacked the arms off a corpse that tried to climb the table, then frantically untied a small, leather bag from his belt. As he threw it to Kellyn, an arm previously severed from a corpse fell over the edge of the table and gripped the front of Zang's tunic.

Kellyn dragged her eyes away from Zang's peril and searched through the bag for a firestarter, found a tiny red crystal and activated it; flames shot a hand's breadth high from its pointed tip. She lit the candle and set it down, then tore curtains from a room off the central corridor. She froze. Outside the window, dozens more corpses shambled toward the palace, and these undead creatures had clearly been in the grave for years, perhaps decades. Many were little more than skeletons draped with the tattered remnants of their burial finery. Sightless eye sockets turned toward the light of her candle.

She dropped the candle onto the drapes piled on the floor. When the cloth failed to ignite immediately, she activated the firestarter again, and soon had a roaring blaze going. No sooner had she returned to the corridor and latched the door than she heard the crash of shattered glass.

"More are coming," Kellyn shouted. "We must retreat."

Zang severed the head from a corpse, then turned to flee as the table splintered and burst. An arm clung to his trouser leg; he slapped it away with the flat of his sword. "Up! Set fire to everything!"

"Are you wounded?" Kellyn asked as they ran, stopping every twenty feet or so to set fire to the floor, rugs, tapestries, anything flammable.

"Yes. So now when I tell you to run, you will listen! There's no hope for me now."

Wounded he may have been, but he was in much better shape than Kellyn, whose body had been badly abused by her father's possession. Zang lent her aid with only his left hand, for the right had suffered a bite wound. "Zang, if the palace burns, the sword spirits' cages will most certainly be crushed. Are we saving the kingdom from an infestation of the undead only to unleash a dozen angry sword spirits upon the countryside?"

"The undead will march unchallenged across the land if enough of them survive this night. The sword spirits—" He paused, grasping the hilt of his sword. Kellyn knew a pang of jealousy; no doubt the mage was using the extra senses provided by his bond with his sword, something now denied to her. "They will be enraged. And they will certainly kill anything in their path, undead or otherwise. But they cannot survive indefinitely without a sword to inhabit."

Kellyn shook her head as they finally found a stairwell and began their ascent to the roof. Her father's army of corpses might perish tonight, but most likely an untold number of innocent Kattenese would join them when the spirits vented their rage.

Micah leaned heavily on Felida. The healer fed him some of the same food she'd given Kellyn, and it helped a little. Not enough, but a little.

"Keep going up," Felida said. "We'll find a window that leads on to the roof, eventually."

Up felt wrong. The servants quarters were that way, and Valdis had known they'd be coming. He'd surrounded the palace with reanimated corpses in case they came by ground. But he'd known from Kellyn's memories that Jirra was a member of an airship's crew. He may have guessed that they might come by air. He'd have placed more defenses up near the roof. Micah would never make it that far. If only the jar of gris hadn't fallen. If only his mother had survived. If only he had Serpent again.

"Wait!" he shouted hoarsely."There may be servants up there," said Micah. "They might be undead, too."

"I know," said Felida. "But we don't have much choice."

"I can defeat them, but I'll need something from my room."

Felida stopped and placed a hand on his shoulder. "There's no more gris. Whatever you're planning, understand that we won't be able to help you recover for quite some time. Days, maybe weeks."

Micah said nothing. He led the way up, leaning on the walls with Felida right behind him. At the landing that led to his room, he exited into the hallway, finding neither traps nor snares. Had his father not considered him much of a threat? He stumbled down the hall, opened his door and fell face first to the floor. Felida knelt at his side.

"What are you seeking?" she asked.

"A stone, shaped like a snake. It should be here somewhere." He tried to rise, to help find Serpent, but he couldn't walk, could barely speak.

Felida left him then, opened the drapes to get a little starlight, and returned within moments. "Is this it?"

Micah tried to take Serpent from her hands, but he couldn't lift his arm. "Yes. Put it around my neck." He clutched the familiar stone, shocked at how relieved he felt, tension in his chest and legs draining away like water from a tub. He breathed deeply. "Help me up."

Felida dragged him to his feet, and he found that he had just enough strength to continue. Serpent felt warm in his hands. He had no way of telling if the stone really gave him the strength to continue, but he chose to believe it had. They returned to the servants' stairs.

They found a high-ceilinged hallway beneath the peak of the roof, stiflingly hot even in the middle of the night. There were two doors, one on each side of the hall. Micah heard shuffling footsteps behind one of them, but nothing behind the door to the left. More footsteps sounded on the stairs behind them. His sister and Zang had finally rejoined the group.

"They're not far behind us," Zang said, panting. He was bleeding from a half a dozen wounds, but Kellyn looked unharmed.

Even though there was no sound coming from the door to the left, Micah opened the door to the right, and immediately a female servant lurched toward him in a bloody nightdress. Micah grabbed her hand and drank her diwa. There were two more of the creatures in the room, a dormitory like space with a dozen narrow cots. Micah finished them both. A portion of his strength returned as he moved to the room's only window and looked out.

"I can't see the airship," he said.

"Stand aside," Felida said. She held her arm out the window and aimed a little blue crystal at the stars. She mumbled something, and the light from the stone became so bright Micah had to look away. The crystal darkened, then shone fiercely again, blinking on and off regularly. "They'll see my signal, but they'll have to lower a rope. The roof's too steep for us to climb out onto it." She looked at Micah. "Why didn't you try the other door?"

"You said there'd be traps. I know how to deal with the undead. Whatever's next door might be very different."

From the other room came a sound of breaking crockery. Like an enormous vase cracking open. Bright orange light then shone from under the door. "I think the other trap has sprung," Micah said.

Kellyn and Zang stood in the hallway, swords drawn and facing the door. No more sound came from within, but the shuffling footsteps of the undead came from the stairwell. Payner and Abbatay threw cots down the stairwell, hoping to slow them down.

"You know what's behind that door, don't you?" said Zang.

"Yes," said Kellyn. "And there's only one thing we can do. Well, one thing that I can do, anyway."

Zang frowned and looked at her with his head cocked to one side. "You can't defeat an unbound sword spirit. Both of us together, healthy and at the height of our powers, would stand little chance. In our current condition, that thing will burn through us like a forest fire through dry leaves."

As if to underscore his warnings, the room on the other side of the door had caught fire. Smoke seeped from under the door, and they could feel the heat out in the hallway. "Just get everyone to the window. Either this will work, or we're all dead. It can't hurt to try."

Zang nodded once and ushered everyone into the other room. Kellyn took a deep breath, then opened the door and stepped inside. The creature that greeted her looked a lot like Shaethe, except that this one seemed to have too many arms, and fewer horns. The spirit stood among the shards of a large, broken vase. It turned its face to her and roared. Kellyn drew her sword and held her arms out as if welcoming an old friend.

"Sword spirit! You have been freed! I am Kellyn; I and my friends have killed the sorcerers who imprisoned you!"

The spirit held perfectly still, like a burning statue. She feared it wouldn't respond, but after a brief silence, it said, "Why are my brothers and sisters still imprisoned, then?"

It pointed at Kellyn and a spear of fire shot through the air. She dove to her left to avoid the flames. "Your rage is great, and greatly justified. How could I hope to reason with a dozen of your kind all at once?"

"You know nothing of my kind!" the spirit bellowed. Flames shot out of its mouth and nostrils, igniting more of the floor and walls.

"But I do! I was once bonded with a spirit named Shaethe. He was like a brother to me. I helped him kill the man who put you in that vase."

"And where is Shaethe now? Your sword is dead. You are lying!" Again flames burst from the hands of the spirit, but this time without aim. The walls and ceiling had become engulfed, and Kellyn found it difficult to breathe.

"My sword is dead, you're right. But it was once—" a fit of coughing interrupted her, and the spirit opened its mouth, revealing fangs and a tongue that lashed the smoky air. "My sword was once Shaethe's home. He died helping me. If you doubt me, examine the sword yourself. No human could make a sword like this one."

The spirit moved across the floor without moving its legs, sliding along like a drop of water on a sizzling pan. It took the sword from Kellyn and examined it. As it was looking at the odd double blade, another thought occurred to her, but she found little enough air to breathe, and speech proved too much.

The spirit gave the sword back. Despite being handled by a spirit of flame, the sword remained cool to the touch. The flames had spread around most of the outer wall of the room. She had to get out of here, and soon.

"What do you want of me?" the spirit asked. When Kellyn slumped to the floor, the spirit waved its arms. Immediately the flames receded, and she found she could speak again.

"This is not your world. Without a home like the sword I carry, you will soon perish. I offer you my sword."

"I was not made for you, nor was your sword made for me."

"It won't be perfect for either of us, not even close. Yet the offer still stands."

"You still haven't told me what you want."

"Spare my friends. Let them leave here unharmed. If you must have vengeance for what has been done to you, take me."

"Why should I spare any of you?"

"Your captor was my father. Shaethe and I killed him. My father released reanimated corpses upon this world, and if left unchecked they will kill all of my kind. I've set the palace ablaze to stop them, but now your brethren will be freed if the palace collapses upon their prisons. They too, will wreak havoc."

"I think not." The spirit paused for what seemed far too long. Kellyn closed her eyes, preparing to face her fate. "I will spare you and your friends for freeing me."

The flames went out with a whooshing sound and a blast of cool air. When Kellyn opened her eyes, the spirit had vanished.

She blinked back tears as the room filled with smoke. She could feel the spirit within her sword. It felt odd, uncomfortable, heavy and unbalanced. But alive.

"Thank you, spirit. Have you a name?"

The sword did not respond, and Kellyn felt a pang of loss. Speech between mage and sword was possible only under special circumstances. Having met two sword spirits in a day, she mourned the absence of direct communication.

"Will you consent to take the name of Shaethe?"

Cool indifference radiated from the sword.

"Shaethe is a great deal better than any other name I could suggest. It is the name of a great spirit, one who died so that my friends and I could live and complete our quest."

The sword assented.Kellyn put Shaethe back in its scabbard as she stumbled for the other room. Micah had already been lifted in a rope sling up to the waiting *Nighthawk*. Jirra spoke quietly with her father and Felida. Payner and Zang looked up as she entered the room.

"I didn't think I'd see you alive," said Zang. He looked at the sheathed sword on Kellyn's hip. "The spirit joined you?"

"Yes. He spared us, and I gave him life as well."

"It will be a rocky relationship. No other spirit will ever fit you as well as your first one. Some mages give up the sword entirely if they lose its spirit."

"I won't."

Another rope had come snaking down, this one with a crewman attached. He had a bundle of ropes tied to his harness. "Come on! Everybody at once! The palace is burning; we need to get out of here now!"

In short order, they were all dangling from the airship, waiting their turn for the skeleton crew to pull them up. Kellyn was last, and she hung looking down at Engvar House as it retreated behind them. On this dark night, the flames would be visible for miles. Someone would come to investigate. With luck, all the reanimated corpses would have followed them into the palace. Maybe they'd all burn before the first people arrived on the scene.

And the sword spirits? Kellyn wondered at the new Shaethe's words. It had seemed unconcerned that the spirits would wreak havoc on the countryside. Kellyn could only hope the spirit was right, but she had no way of knowing.

"Am I right not to worry, Shaethe?"

Her rope jerked as it was finally her turn to be hauled aboard. She felt a sense of agreement coming from her sword spirit. Not warmth, not affection, not the bond she had shared with the original Shaethe. It wasn't the perfect solution, but then, in life, nothing ever was. It was enough, for now, that she was still alive.

The human price of their adventure became painfully obvious in the light of day. They were all rested, bathed, and fed. Payner had escaped with only minor cuts and bruises. Felida and Jirra were also mostly unharmed. Kellyn had suffered burns and cuts, and deeper psychic wounds from the battle with her father, but she was otherwise well enough and needed no further attention.

Abbatay and Zang had each been wounded by the reanimated corpses. They lay in the ship's hold under constant watch in case one of them should die suddenly and attack the rest of the living. Felida bathed their wounds and provided what care she could, but the prognosis was not good. "I have a problem. I can keep them comfortable for a couple of days, or I can keep them alive for a few weeks but in great pain," Felida said. She had joined Payner, temporarily elevated to command of the ship, in the captain's quarters. Jirra and Kellyn sat together on the edge of her father's bed.

"My father wants to live as long as he can," Jirra said. Her eyes were red and puffy from crying. "He wants to live long enough to complete this one last voyage."

Payner nodded, eyes red and brimming with tears. "We need him alive. Magda knows how bad he's hurt, and how many men we lost at Engvar. I don't think she could take losing the captain so soon after all those deaths, and after losing Marshall. This may be her last flight."

"What about Zang?" Kellyn asked.

"He wants to live, too," said Felida. "He told me he needs to give a complete report to the Elders."

"So what's the problem?"

Felida sighed. "I won't have much time to help Micah, and Jirra has no training."

Kellyn sat a little straighter. "I thought he was doing better. I thought that prayer stone helped."

"He drank the diwa of the corpses in the servant's quarters back at Engvar House. Physically, he is doing better. He'll survive. But . . . what he's done has corrupted him. Perhaps in ways he's not aware of yet."

Kellyn nodded. She could see the obvious solution. "You're saying they'll decide to strip his powers."

"I see no other way."

"What about you, Jirra?" Kellyn asked. "Do you see any other way out for my brother?"

Jirra shook her head. "Will that really be so bad? His powers have brought him nothing but pain and suffering. Maybe he'll be able to live a normal life, without magic."

Kellyn shrugged. Normal? What was normal? Micah was just a ten-year-old boy, after all. With everything he'd seen and done, what chance was there that he could ever be normal? She stood. "I'll break it to him, then."

"No, not yet," Felida said. "I promised I'd try to help him when this is all over. And I intend to keep my promise. But I don't want Micah pondering the loss of his powers for the remainder of this journey. He could still be dangerous."

Micah slept fitfully in his hammock, unable to relax even now, four days after they'd escaped. Every time he closed his eyes, he saw hordes of corpses, their faces devoid of expression, lifeless eyes staring without focus. For the one brief time he'd managed to sleep deeply, he dreamt of his mother, telling stories of olden times. He'd awoken sobbing and calling for her.

Waking felt no better. He was now an orphan. Yes, he had a sister, a sister who'd tried to save him. But what did that prove? She was destined to become a mage. And Micah? At best, they'd let him live, but without his magical powers. No one was saying that out loud, but it was obvious. Zang had made his opinion quite clear before they'd assaulted Engvar. The fact that no one was talking about what would happen to Micah once they reached Thurn provided all the proof he needed.

Cowards, he thought. *They should have the guts to say it to my face.* He touched the amulet that clung to his chest like a hideous scab, preventing him from performing sorcery. They hadn't even had the courage to put that cursed thing around his neck while he was awake. Just another of their lies. At least they hadn't taken Serpent from him, though the stone now felt cold, dead, devoid of diwa.

He fantasized about vengeance. About learning everything there was to know about sorcery. He dreamed that he would one day become even more powerful than his father. That he'd conquer the world and make them all grovel at his feet. But he just didn't care enough. No one loved him, and he loved no one.

Someone came down the stairs into the crew's quarters. Micah closed his eyes. The footsteps came closer.

"Micah?" Kellyn said. "Can we talk?"

"I guess."

"The others don't think it's wise for me to tell you this, but I can't put it off any longer."

Micah swung his legs out of his hammock. "I'll save you the trouble then. I know they're going to strip me of my powers. I won't have any talents. I'll be a normal kid. Great."

"Felida thinks that when you drank in the diwa of the corpses, you were corrupted. I think she's right. We've been talking a lot about the nature of diwa. Well, the many natures of diwa, since there's many different kinds."

"Lon said you mages don't know as much about diwa as we sorcerers," Micah said.

"He's probably right. But we're not totally ignorant. The kind of diwa our father used to control corpses is especially dangerous. Felida thinks that unless you're stripped, a kind of infection will set in. That eventually, you'll be killed by it, and become one of the undead yourself."

"Wonderful. So I'm supposed to be grateful, then? Happy?" Micah wanted to continue berating her, but his will evaporated. He asked the question he feared most. "What's going to happen to me?"

"You mean . . . after they take your powers? I'm not sure. I'm only fifteen, so I'm not officially an adult. And my status within the Brotherhood is . . . well, I don't have any idea what they're going to decide to do with me, once we get back to the capitol. But you're my brother. I'll make sure you're taken care of. You'll need an education, a place to stay. I think I may have an idea, there. But whatever the case, I won't abandon you."

"And what if the Brotherhood says I'm not your responsibility? What if they tell you to go on some mission halfway around the world?"

"Then I'll quit. Micah, please believe me: I won't walk away from you. If I have to give up everything, I will. We're family. And we're the only family we have."

Micah lay back down and carefully turned to face the ship's hull. He didn't want anyone seeing him so weak. "We'll see," he said. "Promises are easy to make, but a lot harder to keep."

"Get some rest, Micah. We're getting favorable winds, but we've still got a ways to go."

Mostly, the remainder of the voyage passed without incident. No pirates. No angels. Kellyn wanted to ask Abbatay about the angels, about whatever the captain had thought he was doing and why he'd ordered her to kill them. Not so long ago, though it seemed an eternity. But Abbatay spent his waking hours with his daughter. Jirra never left his side. Kellyn had tried to talk to her; she'd discuss her father's condition and the treatments she and Felida were giving him, but nothing else. And after a while, Kellyn couldn't bring herself to try to get her to change the subject. This was her father, after all.

So she spent the days exercising, climbing the ropes, checking for parasites, helping the skeleton crew with their chores. Felida pronounced her healthy a week into their flight. She felt reasonably well, but tended to avoid the ship's one mirror in the captain's cabin. Her skin still hung loose and gray. Shaethe had taken some getting used to, as well, but her swordplay continued to improve, sharper and crisper than ever before. Somehow it all felt hollow. So many had died, and two more were about to join the dead.

Zang did not survive their journey. He died less than two days' flight from the capitol, out over the Thurnic Sea, and immediately tried to attack the crewman assigned to watch-duty that morning. He and Abbatay had both been chained to their beds for just such an event, so no one was harmed. But someone had to kill him, if that was really the right way to think about it. If you could kill someone already dead.

Disposing of the corpse fell to Kellyn. She hacked Zang to pieces, and very carefully placed the still active body parts in a sack. Magda set her down on a small rocky island with the sack and some firewood. She cremated Zang, placing the mage's sword atop the blaze. The sword glowed white hot before its spirit slipped back into its own realm.

Kellyn felt for any reaction from Shaethe, but the blade remained quiescent. She didn't press the issue. Back aboard the *Nighthawk*, the mood had grown from somber to downright black.

Two days later, they landed in the capitol.

23

Kellyn looked down and saw Jirra's sweating face several feet below her. They had climbed nearly to the top of the west wall of the King's Summer Residence; Brotherhood initiates often made the difficult climb to hone their skills, but today they were alone. She made it to the parapet first and waved at a guard. Just a few beats later, Jirra joined her. They stood in silence for a bit, catching their breath and drinking water from bags at their waists.

"Next time," Jirra said, "I'll beat you."

"I don't doubt it," Kellyn said. "Your first time, and you very nearly reached the top before me." Neither of them mentioned that Kellyn still hadn't regained her full strength. She'd looked a mess when they'd arrived in the capitol, loose pale skin, graying, brittle hair, and cracked, yellow fingernails. She'd shaved her head, and noticed with relief that the stubble growing in was black. Felida had helped her recover a little, but she'd been quite busy, and at any rate the only prescription that could help her was time.

From her backpack, Jirra retrieved a contraption of brass, wood, steel, leather and rubber. She set the oddly jointed thing down on the walkway atop the wall and carefully removed the climbing claws attached to her good knee and the stump of the other leg. She bent to grab the contraption and it unfolded at her touch.

"It's an artificial leg!" Kellyn had exclaimed when she'd first seen it. A lesser sort of spirit had been bonded to it, but no bond with the wearer accompanied the leg. Leather straps at the top, obviously meant to hold the leg in place, writhed like a nest of snakes. They grabbed her leg and pulled the artificial leg snug to her stump. She stood, flexing the device as if it were a real leg.

"I still can't get over how well it works," Kellyn said.

"I hate it," Jirra muttered. "It works just like a real leg, but it feels like I've got a parasite attached to me. It moves, you know? Constantly readjusting its straps. I wish it would just sit still."

"I've never seen one up close."

"Felida says it'll do me some good to have a magical object on my person at all times. Gives me something to focus some of my undefined talents on. Supposed to make my visions clearer."

"Well, does it work?"

"Not yet. She says it takes time. My visions are all jumbled and contradictory. Worst thing is, I can't climb with this thing on, not yet anyway, and there's so many great buildings to climb in the capitol. I end up taking it off and putting it back on constantly. Felida says I should leave it on all the time. Forget that."

Kellyn tentatively laid an arm across Jirra's shoulders. She stiffened at first, then slipped an arm around Kellyn's waist. The top of Jirra's head brushed her cheek, her damp hair tickling her nose. This was the first time they'd been truly alone since arriving in the capitol, and it might be the last. Jirra turned to put her other arm around Kellyn's waist, but after a brief hug, they separated. Kellyn looked out over the city, afraid to speak. She wanted to hold Jirra, to tell her how she felt. But with all the worries in her head, she couldn't bear the thought of rejection.

Her fate would soon be decided. She wished she knew what the Elders were saying to each other about her. But even Jirra couldn't see her future. Seers generally had a hard time in the capitol, protected as it was by many layers of magical wards. At six bells, Kellyn had to go back to the Brotherhood House to hear their decision.

"I wish we could stay here for the sunset," she said. "On a cloudy day like this, it'll be magnificent to watch from up here."

"It can't compare to a sunset seen from a few thousand feet up in the air," said Jirra. Just visible among the clouds were a pair of male airhees. Magda was nowhere to be seen. "I'm glad she decided to live."

One of those males—it was impossible to tell Spot from the other at this distance—was a stray. He'd followed Magda as she brought the *Nighthawk* in for its landing, and now Spot flew with him over the city. If all went well, Magda would have the two mates her species needed. The three of them would mate, and in a few years, she would give birth to a dozen or so baby airhees.

"It's good to see new life coming from all this," Kellyn said.

After a lengthy pause, Jirra said, "What will happen now?"

Kellyn shrugged. "The Elders . . . I truly don't know what they'll decide. But it's really up to Micah. Once I know what my options are, I'm going to give him as many choices as possible. I'll follow his lead. He's my only family."

Jirra grew quiet and very still. Kellyn wondered if the mention of family had reminded her of her father. He'd died just hours after they reached the capitol and reanimated immediately afterward. The Elders had been warned, and a team of mages in full plate armor had met the airship and taken Abbatay into custody. Jirra had gone with them to spend whatever time her father had left at his side. She hadn't yet spoken of his death, or what the armored mages had done afterward. Kellyn could imagine, having disposed of Zang just a couple of days earlier, and the scene in her head wasn't pretty.

"It's getting late," Jirra said.

Kellyn slid a coil of rope from her shoulder. Jirra stopped her with a hand on her chest. They looked at each other for a few heartbeats before Jirra moved closer. They kissed. Kellyn wasn't sure about Jirra, but it was the first time she'd ever really kissed anybody. It felt great, but she was awkward and clumsy. Their teeth clicked together at one point, and they shared a nervous giggle. All too quickly, it ended. Afterward, Jirra looked like she wanted to say something, but she turned away. Kellyn hurriedly tied the rope around one of the square crenellations atop the wall, glad to have something to do to hide her nervousness.

"You go first," she said as she took off her artificial leg. Kellyn nodded and lowered herself to the ground, grinning all the way.

To make their final examination of Kellyn, the Elders ordered her to sit in the center of a large, octagonal room: the Chamber of Truth. Felida drew designs on the wooden floor around her with yellow chalk. The Edlers sat in the shadows on a raised dais at the far end of the room. Through the silence, she could feel them probing her memories, tiny invisible fingers poking and prodding. It wasn't particularly unpleasant, but it made her uneasy. Nothing could be hidden here. Everything would be laid bare. At least they'd be making their decision based on all the facts, not just on others' opinions of what she'd done.

"It is clear," said a man in the shadows after several minutes of wordless examination, "that Kellyn did not, in fact, possess her mother." His words echoed a little in the enormous chamber, but Kellyn could hear him well enough.

"We cannot examine her mother's body," said a woman who may have been Trenna; she couldn't be sure. "Therefore, many of the questions we have must remain unanswered. Whether her sword possessed her mother or not must remain a mystery."

She didn't know who was up there. There were hundreds of Elders within the Brotherhood and the Sisterhood. Any of them might be occupying the traditional twelve seats on the dais. Any of them might have fought against her parents ten years ago. Who knew what biases they might have? Hadn't Zang once said he'd rather just kill her and be done with it, rather than risk setting Valdis Hittrech loose upon the world again? Might one of these Elders be just as cautious?

"What concerns me most," said a different woman, "is her willingness to possess her mother. The fact that she did not in fact perform an act of sorcery does not obliterate her choice to follow Shaethe into her mother's body."

Kellyn wondered if she should respond, and decided she had nothing to lose. "I knew what I was doing," she said, loudly that they might hear. "I was aware of the consequences."

The male Elder did not respond. The first woman said, "The girl tried to salvage her mother. Against all evidence, she felt there was some possibility she might not be evil to the core."

"Yes," said a man. "She 'felt.' This one relies too much upon her feelings, and too little upon cold rationality."

"As did we all, at her age."

"We could do with a bit more feeling, I say," said a new, female voice. Might it have been Felida? Kellyn new a thrill of hope. "If love and compassion do not motivate our thoughts, what good do we bring to the world?"

The Elders whispered among each other then for several minutes. Kellyn couldn't distinguish individual words, and wondered if some sort of privacy spell had been enacted. Suddenly, silence fell over the chamber. Had they reached a decision? She could hardly stand the suspense. After several more minutes, a different voice, a deep, gravelly and male, said, "Initiate, rise and receive our verdict."

Kellyn stood. Her legs wobbled a bit and a bead of sweat trickled down her spine.

"You have passed the test of initiation. Not all tests are as clear cut as those we devise in the Testing Chamber. And yet you have performed as well as we might have hoped. We accept you into our ranks. There remains now only the question of your position among us. Will you move on to the next logical rank of Apprentice? Or will you accept a commission as a Journeyman?"

Kellyn's breath caught in her throat. Journeyman! Granted, she should have reached that rank already. She should have been an Apprentice at age ten, and a Journeyman by the age of thirteen or fourteen at the latest. She felt the temptation to grab the commission immediately, but there was still the problem of what to do with Micah. She'd have to be very careful how she said what she needed to say next.

"Elders," she began, "I would like nothing more than to accept a commission among you. But I have my brother to think of. His fate has been decided: his powers will be stripped. After that, I need to be certain he is being cared for, and treated well. If I am satisfied that I can become a Journeyman without compromising his care, I will accept. But I'm afraid I cannot make that decision right now."

She thought they might be shocked, or angry. Instead, the man spoke softly, "Very well, Initiate Kellyn. When you have made your decision, please inform your former teacher, Magrahim. The commission will wait for you."

Micah lay in a soft bed, feeling sleepy, sore and confused. The healers had done something to him. There were bandages around his head, and a strong medicinal smell in the small room. He lay in a tiny bed, little more than a cot. A chair and a small table took up most of the remaining floor space. A door stood open to his left. To his right, a small window allowed warm, fresh air inside. Outside, he could see rooftops and sky. He knew he was in the capitol, but where exactly? He had no idea.

His head hurt, but not terribly. It had been throbbing when he first woke up, but Felida had given him a cup of some brownish liquid, and the pain had eased. She was nice, and familiar, like maybe he'd known her for a long time. She certainly seemed much more concerned for his well-being than the other healers. Not that the others were rude or uncaring. They were just brisk.

One of those busy young women poked her head into his room. "Good, you're awake. You have a visitor."

He blinked in surprise. No one had visited him here, except the healers. He had no family, and though he was a little confused about the details, he certainly wasn't from Thurn. Most of the people here spoke only Thurnic, which he didn't understand at all. He spoke Kattenese. Of the healers, only Felida and one or two others spoke that language fluently.

A woman of indeterminate age entered his room and sat at the small table. She looked quite a bit older than Micah, with very short, black hair and wrinkled skin, and very familiar. She looked Kattenese, with the narrow eyes of that northern folk. He wondered if she, too, were Kattenese. It would make sense. Felida had said his memories would come back slowly. Micah smiled at the newcomer and craned his neck to get a better look at her. "I'm Micah. Who are you?"

"It's me, Micah. Kellyn, your sister."

Micah's head slumped back to the pillow. He flinched as memories assailed his mind. It was usually like that. Felida would mention a person or a place and things would go 'pop' in his memory. Sometimes the memories were pleasant. Not often. Not this time.

"What are you going to do with me?" he croaked.

"I'm not making decisions for you, Micah. No one is. I'm here to give you some options. For once, I want you to be able to choose your fate."

Things were coming back. Kellyn was a mage, and Micah had been . . . something like a mage. Different, more powerful. He couldn't quite put a finger on it, but he no longer had magical talent, so what did it matter? He pointed at the bandages around his head. "Not making decisions for me, eh? What about this? I didn't choose this."

Kellyn held up her hands. "Neither did I. That decision was made by the Elders. It might even be what's best for you. But that's not why I'm here."

Micah glared. His headache had gotten worse.

"You have three choices. First, the Brotherhood maintains an orphanage. They would accept you, educate you, set you up with an apprenticeship in a trade here in the capitol."

Micah did not respond. Images of a life spent digging ditches or making pottery filled his head. *Or mending fishnets*, he thought. *Or, I don't know, digging rocks in a stupid quarry*. More memories flooded his mind at the thought of a quarry. And an image. A woman with a broad face, neither pretty, nor ugly. *Mother*. But then her face changed, became thinner, more angular. Pretty, beautiful even, but angry. Furious. Evil. He gasped for breath and tears sprang to his eyes.

Kellyn frowned, but otherwise did not respond to Micah's obvious distress. "Secondly," she said, "I could leave the Brotherhood, open a shop as a practitioner somewhere, and you and I could live together as a family."

When Micah said nothing, Kellyn continued. "Or there's a third option. I spoke to a friend of mine, a very powerful friend. He and his wife have no children. They would be willing to take you in, maybe even adopt you. You'd have a very comfortable life with them."

"Who are they?"

"First Minister August Nigh and his wife, Chahn-li. I hope you'll at least meet with them before making your decision."

"What about you? Will they adopt you, too?"

Kellyn shook her head. "No. I'd stay in the Brotherhood if you go with them. We'd still be siblings, but I couldn't be loyal to the Elders and be the daughter of the First Minister at the same time."

"I'll do it," Micah said, thinking he might like to live free of Kellyn's presence. "I'll meet with the Nighs." When he refused to say more, Kellyn rather awkwardly excused herself. Micah lay on his bed for a long time, trying not to remember. Failing. He idly fingered the stone that hung around his neck, but whatever power Serpent might have had, whether or not it had truly given him the strength to keep going back in Engvar, he felt nothing now. But then, he wouldn't feel any-thing, would he? They'd stripped him of his powers. Slowly, he removed Serpent from around his neck, and stared at it for what seemed ages. He flung it out the open window.

Micah sat in a chair with wheels as Felida pushed him through the Royal Palace. It was a grand place, full of statues, tapestries, chan-deliers, and people wearing rich, colorful clothes. The floors were all polished stone. His memories had come flooding back since meeting with his sister. He knew that not all that long ago he would have seen diwa within those stones. He would have been able to seize that power, lift impossibly heavy objects, and kill with a touch. It was gone now, all of it.

Felida rolled his chair up to a set of tall, ornately carved doors. She spoke softly to the guard who stood at stiff attention before knocking. A servant came to the door, bowed deeply, and escorted Felida and Micah into a high-ceilinged room. Though as fine as anything else he'd seen in the royal palace, this room was almost devoid of decoration.

An old man stood from behind a desk covered with papers. He shooed away his servant and waved Micah and Felida over to a couch and a couple of chairs near the window. "Come, come! It's high time I take a break. Sister Felida, I believe? I have read your reports, and I extend the King's gratitude for your excellent service. Most excellent!"

The old man spoke loudly and smiled a lot. Micah felt like he should like him right away, and that made him suspicious. He never liked anyone instantly.

"And you must be Micah." Nigh's demeanor changed. Suddenly, his eyes looked sad and droopy. "The things you've endured, dear boy. Felida? Might I have some time alone with the boy?"

"Of course, First Minister. Shall I wait in the corridor?"

"If you wish. But if duty calls, you have my leave to depart."

"I thank you. Micah? If you need me, send for me at the Sister House."

Micah ignored her. He still believed the healer cared for him, but she didn't have his best interests in mind. No one did.

Nigh watched Felida depart, then pulled a small red crystal from a desk drawer. He'd seen one like it before, back in Kattenwa. Tunni, the pit boss at the quarry, had used something like that for privacy.

"Recognize this, do you?" Nigh said. He smiled again. "It's for show, really. Any competent mage or sorcerer could still spy on us, given sufficient motivation. They will, however, hear an innocuous conversation about your past, particularly concerning your recent adventures in your homeland. There are other, more powerful, magical wards woven around this room. We have complete privacy here, I assure you."

"So what do you want?"

"Excellent question, my boy! Always the best question to ask, especially when someone is offering to do you a favor. As I most certainly am. I wish to adopt you, so that I have someone to whom I may leave my vast fortune when I die."

Micah blinked. "Why me?"

"I'll get to that. You see, Micah, I'm not actually going to die, at least not anytime soon. After you've been fully trained, I will take one last trip in an airship, my ship will disappear, I will be declared dead, and you will inherit everything I own. Meanwhile, I will remake my body to be young again, change my appearance, then come back to the capitol to work for you."

"You're . . . you're a sorcerer!"

"Is it really that surprising?"

"But . . . don't the mages know?"

"Of course they don't know! They've examined me fully on a couple of occasions, and have declared my limited magical talents to be harmless. Many of my political enemies have accused me of practicing sorcery over the years. And the fact that my wife is from the Far Western land of Sook, where sorcery is a respected profession, only adds fuel to their suspicions. All successful people face such charges from jealous opponents from time to time. And since I have been more successful than most, I have faced such accusations more frequently than most. Fortunately, the mages no longer give any credence to my accusers."

Micah sat very still in his chair. He hadn't had particularly good results from dealing with sorcerers so far in his life. He looked at the First Minister the way he might have eyed a poisonous snake.

"I don't know what you want from me. I don't have any talents. Not anymore."

"Ah, that. Yes, the mages have stripped you. Interesting word, 'stripped.' Brings to mind images of permanence, does it not? Strip the bark from a tree, and the tree dies, yes? But that isn't really the best word for what they've done to you. 'Suppressed' might be more accurate."

Micah blinked. He couldn't have been more stunned if he'd been hit in the forehead with a stone. "Are you saying I could get my powers back?"

"It will take time. It will be unpleasant, occasionally painful. But yes, you can become a sorcerer once more."

"So what's your plan? Are you going to kill the king and take his place? Conquer the world?"

Nigh laughed, a deep, hearty sound so full of mirth that Micah laughed right along with the old man.

"Conquer the world? Whatever for? And as for replacing the king, why bother? The king is a halfwit; I already control the kingdom and everything that happens within its borders. And much that occurs beyond our borders, as well."

"But not everything."

"Is that what you think sorcerers do? Sit around thinking of evil plans to bring the world to its knees? Your father was a fool! Have you ever examined his grand design, boy? He would have succeeded, you know, given enough time. The mages were quite right to want him dead. He would have swept away everything in his path, and in doing so he would have ruined the world he wished to conquer. My people have researched his methods and concluded that conquering the world through necromancy would result in the death of at least ninety-seven out of every one-hundred people in the world. Crops would fail, livestock starve, and cities fall to ruin. It would be the end of civilization, perhaps of the human race itself. Your father would have been the emperor of the world. And all of his subjects would have been corpses."

Micah listened, and he found that he agreed. None of that mattered, though. Valdis Hittrech was gone. "So where do I fit in?"

"One of my nicknames around the capitol is 'The Puppet Master.' I pull the strings that make things happen. When the king wants a new law, or a new tax, or an improved harbor, or a treaty with a neighbor, or anything at all, really, he comes to me. I twist arms, make promises, remind people of past favors, bribe, blackmail, and threaten, whatever it takes, to make the king's wishes into reality. My fortune helps, of course, but the best weapon at my disposal is information. Should you join me, you will begin as one of my vast horde of information gatherers."

"A spy?"

Nigh shrugged. "Occasionally. Not exclusively. You'd also be a researcher, perhaps a military commander. You'd go as far as your talents can take you."

"Like Abbatay," Micah said with sudden inspiration. "He worked for you."

"Yes. But he wasn't just an airship captain. Ah, I will miss him! Extremely able, that one. I once thought your sister would be a good candidate for the position I'm offering to you. I thought the blackness within her was innate. Had I known it was your father's soul, none of this would have happened. But I didn't know, worse luck. I thought that if my man Abbatay could put Kellyn into certain deadly situations, her inner nature would come to the fore, and that she could be gradually steered away from the Brotherhood and into my service. Abbatay first brought you to my attention, you know."

Micah narrowed his eyes. His truth sense detected no lies. But then, did he have a truth sense anymore? More importantly, could he really get his powers back? And what did Nigh actually want from him? He hadn't made anything clear yet.

"So what would I have to do? Not airship captain, probably."

"No, but I do have a certain project in mind for you that does focus on airships. Specifically, finding ways to use them in battle. But you'll find out about all that later."

"And what if I say no?"

"Then you'll leave here remembering a very different, completely innocent conversation. I'll still adopt you, and you'll become a dutiful son. But you won't get your powers back, and far less will be expected of you. When I 'die' and come back, I will work for you, secretly controlling your actions, and gradually retake control of my commercial and manufacturing empire. I may even have you adopt me. You'll then lead a prosperous, if a trifle boring, life of wealth and ease. Eventually, I will become so important in the kingdom that the king will offer me my old post as First Minister, and the cycle will begin again."

Micah frowned. Such arrogance! But then, was there any reason for Nigh not to be so confident in his abilities? And could Micah really contemplate refusing the opportunity to work with this man? *After all,* he thought, *I'll be a sorcerer again. And one day I'll take this old man's place. When he fakes his death, maybe I can make sure it isn't so fake.*

"Very well, I accept."

"Excellent!" Nigh stood. "I'll have my people draw up the papers, and present you to the royal court soon afterward. Oh, and you can forget that nonsense about killing me and taking my place. You don't stand a chance. I do, however, admire your ambition. You'll make a good son. Very good indeed."

Kellyn made her way from the Brotherhood's House to the home of the Sisters as quickly as she could. Jirra was due to be accepted into the Sisterhood today and she wanted to have as much time with her as possible before she walked through those doors. Once she went into that building, she'd be very busy. For that matter, Kellyn had a mission of her own now. She'd be leaving the capitol the next morning.

She found Jirra in a courtyard speaking to an old woman. The stooped, wizened crone frowned deeply and laid one spotted hand upon Jirra's shoulder. The two women embraced awkwardly before the old woman turned and limped away. Jirra watched her go so intently that she didn't notice Kellyn until she was standing by her side. Wordlessly, Jirra put her arms around Kellyn's waist.

"Are you well?" Kellyn asked, putting her arms around Jirra's back and kissing the top of her head.

"That was my mother."

"Really? She looked much older . . . than your father." Kellyn silently cursed herself for bringing up that painful subject, but Jirra didn't react.

"She's actually younger than my father. But her life has been very hard. She's made some fantastically poor decisions." Jirra sighed heavily. "Ah well, at least she seems to be sober now. Most of my memories of her involve drinking. Maybe Daddy's death woke her up."

"So, was she just seeing you off?"

Jirra nodded. "I feel like an orphan."

"Hey, I *am* an orphan. It's not so bad. But then, considering who I had for parents, pretty much anything looks good by comparison."

They laughed, but Jirra's chuckle sounded forced. "The difference being I love my folks. Even Mom. She's not a bad person, just . . . flawed."

"What happens next?"

"Well, I do have some good news. You'll never guess who my primary instructor is going to be."

"Oh? Who could that be?"

Jirra looked up at her, pulling away from her embrace. "You're a horrible actor. You already know, don't you?"

"I've got a good idea. Felida, right?"

Jirra smiled. "She's great. She's the way I wish my mom had been. Tough, but caring. Really interested in me. And she's fascinating to talk to! She's had so many incredible experiences. I wish you could get to know her better."

"Maybe we'll all have time for that. But you're about to become really busy. They're going to work you harder than you've ever worked before, you know that?"

"I know," Jirra said. Her smile slipped from her face. "Now, when are you going to tell me that you're leaving?"

"I guess I can't hide anything from a seer, can I?"

"No, you can't. So don't ever try to lie to me, right?"

Kellyn shook her head. "I won't. I leave tomorrow."

"You're part of the Engvar expedition, then?"

"Yes. Magrahim says the sword spirits aren't really in our world; they're on a different plane, but still imprisoned by those vases. We've got to bind those sword spirits to proper swords, and make sure Kattenwa isn't being overrun by reanimated corpses. And on the way back, we're supposed to stop in Roccobin to retrieve Felida's things. That's how I knew she was being transferred here, and it only makes sense that she'll be your teacher."

"Speaking of teachers," Jirra said, "what about Magrahim?"

"He's been chosen to lead the expedition."

"That's great for you then."

"It is. And my friend Alonselle has been assigned to the expedition as well. I just wish you and I had more time."

Jirra stepped closer and kissed Kellyn. They stood like that for a long time, in silence, until Felida entered the courtyard. "It's time, Jirra," said the healer.

Jirra nodded but she never took her eyes from Kellyn's. "This isn't goodbye," she said. "Not permanently, anyway. My visions might be pretty jumbled right now, but one thing is clear: we'll see each other again."

"I look forward to it," Kellyn said. With one last, brief kiss, she saw her off. She stared at the doorway long after she and Felida had disappeared inside. "Can't stand here all day," she muttered to herself. "I'm a Journeyman, now."

She had things to do, supplies to gather and pack. She had a mission in the morning, a bonded sword on her hip, a blossoming romance with Jirra, and just one soul inhabiting her body. And Micah? Micah had the Nighs. What more could she ask?

END

CPSIA information can be obtained
at www.ICGtesting.com
Printed in the USA
BVHW010543220522
637733BV00024B/493